The Light on the Star

To Charlie Bobbish,
all-around good guy and
fellow grad, wishing you
the absolute best,

Steve Dotson
19 January 2006

The Light on the Star

Robert S. Dotson

Library of Congress Number:		2005904358
ISBN :	Hardcover	1-4134-9642-3
	Softcover	1-4134-9641-5

This is a work of fiction. Names, characters, places and incidents either are the product of the author's imagination or are used fictitiously, and any resemblance to any actual persons, living or dead, events, or locales is entirely coincidental.

This book was printed in the United States of America.

To order additional copies of this book, contact:
Xlibris Corporation
1-888-795-4274
www.Xlibris.com
Orders@Xlibris.com

28909

Dedication

For my father, C. Jefferson Dotson, who loved the Army Air Corps, the Army Air Forces and the Air Force; for my cousin, Jefferson Scott Dotson, an American fighter pilot who gave everything; and for my classmates, those magnificent gold tags of the Class of '63.

Prologue

United States Air Force Academy, Colorado

Friday, 23 September 1983

A middle-aged man struggled, breathing heavily, as he climbed the last ten yards to the ridge line of the mountain. Reaching it, he took off his backpack and hat, letting a strong breeze cool the sweat on his head as he surveyed the brown, flat country of eastern Colorado that stretched to the horizon. The Academy's campus was below him to the southeast, two miles away at the base of the Rampart Range, and the white-granite and aluminum surfaces of its buildings gleamed in the mid-afternoon sun.

He heard the sound of jet engines in the distance reverberating against the face of the mountains. Looking to the south, he quickly scanned sections of sky as he had learned to do on his first training flights twenty years earlier. Four F-16s in close formation were streaking northward toward him at low altitude, heading for the cluster of buildings below. Suddenly, one of the jets broke sharply upward, roaring away from the others as its afterburner lit, and climbed vertically until it disappeared from sight into a brilliantly blue Colorado sky.

Good missing-man formation, he thought, shading his eyes. *These kids are as good as we ever were in the cockpit. Maybe even better.*

Using his hiking stick for support, he sat down on a rock, reached into his shirt pocket and pulled out a small photograph of a young man in uniform. *God, we were so young then. And we'd had enough of military formality,* he mused, convincing himself again that being alone on the mountain was more fitting, a better remembrance than the formal memorial service for his twenty-year class reunion that had just ended at the campus in the distance with the wail of F-16s overhead.

Gazing at the pale light of the horizon, he remembered another sky from a haunting day during his late twenties, one he could never quite bury in the recesses of recollection. In moisture-laden air, trailing vortex streamers from its wingtips, a swept-wing jet in camouflage war paint dove in a tight turn toward a dirt road in the rugged wilderness of northern Laos, then rolled out to strafe with its cannon. Streams of tracer fire bracketed the airplane as soon as its wings leveled. Its nose came up, breaking off its attack, and it hemorrhaged flame, rolling slowly as it lost momentum. It rolled over on its back and hit the ground in a fireball.

He sighed deeply as he let the memory run its course this time, not blocking it with another quickly seized thought as he had done often since then. Images of a blood-spattered cockpit and a terrifying flight in weather and darkness came back to him again.

So young, so bitter and so damned hardheaded. Friends first and then barely speaking to each other at the end. How could we have let that happen? Why the hell didn't you listen when I tried to warn you? Things would be a lot different now.

Reaching into his pack, he found the plastic tobacco pouch he had carried on all of his combat missions. Inside it were two of his medals, his Air Force Cross and Purple Heart. He put the photo into the pouch with them and zipped it closed. Pulling himself to his feet with his hiking stick, he stood, and after walking a few searching steps, he chose a rock under a small pine tree. He kicked at it awkwardly to dislodge it from the earth that held it. He knelt down slowly, working his hands down his walking staff to keep his balance, then grabbed the large stone, using all his strength to roll it to one side. Gently, he placed the pouch into the earthen cavity he had uncovered, then moved the rock carefully back into place.

He twisted roughly to a sitting position, reached for his pack and took out a glass and a bottle of cognac. He cut through the bottle's lead seal with his pocket knife, removed its cork, poured a glass and raised it to the sky. *Here's to all of us who fought and to all of you who fought and died.* He breathed the rich aroma of the amber-colored liquid, then took a slow drink, letting its strong flavor flood his mouth and warm his throat. Looking into the distance, he saw the Academy's stadium, and he began to remember how eager they were to start flying when they graduated, when going on to pilot training finally became a reality after four long years of waiting.

Chapter 1

Friday, 22 November 1963

Second Lieutenant Kevin O'Dea rolled his T-37 jet trainer on its back and pulled on its control stick to bring the airplane's nose well below the horizon in an inverted dive. With airspeed increasing rapidly, he rolled upright again, slowing the roll at the end to line up with east-west section lines that separated irrigated Arizona farms on the desert below him. He pushed the jet's two throttles fully forward with his left hand to ensure full engine power, and he let airspeed build as the altimeter unwound, registering an earthward plummet of hundreds of feet per second. As airspeed raced past 200 knots, he pulled the stick straight back, bringing the jet's nose upward through the horizon. Glancing at the g meter on the instrument panel, seeing it register four times the pull of gravity, he tightened his stomach, taking his breath in gasps as the g's came on, to prevent blackout from blood being pulled away from his head into his lower torso and legs.

The airplane's nose shot upward toward the noonday sun, and he turned his head to the left to look at the horizon through the canopy. Passing the vertical, the airplane upside down and beginning a fall to earth, still decelerating, he looked forward again, tilting his head well back, pressing the top of his flight helmet against the head rest of his ejection seat, straining to find the horizon behind him.

Seeing that he had pulled up straight when the section lines came into view again below him, he waited for the top of the canopy to fall to just above the horizon and gently released all rearward pressure on the stick to keep the jet from stalling as airspeed continued to drop. He started a slow roll with smooth, firm pressure on the airplane's sluggish controls, completing the maneuver with the trainer in slow, level flight, its nose well up in an exaggerated attitude above the horizon. He glanced at the airspeed indicator. *Right speed. A hundred knots. A pretty decent Immelmann,* he decided, satisfied with the half loop completed by a half roll at the top. *I've got the good hands today.*

He glanced at the fuel gauge to see how much more time he had to practice the acrobatic maneuvers he had to fly proficiently on a check flight the following week. *Eight hundred pounds of gas left. I'd better get back.* He eased in aileron to start a slow roll and let the jet's nose slice downward toward the desert below. On impulse, feeling airspeed building in the dive from increased sensitivity of the stick, he rolled upright and pulled the nose up sharply, well above the horizon, forgetting the cockpit instruments he had been using for the precise, formal maneuvers he had been practicing, relying only on the feel of the airplane. Climbing steeply, he released all back pressure on the stick, letting the jet float, letting it go ballistic at zero g, and he pushed the stick to the right and held it there. Earth and sky spun ahead of him as the airplane responded with continuous, exuberant rolls to the right, the roll rate decreasing and the nose dropping earthward with each revolution as airspeed bled away in the rolling climb.

When the nose dropped slightly below the horizon, he centered the stick to stop rolling and pulled the throttles back to enter a shallow glide to conserve fuel. *Damn!* he thought, *what could be better than this? Out here by myself doing acro on a crystal-clear Friday afternoon, and I'm actually getting paid to do it.* He looked over at the empty ejection seat to his right usually occupied by his instructor pilot—his IP. *I'm really missing you right now, Screamer.*

He had been unlucky in the draw for IPs. His, Captain Riemer, or Riemer the Screamer as he was known among student pilots, thought that the fates had laughed at him. They had, Riemer believed, thrown him into that special purgatory called undergraduate pilot training—UPT—inhabited by ham-handed rookies who would plunge him to the ground to his death if he were ever unwary. This apparent fall from grace, after three glorious years of flying single-seat fighters in Europe, had made Riemer an ardent disciple of what UPT students called the FSR school of instruction, FSR standing for the three great motivators, fear, sarcasm and ridicule. With the side-by-side seats in the T-37,

Riemer was adept at getting a student's attention with a sharp whack to the right side of a flight helmet or by squeezing an oxygen hose to strangle the air supply to an oxygen mask.

Well, Kevin concluded as he continued his descent, *I can stand anything, even the Screamer, for six months. Besides, flying solo like this makes Riemer just a pimple on a gnat's ass.* He turned up the volume on the radio to hear Riemer's voice more clearly from Rag Top, the call sign of a glass cage near the approach end of the runway that T-37s used for takeoffs and landings at Williams Air Force Base, southeast of Phoenix. Two IPs worked a shift of several uneasy hours there and controlled the landing pattern, hoping that none of the green student pilots under their charge would jeopardize their careers by crashing on their watch.

"Rag Top is landing runway three zero left," Riemer announced. "Altimeter is three zero point zero two. Winds are down the runway at eight knots."

Kevin reached for a small knob on the altimeter and turned it slightly to set 30.02 in its calibration window. The instrument, which worked by sensing atmospheric pressure of the outside air, displayed altitude above sea level when set properly.

After a long, pleasurable glide, he turned the trainer steeply to enter the landing pattern. *The jet feels really good today,* he said to himself, glancing at the airspeed indicator and altimeter, seeing that his speed and altitude coming out of the turn were right on. He flew the airplane around the outer perimeter of the pattern, connecting straight-and-level legs with steep turns, enjoying the sensation of light g loading each time he banked the trainer sharply to change direction, feeling the edge of mastery as he worked its controls. Rolling out of the turn that placed the runway directly ahead, on the initial approach, he pressed the microphone button on the right throttle and called, "Warlock two one, initial," telling the instructor crew at Rag Top that another T-37 was preparing to land.

Riemer responded by announcing the landing information again, ending with, "Winds are down the runway at ten knots."

Ideal conditions, Kevin thought. Over the end of the runway, he rolled the airplane into a steep turn to the left and reduced power with the throttles to begin to decelerate to landing speed. Out of habit, he flicked a switch below the mike button with his left thumb to activate the jet's speed brake, a rectangular panel on the bottom of the airplane that killed off airspeed quickly when it was extended into the airstream.

As the jet's nose swept horizontally, just above the horizon in the last part of the turn, he rolled out on the downwind leg of the landing pattern, placing him on a heading opposite to the runway's. He extended the trainer's landing gear quickly by firmly lowering a large, round handle on the instrument panel, and checked for three green lights just above the handle that told him all three wheels were down and locked. Continuing to hold altitude as the runway dropped behind him, he looked over his left shoulder to time his last turn. With the end of the runway a half mile behind, he felt for the flap lever without looking for it, moved it to full down to extend the jet's wing flaps and rolled into a shallow left bank to begin a final turn to landing. He pressed the mike button and called, "Warlock two one, gear check, full stop," telling Riemer that he had visually confirmed the three green lights and that he was ending his flight.

As the airplane turned and descended, the runway appeared to rotate slowly and flatten, its long line of pavement moving gradually from the left side of the canopy toward the windscreen. He felt good. He was comfortable with the jet, instinctively staying ahead of it, anticipating the next movements he would have to make with the stick and throttles.

He rolled slowly out of the turn as the jet's nose came around to the runway heading, finding the right feel on the stick, pointing the airplane to fly toward the edge of the landing pavement ahead. His senses sharpened as he closed the distance, and he made fine, quick movements with the stick to stay on glide path. He eased the throttles forward to hold final-approach speed at 100 knots, and he looked quickly in and out of the cockpit, holding glide path and checking airspeed.

The end of the runway began to rush at him. He shifted his vision to look down its length to the far end for better depth perception. *Easy, easy*, his senses told him. He eased the stick back, slowing the upward movement of the horizon in the windscreen. When the picture in the windscreen looked right, he pulled on the throttles, moving them slowly, completely back to idle power. With gentle pressure on the stick, he let the jet settle until he sensed the runway just inches below the landing gear. Increasing the pressure with his right hand to hold the airplane just off the concrete, he kept the stick coming back slowly as airspeed fell off. *Back. Back. Easy. Easy. There.* The jet's two main wheels touched lightly, and he looked to his right quickly to see that he had landed directly in front of Rag Top, the prescribed landing point. *A grease job. Man, I must be unconscious. Nothing can go wrong today.*

On the landing rollout, he eased the stick forward to lower the trainer's nosewheel gently to the pavement and worked rudder pedals with his feet to keep the slowing airplane headed straight down the runway. *I hope my check ride next week goes this well,* he thought, as the airplane decelerated and rolled toward a taxiway at the far end. Relaxing as the jet slowed, he became aware of dampness from sweat under his flying suit that was always there after a flight, even in an air-conditioned cockpit, telling him that an hour and a quarter in the air demanded more from him than he had felt at the time.

Up ahead, on his right, a T-38 turned off the outside, parallel runway. The jet came to a stop to wait for him to clear the inside runway before crossing it behind him on the way to the parking ramp. *The White Rocket,* he said to himself, approving of the nickname that student pilots had attached to the sleek, white-painted jet trainer officially known as the T-38 Talon. For many of them, those headed to bombers, transports and tankers after UPT, it would be the highest performing airplane they would ever fly. *You're just three months away.*

As the last taxiway neared, he pushed on the tops of the rudder pedals to test his brakes. Feeling good braking, he pushed on the left rudder pedal, turned onto the taxiway and changed radio frequencies. "Williams ground," he transmitted, "Warlock two one is down."

"Williams ground control, roger. Two one is cleared to the ramp."

He quickly raised the jet's speed brake and flaps and turned off electrical switches, cleaning up the airplane while scanning rows of parked T-37s ahead for a crew chief standing in front of an empty parking space. Seeing his man, he turned off the taxiway and onto the parking ramp.

Nearly abeam the empty space, he turned the nose of the airplane toward its crew chief and applied brakes to slow to a crawl. Casually, the man ahead began motioning him forward with upraised arms then crossed his wrists above his head and clenched his fists to signal a stop.

Kevin responded with the brakes and, pulling the throttles to off, looked at two columns of small, matched dials in the center of the instrument panel. The needles in all of them began dropping as the airplane's two engines unwound, as fuel stopped flowing to them, and the flames inside that gave them fiery life were snuffed out. He raised the jet's canopy, felt warm outside air invade the cockpit and smelled a faint kerosene aroma from spilled jet fuel when he unfastened his oxygen mask. A bright sun made him squint when he raised the shaded visor covering his eyes before removing his flight helmet. He paused for a moment to enjoy them, the sensations of a flight's ending, the sound, odor and bright light of a busy airfield.

The crew chief, wearing ear-muff noise suppressors to protect his hearing from the high-pitched whine of the T-37's engines, walked leisurely to the left wing of the airplane, pushed a yellow wooden chock around the wheel of the landing gear with his foot, then approached the open cockpit. "Good flight, sir?"

"Great flight, chief," Kevin said as he finished shutting down the cockpit.

"How's the bird, sir?" the enlisted man asked, removing his noise-killing ear muffs, barely concealing his concern that another spastic student pilot might have damaged the airplane he considered his own.

"No discrepancies. You've got a good-flying jet here. It gets my vote for champ of the ramp," Kevin replied as he handed his helmet to the crew chief and unfastened his lap belt.

"Thank you, sir," the crew chief said appreciatively, pulling shoulder straps that connected to the pilot's lap belt out of the way to help him out of the cockpit.

Kevin stood up, and holding on to the trainer's windscreen to support the extra weight of his parachute, he stepped backward out of the jet to lower himself to the ramp. He signed the jet's maintenance record, then picked up his flight gear from the left wing where the crew chief had stuffed it all into a protective cloth bag and said, "Thanks, chief. I hope I get your airplane again sometime when I'm out solo."

"Glad you enjoyed it, sir."

He began walking toward a one-story building beyond the ramp, careful to stay in front of the parked airplanes to avoid jet blast from any that might have engines running. A sign at the entrance announced the building to be the 3526th Pilot Training Squadron. He walked inside and went through a second door under a sign that designated the room where pilots stored their flight gear as Life Support. He found two bare arms on a tall rack welded together from two-inch pipe, and letting his parachute fall off his shoulders onto his forearms, he slid it onto the lower pipe. Ending his post-flight ritual, he took his helmet out of its bag, slid the bag's cloth handles over the upper pipe and placed his helmet on the top pipe's padded end.

I could use a cup of coffee, he thought, deciding to put a pleasurable finish on a good mission. He walked to the end of a long corridor that separated the coffee room from Life Support, passing flight rooms where instructors held court at gray-metal, government-issue tables topped with plexiglass. There, as artists with grease pencils, they explained and diagramed mysteries of the air for their students in pre-mission briefings and after-mission debriefings.

He was surprised to see the coffee room so crowded. Normally, four or five students might be found there, taking a break from studying flight manuals in the flight rooms, exaggerating their aerial exploits with flat hands moving in front of them, simulating airplanes in flight, amusing others drinking coffee who knew better. At the coffee bar near the far wall of the room, decorated with numerous coffee cups hung on wooden wall panels behind two large brewing urns, one of the students held a hand-size, battery-powered radio while the others stood and listened closely.

Seeing Ed Walker, a classmate from the Air Force Academy, on the edge of the crowd at the doorway, Kevin walked up behind him and asked, "Hey, Ed, what's going on?"

Ed turned around, his face colorless and drawn.

"Jesus, Ed," he said in a low voice, startled at what he saw. "What's wrong?"

"President Kennedy's been shot," Ed whispered.

"Oh, god, no!" he blurted out.

"Quiet!" the man with the radio shouted. "There's another announcement."

As Ed turned toward the radio again, Kevin strained to listen. Through the crackling static of its small speaker he heard a weak voice say, "President John F. Kennedy died at approximately one p.m. central standard time here in Dallas. He died of a gunshot wound to the brain. There are no other details of the assassination."

A few in the room erupted with profane outbursts while the rest stared in bewilderment. Stunned, he couldn't believe what he had just heard, and the elation he felt from flying so well faded quickly away.

Chapter 2

Friday, 22 November 1963

Kevin sat alone in his darkened room, watching still images of a charismatic JFK from early in his presidency move at a funereal pace, one slowly after another, across a cold-blue television screen. Still not quite believing what the off-screen narrator was saying, Kevin's thoughts wandered to an early-June day, six months before at the Air Force Academy, when the first president ever to address a graduating class there was about to arrive.

Dressed in their parade uniforms, white hats, blue tunics, white trousers and gold sashes, the 499 graduates of the Class of 1963 sat patiently in two rectangles of chairs at the center of the grass playing field in Falcon Stadium. During the previous hour, they had marched individually to the platform in front of them to receive their diplomas and commissions as second lieutenants. The stadium's stands were filled with families and friends eager to have their young President arrive to give the ceremony a memorable conclusion with a Boston-accented commencement address, and while they waited in cool mountain sunshine, the Academy's band played a medley of military marches.

Kevin surfaced from daydreaming about Teresa and looked up when he heard the sound of rotor blades smacking the air. The President's helicopter swept low over the assembly from the south and landed in a parking lot behind the stadium. As the crowd began to cheer in anticipation, the cadet wing commander stepped to the platform microphone and called the graduates to attention and to present arms.

When the President's open-top limousine entered the stadium, the band sounded "Ruffles and Flourishes" followed by "Hail to the Chief," but Kevin could hardly hear the music over the thunderous cheering of the spectators when they erupted at the sight of JFK. The President's car moved slowly around the perimeter of the field, and his rugged smile and upraised arm kept the crowd on their feet and sustained their cheering and applause.

When his car stopped at the speakers' platform, President Kennedy, clearly enjoying himself, stepped out quickly and continued to wave as he made his way to his seat. Other dignitaries followed from two other cars in the motorcade, and when they had all had found their places on the platform, the cadet wing commander called for the Class of '63 to order arms and to be seated. The Academy's senior officer, its superintendent, a two-star general, stepped to the microphone, introduced the officials on the platform then called the class's ranking cadet forward again.

The cadet colonel said, "Mister President, I have the honor to inform you that, by acclamation, you have been elected to be a member of the Class of 1963, to be our classmate." He turned toward the President and presented him a diploma plaque. The spectators loved it and cheered loudly, while the graduates added vigorous applause from nearly a thousand white-gloved hands that sounded like hundreds of sails snapping in the wind.

When the wave of approval faded, the superintendent took the microphone again and said, "Ladies and gentlemen, the President of the United States."

The crowd responded enthusiastically, but this time with more applause than cheering as the proceedings took on a more formal tone. The President rose from his seat, and after shaking hands with the general, strode to the microphone. With the response from the crowd just past its peak, he recognized the others on the platform, including the Air Force's senior-ranking officer, its four-star chief of staff, legendary General Curtis LeMay. The President began:

> Fellow graduates. I want to express my appreciation for becoming an instant graduate of this Academy, and consider it a high honor. Mister Salinger, Press Secretary of the White House, received the following letter several days ago:

The White House
1600 Pennsylvania Avenue

Dear Sir:

Would you desire to become an honorary member of the Air Force Cadet Wing for granting one small favor? Your name, Mister Salinger, shall become more hallowed and revered than the combined memories of generals Mitchell, Arnold, and Doolittle.

My humble desire is that you convey a request from the Cadet Wing to the President. Sir, there are countless numbers of our group who are oppressed by Class Three punishments, the bane of cadets everywhere. The President is our only hope of salvation. By granting amnesty to our oppressed brethren, he and you could end our anguish and depression.

Please, sir, help us return to the ranks of the living so that we may work for the New Frontier with enthusiasm and vigor.

The President chuckled along with the crowd and continued:

It is signed "Sincerely, Cadet Marvin B. Hopkins," who's obviously going to be a future general.

As Mister Salinger wants to be honored with generals Mitchell, Arnold and Doolittle, I therefore take great pleasure in granting amnesty to all those who not only deserve it, but need it.

Kevin smiled as he recalled the crowd's high-spirited approval of JFK's deft opening. He could still remember the speech's high points, especially the closing that brought the graduates to their feet with loud applause. President Kennedy concluded:

I want to congratulate all of you who have chosen the United States Air Force as a career. As far as any of us can now see in Washington in the days ahead, you will occupy positions of the highest responsibility, and merely because we move

> into a changing period of weapon technology, as well as political challenge—because in fact we move into that period—there is greater need for you than ever before. You, here today on this field, your colleagues at Omaha, Nebraska, or at Eglin in Florida, or who may be stationed in Western Europe, or men who are at sea in ships hundreds of miles from land, or soldiers in camps in Texas, or on the island of Okinawa, they maintain freedom by being on the ready. They maintain the freedom, the security, and the peace not only of the United States, but of the dozens of countries who are allied to us who are close to the Communist power and who depend upon us and, in a sense, only upon us for their freedom and security. These distant ships, these distant planes, these distant men keep the peace in a great half-circle stretching all the way from Berlin to South Korea. This is the role which history and our own determination has placed upon a country which lived most of its history in isolation and neutrality, and yet in the last eighteen years has carried the burden for free people everywhere.
>
> I think that this is a burden which we accept willingly, recognizing that if this country does not accept it, no people will, recognizing that in the most difficult time in the whole life of freedom, the United States is called upon to play its greatest role. This is a role which we are proud to accept, and I am particularly proud to see the United States accept it in the presence of these young men who have committed themselves to the service of our country and to the cause of its freedom.
>
> I congratulate you all, and most of all I congratulate your mothers and fathers who made it possible. Thank you.

Kevin remembered the pride he had felt later in the ceremony when he and his classmates raised their hands, with their commander-in-chief looking on, to take their commissioning oaths.

> I, Kevin Patrick O'Dea, having been appointed a second lieutenant in the United States Air Force, do solemnly swear that I will support and defend the Constitution of the United States against all enemies, foreign and

> domestic; that I will bear true faith and allegiance to the same; that I will take this obligation freely, without any mental reservation or purpose of evasion; and that I will well and faithfully discharge the duties of the office on which I am about to enter. So help me God.

A few minutes later, they ended the ceremony by hurling their parade hats into the air after receiving the order, "Gentlemen, you are dismissed!" Kevin made his way toward the stands, shaking hands and giving best wishes to his classmates. Seeing his family and Teresa at the railing, he ran up concrete steps to greet them.

"Congratulations, Lieutenant," his father said with a wide smile, shaking his hand firmly.

"Thank you, sir."

"Come here, handsome," his mother beamed as she hugged and kissed him.

"You look great!" his younger brother Sean declared when his turn came and grabbed him around the shoulders.

"Thanks, Sean. Having a good time?"

"Jesus, this is just great! Kennedy was terrific!"

"Sean!" his mother said sternly. "You watch that swearing."

"Sorry, Mom," his brother replied, grinning, his face reddening beneath his freckles.

Teresa had waited at a distance for his family to greet him first. He walked over to her, embraced her, and received a modest kiss on the cheek in return. "Where's that Spanish passion?" he teased under his breath.

"Later, my love. This is your mother's moment," she whispered.

"Well, folks," his father said, looking at his watch, "let's get this formation together. We've got a plane to catch in three hours. We'd better get to the officers' club for some lunch before it gets too crowded."

"Sounds good, Dad."

As they walked toward a stadium exit, Kevin dropped behind the others and walked with his mother. "Isn't she something, Mom?"

"Kevin, Teresa is lovely. Over the last few days I've seen real substance there."

"I'm glad you think so. I'm going to ask her to marry me tonight." She put her arm around his waist and hugged him as they walked. "That's marvelous. I'm really happy for you, Kevin."

"God love ya, sweet mother o' mine," he said in a brogue, kissing her on the cheek.

After leaving his family at their rental car, he walked across the parking lot with Teresa toward his car, her arm in his, and said, "Mom thinks you're okay."

"Just okay?"

"No, a little more than that. Actually, she thinks you're wonderful."

"I'm glad," she said as they reached his car, "because I feel the same way about her son."

She put her arms around his neck and gave him a moist kiss firmly on the mouth. Leaning back in his arms, she asked, "And what do you think of Spanish passion now, my Irish skeptic?"

"It just gets better and better."

Kevin looked at his watch. *Thirty more minutes,* he thought, impatient to make his weekly pre-arranged phone call to Teresa. As he thought about her, he remembered the double date at the end of his junior year that had changed everything. He had driven to Denver with his roommate, Ed Walker, to meet Ed's fiancee, Clare, and a blind date. Clare had insisted for weeks that he meet this new woman, and he had finally given in.

Blonde Clare Rossetti had driven high-school boys crazy in her cheerleader's sweater, and she had fallen for Ed Walker when he played starting linebacker with a cool ferocity, a year before he became a cadet. He had given up football reluctantly after making the Academy's freshman team, when two concussions had threatened to keep him from going to pilot training.

Clare welcomed Ed with a kiss and then made the introduction, ending with, "And Kevin, this is Teresa de la Cruz."

He was completely unprepared for her. Her dark eyes transfixed him. He tried to say something, but for a telling fraction of a second, he couldn't make a sound. After clearing his throat, he mumbled, "Hi."

"Hi, Kevin," she replied softly, with none of the false gaiety he expected when the nervousness of first meeting did its usual straining work on conversation. "Clare has told me a lot about you."

"Clare would know," was the best he could manage, unable to say anything remotely clever. "She says that you can be mysterious at times," she said with a perplexed smile, trying to draw him out.

"Not really," he muttered, not believing the drivel, the conversational crutches, coming out of his mouth.

"Yeah, well, we'd better move it if we're going to make the show on time," Ed interjected, seeing his classmate's plight and coming to his rescue. "Teresa, allow me," Ed continued, opening the driver's-side door to help her into the back seat of his car.

As he and Clare walked around to the passenger side, he said to himself angrily, *O'Dea, you jerk, you've been through this nice-to-meet-you stuff a hundred times. What the hell's wrong with you?* Then, noticing Clare's impish smile, he glared at her and asked in a low voice, "What's so damned funny, Clare?"

When the others couldn't hear, she whispered delightedly, "You, Kevin. She knocked you flat on your ass, didn't she, lover boy."

Yeah. Pretty completely, Kevin admitted to himself. *God, she looked beautiful graduation night.*

After finishing a quiet dinner, he looked at her silently for a moment, then smiled and said, "I couldn't imagine life without you now. Do you see what a lovesick fool you've made out of me?"

"Then this must be the table for two lovesick fools."

He took her hands in his and said softly, "I want to be with you always. Could you love me for that long?"

"Longer."

He reached inside his jacket, found the ring and put it on her finger while she looked into his eyes. She smiled again, and a single tear glided over her cheek. She closed her eyes for a long moment, then looked at the ring.

"No more tears," he said, brushing her cheek with the backs of his fingers.

"It's how you know a Spanish girl is deliriously happy," she said, then took his fingers and pressed them to her lips.

"I just don't want you to cloud up those beautiful eyes. They're what nailed me the first time I saw you."

After they had sat silently for a while, holding hands, she said, "I know that it sounds completely old fashioned, but my father expects you to ask his permission for us to marry. Could you come to Durango in August to meet him, on your way to pilot training?"

"Sure. Will he be tough on me?"

"Spanish fathers think it's their role in life to be tough where their daughters are concerned, but Juan will be a big help," she said, referring to her older brother, a seminarian a year away from ordination as a Jesuit priest. "He's anxious to meet you. I've asked him to come home to our ranch from the seminary this summer to guide you through everything, and my father actually listens to him. Anyway, even Spanish fathers can't stand in the way of what's meant to be."

But they can put a real twist in your life, Kevin thought as he looked at his watch again. Seeing that he had more time to kill, he let his thoughts drift to his trip to Durango, Colorado, three months earlier.

Following Teresa's directions, he had found the gravel road she had described, and he turned off the highway into a narrow creek valley resting between two high ridges covered with pines. After a mile of slow driving, climbing gradually toward mountain peaks in the distance, he saw a house with rough-lumber siding and a steeply pitched, cedar-shake roof across the creek. He turned toward it, crossing a sturdy wooden bridge.

"You'll love the Abramssons. They were wonderful to Juan and me growing up," Teresa had said, after explaining that the Spanish ways of courtship would not allow a suitor to stay under the same roof as his intended.

She had gone on to say that her neighbor, Karin Abramsson, had spent many hours with her and had shared mothering her with Juanita, the family housekeeper who had died when she was twelve. After that, she had said, Karin had guided her through her teenage years over sessions at a loom teaching her the weaver's art. Jakob, Karin's husband, had welcomed Teresa's visits as much as his wife, she had told him, probably because they filled a void for the childless couple. She had recounted many of their conversations in front of the Abramssons' fireplace as Karin knitted, as the aroma from Jakob's pipe mingled with the scent of a wood fire. She had laughed when she said that these evenings had invariably ended with Karin, the impeccable Swedish housekeeper, reminding her husband to clean up stray wood shavings around his chair that he had carried in on his clothing from his cabinet shop in a barn behind the house.

Kevin climbed a set of wooden steps after parking his car and knocked on a hand-carved front door. A woman in her mid-forties, with light-blue eyes magnified by wire-rimmed glasses, her graying blonde hair in a bun, opened the door wide and said, "You must be Kevin. I'm Karin. Welcome. Please come in."

He liked the feel of the room. Its beamed wooden ceiling paralleled the pitch of the roof line, and its white walls were decorated with intricate, hand-done stencils at the tops and corners. Wool wall hangings done in Scandinavian blues took up the center spaces. One wall, opposite a large stone fireplace, was filled with books.

"Thank you," he said. "Beautiful room."

"Thank you. A little bit of Sweden in Colorado. Make yourself comfortable, Kevin," she said, motioning to chairs near the fireplace. "I'll go get Jakob from his shop. He's anxious to meet the man who's stolen Teresa's heart."

Jakob Abramsson beamed heartiness as his long strides carried him into the room with his hand extended. "Welcome to the mountains, Kevin."

He returned the firm grip of the taller, older man with tousled gray hair. "Thank you, sir."

"Sir? My goodness. You'll make me feel more ancient than I am. Please call me Jakob. How was the drive from Denver?"

"All trips should be that good on the eyes. I drove with the top down the whole way."

Karin walked into the room from the kitchen carrying a large tray and said, "You must be hungry after driving all day." She set the tray down on a coffee table in front of the fireplace and said, "Swedish beer and smorgasbord."

"You shouldn't have gone to all this trouble."

"It's easy after years of practice. Besides, we'll be having another guest shortly. I called Juan after you arrived, and he'll be here soon."

"It'll be good to meet Teresa's brother. I feel like I'm flying a little blind here."

"Juan will be a good navigator for you, Kevin," Jakob said. "He understands Miguel probably better than anyone, and he wants tomorrow to go smoothly for you and Teresa."

"The way Teresa's talked about him, Juan sounds like a great guy," Kevin probed.

"He is," Karin replied. "He was very popular in high school. He played sports and was the student-council president, and it came as a complete surprise to everyone when Juan, of all people, announced that he wanted to go into the seminary."

"Mostly, it surprised a number of girls who had hopes of catching him," Jakob added. "Of course, his father was very pleased."

"Teresa says that her father's pretty traditional," Kevin said.

"Well, he's a good man who works hard, and Miguel was very helpful to us when we moved here from Minnesota," Jakob answered. "Probably the best thing he's done is to raise two exceptional children without a mother."

"Teresa tells me, though, that after her mother died, she was raised in a kind of cooperative effort."

"We sort of adopted Juan and Teresa," Karin said. "They spent a lot of time with us, and we enjoyed watching them grow."

"Yes," Jakob chuckled, "we introduced a little Swedish leavening into the Spanish baking. I remember once when Teresa discovered the tradition of bundling in a novel we had loaned her from our library," he said, waving at the wall of books at the other end of the room. "She said that it must be a sinful practice. Karin assured her that it was possible for an engaged couple to be bundled in the same bed and still be good Christians, especially if they're Swedish Lutherans. When Teresa finally understood our secret, and blushed the deepest shade of red you ever saw, it was priceless."

Karin smiled at the memory and said, "Over time, as Jakob and I talked with them about anything and everything, they seemed to look at things a little less narrowly. I remember—" she began, but was interrupted by a knock at the door. "That must be Juan," she said, as she rose to answer it.

"Hi. I'm back for that feast you promised this afternoon," Juan said to Karin as he entered, and seeing the two men at the fireplace, he moved through the room toward them with the ease that came from many previous visits. Wearing jeans, western boots and a faded western shirt, Juan looked very much at home.

Jakob said, "Karin and I were just explaining to Kevin here how we introduced unorthodox Swedish opinions into young Spanish minds."

Juan laughed easily and said, "Well, Kevin, you can see how difficult it is dealing with heretics, without the Inquisition around anymore." Juan extended his hand and said, "Delighted to meet you finally."

Karin joined them from the kitchen as they sat down, bringing another beer for Juan. "The reason I wanted to meet you here," Juan said, looking at Karin, "is to have our talk over the best food and drink in town. After the fare at the seminary, this is heaven."

As Juan reached for one of the sandwiches made from dark bread, Karin said, "The boy may be Spanish, but he has a Swedish soul."

"A couple of hundred herring sandwiches over the years will do that to you," Juan said. "So, Kevin, what have these two been telling you to tarnish my priestly image?"

"They've been telling me that you are the greatest director of meetings of all time, and that tomorrow's flawless performance will reflect the usual Jesuit skill behind the scenes," he said, feeling his anxiety beginning to build.

"Well, everything's set for ten in the morning. I'll be looking very official in my new cassock, and as courtesy requires, Father and Teresa will be dressed like they're going to church. I will introduce you to him and we'll start from there. After some preliminary pleasantries, you will ask for his permission to marry Teresa, and then you'll respond to his objections."

"Objections?"

"Yes. There's a kind of mildly combative style that's expected in this situation. He's expected to raise objections, and you're expected to respond to each of his concerns. The tone you should take is to be very respectful, but firm."

"Do you have any idea what he'll object to?"

"Oh, he'll say, for example, that Teresa can't marry until she finishes college, even though he already knows that you don't plan to marry until next year. Then, you'll say something like, of course, sir, we wouldn't dream of marrying until next year. That sort of thing."

"So, this'll be a piece of cake."

Juan and Karin exchanged a quick glance. "Kevin," Karin said, "you have to realize that this will be a very difficult meeting for Miguel. He'll be asked to give up his only daughter who came into his life after two miscarriages and the death of his wife in childbirth. His attachment to Teresa is, understandably, very strong. That attachment will be at the center of any other difficulty he might raise."

Jakob added, "He's known for a long time that this day would come, but human nature being what it is, he'll probably find it very difficult to accept."

"I'm sorry, Juan," Kevin said. "Teresa told me about the death of your mother, but I didn't know the rest."

"From what I've learned over the years, my family's move here from Spain, just before the civil war there, was very difficult for her," Juan replied. "Her family was very pro-Franco, but my father developed sympathies for the Loyalists after he and my mother were married. Her parents' strong feelings about the war magnified their differences with my father over his political views, and she became estranged from her family. She never returned to Spain after the war, and she became very depressed at times. So, Kevin, I hope that you can see that this meeting tomorrow will be a very emotional experience for my father, even though he'll do everything he can to hide it. After watching him for the last few days, I know he's brooding about something, but he won't talk about it."

Feeling uneasy, Kevin asked, "What might he object to where I'm concerned?"

"Since you and Teresa are both Catholics, the biggest potential issue in Miguel's mind has been resolved," Jakob said, striking a match. "On the surface, nothing else would appear to be a problem. So, the question is: what might he plausibly make into a problem?" He paused to take several draws on his pipe and continued, "After Teresa came home for the summer and told us about your engagement, Karin, Juan and I talked over the phone about tomorrow's meeting. We believe that he might object to your profession."

"What do you mean?"

"Both Teresa and Juan were too young to remember the Second World War, but Karin and I remembered Miguel being very strongly affected by the bombing of cities that killed so many civilians—on both sides."

"What are you saying, Jakob? Is he a pacifist?"

"No, it's more tangled than that. He was grateful that Hitler and Mussolini were crushed after they supported Franco during the war in Spain and caused so much death and destruction throughout Europe later. But the civilian casualties troubled him greatly. After what the Germans did in bombing Guernica and other Spanish cities, he expected their air attacks on London and Coventry, but he couldn't believe it when Hamburg and Dresden were destroyed by allied firebombing. It made a deep impression on me when he said once, after Dresden, that military men are all the same under the uniform. I tried to argue with him. I told him that the fascist regimes in Germany and Japan were the most evil powers ever to appear on the face of the earth and that almost anything was justified in destroying them, but he wouldn't listen."

"Jakob, you're not serious. Are you saying that he might actually lump me in with fascists?"

"Kevin," Juan added earnestly, "we're not saying that it's logical or even reasonable for him to believe that all military men think and act alike. But, in the emotion of this meeting tomorrow, since he has nothing else to grab on to, this could be something that he might use as a pretext when the real issue is Teresa. We just want you to be prepared for it and not to let him surprise and anger you. He would call any display of anger on your part disrespect, and that would complicate things a lot."

"Juan, even the idea of equating me, or men like my father who fought them, to those goose-stepping bastards is just plain crazy," he said heatedly.

Karin said, "Kevin, I can understand why you're upset by this, and I want to tell you something that's very important. Teresa had no idea that her father might feel this way, since it all happened so long ago, and he's not the most open man when it comes to discussing things like this with his children. After the three of us talked with Teresa a few days ago, she was also upset and told us that she hopes her father won't dredge up any of this tomorrow. You should know, though, that if he does and if things go badly, she won't let her father prevent her from marrying you. So, in a very real way, it will be Miguel who'll be on trial tomorrow, not you. Teresa is hoping, though, that she won't have to choose you over her father. She loves you both very much."

"But, if that's Teresa's decision, won't he have to live with it?"

"Kevin," Juan said quietly, "there are many good qualities that a Spaniard can possess, but an extreme sensitivity to perceived disrespect from his children isn't one of them. There are many stories about Spanish parents renouncing their adult children for the rest of their lives for things that would be considered completely absurd here in America. My mother's story is only one of them."

"Well," he said with a deep sigh, "then let's hope that things go well tomorrow."

"Kevin," Jakob said, "I hope that you're not angry that we've waited until now to tell you all this, but we didn't want you to worry all summer about something that might or might not happen tomorrow. Over the last few months, I've collected some articles on British and American bombing campaigns that cover the controversies evenhandedly."

"Thanks, Jakob. I'll definitely read them tonight."

"Kevin," Juan said as he stood to leave, putting his hand on Kevin's shoulder, "all three of us here want tomorrow to be a good day for you and Teresa. I want you to know that I will do everything I can to get my father to bless your marriage to my sister."

The next morning, he drove across the Abramssons' bridge to take the unpaved road farther into the mountains, and he thought again about the articles Jakob had given him to read. They had described starkly the staggering effects of total war in which nearly thirty million civilians around the world had lost their lives.

In answer to the 70,000 killed by German aerial attacks on Great Britain, the Royal Air Force had conducted campaigns against cities in Germany in night raids with incendiary bombs that, at their most destructive, had gutted Hamburg and Dresden. They had incinerated 50,000 people in each city in one night. American bombers, which for the most part had concentrated on precision bombing of military and industrial targets in daylight raids in Europe, had dropped incendiary weapons in area attacks at night against Japanese cities. Traditional targets in Japan had been more scattered among residential areas than in Europe, and high-altitude, precision bombing in attacking them had proved ineffective. As a consequence, Curtis LeMay, then a two-star general commanding American bombers in the Pacific, had sent his B-29s on low-altitude fire raids against highly flammable urban centers in Japan. In one night raid on Tokyo in 1945, close to 100,000 had perished when a fire storm swept over the city. The atomic attacks on Hiroshima and Nagasaki five months later had wiped out nearly twice that number. The Japanese had paid an enormous price for their aggression, barbarity and atrocities throughout Asia and the Pacific.

Kevin remembered then that his classes in military history on World War II hadn't dwelled on civilian casualties. They had focused mainly on the technical aspects of the European air campaigns, describing how systems of targets had been developed by American airmen and then attacked. The emphasis in his textbooks had been on allied attempts to cripple the entire Nazi war machine by concentrated strikes on its most vulnerable components, aircraft factories, oil refining plants and distribution facilities, as well as transportation networks, in hopes of finding an Achilles heel. Jakob's articles that centered on civilian deaths on both sides in attacks on cities were sobering.

The road continued its gradual ascent up the valley for another mile before it ended. The ridges on either side flattened slowly to meet the base of the mountain ahead of him, forming a large pasture, where sheep grazed behind a white masonry house with a roof of orange tiles and weathered wooden outbuildings of a working ranch. He parked at the end of the road, away from the house, and opening the car door, delaying getting out, he looked at the knot in his tie once more in the mirror to center it. He hand-brushed the shoulders of the coat to his suit that Karin had insisted on pressing for him, then looked at his watch again. *Ten o'clock. Here we go into the wringer.* Unable to delay any longer, he swung out and closed the door.

He walked up to a heavy front door made of wooden planks, and Juan, dressed in a black cassock, opened it immediately after he knocked. "Good morning, Kevin," he said warmly, but formally. "Please come in and join us in the parlor." Then he whispered, "Remember, respectful but firm."

The front door led to a dimly lit hallway with a stone floor that connected the isolated parlor at the front of the house to the living area in the rear. There was another door at the far end of the hall, and the entry to the parlor was the only opening in the corridor. He followed Juan through a doorway framed in hand-carved beams and saw a white-walled room with few wall decorations and dark leather furniture. Teresa was sitting in a chair along the far wall, wearing the pale-blue dress that she had worn the day of their engagement. Despite her welcoming smile, she remained seated in apparent deference to protocol.

Her father rose from his place on a sofa perpendicular to Teresa's chair along the long wall of the room, opposite tall, narrow front windows. He was a head shorter, and his graying black hair was matched by the mixture in his mustache. His wide tie and the wide lapels of his dated suit disclosed a man with little regard for fashion, and his stony expression did not change as Juan moved to a chair opposite Teresa's flanking the couch.

"Kevin, please take this seat," Juan said, gesturing toward the remaining chair facing the couch across a heavy pine coffee table. "Father, may I present Kevin O'Dea. Kevin, I am pleased to introduce you to my father, Miguel de la Cruz."

"Good morning, sir."

"Good morning," the older man replied as he nodded curtly. He did not change expression or offer his hand before he sat down again.

This is not going to be easy, Kevin said to himself as he took his seat, feeling moisture on the palms of his hands for the first time.

"Juan tells me that you have come all the way from Washington to visit with us, Mister O'Dea," Teresa's father said with an accent.

"Yes, sir. All together, I've traveled for four days. The last day, from Denver to Durango, was by far the most enjoyable."

"The mountains are, of course, very scenic. How long do you intend to be in Durango?"

"Sir, I intend to leave on Saturday for Arizona."

"Tell me, Mister O'Dea, what is the purpose of your trip here?"

He swallowed and said, "Sir, I have come to ask your permission to marry your daughter."

"I see," the older man said with no change in expression. "Tell me, how long have you known each another?"

"We met a year ago, sir."

"That is a very short time."

"In that time," Kevin replied quickly, remembering Juan's instructions to address each objection, "I believe that we have come to know each other well and to respect each other."

"I see. Well, in any case, Teresa cannot possibly marry until she finishes her education."

"I agree, sir. We would wait until next year."

"Yes, Father," Juan added lightly, "I insisted that they not marry until I am ordained and can properly officiate."

"Yes, yes," the older man continued impatiently, brushing past his son's attempt at conviviality. "I am told that you are a Catholic, Mister O'Dea. Are you a practicing Catholic?"

"Yes, sir."

"And your family, Mister O'Dea. Tell me about them."

"Sir, my parents live in Arlington, Virginia near Washington, and I have one brother. My father is an attorney who works on congressional relations for his company," Kevin said, deciding not to mention his father's earlier twenty-year career as an Air Force officer.

"I see. And how would you support my daughter?"

Kevin felt the older man's eyes boring in as he asked the question. "Sir, I plan to pursue a career in the armed forces. I was commissioned as an officer by President Kennedy in June."

"You are a soldier then. I left Spain to get away from Franco and the others in the army there. Why would I want a soldier in my family now?"

Kevin looked at Teresa and saw her lips tighten as she looked at her father. He turned toward the older man again and said, "Sir, I don't see how you can compare military service in this country to a revolt by the army in Spain nearly thirty years ago. American officers take an oath to defend the Constitution. They don't lead rebellions against it."

"Do they also have different attitudes, Mister O'Dea?" her father asked with an edge to his voice. "Are they immune to the arrogance and indifference to slaughter that seems to follow military men, wherever they come from?"

He looked at Juan, who looked down and sighed visibly at the question. He felt his own anger begin to stir, but he struggled to control it, knowing that his adversary wanted him to rise to the bait. "Sir, with respect, I don't know what you mean."

"Mister O'Dea, I saw enough brutality in war when you were a child to last me for a lifetime. I don't need to be reminded of it by having a son-in-law who wears a uniform."

"Sir, I still don't understand what you mean."

"Then let me be clear. I expected Americans and the English to conduct themselves with elementary humanity in fighting the Axis powers after the war in Spain, but instead, they resorted to the wholesale killing of civilians by bombing cities with their air forces. The worst of the immorality came in the atomic bombing of Japan. That should be plain enough for you, Mister O'Dea."

Well, I guess the gloves are off now, he decided. "Mister de la Cruz, are you telling me that you see no difference between the fascist regimes that caused the deaths of millions of people by resorting to war and to genocide and the nations that fought to defend themselves?"

"No. I am telling you that the military men on both sides acted like savages and that I don't want my daughter to marry someone in the military."

He looked at Teresa and saw that she was seething. Looking back at her father, he said, "Sir, the air attacks you spoke of were intended to force the German and Japanese governments to surrender, to save the lives of maybe a million allied soldiers by avoiding the ground battles necessary to occupy Germany and Japan. An earlier end to the fighting would also have saved many enemy lives, civilian as well as military. Bombing didn't work in Germany to force a surrender because Hitler was apparently willing to fight to the last German, but it did work in Japan, and it made an invasion with huge casualties on both sides unnecessary."

"That all sounds very noble, Mister O'Dea, but I think you are being very naive."

"Sir, if what you're saying is that revenge played some part in the allied bombing of cities, you're probably right. But, if you're going to condemn the men who planned and flew those missions, why don't you also condemn the British and American governments that authorized them? Sir, President Truman directed the bombing of Hiroshima and Nagasaki, and from everything I've read, the allied bombing campaigns had wide public support as a way to shorten the war and end the killing."

"Not everyone supported the extermination of human beings by destroying cities through bombing," the older man said firmly.

"Kevin," Juan said softly, "surely you are troubled by the huge losses of life caused by those bombings."

He looked at Juan, whose face seemed to be pleading for any concession to try to rescue an encounter that was fast careening out of control. He lowered his voice and said, "Anytime thousands of human lives are snuffed out in one stroke, anyone with any humanity at all has to be troubled. The more I learn about all of it, everything from the battle deaths to the Japanese atrocities to the German death camps, the more tragic, unbelievable and unreal it all seems to me. I hope we never see anything like those things again, but I know that good intentions won't be enough to prevent them if they ever start to come back. That's why I've chosen to wear a uniform. To prevent them."

"Again, very noble, Mister O'Dea, but also very naive," the older man said as he rose from his seat. "I do not believe that we have anything more to say to one another, and I have work to do. Juan will see you out," he said as he walked to the doorway.

"I have something to say, Mister de la Cruz," Kevin said, getting to his feet, his voice rising and hardening. "I want you to know that I love Teresa deeply and that I will follow her to the end of the earth if I have to."

Her father turned at the doorway and said angrily, "You, young man, are disrespectful and arrogant. Can the other military attitudes be far behind? Please leave my house at once!" He turned again and walked out of the room with long paces that echoed in the hallway, that stopped with the slamming of a door.

Kevin said nothing further after Juan rushed over to him and grabbed his arm to choke off any reply. As Juan released his grasp, Teresa came to him quickly and embraced him. "Oh, Kevin," she said, "please forgive Juan and me for bringing you into this. We are completely humiliated."

Before he could reply, Juan added, "Kevin, I've never seen him behave this way. It was appalling. Please accept my deepest apology on behalf of my family."

He could see the hurt in her eyes before he kissed her and said softly, "I've really missed you."

"You're all I've thought about," she replied, kissing him again.

Dropping his arm to her waist as he turned toward Juan, he asked, "What do we do now?"

"Kevin, I know that things might appear to be completely hopeless at this point, but I don't think they are. Please give me some time to reason with him. I think, though, that it would be best if you left now."

"All right, Juan, but I meant what I said."

"I know, and I'm glad you feel as strongly as you do about each other," Juan replied wearily, "but I've got some hard work ahead of me."

"I'll call you tonight after we've had some time to talk to him," Teresa said, taking him in her arms again. "I'm glad you're willing to, but you will never have to go to the end of the earth to find me."

The next morning, Karin entertained him after breakfast with a demonstration at her loom while he waited for Teresa. "Teresa and I have been working on this piece over the summer," she said. "What do you think of it?"

Red and orange were woven subtly with the more traditional Scandinavian shades of blue that predominated, and the effect appealed to him. "I like it a lot," he said.

"Do you know anything about weaving, Kevin?" she asked while she looked closely at the fabric slowly taking form on the loom frame.

"Practically nothing."

"Then trust me when I tell you that Teresa has real talent in this medium."

"I had no idea. All I know is that she's an art major, and she dragged me off to a couple of exhibitions of paintings in Denver last year, but I've never seen any of her work."

"Her college courses are giving her a good general foundation, but this is where she has genuine promise."

"She continues to amaze me."

Karin stopped when she heard Teresa call from the front of the house, "Karin?"

Kevin followed Karin to the front door and was pleased by what he saw. He had seen Teresa in jeans before, but the addition of the new touches, western boots, a long-sleeve shirt with pearl buttons and a broad-brimmed hat, with her hair pulled back, gave her a new look that he found natural and appealing.

Karin gave Teresa a maternal embrace and said, "I am so sorry about yesterday. How are things this morning, sweetheart?"

"Not much change," she said after Karin released her. "And Father left early this morning for Grand Junction all day on business."

"Well, maybe he needs some time alone to think things over," Karin replied.

"Maybe so," Teresa said as she walked over to him and brightened as she took his hand. "Ready to go riding?" she asked.

"Ever since you called last night."

"Good. I have some beautiful places to show you, and I've packed a picnic lunch for us."

"Have a lovely time," Karin said, holding the door.

He followed her through the doorway and down the wooden steps as Karin closed the door behind them. Approaching two horses whose reins she had tied to a light post, Teresa pointed to the larger, brown one and said, "This handsome, gentle fellow is yours. He's called

Francisco. This one," she said, untying the reins of a smaller gray horse, "is Risa. It means laughter in English. She has quite a personality."

"We could use a little laughter after yesterday," he said as he untied the reins of his mount.

"I promise you that today will be much better than yesterday," she said after swinging up easily into her saddle.

He fumbled briefly, trying to get his hiking boot into a stirrup, and he mounted awkwardly on his second attempt. "I guess I'm ready."

As Teresa turned her horse, the mare pranced sideways for several steps before Teresa stopped her with a sharp movement of the reins. "Now you see what I mean about Risa's personality."

He turned the larger horse easily to follow the livelier gray, and he saw an embroidered bag tied behind Teresa's saddle. "What's in the bag?" he asked when he came up beside her.

"It's our picnic blanket. Our lunch is in the saddlebags behind your saddle."

They traveled along a wide, well-worn path by the creek to the pasture he had seen the previous day. They crossed it, skirting the trees on its boundary, and took a trail through an aspen grove toward the peak of a distant mountain. Moving in front of him, she turned in her saddle and said, "We'll have to go single-file from here."

The ascent was gradual, and the horses climbed without laboring. He soon found himself stealing long looks away from the scenery to watch Teresa's hips and back sway easily and sensuously with the slow, steady pace of the mare.

After about thirty minutes of leisurely climbing, the trail to the summit converged with a stream, and they paralleled it for a half mile. With another half mile left to the top, the trail crossed the stream, but Teresa turned to follow the stream bed that flattened out and widened as it changed direction to cut across the slope of the mountain. She led them through the shallow water of a barely moving current for a quarter of a mile, at times leaning over to clear the branches of trees that lined the stream banks. They came out into a clearing around a small pond that was bordered on the far side by a sheer wall of rock to the peak. Small groves of aspen were close to the banks, and pines were farther back. The leaves of the aspen shimmered in the breeze.

"This is the place where I come to be alone with my thoughts. What do you think of it?" Teresa asked as she dismounted and tied her horse to a small tree near the stream to allow the mare to drink.

"Let's never leave," he said, after getting down and tying the larger horse to the same tree.

"I knew you'd like it," she said, taking his hand. "It's so peaceful. I came up here yesterday after Juan and I tried talking to Father."

"You told Karin that nothing much has changed."

"It's all so unfair."

"Well, as President Kennedy is fond of saying, life isn't fair."

"It's not only unfair, it's stupid to hold you responsible for things that happened twenty years ago."

"My three advisers tell me that what's really going on with your father is something else. He doesn't want to let you go."

"Kevin, I love my father, but he's wrong to do this. And he's wrong about you."

"Are you sure that you're not just being blinded by love?"

"I've been made wiser by love. Before I met you, I dated a boy in Denver, at Regis College, and I thought that I loved him. He was warm, funny and very attentive. He was also a coward. When his social-climbing parents found out about me, they threatened to stop supporting him. It seems that they didn't want anyone named de la Cruz as a possible daughter-in-law. So, he broke up with me. He would never have stood up to my father the way you did."

"Well, I just have the advantage of more training and experience in taking abuse."

"No, it was courage and honesty, and you were magnificent. That's what Clare saw in you. She told me that I should forget that creep and his bigoted parents. She said that she knew someone who could make me forget him. She was right about you. Kevin, I've felt strong currents pulling us together since the night I met you. I've never felt anything like this before."

"Well, after you graduate, we can get married whether your father likes it or not."

"I don't want you to wake up one morning, realize that you shouldn't have to put up with any of my father's nonsense and stop loving me because of it."

"That would never happen."

"The truth is that it can happen—and has happened to other people. I don't want to risk losing you. That's why I want to go with you when you leave tomorrow."

"You mean elope?"

"I want a church wedding when we can arrange it, but that can come later. I can pack a few things tonight, and we can drive to Nevada early tomorrow to make everything legal. We're both over twenty-one, and no one can stop us."

"What about your last year of school?"

"I can transfer to finish. Kevin, forget all these imaginary obstacles and say that you'll do this for us. For us, Kevin."

"Teresa, of course you can go with me if that's what you want. I'd marry you right now if I could."

Teresa unbuttoned her shirt pocket and removed a plain wedding band. "This was my mother's. I don't want to make my real marriage promises to you in some wedding chapel in Nevada. Would you marry me here, Kevin, here in this beautiful place that means so much to me?"

He looked into her eyes and said quietly, "I'd marry you anywhere."

She removed her hat and dropped it to the ground. She took his hand again, intertwined her fingers with his and said, "I love you, Kevin, and I promise to honor you every day of my life. I will always be faithful to you as my husband, and I will be yours, no matter what life brings to us. I will cherish you as long as my soul lives."

He took the ring from her, put it on her finger and felt lightheaded as he struggled for words. "Teresa, I love you . . . and I will for the rest of my life. I will respect you . . . and always see you as the greatest gift I've ever been given. I will be faithful to you . . . no matter what the future holds for us. I will honor you as my wife . . . and I am bound to you forever." She put her arms around his neck, and he pulled her close as desire for her surged within him. She responded to him eagerly and kissed him hungrily as their arms tightened around each other. Then, breathing deeply, she pulled away from him and walked to the gray mare that ignored her and continued to eat tall grass by the edge of the stream. She untied the bag from behind her saddle, and opening it, pulled out a quilt with the same rich embroidery as the pattern on its cover.

"Our housekeeper Juanita and I sewed this when I was a young girl. I had a favorite fairy tale about a handsome prince coming to take me away one day that she told me over and over, and she said that if he came in winter, I would need a blanket to keep me warm. So, we made this together. It took us nearly three years to finish it. We worked on it mostly in winter to pass the hours in the long darkness, and I put it away after we were done. It's never been used." As she started to walk toward the pines, she said, "Wait a few minutes, and then come after me."

He was caught and lifted by an irresistible, primordial wave. It gathered strength while he waited, and it carried him toward her in its upward arc when he followed her. He felt it breaking, rushing him forward, its eventual flowing and ebbing to become the ancient, urgent rhythm of life.

He found her lying on a bed of pine boughs among the trees, waiting for him, the quilt doubled over her and her long, dark hair down, framing her glowing face. Feeling his own face flushed as he sat down with his back toward her on the edge of the blanket, he began to undress. Freed of his clothing, he moved under the covering to be with her, and her touch electrified him, overwhelming his senses. He looked at her, in so many ways still a mystery to him, and feeling as if he were stepping from a high, safe place into a sweet oblivion, he whispered, "You are so beautiful. So completely, wonderfully beautiful."

The next morning, Kevin looked nervously at his watch after driving for a dusty mile and stopping his car at the intersection with the highway to Durango. He hoped the wrath of Miguel de la Cruz wouldn't fall on Karin and Jakob. He had told them nothing about the elopement so that they could claim complete ignorance when questioned.

A pickup truck raised dust behind it as it made the last turn to the highway. Kevin got out of his car. He was surprised and began feeling apprehensive when he saw Juan at the wheel and Teresa in the passenger seat. Juan braked the truck to a skidding stop, and he and Teresa got out. She was radiant, and her unshaven brother looked like hell.

Teresa came to him, took his hand as she kissed him on the cheek and said, "Hello, love. Juan has something he wants to tell you."

"Kevin," Juan said wearily, "I've been up all night with my father. There was a lot of screaming and shouting, but in the end, he agreed to give his permission for you two to marry."

"Juan, I'm completely stunned. I never thought he would, not after what happened two days ago."

"I hope I never have to go through anything like that again, but I wouldn't let him refuse to talk about what he had done to you. At first I tried logic and reason, but that didn't work. We really began to get at the truth when I called him cowardly for not answering your arguments and bolting from the parlor. I still can't quite believe I did it, but I kept going after him even when he bellowed that I was being disrespectful and to shut up. It sounds much more cataclysmic in Spanish. Anyway, I finally broke through, I think, when I told him that he was deceiving himself to think that he could keep the two of you apart and asked him if he wanted to do the same thing to Teresa that my mother's parents did to her."

"Juan, I don't know what to say."

"Kevin, say that you'll forgive my father and forget what happened on Thursday. We both know what was going on. It may not be entirely clear to you now that you need to do what I'm asking, but my sister's real happiness with you, and yours too, depend on your being able to see wisdom here."

Kevin looked into Teresa's eyes and asked quietly, "Is this what you really want?"

"I think Juan is right," she said softly, tightening her hold on his hand.

Juan added, "He's even agreed to a form of public penance. I insisted that he give a dinner for you and Teresa and invite Karin and Jakob. Will you delay your trip for a day and dine with us tonight?"

"Yes, of course I will," he said, half reluctantly. He turned to embrace Teresa and whispered, "After yesterday, I am going to find out what aching to be with you really means."

Time to call, Kevin decided, checking his watch again. He left his room and made his way between two rows of barracks, originally built during Word War II, that had been converted into eight, two-man apartments to house student pilots. Walking toward the locked, darkened officers' club ahead, closed out of respect for their fallen commander-in-chief, he saw that the phone booths near the club's entrance were empty. On any other Friday night, the building would have been crowded with men in flying suits at the bar, putting a loud end to another week of soaring in desert skies. He entered a booth, lifted the phone receiver, spun the last hole of the phone's rotary dial up to its brass stop, and let it unwind. The operator who answered connected him to the pay phone in Teresa's dorm where she stood waiting anxiously.

"Hello," she said after one ring.

"Hi," he said, recognizing her voice. "I love you, Mrs. O'Dea."

"Hello, love. I really am glad to talk to you tonight. It's been such a horrible day."

"Are you okay?"

"I was pretty weepy earlier, but I'm all right now. All those people on television just crying and crying."

"Yeah. I know."

"I had to stop watching. Are you okay?"

"I'll be all right. I still can't quite believe it. He seemed larger than life six months ago at graduation. I never thought he'd be the first of our classmates to die."

"Some of the girls here are very upset. Clare's locked herself in her room and won't come out."

"Clare?"

"Remember? I told you once that Clare's really a softie behind that facade of hers."

"Will she be all right?"

"She's done this before, after major fights with Ed. She'll let me in after a few more hours."

"And I always thought that Clare was the tough one."

"We're both softies, really. I miss you so much."

"I knew that being away from you would be bad, but not this bad."

"Somehow, I can't escape this feeling that today is just the beginning of something. It's very strange. I can't explain it, but it makes me feel like I have to be close to you. Is there any chance that you can come to Durango next week for Thanksgiving? Dinner's at Karin's this year."

"I'll try, but it'll be tough to get next Friday off. We'll probably be standing down from flying on the day of the funeral next week, and I don't know what that'll do to the flight schedule. I'm a little ahead of the other guys at my table, though, and maybe I can weasel Friday off out of my instructor."

"I know a place where we can slip away and be husband and wife again for a while."

"No fair. You're going to talk me into becoming a deserter. It's a bad way to start a military career."

"If you can't come to Durango, I'll go down there on Friday. I just need to be with you next weekend. Can you call me here Tuesday night and let me know? I'll be home Wednesday night. You can call me there if you miss me on Tuesday."

"I'll call you on Tuesday, same time, and I'll miss you on Tuesday, just like every other day of the week. I can't wait to see you. Love you."

"Love you too. Bye."

"Bye."

He hung up the phone and pocketed the coins he hadn't used from the booth's metal shelf. Walking back to his room, he noticed that the stairs to the student pilots' apartments, normally occupied by Friday-night revelers who had gotten an early start at the club and had moved on, were mostly deserted.

They're probably still watching the tube to hear more about that guy they arrested. What's his name? Oswald. Lee Harvey Oswald, he remembered. Ahead, he saw a solitary figure drinking from a beer bottle, sitting on a stoop to a bottom-story apartment. As he got closer, he recognized his Academy classmate, Sam Prentiss. "Hey, Sam. What're you doing out here all by yourself?"

"Hey, Kev," Prentiss replied through his crooked smile. "I had to git out here, away from all the knee-deep bullshit inside," he said with a slight slur in his Mississippi drawl.

"What's happening now?"

"Well, a little while after they arrested Oswald, one o' those slick TV boys started talkin' about—git this—the possibility of a lone assassin. And, on top o' that, our classmate, good ol' Dave Mercer, the North Dakota boy scout, starts buyin' it. Well, I told ol' Dave that he was full o' shit and came out here. The President gits shot from long range with Secret Service agents crawlin' all over the place. And one guy did it? Come on. Can you believe that shit?"

"I don't know, Sam. I haven't gotten that far yet. I'm still pretty numb."

"Well, I reckon you got to be born and raised southern to have a good ear for bullshit. It's a way o' life in Mississippi, you know. Where're you headed, anyhow?"

"Back to my room, I guess. I need a beer."

"Well, son, you're in luck. I just happen to have a spare," Prentiss said, producing a second bottle from behind his back. "Pull up a step, and sit a spell."

"Thanks, Sam," he said, accepting the bottle and sitting down.

"You know what, Kev?"

"What, Sam?"

"I think it'd do both of us a lot o' good to go flyin' tomorra. I'm talkin' about real flyin'. Open-cockpit flyin'. Blow all this fuckin' stuff from today right out o' our heads."

"And just how would we do that?"

"Didn't you know? I got me an airplane. My daddy gave it to me for graduation."

"Sounds interesting."

"Yeah. It's a Stearman Kaydet. The same kind o' two-winger he trained in back in forty-three."

"Your dad was a pilot?"

"Damn right. He flew Mustangs in the big one. In the ETO, as he likes to say, when all his ol' squadron buddies come over to the house and git drunk. Drives my momma, the ex-debutante, crazy. Anyhow, that's the European Theater o' Operations to peckerwoods like you and me, which, accordin' to Daddy and the boys, includes anyone who ain't gunned down a kraut in the air."

"So, your old man was a warrior."

"Yep. He nailed four o' Goering's boys before it was all over. Even shot down a Me-262 jet in the landin' pattern. He was really pissed that it all stopped before he got five to make ace."

"What's he doing now?"

"He's in the car bidness with my gran'daddy. They make a helluva lot o' money peddlin' cars, and they've got it pretty good. But you know what?"

"What?"

"Daddy says that the best time o' his life was when he was flyin' Mustangs in the ETO."

"Well, it was a great airplane."

"So's the Stearman. Daddy and me flew it all the way out here from Mississippi. We had one helluva time. Took us a week. We raised hell all over Texas along the way. Shut down the bars every place we landed. So, how about it, Kev? Let's put some leather helmets and goggles on tomorra mornin', go do some honest acro and forgit all this shit on TV."

"You've sold me, wild man. Let's do it."

"Good. Oh. And there's somethin' else."

"What's that?"

"You're gonna love the takeoff. I keep it in a hangar out at a cropduster's place near Florence. The takeoff goes right over the prison. And you know what?"

"What, Sam?"

"When you see them miserable sonsabitches in the yard when you fly over, it don't make no difference how bad you feel. You see pretty quick that you got it good compared to them. And that, my friend, is no bullshit."

* * *

The next morning, Kevin sat in the front cockpit of the Stearman as Prentiss taxied his yellow biplane onto the cropduster's dirt runway. As the nose came around, Sam brought the throttle up to full power without stopping to line up, and the wind coming over the windscreen from the propeller felt good to Kevin as they started the takeoff roll. He glanced down at the stick and saw it move quickly forward and back as Prentiss lifted the tail off the ground, letting the airplane roll only a short distance on its main gear before it became airborne.

Prentiss leveled the airplane at fifty feet above the ground and accelerated, keeping the throttle fully forward. Directly ahead, Kevin could see a long chain-link fence topped with razor wire that enclosed a compound of buildings behind a high masonry wall. At the fence, Sam pulled the nose up to go sailing over the wall in a climb and started a smooth aileron roll. As they passed directly over the prison yard with the airplane inverted in the roll, men in orange coveralls below began waving frantically. He looked into the mirror above his head and saw Prentiss wave casually back. Sam completed the graceful roll past the far side of the fence in a slight descent and then eased the nose up to start a climb to altitude, a wide grin on his goggled face.

Sam's right, Kevin decided. He felt his mood begin to brighten as they climbed in the simplicity of a crisp desert morning, with fresh, cool air flowing around him.

Chapter 3

Monday, 22 June 1964

The dry desert heat hit him in the face like a furnace blast. Kevin closed the door to his air-conditioned room, put on his flight cap and looked at his watch. *Ten minutes to get to the flight line.* He hurried down the steps on the way to his car in a parking lot behind the building.

"Hey, Kev," Sam Prentiss called out behind him. "Can you give me a lift to the flight line? My 'vette's in the shop."

"Sure," he yelled back. "Come on."

Prentiss ran to catch up with him. "Can't wait to do some of that two-ship," he said, using the shorthand for two aircraft flying in formation, the phase of formation training before four-ship in the T-38.

They put their briefcases stuffed with flight manuals into the car's jump seat and got in. Kevin started the engine, and the voices of the Dixie Cups came out of the radio, ending their number-one hit, singing, " . . . and we're gonna get ma-a-arried. Goin' to the chapel of love."

"They're singin' about you, Kevin boy," Sam chuckled. "When're you and that honey o' yours gonna tie the knot, anyhow?"

"A little over two months from now. End of August. Are you going to give us a fly-by after the ceremony in the Stearman?" he asked facetiously, pulling out of the parking lot.

"Hell, I will if you want me to. Even better, you can take it and fly off into the sunset with your honey. Damn, now wouldn't that be somethin', readin' in the society section o' the paper: And the bride looked lovely in her white dress, with her white veil flowin' out o' the cockpit, over the top o' her goggles, as she flew away." Sam broke out laughing, very pleased with himself and the image.

"And all I asked for was a fly-by," Kevin said, grinning.

"Well, you're flyin' the Stearman pretty good now. You're gettin' a nice feel for the airplane."

They pulled into a parking lot at the flight line as the Beatles were ending "Love Me Do." As Kevin hunted for an empty space, the disk jockey said, "And now, here's Jerry with the news at five minutes before the hour."

"From Washington, FBI Director J. Edgar Hoover announced that agents from the Bureau will move swiftly to investigate the disappearance of three civil rights workers reported missing this morning in Mississippi. Closer to home—" He cut the announcer off in mid-sentence as he turned off the ignition after parking.

"They're dead, and the fuckin' Klan did it," Sam said with an edge to his voice.

"What?"

"Those three guys missin' back home. The fuckin' Ku Klux Klan killed 'em."

"What makes you so sure?"

"I just know, that's all. Kev, I love Mississippi. One o' these days I'm gonna be back there, sellin' cars with my daddy. But, I've got to tell you, some bad shit happens sometimes back home, and the Klan's usually right in the middle of it."

"Well, they've only been missing a little while. Maybe they'll turn up. Anyway, Sam, we've got to get our heads on straight." Trying to jolly Prentiss out of a darkening mood, he joked, affecting Sam's drawl, "We got to go do some serious aviatin'. We ain't got no time for no deep thinkin', now. Heah?"

It seemed to work as Prentiss responded with a grin. "Okay, Kev. Let's go do it."

They walked to their flight room and looked at the afternoon schedule posted on a plexiglass board in grease pencil. "Outstandin'!" Prentiss exclaimed under his breath, "We're in the same two-ship, and we got the first takeoff time."

Kevin saw that their flight commander had decided to fly with them, taking the place of their normally assigned instructors. "And we've got Gentleman Jim," he replied in a low voice. Easygoing and self-assured, Major James Sherman was a gifted teacher whose presence in an airplane practically guaranteed a good day in the air. They walked over to his table.

"Good afternoon, sir," they said to the tall, blond Nebraskan.

"Good afternoon, gentlemen," their flight commander responded, motioning for them to take seats. "It looks like a fine day for formation flying. Weather in the area is reported as scattered cumulus with tops at fifteen-thousand feet. So, no problem there. Let's get right into the briefing."

Engine start, taxi and takeoff went smoothly, and an hour after the briefing ended, Kevin led a flight of two T-38s over barren Superstition Peak, headed eastward toward the pine-forested high country of southeastern Arizona. Prentiss, flying solo, held close formation on Kevin's wing as the lead jet maneuvered through billowy cloud columns that softened the rugged terrain below them.

"Very nice takeoff and departure, Kevin," Major Sherman said from the rear cockpit over the intercom, making conversation to fill up dead time during their climb to working altitude.

"Thank you, sir."

"What kind of assignment are you looking for out of UPT? We'll be deciding in a few weeks."

"I want to go to fighters, sir."

"Well, Kevin, there's a dirty little secret you need to know about. The generals who command the bombers and the transports will burn up a lot of their quotas for UPT graduates on your class. They want to get career-minded folks to fly their heavy airplanes, and they hope, by getting you Academy guys into their cockpits, that they won't lose so many to the airlines down the road."

"Sir, are you saying that we won't have any fighter assignments for our class?" he asked, continuing to scan the sky ahead for other airplanes.

"No. There'll be a couple of assignments to single-seaters. But they'll go to the naturals, like Prentiss out there, at the top of the class. The other fighter assignments won't be nearly as attractive. With this new, lame-brain policy out of the Pentagon, we'll be sending UPT graduates, instead of navigators, to the back seats of F-4 Phantoms. They'll sit in the back seat, work the radar for the guy in front for a couple of years and watch their pilot skills rot away over time."

"You're not painting a very happy picture, sir."

"Well, Kevin, I'm afraid it's the real world. Have you thought about being a UPT instructor?"

"No, sir."

"You should. You'd do a lot more piloting by flying the T-38 than you'd do in the F-4. Besides, you've got good hands and the temperament for teaching. Not everyone has the patience to do the job well."

"It's not something I've really thought about, sir."

"Why don't you think about it. You'd be able to go to fighters after you finish your tour as an IP. It's a natural progression. I'm doing my recruiting bit for Training Command today, and I'd like to put in a recommendation for you, if you decide it's the way to go."

"Thank you, sir. I'll give it some thought."

They reached the formation working area. As he had been briefed, Kevin began maneuvering the flight in lazy, rolling climbs and descents with his wingman in close formation, the staggered wingtips of the two jets almost overlapping, their fuselages twenty-five feet apart, gaining and losing a mile or more of altitude with each segment of the aerial roller-coaster. As he pulled through the first dive, Kevin looked out to see how well Prentiss held position as the g's came on, inflating the bladders of the g suit he wore, squeezing his legs and stomach to keep blood from pooling away from his head. Prentiss was right with him, holding steady position. Sam was welded to his wing as the flight went through a long series of climbs and dives.

"The man's as good as his IP says he is," Sherman said. "Okay, Kevin, let's conclude the wing work and do a pitchout and rejoin."

"Yes, sir." Kevin leveled the flight and headed eastward at 25,000 feet to stay well above the building clouds. Looking back at Prentiss, he twirled his right index finger above his head to signal a pitchout. Sam nodded in reply. He rolled his airplane steeply away from Prentiss and advanced the throttles to hold altitude and airspeed as he turned 180 degrees to head westward. Prentiss delayed his turn, following five seconds later.

Kevin completed the pitchout and rolled out with Prentiss a mile in trail. Signaling a rejoin by rocking the airplane's wings, he set up a shallow turn to the north. Kevin looked behind to see Prentiss's T-38 move to the inside of the turn to cut off the leader. Below them and to the right, he saw two other T-38s in close formation headed to the east, two white darts lit by the sun, sailing away together across the green of mountain pines.

"Friendlies at four o'clock low, sir," he advised Sherman.

"Roger, I have them."

Seeing the other trainers streak silently away, out of sight, he looked up again at Prentiss's jet silhouetted against the horizon. At half a mile out, Sam was closing very fast.

"He's got a lot of overtake on us," Sherman said, evaluating the closure rate. "Let me have the airplane, Kevin, in case we have to move out of the way at the end, if he can't slow down in time." Sherman shook the control stick lightly from the rear cockpit.

Kevin answered by shaking the stick from the front cockpit. "Your airplane, sir."

"Okay, I've got the airplane. Now let's see what happens. If he's out of control, he could go smoking right past us. Or, he could panic, pop out his speed brakes, yank his throttles to idle, kill off all his airspeed and drop out of the sky like a rock."

Kevin took his hands away from the stick and throttles and concentrated on the last part of the rejoin. At a quarter of a mile, he saw two speed-brake panels extend from the bottom of Prentiss's jet. The closure rate slowed rapidly, and with speed brakes retracting, Sam continued to move effortlessly to close formation on the leader's right wing.

"Outstanding rejoin," Sherman said. "But I'll have to tell him to take it slower on his check ride. He'll scare the pants off his check pilot if he comes in that fast. Okay, I've seen enough. Let's give Prentiss the lead so you can get a little wing work."

"Yes, sir." Kevin took control of the airplane from his instructor again and worked the rudder pedals, making the jet fishtail, then pointed forward, signaling Prentiss to take wider spacing and to take the lead. Sam nodded, acknowledging the visual signals. Kevin reduced power slightly to slide into close formation on the new leader.

Prentiss rolled away from him to start the rolling climbs and descents that Kevin had led earlier. Kevin worked the stick and throttles hard to hold position, but in the troughs of the dives, as airspeed and g loading increased, he over-controlled his airplane, causing it to porpoise slightly as he tried to stay steady on the leader's wing. *Damn it, O'Dea, you ham hand! Stay in position.*

"You're holding position pretty well," Sherman advised, "but you start to bobble at the bottom of the dives when the g's come on. Your stick's probably too light. Put in some nose-down trim to make it heavier and less sensitive."

Kevin thumbed the trim button at the top of his stick grip at the end of a rolling climb. Coming down the back side, he felt a much-increased weight in his right hand as airspeed increased, but this time, the heavy stick damped out the oscillations that had frustrated him earlier. *So that's the secret.*

"That's it," Sherman said. "A little more heaviness in the stick will let you fly wing in this kind of maneuvering a lot better."

"Yes, sir." Feeling more comfortable, he concentrated on the climb that was coming as they pulled through a dive. Out of the corner of his eye he saw two white streaks.

Without thinking, he snapped his jet violently away from Prentiss and pulled hard to gain separation.

"What the hell are you doing?" a surprised Sherman yelled.

Without answering, he reversed his roll quickly and climbed. Below them, two T-38s streamed black smoke as they plummeted earthward in fiery, diverging arcs. A third jet, missing a large part of its vertical stabilizer, was in a flat spin behind them, falling like a fluttering leaf. Speechless, Kevin saw the spinning jet's canopy blow off and its ejection seat rocket upward. Within seconds, a parachute opened.

"Sweet Jesus," a stunned Sherman whispered as the mid-air collision unfolded toward its deadly ending below them. "I have the airplane, Kevin," he said after a few seconds in a low, flat voice.

"Your airplane, sir."

"Williams tower," Sherman transmitted over the emergency radio channel, Guard channel, "this is blue lead on Guard. There's been a mid-air in the formation area. Three T-38's have crashed."

"Blue lead, this is Williams tower on Guard!" an answering voice said urgently. "Say your position. We're scrambling the rescue helicopter."

Oh, god. Ed was in the flight that took off right after us, Kevin remembered.

"Blue lead is east of Williams, on the zero-eight-five radial at sixty-eight miles. I see one—no—two parachutes."

"Blue lead, this is Williams tower. Do you have enough fuel to remain on scene until the rescue helicopter gets out there?"

"Williams tower, this is blue lead. Affirmative. We'll stay until the helicopter gets here."

Below them, three crooked shafts of swirling black smoke reached into the sky from burning crash sites as the two parachutes continued to descend slowly.

* * *

That evening, Kevin approached a captain wearing a starched white dress on duty at the nurses' station in the base hospital. She looked all-business.

"Can I help you, Lieutenant?"

"Yes, ma'am. I've heard that Lieutenant Ed Walker and Lieutenant Sam Prentiss have been admitted. I was in one of the flights involved in the mid-air this afternoon. I'd like to see them if I can."

"They're resting, and Lieutenant Walker's been sedated."

"Is he okay?"

"A broken arm and some nasty scrapes and bruises from the ejection, but he's all right otherwise. He's very lucky. Prentiss is even luckier. Hardly a scratch."

"Could I take a quick look? I'm going to be calling Lieutenant Walker's fiancee in a few minutes, and it'll help a lot if I can say I've seen him. I'm going to be his best man."

"Okay," she said, seeming to soften a little. "Just a few minutes. But don't do anything to disturb him. He's in the third room on the left."

"Thank you, ma'am."

As he walked down the hall, Sam Prentiss called out to him from a room on his right. "Hey, Kev!"

Kevin stopped at the doorway and looked into the room where a bored Prentiss, sitting on the edge of his bed, was flipping playing cards toward a bed pan on the floor several yards away. "Hey, Sam. Are you okay?"

"Yeah. One of my knees is a little sore. Must have banged it against the canopy rail on the way out."

"I'm glad you're all right, man."

"Yeah. They're lettin' me out tomorra, so I guess there's nothin' serious."

"I'm glad to hear it. Listen, I've got to look in on Ed. I'm going to be calling Clare in a few minutes."

"Sure. Go ahead. I'll see you tomorra at the flight line, after I finally get all fifty-two of these suckers into that bed pan."

"Okay, Sam. See you tomorrow."

He walked on to Ed's room and looked through the door. Ed was covered by a sheet, his arms out, sleeping restlessly. His right arm was in a cast, and there was a massive purple bruise on his left forearm.

Kevin stood silently for a few minutes watching his classmate, until he heard someone whisper behind him, "Lieutenant." He turned and saw a man wearing a white lab coat over his uniform, with gold oak leaves on the collar, motioning to him at the doorway. A black name tag on the coat was engraved with Dr. Silverman.

He followed the flight surgeon to a place in the corridor away from Ed's room. "Sir, the nurse said I could see him for a few minutes if I didn't bother him."

"Yes, she's filled me in."

"She said he's okay," he said quietly, hoping for more information.

"Physically, yes, but we'll have to see how he handles the emotional end of it. He's had a pretty traumatic experience. Is he tough, Lieutenant O'Dea?" the doctor asked, glancing at the name tag on Kevin's flying suit.

"Yes, sir. Very tough."

"Then he'll want to get back in the saddle and fly again. I've seen it before after accidents. The hard cases want back in, and the others pack it in. So, he and Prentiss are both tough guys."

"Yes, sir."

"Well, we'll have to see."

"Sir?"

"As far as I can tell, he didn't come through this as easily as Prentiss seems to have done. One very cool customer, our Mister Prentiss. Lieutenant Walker, on the other hand, seems to have had the living hell scared out of him. He was pretty shaken up, and we had to sedate him. From what I've pieced together so far, he was leading his flight when they hit yours from behind. Apparently, he holds himself responsible. The two pilots in the other airplane were probably killed on impact with Prentiss's jet, likely decapitated, and I'm guessing that it won't be easy for your friend to live with that."

"No, sir," he agreed, after hearing his first account of the accident.

"You told the nurse that he's engaged."

"Yes, sir. His wedding's in September."

"Is it timed to come after his graduation from UPT?"

"Yes, sir."

"Well, Lieutenant, he won't be graduating in September. With the broken arm, I'm going to ground him for at least five weeks before I even begin to think about letting him back in a jet. He'll wash back to the next class even if everything goes well. That'll also give us some time to see if he can pull things together."

"I understand, sir."

"By the way, it would be better if the wedding were in a few weeks rather than a few months. He's going to need a lot of support to cope with this. I don't think he'll ever quite get over it. It'll probably be one of those lifetime things, but if his luck holds out, he'll be able to deal with it and not go over the edge. Think about that when you talk to his fiancee. We'll release him in a few days."

"Yes, sir," he replied, sensing that the doctor had said all he was going to say. "Thank you, sir."

They parted, going in opposite directions in the empty hallway. As he walked out of the hospital's main entrance toward a pay phone that he had seen on his way in, he began rehearsing his call to Clare. He consoled himself. *As bad as this is going to be, it's a lot better than it would be if Ed were in the other airplane.*

He put in the coins and the operator connected him.

"Hello?"

"Hi, Clare. It's Kevin."

"Why, Kevin," she said breezily, "what a surprise. Are you needing more advice on how to woo a Spanish woman? It'll have to be quick. I'm waiting for a call from Ed."

"No, Clare."

"What is it?" she asked with a trace of alarm in her voice.

"Ed's all right," he answered, hoping to soften the blow to come.

"Oh, my god, Kevin, what is it? You're scaring me."

"He's in the hospital, but he's okay. I've just seen him."

Her voice took on a tone of panic that he hadn't heard before. "What's happened?"

"He had to eject out of his airplane this afternoon, but the rescue guys got to him fast. He's hospitalized. Under observation."

She started crying. "Oh, no!"

His gut wrenched as he listened to her, but he kept talking. "He has some scrapes and bruises . . . and a broken arm, but he's okay."

She blurted out, "If he's so damned okay, why hasn't he called me? Tell me everything. Now, Kevin!" she demanded.

"He's sleeping. They gave him some stuff to put him to sleep." He paused and then said the hardest part quietly, "He was in a mid-air collision with another airplane."

She was frantic. "Oh, my god. I'm coming down there. I've got to go." She hung up.

His heart was pounding as he walked from the phone booth. *I'll call her parents in a little while to get the flight information,* he decided. *I'll pick her up at the airport tomorrow.*

As he walked to his car, he heard the sound of a T-38 taking off for a night flight. He looked up and saw a white airplane speeding into the twilight sky, trailing two bright-orange cones of flame from its afterburners. Then the orange lights disappeared.

He thought for a while about the casualties along the way. Six of his classmates at Williams had washed out, unable to adapt to the air. The same story was being repeated at the other seven UPT bases. *And now two of us dead. One today and one last year,* he thought, remembering his classmate who had crashed his T-37.

A second T-38 lifted into the darkening sky. He looked after it and then walked away as the thought came to him. *This is a rough business.*

* * *

The next morning, he hugged Clare when she came through the airport gate and prolonged holding her.

"I'm sorry I hung up on you," she said. "I'm a mess."

"Naah, you were just being your ornery self," he kidded, trying to lift her spirits.

"Thank you for meeting me."

"You didn't think I'd leave you alone with all these low-life Phoenix cowboys hanging around, did you?"

She smiled weakly as he took her bag from her and held her hand to take her to his car.

After they got in and started out, he turned off the radio and let her be silent for a while as he drove. They left Phoenix, headed eastward toward Williams.

"Tell me he's really going to be all right, Kevin."

"He will be, Clare. Ed's strong. You know that."

"Yes. It's why I love him so much," she replied, and then lost herself in thought for the rest of the drive in the cool desert morning.

Ed was awake when they entered his room. "Hi, babe," he said groggily, surprised to see her.

She kissed Ed, held him and said, "I love you, you big ox."

Ed hugged her back, showing the full extent of the cuts and bruises on his arms.

Clare sat next to him on his bed and held his hand. "The nurse said that you'll be released the day after tomorrow."

"Yeah? I'll be glad to get out of here." Ed looked over at him. "Hey, Kev."

"How're you feeling, big man?"

"I'm okay."

He saw the look of a wounded, hunted animal in Ed's eyes. "I'm really glad to hear it." He managed a smile and said, "Well, I knew if I waited long enough, I'd catch you two in bed together eventually. Now that I've seen you, I've got to go tell everybody. I'll come back in about an hour." He waved as he left.

When he returned, Clare was already outside, waiting for him on a bench near the main entrance. She stood when she saw him and walked to meet him.

"I had to leave so that they could give him some tests," she said when they met. "Hold me for a minute, Kevin."

He put his arms around her and she began sobbing quietly against his chest.

"He wants to fly again," she said.

"I knew he would," he replied softly.

"But why would he, after this?"

"If I were in there, I'd be saying the same thing."

"I just don't understand it. What am I going to do?"

"I think you already know what you have to do. He's going to need you now more than he's ever needed anyone."

"What are you saying, Kevin?" she asked, pulling slowly away from him, drying her eyes.

"He's going to be grounded until they see how well he recovers. That's what his doctor told me last night. If they don't let him fly again, he won't be the same man you fell in love with, Clare. I can promise you that. He won't be."

"How can he do it, Kevin? All his brave talk didn't fool me. He looks scared to death."

"He can do it if you help him, Clare. He hasn't come this far to give up now."

"What should I do?"

"His doctor told me last night that it would be better if you two were getting married in a few weeks rather than after UPT. I think he's right. Can you do that?"

She didn't say anything at first, but then murmured, "Yes."

"After he's released, take him back to Denver and move up the wedding. Love the hell out of him on your honeymoon, and then come back here to be with him when he starts flying again."

"All right."

"Teresa and I will do anything that you need help with to get you settled down here. And I'll call Teresa's brother, Juan, and ask him to help you with the wedding arrangements if you run into any roadblocks with the Church in Denver. Deal?"

"Deal."

He embraced her again and said, "I promise. Everything's going to be okay."

"I hope so, Kevin. I don't think I could take anything more than this."

Chapter 4

Tuesday, 4 August 1964

Clare, Ed and Kevin were finishing dinner in the kitchen of the Walkers' recently rented apartment in Chandler. They were seated at a dinette table that showed its age. It had been used by many other student pilots and their wives before them, and it barely fit into the small room.

Clare asked, "How about another helping, Kevin?"

"Thanks, but two's enough for me. You make a great lasagne, Clare, but I've reached my limit."

"Well, you do know how to compliment an Italian girl," Clare said as she stood to clear the dishes away.

"Yeah," Ed said. "There's no stopping her now. She's got the wedding loot up and running, and this place'll be pasta central before you know it."

"You guys look like you made a good haul on wedding presents," Kevin said.

"We even have two extra blenders," Clare said as she came back to the table after taking three dishes of strawberries out of an ancient refrigerator.

"Well, I guess a house can't have too many margarita makers," Kevin said, taking his dessert from Clare.

"So," she asked, "how are things going on the groom's end of your wedding? We're getting into countdown territory now with less than a month to go."

"Everything's on track. The rehearsal dinner's all set, and I've been running around to tie up some loose ends for Teresa and Karin in Phoenix."

Ed said, "We took a break from unpacking boxes on Sunday and drove up to Sedona. We saw the chapel while we were there. Great place."

Clare added, "It's really beautiful. I've never seen anything quite like it. The picture Teresa showed me didn't do it justice."

"Yeah," Kevin agreed. "Juan, the indispensable man, found the perfect place. We were sitting around the fireplace at Karin's house last Christmas, and Juan just casually mentions that he has this priest friend who runs religious retreats at this little chapel in Sedona. Then, like it was no big deal, he said he could arrange it for us if we'd like to use it. Naturally, Teresa fell in love with the place the first time she saw it."

"That's the artist in her," Clare said.

"Well, folks," Kevin said, looking at his watch, "I hate to eat and run, but I've got to do some planning for a navigation flight I've got early tomorrow morning."

"Are you sure you can't stay for coffee?"

"I'll take a rain check, Clare. I've really got to get back."

They stood up together, and Ed said, "I'll walk out to your car with you."

"Okay," Kevin said and then kissed Clare on the cheek. "See you later, comely babe."

"That's why I like having you around, you sweet-talker. Bye."

The two men walked outside to Kevin's car, and Ed said, "Kev, I want you to know that I really appreciate everything you've done for Clare and me."

"What the hell good's an old roommate if he won't do a little apartment hunting while a guy's on his honeymoon?"

"You did a lot more than that, and I'm grateful."

"It's the least I can do, Ed-man. We're all pulling for you. You know that."

"Yeah."

"How'd it go this morning, getting back in the saddle?"

"A little rocky. The landings were a little rough, but I'll be okay after a few more flights. I didn't come back here to get bounced out, not after all that shit we swallowed for four years at the zoo," Ed said, using cadet slang for the Air Force Academy.

"Absolutely," Kevin said, extending his hand.

Ed took it firmly and said, "I really mean it, Kev. Thanks for everything."

Kevin got into his car, started the engine and drove off, waving to Ed as he left. He turned up the volume on the radio to listen to Frankie Valli and the Four Seasons harmonizing in the middle of "Rag Doll." "Ooo, I love you just the way you are," they sang. *Damn, these guys are terrific. "Walk Like a Man." "Candy Girl." Great stuff.*

After stopping at a traffic light in the center of town, he accelerated, turning onto the road to Williams. The Supremes finished "Where Did Our Love Go," and a disc jockey said, "There you have it, desert dudes and dudettes, the number-one song in the country. Now for the headlines at the top of the hour. Less than an hour ago, President Johnson announced from Washington that American carrier planes have attacked North Vietnam. They hit bases used by torpedo boats that fired on American destroyers in international waters this morning, for the second time in two days."

Pretty ballsy for a little dip-shit country in the middle of nowhere.

"Earlier today, also from Washington, a spokesman for the Federal Bureau of Investigation said that three bodies were recovered from beneath an earthen dam near Philadelphia, Mississippi. While the FBI hasn't issued a positive identification yet, all indications are that they're the remains of three civil-rights workers missing since late June."

God, that's a shame. It looks like Sam knows Mississippi all too well.

Chapter 5

Saturday, 29 August 1964

Kevin's head still hurt, but the throbbing had dulled after the six aspirin he had taken began to work. The warmth on his outstretched body from the sun behind him felt good, but he kept his eyes shut behind his sunglasses to avoid its light.

"Hey, Kev," someone called to him.

He squinted through one eye and saw his Academy classmate, Charlie Rasmussen, with his flaming red hair approaching from the entrance to the swimming pool. Rasmussen, one of the top graduates of the Class of '63, had delayed his entry into pilot training by six months to complete an accelerated course in international relations at Georgetown University to earn a master's degree.

"Hi, Charlie."

"Well, Kev, it looks like you have a bad case of the morning after the night before," Charlie said, grinning, standing over him, apparently enjoying his distress. "But let me assure you that you had a great time last night."

"Yeah? I don't remember much after midnight," Kevin said, slowly opening his eyes.

"That's when things got going strong," Charlie told him as he dragged a lawn chair closer to the edge of the pool.

"Hey, Charlie. Could you lift that chair, instead of scraping it along the concrete? It sounds like you're building a road."

"Sure, Kev. I've really got to hand it to Sam Prentiss. The man knows how to throw a bachelor party."

"Right now, I feel like killing him."

"Well, I've got to say that I never saw anything like last night when I was in grad school. In fact, the guys in my UPT class are complete wallflowers next to you guys."

"Your class'll probably get a little crazy too when you get near the end of training. What's that you're reading?"

"It's a back issue of *Time.* It's got a long article on the North Vietnamese attacks on our destroyers in the Tonkin Gulf and our air strikes on their torpedo-boat bases."

"What do you make of all that, now that you're an international-relations expert."

"Well, the first thing is that we can't allow a half-assed country like North Vietnam to attack our ships in international waters and get away with it. If this article is accurate, we launched sixty-four sorties from two aircraft carriers and ripped up four targets pretty badly. Even though we lost two airplanes, it looks like we caused a lot of damage. Hopefully, Ho Chi Minh will remember that the next time he starts thinking about anything major, even in South Vietnam. We've always got the air-strike option."

"Interesting."

"Then there's the broader message."

"What do you mean?"

"When we showed the Soviets and the Red Chinese that we're willing to fight to protect ourselves, we gave them something to think about before they try anything in Europe or somewhere else in Asia. If we'd shown weakness in the Tonkin Gulf, there would've been a greater chance of their probing us somewhere else. And, of course, there's domestic politics."

"You mean the election campaign."

"Yeah. With only two months to go until the election, Johnson couldn't give the opposition an opening—not with the Republicans running around the country saying that he's screwing up in Vietnam by not taking the fight to the North Vietnamese."

"Will it come to that, do you think?"

"Very possibly. It may turn out that the only way to win in South Vietnam is to hit the North Vietnamese with air strikes, to force them to negotiate a settlement. I looked at Vietnam when I did my thesis on counterinsurgency at Georgetown. I think it's going to be a very tough job to beat the Viet Cong guerillas in the South."

"You'd better give me the short version. I don't think my head could absorb much more this morning."

"Okay. If you look at the suppression of the Communist guerillas, the Huks, in the Philippines in the late forties and early fifties as a successful model for counterinsurgency, you see some key things. First, because the Philippines are isolated geographically, the Huks had no real outside source of supply. Then, the Philippine government did a good job of isolating the guerillas politically by responding to popular grievances. The last thing is that the government supported and used its military well, and they won the fight on the ground. The end result was that the Huks were defeated without overt American involvement."

"I think I'm beginning to understand where you're coming out."

"Yeah. The situation in South Vietnam's about as far from favorable as you can get. The North Vietnamese have an established supply route to the guerillas in the South. Added to that, the political situation is about as screwed up as it can be. After Diem was assassinated last November, there've been two military governments, and the country is as divided as it ever was among the various factions, like the Catholics and the Buddhists. There're something like sixty different political parties. It'd be tough for any government to work. And the South Vietnamese military's performance in the field isn't exactly anything to write home about."

"So, in this one, the American role goes overt."

"I'd say sixteen thousand American military advisers there now, with more to come, is pretty overt."

Kevin saw Sam Prentiss rounding the corner of the officers' club on his way to the pool. "Well, here he comes, the party guy himself. Don't tell Sam that we've been talking about Vietnam, or else he'll go on and on about how we should've nuked the Vietnamese when they surrounded the French at Dien Bien Phu."

"Hi, Charlie. Hey, Kev," Prentiss called out, grinning. "It looks like you're comin' back from the dead."

"No thanks to you, you son of a bitch," Kevin replied with a wry smile.

"Well, hell, Kev. I swear. If I'd remembered that you Yankee boys can't drink worth a shit, I would've stopped fillin' up your glass and makin' all them toasts," Prentiss protested, looking completely without remorse. Enjoying the memory, he said, "Man, you were in bad shape when we poured you into bed last night."

"Yeah," Charlie added, heeding Kevin's advice and slipping his magazine, front cover down, under his chair. "It took three of us, but Ed Walker did most of the heavy work."

"Oh, fabulous," Kevin said. "I can't wait to get an ear full from Clare, Ed's wife, at the rehearsal dinner tonight. She'll be merciless."

"How's Ed doing, by the way?" Charlie asked. "All he said last night when I asked him is that he's only barfing after every other flight now, instead of after every mission. He changed the subject pretty fast."

"He's gutting it out," Kevin answered. "He's almost finished with two-ship now. He'll be okay after four-ship, but I don't look for Ed to be asking for an assignment after UPT with a lot of formation flying."

"Man," Charlie mused, "I don't know how I would've handled a close call like that."

"Well, Charlie," Sam said, "that's ancient history. What's goin' on this mornin', anyhow?"

Charlie said, "While Kev here's been doing his imitation of a corpse, I've been ogling Kelley, the sun-goddess lifeguard. She's the only reason I come out here to burn the hell out of my pale, freckled body. Great shoulders."

"Shoulders?" Sam scoffed. "Now, I've heard o' boob men and leg men. But shoulders? Charlie, goin' to grad school right after graduation really screwed you up."

"Naah," Charlie countered, "It started way before then. Did either of you ever see *Rear Window?"*

"Sure," Kevin volunteered. "Jimmy Stewart. Great movie."

"No," Charlie corrected him. "Grace Kelly; great movie. Now there, gentlemen, is a woman with a set of shoulders."

Sam was getting impatient. "Well, have you made your move on the lovely lifeguard, or are you still contemplatin'?"

"I've talked to her a little around the pool. Maybe I'll get my courage up when I get to be a big T-38 jock next month like you guys."

"Too late," Kevin said. "She goes back to Arizona State next week."

"Charlie," Sam added, shaking his head, "she's been lifeguardin' for almost three months. And all you've done is talk around the pool? Man, you scholars need some real help with the killer instinct. Need some advice from a fighter pilot on how to hustle the ladies?"

"Don't listen to him, Charlie," Kevin said. "Sam was insufferable before he got his assignment to fighters. Now he's completely off the chart."

"Well, now," Sam retorted. "Who did Kandy invite up on stage to dance last night? Did she ask Kevin, our future T-38 IP puke, or me? I rest my case."

Charlie laughed. "I'll have to admit it, Sam. You had some great moves on stage last night. But we spectators were a little surprised that, unlike Kandy, you kept some of your clothes on. So, Kev, are you going to be an IP here at Williams?"

"No, I'm going to Laughlin in Del Rio, Texas. They're just starting to get T-38s there. I'll be going to Randolph first, though, to get checked out as an IP," he added, referring to an air base near San Antonio, Texas.

"Back to this other matter," Sam insisted. "It's a sad, sad situation. Kev, what're we gonna do to help our friend the scholar improve his chick skills? Should we take him to a Steve McQueen triple feature?"

"I think I have something that might work. Charlie, are you bringing anyone to the wedding tomorrow?"

"No, I hadn't planned to."

"Okay. I'm going to have to leave now to finish packing. After I go, separate from Sam here, of the bad reputation—to keep whatever dignity you have left in Kelley's eyes after associating with him. Then go over there and strike up some of that talk around the pool you're so good at. Then, after a while, casually invite her to the wedding. Tell her that the bride and groom, especially the groom, hope she'll attend. Today's her last day of lifeguarding, and it's beautiful up at Sedona. A wedding and a reception should be safe enough for her to take a gamble on a first date with you. Should be a piece of cake, even for a Georgetown guy. What do you think, Sam?"

"I think it's downright brilliant, 'cept for the part about my reputation, o' course."

* * *

On Sunday, Juan stood in white vestments before Teresa and Kevin, in front of an altar. Behind him, a late-afternoon sun illuminated the red rocks of Sedona, visible beyond the sanctuary through a towering wall of glass held together by a massive red-stone cross at its center.

"Father," Juan intoned with his arms upraised, "You have made the bond of marriage a holy mystery . . . ."

After Juan completed the introductory prayers, Ed read the ageless verses of love from the Song of Songs and the first letter of John. "Hark! My lover . . . ," Ed began in a strong voice.

He looks good, Kevin thought. *More like his old self again. Clare's definitely got the magic.*

When Ed was done, Juan came to the lectern to read the gospel. Looking at the two of them, he smiled and began, "From the holy gospel according to Mark: Jesus said, 'At the beginning of creation, God made them male and female . . . .'"

Kevin looked at Teresa as she smiled warmly at her brother. *Where would we be now without Juan?*

When he was done with the reading, Juan returned to the center of the sanctuary and bowed his head. Then, speaking from the heart to the congregation, he said, "There is, of course, no sermon today, because we are now at that place in the Mass where Teresa and Kevin will exchange their marriage vows. Anything that I might say would pale completely into insignificance in comparison. But, I must tell you, I have reflected on the journeys of these two souls, moving inexorably toward one another, as seen by the mind of God since the beginning of time." His voice faltered briefly, and he continued, "It is a profound thing, and I am completely awed by it. And, so, I ask Kevin, do you take Teresa . . . ?"

Some part of him listened carefully to Juan, but as he looked at her, Teresa flooded the highest levels of his awareness. She looked more beautiful than he had ever seen her. The ageless question Juan was asking him didn't seem to matter. He had already promised her everything a year before in the mountains of Colorado. "I do," he answered, dimly aware that her brother had stopped speaking.

As Juan turned to his sister to ask the same question of her, Kevin looked at Teresa and Clare standing together. Seeing the two of them, he thought about the introduction two years earlier. *A glimmer of something that changes lives.* He wondered if he would ever quite know what left him almost speechless when he saw her for the first time. It always seemed to be just beyond his understanding, just beyond his grasp. *Some kind of recognition, maybe. There for an instant and then gone.* It was just too elusive.

"I do," she answered Juan.

Kevin's brother, Sean, the best man, handed him her ring, and he put it on her finger, next to her mother's wedding band that he had placed there a year before.

The vows completed and the rings exchanged, Juan continued with the traditional prayers of the Mass. Having heard them many times, Kevin responded from instinct as images from the past two years moved strongly through his thoughts. He saw their lives beginning to weave together, Teresa's, his, Juan's, Clare's and Ed's. *Going where, I wonder?*

The minutes seemed to quicken, to compress. Then, in a final rush of words, he heard Juan say a final blessing over them. When time elongated again, Mass was over and Teresa turned toward him. He raised his hand to touch her cheek lightly while he kissed her. She took his hand and squeezed it tightly as they began walking through the aisle.

At the back of the chapel, they went downstairs to wait for their guests to assemble outside. A few minutes later, Ed came down and asked, "Are you guys ready? The car's in place, and Clare's lined up all the rice throwers."

"Okay, we're all set," Kevin said, and Ed left. "Are you ready to move among your adoring public, oh gorgeous one?"

She smiled. "Will I be safe? Clare's told me about your classmates at your bachelor party."

"Don't worry. That was just momentary insanity. Besides, I've got six armed men outside to protect you."

They climbed the stairs, and when they reached the top, Ed barked a command. Six sabers flashed upward, forming an arch just beyond the chapel's entrance. They walked under the crossed blades and then hurried down a curved walkway to a parking lot as rice began to fly. Halfway down, Kevin saw Charlie Rasmussen and Kelley standing by themselves behind a parked limousine at the bottom of the walk. Charlie was holding a signaling mirror to his eye, aiming the sun's reflected rays toward the south.

Strange, Kevin thought. Beginning to understand, he looked southward, just above the horizon, and saw a biplane circling soundlessly. He stopped and said to Teresa, "Let's wait here for just a second."

"Is anything wrong?"

Pointing, he said, "No. In fact, it's perfect. It's Sam Prentiss."

Holding hands, they watched as the yellow airplane dropped silently from its orbit and headed toward them. When it was a mile away, with the sun making a silver disk of its spinning propeller, they heard the sound of an engine at full power as Prentiss raced along the valley floor. At a quarter of a mile away, Sam pulled the nose of the Stearman up and, gaining altitude, rolled lazily once before waving, roaring away toward Oak Creek Canyon to the north.

Chapter 6

Sunday, 7 March 1965

A blanket of clouds covered central Texas below two T-38s flying in route formation, two wing spans between the wing tips of the two jets, headed south at 25,000 feet. Kevin was flying in the rear cockpit of the wingman's jet, and Josh Pemberton, Kevin's senior-year roommate at the Air Force Academy, was leading the flight from the rear cockpit of the lead airplane. A wisecracking Yankee from Maine, Pemberton could always be counted on to find irreverence in any situation. He had completed UPT at Vance Air Force Base near Enid, Oklahoma, and both he and Kevin were nearly finished with the advanced checkout course at Randolph Air Force Base, near San Antonio, Texas, that would make them fully qualified IPs in the T-38.

Kevin reached into a metal map case to his right and took out a booklet bound at the top. His eyes moving between the lead jet and the booklet, he turned to a page with a diagram of an instrument approach into Randolph. He fastened the booklet onto a small metal clipboard strapped to his right leg and scanned the page between glances at the flight leader.

Reaching forward to the stack of control panels for his jet's radios between his legs, under the instrument panel, he changed the channel on the panel marked TACAN—shorthand for tactical aid to navigation, a station in a network of radio transmitters used by military aircraft to navigate across long distances at high altitude. With the change in channels, a white arrowhead on the edge of the compass dial on his instrument panel stopped pointing in the direction of the TACAN station at Austin, Texas behind the two jets, and swung clockwise around the dial. It stopped at a heading of 230 degrees on the dial when the airplane's TACAN receiver locked onto the station at Randolph to the southwest. A small window above the compass dial then displayed 32, the nautical-mile distance to the Randolph TACAN, calculated by distance-measuring equipment—called DME—within the receiver.

"When I called my wife last night," Kevin's IP, Major Bill O'Rourke, said from the front cockpit over the jet's intercom, "she said that the weather in San Antonio's been rotten since we left on Friday. Not much activity on the golf course. So it was a good weekend to get your cross-country flights done. Only two more rides to go before we make you a full-fledged IP."

"Yes, sir. It's good to be close to finishing. You folks at Randolph run a good checkout program for new IPs. I've learned a lot."

"Well, Kevin, you'll be teaching students in a few weeks, after you get back to Laughlin. That should give you enough time to find a decent apartment in Del Rio before you get started. What do you think of life on the Rio Grande so far?"

"As Texas towns go, Del Rio isn't San Antonio or Austin, but I think my wife and I'll like it. It looks like we can get by there reasonably well on a lieutenant's pay."

"And as UPT bases go, Laughlin isn't exactly Williams either. But the housing on base is better. Did you know that U-2s used to fly out of Laughlin to make their high-altitude runs over Cuba?"

"Yes, sir. I'd heard that."

"Well, they gave the U-2 boys pretty good housing. After the U-2 operation got moved out, Training Command inherited Laughlin from SAC," O'Rourke said, referring to the Strategic Air Command, the Air Force's premier combat command, home to bombers, tankers, nuclear-tipped intercontinental missiles and high-altitude reconnaissance aircraft. "You'll be able to live in some fine quarters on-base one day, after about a year on the waiting list while you live off-base."

An air traffic controller at Fort Worth Center interrupted them with a radio call. "Boxer three zero flight, descend and maintain one five thousand."

"Boxer three zero flight, roger," Josh Pemberton replied over the radio, acknowledging the order to change altitude. "Boxer three zero is out of flight level two five zero for fifteen thousand." Josh looked over at Kevin and signaled a throttle reduction by showing a fist, fingers rearward, that he pulled toward the rear of his airplane. Kevin nodded in reply and moved his throttles back to maintain position on Josh's airplane as they descended.

A minute later, the air traffic controller called them again to assign a new radio frequency. "Boxer three zero flight, contact San Antonio Approach Control now on two, twenty-one, point one. Nice workin' with you. Good day."

"Boxer three zero, roger. San Antonio Approach on two, twenty-one, point one. Good day, sir." Josh paused and then called, "Boxer three zero flight, go two, twenty-one, point one."

Telling Josh that he had heard the command, Kevin responded tersely over the radio, "Two." He reached forward to the top control panel in the stack and dialed 221.1 into its frequency selector.

Making certain that both of them were on the same frequency, Josh called, "Boxer three zero flight, check."

"Two," Kevin answered.

Hearing that his wingman was with him, Josh continued, "San Antonio Approach, this is Boxer three zero, flight of two, passing seventeen thousand for one five thousand."

The new controller at San Antonio Approach Control responded, "Roger, Boxer three zero. Squawk ident," the controller directed Josh, telling him to activate a switch on his airplane's transponder, to make the unique radar signal it broadcast blossom in intensity, to make the signal stand out from other radar returns on the controller's radar scope. "Boxer three zero, radar contact. Continue descent now to one two thousand. Say your request."

"Boxer three zero continuing descent to twelve thousand. Boxer three zero requests radar vectors to an ILS approach at Randolph," Josh said, asking the controller to maneuver the two airplanes to the instrument landing system—the ILS—at Randolph. The ILS transmitted an electronic cone, a funnel, with its apex just short of the approach end of the landing runway. A proficient pilot could fly an ILS approach to bring an airplane precisely through weather to a point two hundred feet above the ground, at half a mile from the runway's approach end.

The controller replied, "Roger. Randolph is landing north on runway three two. San Antonio altimeter is two niner, eight seven. Randolph reports six hundred overcast, visibility one mile in light drizzle. Winds are calm."

Josh confirmed, "Roger, two nine, eight seven. Boxer three zero flight, descent check."

As they continued to descend toward the solid deck of clouds below them, Kevin put 29.87 in the altimeter's calibration window and accomplished the other items on a checklist clipped to the left leg of his flight suit. He attached a red clip on his parachute for low-altitude ejections to its D ring and gave the clip a confirming tug. "Check your altimeter and D ring, sir," he advised O'Rourke.

"I'm all set up here, Kevin."

Josh called, "Boxer three zero flight, fuel check. Lead has twelve hundred pounds."

"Two has eleven hundred."

Josh leveled the flight as directed at 12,000 feet. Kevin glanced inside at the white arrowhead on the compass dial again and saw it pointing to his right wing. They were passing east of Randolph with 16 miles showing on the DME. Taking advantage of the lull in the descent, he set up his ILS receiver and instruments for the approach into Randolph, alternating glances between the lead jet and his instrument panel.

"Okay, good. You're set to fly the ILS separately if you lose the leader in the weather. You're staying ahead of the airplane," O'Rourke observed from the display in his cockpit that matched the settings made from the rear seat. "By the way, have you ever flown an approach on the wing in actual weather?"

"No, sir."

"You were spoiled by too much of that clear desert air at Williams I guess. Okay. You'll be able to see the other airplane just fine once we're in the soup. If you do lose the leader, though, just remember the lost-wingman procedures and get some separation from the other jet. Since we'll be on the outside of the turn onto final approach, all you'll have to do is to roll out of the turn and climb a little to get away from him."

"Yes, sir."

"One other thing. Do you still have your sun visor down?"

"Yes, sir."

"I'd recommend putting it up now, before we get into the murk. After that, you'll want to keep your hands on the stick and throttles as much as you can."

"Yes, sir." *Another secret of the trade.* He slid the sun visor on his helmet up, away from his eyes, and squinted to lessen the glare from the sun behind Josh's jet.

The approach controller called them again, "Boxer three zero, descend and maintain five thousand. Turn right to two three zero," the disembodied voice directed, telling them to turn westward, beginning a series of turns in a loop that would eventually point them northwest, toward the landing runway at Randolph.

"Boxer three zero, roger. Leaving twelve thousand for five thousand. Right to two three zero." Josh rocked the wings of the lead aircraft as he began descending again and then started a shallow right turn.

Responding to Josh's wing-rock signal, Kevin moved to close formation on the leader's left wing, almost overlapping their staggered wingtips. He was in position, ready for the cloud layer rushing up at them. From his cockpit, the red wing light on the lead jet's left wingtip appeared to nestle into the lower-left corner of the white star in the center of the insignia painted on the air intake of the lead T-38. The light blocked out a wedge of blue formed by the boundaries of the star and the blue disk behind it. *Now let's see if I can keep it there in the weather.*

The bumpy deck of clouds engulfed them. Swallowed by vapor at 8,000 feet, he sensed motion stopping abruptly, as speed, so apparent when they skimmed briefly across the billowy hillocks on top of the cloud layer, vanished to the senses in the milky world where they seemed to hang suspended. Only small rivulets of moisture sliding horizontally along the canopy suggested that they might still be moving. He felt slightly disoriented in this strange, new place, and with his senses heightening, he clung tightly to Josh's wing. *Keep the light in the corner of the star.*

The controller's voice reached them in their white nether world. "Boxer three zero flight, turn further right now, to a heading of two eight zero. Descend and maintain four thousand."

"Boxer three zero, roger. Right to two eight zero. Out of five for four thousand," Josh answered the controller, his voice quickening as he closed on the ILS cone.

The controller said, "Boxer three zero flight is cleared for the ILS approach to runway three two right at Randolph. Report wheels down at the outer marker," he added, referring to the point where the final, most-critical leg of the approach commenced.

"Boxer three zero, roger. Understand cleared for the approach. Boxer three zero, gear down, now."

At Josh's command, Kevin reached out quickly by instinct for the landing-gear handle with his left hand and lowered it firmly, keeping his eyes locked on the leader's airplane, moving his hand back to the throttles as quickly as he could, to maintain position on Josh. Things were happening fast. He worked the stick rapidly, making small, aggressive motions, thumbing the trim button to maintain position, as the feel on the stick changed rapidly from the lowering landing gear. "Boxer three zero, full flaps, now."

His left hand found the flap lever, moved it to full down and then flew swiftly back to the throttles. The airplane tried to balloon as the flaps lowered, but he anticipated it and counteracted it with smooth, aggressive pressure on the stick, working the trim button in bursts.

After Josh rolled out of the turn, things seemed to slow down. Kevin glanced inside the cockpit and saw that they were on the final-approach course. Out of the corner of his eye, he saw a green light on the instrument panel begin to flash, indicating that they were over the outer marker. Gradually, he moved his throttles back to maintain position as Josh intercepted the glide slope to the runway at Randolph. He glanced inside the cockpit again for the three green lights above the gear handle. "I've got three green, sir."

"I have three green up front, Kevin," O'Rourke answered.

Josh transmitted, "Boxer three zero flight, outer marker. Gear check, lead."

Gear check, two," Kevin radioed back.

"Roger, Boxer three zero flight," the controller replied.

Josh added, "The number-two aircraft will land out of this approach. Lead will fly another approach."

"Roger," the controller answered. "Number two aircraft is cleared to land. Boxer three zero lead, on missed approach, climb runway heading to four thousand. Contact San Antonio Approach on this frequency. Acknowledge."

"Roger. Two cleared to land. Lead to four thousand. Runway heading. San Antonio on this freq," Josh replied, speaking rapidly as he came down the glide slope, working hard to hold the two jets in the center of the ILS cone as they flew through its narrowest section.

Suddenly, brown earth appeared under them as they dropped out of the cloud layer. Kevin glanced ahead to pick up the runway and then back at Josh to hold position. Josh pointed toward the end of the runway ahead with his left hand, and Kevin gave him an answering nod. Josh turned away from him, and Kevin turned his full attention to the runway coming up at him.

He checked his airspeed quickly. *On speed—155 knots.* Making fine adjustments on the stick, thumbing his trim button, he refined the jet's glide path, aiming the T-38 to fly toward a point just short of the runway's threshold.

One more time, he said to himself as he checked the three green lights for gear down and locked. Looking past O'Rourke's helmet at the runway, his view partially obscured from the rear cockpit, he got ready to flare the jet into a landing. Seeing the right picture, he slowly brought the stick back and reduced power. The airplane's nose started up, but the main gear touched down on the runway prematurely, ten knots above landing speed. *Damn it!*

On the landing rollout, O'Rourke observed, "Nice approach on the wing for your first time in the weather, Kevin. Josh could have made it a little easier on you by slowing down sooner and getting the gear and flaps down earlier than we did. We were a little bit less than perfect there when we had to rush the turn onto final approach. One last thing. Did you notice that you touched down a little fast?"

"Yes, sir."

"Well, that can happen when you make a landing off the wing. You don't have as much time to set up for the flare. So, you just need to be aware that it's a potential problem and concentrate hard on the touchdown next time. With a wet runway like this, if the touchdown's long, a hot landing can make getting stopped a little sporty."

"Yes, sir."

"All in all, though, it was a good trip this weekend," O'Rourke said, relaxing, and then added, "for two micks roaring around the country together in the same jet."

"Yes, sir," he laughed. "I enjoyed it too." They taxied to the parking ramp, shut down the engines and returned the airplane to the custody of its crew chief.

Forty minutes later, the debriefing done, Kevin walked out of the squadron building with Josh. Teresa was waiting for him in the parking lot.

"Do I see Teresa sitting in a Chevy station wagon?" Josh asked in exaggerated, feigned surprise.

"Yeah. I bought it last week. Expectant mothers fit better in a wagon than a two-seater."

"Oh, where is that dashing Kev of yesteryear? The one who drove a sports car."

"He traded it in for maturity. You're still driving a Corvette, right?"

"Ouch! That was nasty. One more of those, and people'll start thinking you're a Yankee from Maine."

Teresa stayed in the car, out of the drizzle, and rolled her window down as they approached. "My, those young Air Force pilots are handsome. Welcome home, love. Hi, Josh."

Kevin leaned in and kissed her through the open window. "How's the mom?"

"I'm good. How was the cross-country?"

"Good. We got a lot done. We should finish up this week for sure."

"Did he behave himself, Josh?"

"Absolutely. The man's no fun at all on a cross-country," Josh assured her.

"Why don't you join us for dinner? I'm cooking Mexican tonight and there'll be lots."

"God, it'd be great to escape another night of bachelor slop. I'd even bring some beer. Are you sure it's no trouble?"

"None at all. We'd enjoy your company. Besides, since you're going to be with us at Laughlin for the next three years, we should get to know one another better. You can tell me more of those stories about Kevin during the summer before pilot training."

"Okay. I'm easy. I'll always rat on a classmate for food."

Teresa laughed. "How about around seven?"

"Ayuh," Josh replied, deepening his Maine accent. "Sounds promisin'."

* * *

Kevin answered the knock on the door. "Hey, Josh. Welcome."

Josh entered and held out a six pack of beer. "As promised, I present the sacramental brew of Texas. Lone Star long-necks." He surveyed the small living room of the furnished apartment rented by the month and asked, "What's this contraption?"

Teresa answered from the efficiency kitchen, "It's a loom. We bought it second-hand from a woman in San Antonio."

Kevin added, "Now you see why we need that Chevy wagon. Teresa is a finder and keeper of much stuff."

"Well," Josh bantered, "I know you married folk have to be frugal. But, Teresa, isn't there a better way for Kev to get new underwear? Without you weaving it for him, I mean."

Teresa laughed. "For your information, mister smart guy, I just sold a wall hanging I made on that contraption to a gallery in Austin. It's my first commercial success as an artist."

"No kidding," Josh replied with admiration. "I'm impressed."

Kevin was about to heap praise on his wife's talents, when she cut him off by blurting out, "Oh, my god!"

He rushed into the kitchen with Josh behind him. Teresa was frozen still, staring at a small television set on a counter near the kitchen table. On the screen, there was a wild melee at the foot of a girdered bridge. Uniformed men in hard hats and gas masks were charging through the crumbling ranks of people holding their hands over their heads to ward off blows from police batons. Many were on the ground. Others were running to escape.

" . . . as the Alabama state troopers on foot charged the marchers," an off-screen announcer reported. "Shortly afterward, they fired tear gas. Then a second wave, this time county sheriff's deputies on horseback, made their assault, scattering those farther back."

"Holy Mother of God!" Kevin exhaled.

The scene was riveting, capturing the raw fury of the attackers, the searing pain of those being beaten bloody and the panic-blind flight of others trying to escape, all framed by wispy clouds of tear gas. An anchor man appeared on the screen next and said, "That footage is just in from Selma, Alabama, where, earlier today, marchers who had hoped to travel from Selma to Montgomery to dramatize their support for federal legislation for voting rights were brutally stopped by police. No doubt we'll be hearing much more about this in the days to come."

"Halfway around the globe," the anchor man continued, "American involvement in the war in Vietnam appears to have reached a turning point. We have a report from our correspondent at the air base at Danang in South Vietnam."

The scene shifted to a man in a bush jacket and hat with a microphone in his hand. Behind him, bomb-laden jets were taking off at intervals. "An announcement just out of the Pentagon indicates that the first American ground-combat units will soon arrive here in South Vietnam. Two battalions of marines will dig in around Danang to provide perimeter security for the intensive air operations you see launching from the runway behind me. This is the main air base in South Vietnam from which American fighter-bombers five days ago flew the first strikes against North Vietnam in what is being called Operation Rolling Thunder. In response to raids by Viet Cong guerillas last month against barracks at Pleiku and Qui Nhon, resulting in the deaths of thirty-one Americans, Air Force fighter pilots flew over one hundred sorties to hammer targets that support the flow of men, ammunition and supplies to the Viet Cong from across the border. But this first Rolling Thunder mission was no walkover. Five Air Force jets were shot down, an unusually high loss rate, although four of the five pilots were rescued. As the air war picks up momentum, the stakes in Vietnam continue to grow. This is Peter Holmes reporting from the combat zone in South Vietnam."

Teresa turned off the television and said quietly, "Dinner's ready."

"That first piece looked like something out of czarist Russia," Kevin said, pulling Teresa's chair out for her. "Like Cossacks on horseback cutting down peasants. I guess law enforcement takes on a different meaning in Alabama." He sat down with Teresa and Josh.

"It's not just the police," Josh said. "It's a pretty broad-based attitude, and feelings run close to the surface in Alabama."

"Have you ever been there, Josh?" Teresa asked.

"No, but I got a close-up view of how Alabamians think when I was in Maine during the summer four years ago. The summer of sixty-one. Do you remember what the big national story out of the South was then?"

"It doesn't come to mind," Kevin replied as Teresa shook her head.

"Well, that was the summer of the freedom rides. Do you remember? People on chartered buses riding through the South to protest segregated bus stations?"

"Vaguely," Kevin said.

"For me, though," Josh continued, "it was mainly the summer of Becky Carter. Two of the guys from my old high-school crowd and I went down to Camden, as usual, to meet girls on summer vacation. Our main hunting ground was this mountain outside of town with a hiking trail to the top. Mount Megunticook."

"Only in Maine could you find a name like that," Kevin added.

"Yeah, great name. But the view was even better. On a clear day, looking down on the church steeples in Camden, with the harbor full of sailboats, you'd swear that the scene was right out of some guide book on New England. The best thing, though, was that the girls who climbed the trail wore shorts, and you could see some great legs along with the scenery."

Teresa smiled. "You boys in flight suits really do have one-track minds."

"Even boys without flight suits. Anyway," Josh continued, "we met these three girls from Alabama on top of the mountain, and we went right into our Maine-guide routine. I paired up with Becky. It was instant chemistry. She was this saucy thing, and that accent of hers just made me melt. We started going out just about every night, and she'd laugh like hell every time I'd go into my caustic-boy-from-Maine number. She called me wicked. Took her about five syllables to say wicked. I even started talking to her about going down to Alabama to see her after she went home. I don't remember now just how it got started, but one night I made some crack about one of the freedom-rider buses being burned up in Alabama. Something about the Klan running out of firewood and using buses instead. Becky got defensive in a big way, and I didn't have the good sense to stop. I thought I was in rare form that night, and so I made another smart-ass remark about Alabama. She got really cold. She stared at me with this look that could kill and said, 'You sanctimonious Yankees think you know it all, don't you. Let me tell you something. With all your high-and-mighty opinions on the nigras, I haven't seen one black face in Maine since I've been here. But you're always ready to meddle in things you don't understand.' She got up and left the restaurant right in the middle of the dinner. I tried to see her after that, but I found out later that she left for home the next morning."

"Maybe it was for the best," Teresa offered.

"Maybe. Later, when I thought about it, it seemed kind of ironic. Like I couldn't escape Gettysburg."

"Gettysburg?" Kevin asked.

"Well, Kev, you remember how I used to go on and on about my ancestors who fought in Lawrence Chamberlain's regiment, the Twentieth Maine, when he won the Medal of Honor at Gettysburg."

"Yeah. How could I forget."

"The people they fought that day were in two regiments from Alabama. Well, anyway, on to the future," Josh said, raising his glass of beer. "May I meet a woman while I'm at Laughlin who's half as terrific as Teresa."

Teresa smiled. "You've just guaranteed yourself many free meals over the next three years."

"Ayuh," Josh replied, picking up a taco, speaking downeastern, "We Mainers may be daft, but we ain't stupid."

Their conversation turned to Laughlin and the prospects for housing that wouldn't break their budgets. As always, Kevin and Teresa laughed readily at Josh's sardonic commentary on everyday Air Force life in Texas, and their back-and-forth banter easily filled up the rest of the meal.

After Josh left, Kevin gathered the dishes from the table, put them in the sink and started the washing. "Good dinner, love."

"Not such a good night for news, though."

"Yeah. That stuff from Alabama was pretty rough."

"And there was the piece from Vietnam."

"It looks like we're finally getting serious with the North Vietnamese."

"I'm worried about that, for some reason."

"Why? Now that we're hitting them with air strikes, I think we might finally see some progress in settling the guerilla war in South Vietnam."

"I mean I'm worried about your having to go there."

Kevin smiled. "Love, we have a three-year tour at Laughlin ahead of us. This little dustup in Vietnam will be over long before then." He dried his hands and moved behind her, putting his arms around her and kissing the back of her neck. "Besides, the most important thing right now is for me to show you how much I missed you this weekend."

Chapter 7

Friday, 10 June 1966

Kevin tossed his flight cap onto a couch as he came through the front door of his newly assigned house at Laughlin Air Force Base. "Daddy's home, Mary Clare." Kneeling down on one knee, he held his arms out to the toddler who walked unsteadily from the kitchen toward him. He picked her up, nuzzling his face against her neck, and his dark-haired, blue-eyed daughter squealed with delight.

Teresa came out from the kitchen. "Save some of that love stuff for the mom."

"Absolutely," he said, putting one arm around her and kissing her while holding his child in the other.

"How was flying today?"

"Good. Both flights went well. I was up with my two best students. How's the unpacking coming?"

"Most of the boxes are done. We should be able to finish the rest tomorrow. I've cleared enough room in the spare bedroom to set up the two looms. Can you help me with them tomorrow?"

"Sure. By the way, I ran into Josh at beer call at the club. I know we're still moving in, but I invited him and Elena over to watch the air show tomorrow afternoon. It'd be a shame to waste the great view of the airfield we have from our new front lawn and make them fight the crowd at the flight line. Besides, Josh offered to bring beer."

"Well, impulsive one, you'll have to work very hard tomorrow morning to help me get the house presentable for company."

"It's a deal."

"Anyway, I suppose we should encourage this romance. I like Elena much better than that airline stewardess Josh was dating last year."

Mary Clare began squirming. Kevin put her down, and she wobbled her way to oversize plastic blocks scattered on the living-room floor. "Da da!" she insisted after sitting down firmly, stiff-legged, among them.

"Okay, sugar. Daddy will play blocks with you."

"I'll finish getting dinner ready," Teresa said, returning to the kitchen. "I found some fresh fish at the commissary today."

"Good. I'm starved," he answered as he sat down and began putting blocks in stacks for his daughter to demolish with giggling glee.

The television across the room was on. He looked at his watch and saw that the evening news was half over as a commercial ended and an anchor man from New York returned to the screen. "We turn now to the war in Vietnam with a report from our correspondent, Peter Holmes."

The reporter appeared in his signature bush jacket and hat and spoke loudly into his microphone above the din of helicopters behind him. Red crosses on white-square backgrounds were painted on their sides and noses. "I am near the town of Dak To in Kontum Province witnessing the close of an extraordinary chapter in valor. Behind me, med-evac helicopters, called dustoffs, are carrying out wounded troopers from an infantry company of the fabled Hundred and First Airborne Division. These men fought their way out of a trap after being surrounded by a regiment of North Vietnamese."

The camera shifted to a group of three young soldiers, one with a bloody bandage around his head and the other two with leg wounds, and zoomed in on their faces as they struggled to get up from the ground to board one of the helicopters. The camera then returned to Holmes who continued, "The fighting was so intense and close-range that the company commander called down napalm on his own position from Air Force fighters overhead. The air strikes blasted an escape route through the enemy. The officer who commands these soldiers is none other than Captain William Carpenter, the All-American football player who captained the nineteen-fifty-nine West Point team and who gained national attention as its lonesome end."

Ducking his head under whirling rotor blades, Holmes walked to a helicopter taking on wounded. At its side door, a helmeted soldier with captain's rank sewn on the collar of his fatigue uniform was helping them aboard. Holmes approached him. "Captain Carpenter, how do you feel now that the battle is over?"

Carpenter looked coolly professional and impatient. "I'm just happy as hell to have my men out of there. If you'll excuse me now, please, I've got to see to my soldiers."

Ducking again, Holmes walked away and straightened up when rotor blades were no longer overhead. Using the lifting helicopter as background, the reporter shouted into his microphone above the noise to end his report. "If anybody had any questions about the courage and skill of today's American soldier in combat, what you see going on behind me should answer them fully. This is Peter Holmes reporting from the combat zone in South Vietnam."

"Dinner's ready," Teresa called from the kitchen.

Kevin turned off the television and picked up his daughter to carry her to a small dining area off the kitchen. He strapped her into her high chair and attached its tray. She struggled to avoid the bib he tied around her neck. "No!" she wailed, trying to push it way.

Teresa brought Mary Clare cookies to pacify her and then carried out two plates, placing them on a dining table nearby.

"Looks delicious, love," Kevin said as he pulled out her chair to seat her.

"I've used some new spices. Tell me what you think."

He sat down and took a bite of the fish. "It's very good."

"I'm glad you like it. A wedding invitation came in the mail today. One of your classmates, I think."

"Really? Who?"

"Charles Rasmussen. The bride to be is a Kelley Monahan. Do I know them?"

"They were at our wedding. In fact, it was their first date. Charlie was the one with the bright-red hair who signaled Sam Prentiss with the mirror."

"Oh, now I remember. His date was very attractive."

"Yeah, she'd bowled Charlie over pretty completely by the time he asked her out. I'm glad that things worked out for them." He looked down at his plate and pushed at the food with his fork absent-mindedly.

"Kevin, I thought you were starving. You've hardly touched your dinner. Don't you like the fish?"

"It's good. It really is. Something seems to have happened to my appetite."

"What's wrong, love?"

"I don't know. I guess that piece on the news from Vietnam hit me a little hard. Those soldiers they showed who were all shot up looked like they weren't even twenty years old. Just kids. And here I am, a career officer, sitting safely back here. In a way, it makes me feel like I'm hiding out."

"Kevin, you are not hiding out."

"Then why do I feel this way?"

"If, god forbid, this war continues past the end of our assignment here and you're assigned to Vietnam, you'd go, wouldn't you?"

"Yes."

"Then I don't understand what's bothering you."

"Somehow, waiting for them find me and send me doesn't seem to be good enough."

"What would be good enough?"

"For me to volunteer for a combat assignment."

"Why would that be enough?"

"Because I couldn't do anything more than that."

"What would that mean?"

"It means that I'd go to the personnel office and fill out a volunteer statement. I'd be given an assignment sooner than I'd get one in the normal cycle. Maybe six months to a year sooner. I'd also be given priority over non-volunteers for assignment to the types of airplanes I list on the volunteer statement."

"I mean what would volunteering mean where we're concerned?"

"I don't understand what you're asking."

"When the first assignments to Vietnam started coming to Laughlin, I talked to the some of the wives about them. That's when I first heard about volunteering. A few weeks later, we went to the movies and saw *Doctor Zhivago* together, and something that the Alec Guinness character said about men going off to war stayed with me. He said that happy men don't volunteer. I didn't say anything to you then because you hadn't said anything about volunteering. But I'm asking you now. Are you unhappy, Kevin?"

Mary Clare became restless in her high chair and reached out to Teresa. "Mama."

"Come here, baby." Teresa took her out of the chair and held her on her lap, looking at him, waiting for an answer.

He felt the question stab him deeply. "I've never been this much in love. I couldn't imagine life without the two of you, and I'd rather lose an arm or a leg than lose either of you. I'm not someone looking for escape or adventure."

A look of sadness came over her. "But you're not content, are you. The burden of the idealist."

"You married a soldier, Teresa," he said quietly.

"I married the good, decent man I was meant to marry. He happens to wear a uniform."

"Sometimes, soldiers have to fight."

"And do you think that I shouldn't be worried by that? You could be killed or terribly wounded."

"Teresa, this has been eating at me for weeks. It's not something I want to do. It's something I have to do for self-respect."

She said nothing for a moment. Then she told him quietly, "I sensed something going on, but I didn't know what it was. Sometimes, I just don't understand how you look at things. I love you, Kevin, and I always will. But don't expect me to play the perfect little Air Force wife who smiles and says do whatever you want to do, honey. This hurts." She stood up with the baby and walked into the kitchen. "I'm going to take Mary Clare for a walk."

* * *

The next afternoon, Kevin answered a knock on the front door. "Welcome to our new digs," he said as he opened it for Elena and Josh.

They entered, and Josh held up two six packs of beer. "These are a practice housewarming present. The real thing comes later. Where do you want them?"

"Here. Let me take them."

Teresa joined them from the kitchen. "Hi, Elena. Hi, Josh."

"Your house looks lovely," Elena said. "I hope we're not visiting you too soon after your move."

"Not at all," Teresa assured her. "We've learned how to settle in quickly."

"Where's the princess?" Josh asked.

"We've just put her down for her nap," Teresa answered. "She'll be awake in a few hours, and I'm sure she'll be excited to see you."

"Can I help you with anything?" Elena offered.

"Well, I'm putting the finishing touches on our lunch. Let's go into the kitchen while Kevin and Josh move the lawn chairs from the patio to the front yard."

"Okay, Maine man," Kevin said. "We have our marching orders. Follow me." Moving the beer to one arm, he led Josh to the patio, through a sliding-glass door on one wall of the dining area. He closed it behind them, so Teresa and Elena couldn't hear. He put the beer on top of a cooler and, beginning to stack the lawn chairs, said casually, "Elena's looking awfully nice today. How're things?"

"Ayuh. Looks promisin'," Josh replied, slipping into downeastern. "I should've gotten a clue from you much earlier about the charms of Latin women."

"And how're you and the good Doctor Castillo doing?"

"I think he's coming around. For a Mexican father, he's actually fairly evolved. Maybe medical school had a broadening effect. Anyway, it also helps that Elena has two older, married sisters who beat up on him regularly to support our cause."

"Good. Josh, would you put the beer in the cooler and haul it out to the front yard while I carry the chairs? We always let our guests do the heavy work."

"Very clever. You have a genuine gift for exploitation. You'll probably be a general someday."

They moved the chairs and cooler to the edge of the front lawn, next to a street that circled the housing area. The three parallel runways of the airfield were a little over a mile distant to the east, and the houses overlooked them from a slight hill.

"You've got a great view of the air patch from this corner lot," Josh observed as he put the cooler down on the grass.

"Yeah. And it's a great day for an air show," Kevin replied, taking his sunglasses out of his shirt pocket. "Not a cloud in the sky. I'll be right back. I've got to get a card table for the food."

When Kevin returned, Josh had unstacked the chairs and had opened two bottles of beer. He handed one to Kevin. "Let's get started. Long-necks forever."

"Amen," Kevin replied, clinking his bottle against Josh's and taking a long drink. "Let me ask you something," he said as he put the card table down and rested it against one of the chairs.

"Okay. Shoot."

"Do you and Elena talk much about the war?"

"Not very much. Right now, if we get into anything serious, it's mostly about religion. You rosary rattlers do make it tough on a poor Presbyterian heretic like me to accept associate membership in your Roman club. Having to bring the kids up Catholic and all that."

"Maybe you should talk to my brother-in-law, the miracle-worker Jesuit priest. He's coming for a visit next month. He's a good guy. You'd like him."

"Maybe I will. Anyway, where the war's concerned, we hope that it won't last much longer. If we do decide to walk down the aisle together, I'd hate to have to leave her on the church steps to run off to Vietnam. I never thought it would go on this long."

"Yeah. Sam Prentiss has already done his combat tour. He flew his hundred missions in six months. He's at McConnell now, instructing in the gunnery school there," Kevin said, referring to the air base near Wichita, Kansas. "I saw him on a cross-country a few weeks ago."

"How's old Sam doing?"

"He likes all the extra flying time he's getting, pumping out replacements for the war, but he isn't too shot in the ass about being an instructor. He said that he'd rather be in a real squadron somewhere with a real mission."

"Well, that's Sam for you."

"It's not just him. I was in the bar drinking with him at the club on Friday night after we landed. After a while, this guy in civilian clothes came over and started giving me a ration of shit about the Training Command patch on my flight suit. He was pretty drunk, and Sam told him to get lost. The guy got pretty surly, and Sam shoved him toward the door. As he was leaving, he yelled back to me, 'You're nothing but another miserable REMF.'"

"What the hell is a remph?"

"I asked Sam, but he wouldn't tell me at first. He said to forget about it, because the guy was just a loudmouth who'd just gotten to

McConnell after flying his hundred missions up north. But I kept after Sam until he told me. Finally, he said that it's an Army expression that's been getting around. It means rear-echelon motherfucker, a guy who hides behind the lines while other guys do the fighting."

"Man! Nasty one."

"Yeah. And I'll have to admit that it got to me a little."

"Well, kemo sabe, we'll have to continue this at another time," Josh said in a lowered voice, nodding his head toward the house. "Here come the ladies. We'd better clean up our act."

"Yeah. And I'd better do my job and set up the table."

Teresa and Elena set down the dishes they were carrying on the card table. "Sandwiches and enchiladas to go with the beer. Kevin, could you bring out the tray with the rest of the dishes and utensils?"

"Sure, love."

When he returned, he saw six F-100s beginning to taxi for takeoff on the flight line in the distance. Their distinctive paint schemes and highly polished aluminum surfaces made them stand out from the plainer, duller T-37s on the parking ramp in the foreground. "Elena, have you ever seen the Thunderbirds perform?" he asked, setting down the tray he was carrying.

"No, this is the first time."

Josh added, "I told her that she'd get some idea about how we earn our pay by trying to teach spastic guys who flunked phys ed how to fly formation."

Kevin laughed. "Well, everybody has to start somewhere. These guys, though, being the Air Force's official air-show team, are pretty much as good as it gets."

They filled their plates and sat down on the lawn chairs as the six jets taxied onto the runway. Black smoke billowed momentarily behind the airplanes when their pilots increased power for takeoff, and the roar of the engines arrived a second later, confirming the lag between sight and sound. The four jets in front began rolling and cones of fire appeared behind them, with the hard-light bang of their afterburners sounding afterwards. After a long takeoff roll, the airplanes lifted off. As their landing gear folded upward, one of them moved sharply from a takeoff position on the outside of the formation into the slot directly behind the leader, between the two wingmen, forming a diamond with the four F-100s. The remaining two jets followed half a minute later.

"Isn't it dangerous for that plane to be moving sideways like that when it's so close to the ground?" Elena asked about the slot man's maneuver.

"Well," Josh replied, "it's not as dangerous as it looks because the airplanes are climbing when he does it, but it still takes a pilot with a lot of skill and experience to do it safely."

They watched the four jets in the lead fly a wide turn back toward the airfield. As they came around to line up with the takeoff runway, they gradually lost altitude until they seemed to be skimming the ground, moving very fast.

Nearing the perimeter of the airfield, the jets began to trail white smoke. A few seconds later, they pulled up into a gentle climb and then rolled effortlessly in unison, holding a tight diamond formation. After completing the roll in a slight descent, they made another wide, climbing turn away and extinguished their smoke trails to fly out of the crowd's sight, to set up for their next maneuver. Then, surprising many of the onlookers, the two solo jets suddenly reappeared at opposite ends of the airfield, trailing smoke, and flew past each other over the center of the runway, apparently barely missing one another.

"That looked really close," Elena said to Josh.

"It is pretty close for two jets moving at that speed, but there's actually more separation between them than there appears to be."

In less than a minute after the two solo airplanes disappeared, the four in the diamond formation returned, their reappearance timed to keep the crowd's attention from wandering. For their second maneuver, they pulled into a tight loop together, tracing a circle above the crowd with their smoke trails, leveling out at the bottom very close to the ground. Climbing again, the four flew away to the east, and in tight choreography, the two solo jets followed quickly with another low pass along the runway to minimize dead time in the show. This time, they flew in formation together, with the leader upside down and the wingman upright.

The show continued for another thirty minutes, with the four lead jets performing increasingly intricate variations of rolls and loops, followed by the solo airplanes flying daring individual maneuvers at low level along the runway.

"I think the next pass will be the grand finale," Kevin said to Elena. "It's pretty spectacular. It's called the Bomb Burst."

The four jets in diamond formation became easily visible again southeast of the airfield when they turned on their smoke. They pulled straight up over the center of the runways, making a vertical column of their combined smoke trails.

Josh picked up the commentary. "At the top, they'll break in four different directions."

The smoke trails separated as the four jets rolled onto their backs and took up different headings, lining up with the four cardinal directions of the compass.

Pointing, Josh continued, "Okay, Elena, look over there to the north."

Barely visible at low altitude in the far distance, one of the solo jets was streaking just above the horizon toward the crowd. Its smoke trail appeared, and it began a sharp pull-up.

"He's going to fly a rolling, vertical corkscrew right through the smoke of the other airplanes," Josh told her.

The solo jet zoomed upward, and halfway to the vertical, a momentary flash of bright-orange flame engulfed it. Kevin and Josh were on their feet instantly.

"Bail out! Bail out!" Kevin shouted.

The jet looked like a beautifully plumed bird caught on the rise by a hidden hunter. Mortally wounded, it quickly lost momentum as it continued upward, decelerating toward its death plummet. A puff of gray smoke appeared above the stricken airplane as its pilot ejected, and a few seconds later, the orange and white panels of his parachute bloomed above him.

Teresa and Elena, now comprehending what had happened, stood up. "Oh, my god!" Teresa whispered as she grabbed Kevin's arm.

Speechless, the four of them watched as the doomed machine reached the top of its arc and began a final dive to the ground. Both of its wings were torn off. A missile plunging to earth, it crashed half a mile away, raising a large cloud of brown dust from the scrub-covered ground between the housing area and the runways.

"Well," Josh wisecracked nervously, "the Thunderbirds always put on a great show, but this new routine of theirs is a little costly in airplanes."

Not smiling, Teresa glanced at Josh and then looked at Kevin. "I'm glad that the pilot got out safely." After a pause she added, "I'm sure that when he volunteered for this assignment, he never believed that anything like this might happen to him." She looked away, toward the airfield.

Looking like specks in the sky to the east, the five surviving airplanes abandoned their final maneuver and rendezvoused in an improvised rejoin. In a subdued ending to their performance, the pilots avoided further high-g maneuvering that had brought down one of their comrades. They did not perform the exuberant high-speed entry at low altitude into the landing pattern and the crowd-pleasing snap-up to downwind that they normally flew to close their show. Jolted by the accident, they entered the pattern instead with an ordinary initial approach and made routine, lazy pitchouts to downwind to land without fanfare.

Chapter 8

Friday, 26 May 1967

To the west, a setting sun gave a red glow to scattered clouds over northern Virginia. Kevin enjoyed the sight for a moment then looked ahead again toward a darkening sky to clear his flight path.

"Speedy four zero, you have traffic at three o'clock, two miles, level at ten thousand," an air traffic controller from Washington Center advised.

Kevin looked to his right and saw an airliner, its red fuselage lights flashing below him in the distance. It floated across a twilight sky like a stately, winged galleon, on its way to Washington National Airport. "Speedy four zero, roger. I have a visual on the traffic."

Shut off from the outside world by a canvas hood that covered his canopy, Second Lieutenant Rob Johnson scanned the lighted dials on his panel of instruments in the dark of his rear cockpit. He concentrated on the instrument approach he was flying into Andrews Air Force Base, well across the Potomac River to the east of Washington's commercial airport.

The controller called again. "Speedy four zero, contact Washington Approach Control now on two, ninety-four, point five."

"Speedy four zero, roger," Rob answered, "Washington Approach on two, ninety-four, point five." He changed the frequency in his radio and transmitted, "Washington Approach, this is Speedy four zero, level at twelve thousand."

"Roger, Speedy four zero. Squawk ident."

"Speedy four zero, ident."

"Speedy four zero, radar contact. Turn right now to a heading of zero eight zero. You are cleared for the ILS approach to runway zero one left at Andrews. Descend and maintain three thousand until established on the final-approach course. Report the outer marker with wheels down."

"Speedy four zero, roger. Right to zero eight zero. Leaving twelve thousand for three thousand. Understand cleared for the approach." Rob pulled the jet's throttles back and extended its speed brakes to descend quickly, to get down to approach altitude at a comfortable distance from the airfield. He turned northward, toward the ILS cone at Andrews, when a needle on one of his instruments began moving, telling him to turn left to line up with the landing runway twenty miles away.

"Good intercept of the final-approach course," Kevin said. "What altitudes are you looking for now?" he asked, quizzing his student, making sure there would be no mistakes in the congested airspace around Washington.

"I've got to be below four thousand at fifteen miles and above two thousand at the outer marker, sir," Rob answered, interpreting a complex diagram depicting the approach, strapped to his right leg on a small metal clipboard and illuminated by a miniature flashlight attached to the right wall of his cockpit.

"Right." Kevin was pleased as he watched his strongest student staying ahead of the airplane, flying the approach well and handling the radio with ease. *This kid really has the good hands.*

At seven miles on the DME from the Andrews TACAN, Rob lowered the jet's gear and flaps. A green light on his instrument panel began flashing half a mile later, and he called on the radio, "Washington Approach, Speedy four zero is at the outer marker. Gear check."

"Roger, Speedy four zero. You are cleared to land."

"Roger, Washington. Speedy four zero is cleared to land."

"All right, Rob," Kevin said, "I want you to fly this approach right down to minimums. Call out decision height at two hundred feet, and I'll take the airplane to land. Come out from under the hood after I take over. All set?"

"All set, sir."

Rob kept the needles on the ILS instruments centered and airspeed steady down the glide slope, the last, most-sensitive phase of the approach. Ahead of them, a long pathway of high-intensity approach lights beckoned, pointing unmistakably to the safe channel of the runway beyond a sea of scattered lights between them and the airfield.

"Decision height, sir."

"Okay, Rob. My airplane," Kevin said, shaking the stick slightly. "Very nice approach."

"You have the airplane, sir. Thank you." Rob let go of the stick and pulled his instrument hood to the rear of his canopy, behind the head rest of his ejection seat.

Kevin swooped in over the approach lights and flared the jet into an easy touchdown, and the airplane settled gently on its main landing gear as its wings lost lift with slowing speed. He lowered the nosewheel lightly to the runway, and the trainer's landing light flooded the pavement ahead as he slowed to taxi speed.

"Nice landing, sir."

"Thanks, Rob. For some reason, I seem to have good luck with landings at Andrews, even at night. Maybe it's a welcome-back thing."

"Yes, sir. It's good to be home, even if we had to refuel at Columbus to get here."

"You didn't like Columbus in particular, or is it SAC bases in general?" Kevin asked as he turned the airplane onto a taxiway.

"It's Mississippi, sir. The place gives me the creeps. I guess it's this thing about a black guy born and raised in Washington being in the Deep South."

"Well, on the way back, it's pretty much either Mississippi or Arkansas for refueling on a direct route. But I suppose we could go a little out of our way and gas up in Alabama, if you'd prefer that."

Rob laughed. "Great choice, sir."

"I guess that means you wouldn't want to whistle a few bars of "Dixie" after I talk to Andrews ground."

Rob laughed louder. "Sir, you're too much."

Kevin took control of the radio in the front cockpit and dialed in a new frequency. "Andrews ground, this is Speedy four zero, close out our flight plan."

"Roger, Speedy four zero," the ground controller replied. "You are cleared to the transient ramp. The follow-me truck will assist you in parking."

Ahead, a pickup truck sped toward them on the taxiway, flashed its lights and then reversed course. A large white placard was bolted onto the rear of its cab, and the words, FOLLOW ME, in black, were illuminated by the T-38's landing light when the truck turned around.

"Speedy four zero has the follow-me in sight," Kevin advised the controller. "Okay, Rob, let's go cold mike on the intercom and pop the canopies."

"Okay, sir."

Kevin turned off his intercom switch and raised his canopy. He unfastened his oxygen mask, letting it dangle from one side of his helmet, and enjoyed the silence and the evening breeze on his face as he followed the truck slowly south. Nothing else disturbed the still sky harbor, a military airfield on a Friday night after scheduled flying had stopped. On his right, floodlights illuminated a large fleet of transports bedded down for the weekend, some with protective covers over their engines, that stood ready to wing the President and senior officials of the federal government anyplace around the globe that might call them. On his left, solitary lamps at intervals on the ground, some white, some blue, outlined silent runways and taxiways in the darkening expanse of the airfield's center. The absence of city lights on the horizon added to the feeling of tranquility he drew from the airfield at night rest.

The follow-me truck turned right near the far end of the ramp toward an area occupied by an odd assembly of Navy and Air Force jets, their markings indicating many different home bases. It made a second turn, driving through and beyond the parking space intended for the T-38, and its driver jumped out after braking to a quick stop ahead of them. Kevin followed the route of the truck and slowed down as the driver in white coveralls ran back toward him with lighted wands in his hands to motion the jet forward over the last few feet. The wands crossed and Kevin stopped the airplane, pulling throttles off at the same time to shut down its engines. He turned on his intercom again. "Let's call it a flight, Rob. Don't forget your seat and canopy pins. Mine are in. I'll see you on the ground."

"Okay, sir."

Kevin turned off the battery switch and sat still for a moment in his darkened cockpit, looking at the airplane parked to his left. It loomed over the T-38, its size and camouflage paint scheme making the smaller white jet look somehow trivial in comparison. The F-105 had a menacing, hulking look to it in the night shadows cast by the ramp's floodlights. *You look like you're going to be a brute to fly,* he thought.

A metallic rattle on the side of his silent airplane interrupted his musing. Seeing that the truck driver had pulled out the jet's fold-away steps below the cockpits, he took off his helmet and unfastened the rest of his flight gear to leave it in the airplane for the weekend.

"Welcome to Andrews," the truck driver said. "Are you boys going to stay awhile, or are you going to gas and go?"

"We're done for tonight," Kevin answered.

"Okay. Why don't you hand your stuff down to me, and then we'll button up your jet."

Kevin pulled a folded-up clothing bag from a recess on the left side of his cramped cockpit and lowered it to the driver. From niches on the right side, he retrieved a wad of streamers attached to safety pins for the airplane's landing gear, along with its maintenance record, and handed them down. Feeling stiff from two hours strapped to an ejection seat, he stretched as he stood up on its seat cushion before clambering out of the cockpit onto the flimsy foot holds on the airplane's side. He was glad to feel solid ground when he stepped down to the concrete ramp.

He took a small flashlight from the leg pocket of his flight suit and walked to the wing where the driver had left the jet's book of maintenance forms. He was filling them out when Rob and the driver joined him. "We'll be leaving early Sunday morning," he told the man from transient alert. "All we'll need is a full load of gas. Everything else's okay," he added, handing the book to the driver.

"These jets don't break as much as the old prop jobs did," the man in white coveralls said, making conversation. "Seems like something broke every time they went up when I was a crew chief."

Kevin took the invitation to delay for small talk, guessed at the man's age and asked, "Were you in the war?"

"Yep. B-17s in England. Got out and worked for the post office for a while after it was over, but I started missing the flight line. Grabbed this job when it came open. Been doing it ever since. Airplanes get in your blood, I guess."

"I guess so."

"Now don't worry about a thing, Captain. I've already put the pins in the gear, and I'll close the canopies for you. You'll be all set to go on Sunday morning. I'll be on shift then."

"Thanks," Kevin said as he picked up his bag of civilian clothes from the ramp. "We'll see you then."

Rob picked up his clothing bag and joined him, walking between two rows of parked jets toward a brick building a hundred yards away on the edge of the ramp. An illuminated sign over its flight-line entrance announced it to be Base Operations—base ops in pilot parlance.

"That old guy's a character," Rob observed as they walked.

"Yeah. A lot of the guys on the transient-alert crews are civilians who've been around a while. You run into some interesting old timers every now and then. By the way, how're you getting home from here?"

"I'm going take a cab, sir. My mother doesn't drive."

"Where does she live?"

"In Southeast, sir. Near Capitol Hill. On Fourth Street."

"That's not far out of the way to my parents' house. My dad's picking me up, and we can drop you off."

"Really, sir. I can take a cab."

"Well, this far out, you'd have to call and wait. Besides, a cab would have to find its way through the maze here at Andrews to pick you up. It might never get here."

"Okay, sir. If you're sure it's no trouble."

"No problemo."

Kevin's father was waiting for them at the entrance, and he extended his hand to his son when the two pilots came inside. "By god, it's that brand-new captain. How was the trip up?"

Kevin smiled. "Another great day in the air-machine business. Dad, I'd like you to meet Lieutenant Rob Johnson. Rob's a native Washingtonian. Rob, my father, Colonel O'Dea."

"A pleasure, Rob."

"My pleasure, sir," Rob said, shaking the older man's hand.

"Kevin, do you need to check with the weatherman or the flight-planning folks before we leave?"

"No. We're all set to go. We can do all that on Sunday morning. Dad, I've told Rob that we can give him a lift into town. It's right on our way. Near Capitol Hill."

"Sure. Easy to do. Let's go."

The car was parked just outside the street entrance to the building in a spot reserved for general officers. They got in, and Kevin chided his father, "Bending the rules a little, are we, Colonel?"

"Well, it's so damned deserted out here tonight, I thought the generals wouldn't mind. Besides, all the air policemen are probably hanging around the enlisted club tonight to keep the drunks from driving." He drove off toward a chain-link fence separating the flight-line ramp from the streets along its boundaries, that seemed to solidify slightly in the headlights. Skirting the fence, he turned onto a road that paralleled a long row of large hangars on the west side of the ramp to travel to the main gate. "Where did you refuel on the way up?"

"At Columbus," Kevin answered. "Ed and Clare Walker came out to base ops to see us while we gassed up. He'll be on his way to Thailand, to the B-52 base at U Tapao, after their second baby's born in a couple of months."

"It's a crazy, damned war. We're sending fighters over North Vietnam to do strategic bombing, and we're using B-52s for tactical strikes in South Vietnam. More of Mister McNamara's brilliant strategy, no doubt. I don't know why Lyndon Johnson kept that jackass on as Defense Secretary. Well, I'm starting to rant and rave. A bad thing to do when you're driving. How're you liking pilot training, Rob?"

"I'm really enjoying it, sir."

"Kevin said you're a Washingtonian. Did you go to college in town?"

"No, sir. Actually, I followed in your son's footsteps. High school at Gonzaga in town and then the Academy."

"Well, well. It's a small world. Did you always have a hankering to fly airplanes like he did?"

"No, sir. One thing kind of led to another. I was on the baseball team at Gonzaga, and I was hoping for an athletic scholarship somewhere. But then I got a dose of the real world and found out that they're few and far between for baseball. Football players get most of them. So, the principal, Father Mulcahy, helped me out by getting me hooked up to the Gonzaga-alumni network. He found an officer in the athletic department at the Academy who got interested in recruiting me. They led me through all the hoops to get an appointment. After I got there, going on to pilot training seemed to be the next logical step. By then I'd figured out that I probably wasn't going to make it to the majors, after my batting average dropped when I started trying to hit against college-level pitching."

"We had a couple of major-league ball players in my bomb group in the Pacific when I flew B-29s," the elder O'Dea began as they drove through the main gate. He told them about pick-up baseball games between missions to cope with the tedium and isolation of his air base on the island of Tinian, before recounting the stories of the two ball players, one of whom had been shot down and captured before returning to baseball after the war.

Before long, the Capitol Building came into view as they crossed a bridge over the Anacostia River into Washington from the south. "I know I'm home when I see the dome," Rob said. Following his directions, they soon stopped in front of a modest row house. "I enjoyed meeting you, sir. Thanks for the ride."

"A pleasure, Rob."

"Why don't I pick you up Sunday morning on my way out to Andrews," Kevin said. "About seven."

"Yes, sir. If you're sure it's no trouble."

"You're right on the way."

Rob got out and ran up the steps of a lighted stoop. He knocked, and a gray-haired black woman answered, after pulling back a curtain at an adjoining window to inspect her caller. They pulled away as he entered the house and embraced his mother at the door.

"Did you know him at Gonzaga?"

"No, I didn't know many of the freshmen when I was a senior. But after he got his appointment to the Academy, Father Mulcahy sent me a letter and asked me to keep an eye on him. I didn't really have to do very much. Rob did fine on his own."

"What kind of pilot is he?"

"He's good. The best student I've ever had, as a matter of fact. He's near the top of his class. Probably that better-than-average hand-eye coordination that made him a baseball player."

"Is he a good officer?"

"He's very sharp."

"Then he's got a very bright future. What about your future?"

"Well, I have some news. I got my new assignment this week. It's F-105s. I report to McConnell in January for gunnery school."

"It's time that you moved out of that Training Command backwater and into a front-line unit. I would've never believed it a few years ago, but even fighter pilots have become respectable in this mixed-up war."

"Like you said, they're the ones carrying the mail up north."

"There's a lot more that needs to be delivered. I still can't believe that we held back from hitting targets around Hanoi and Haiphong harbor for so long. That sanctuary business was just mindless. A hell of a way to fight a war, sanctuaries and bombing halts for weeks at a time."

"I guess the days of sanctuaries are pretty well over now. I was just reading that we hit a power plant near the center of Hanoi for the first time."

"It's about damned time. Well, we can talk more about this later. On to the important news for the expectant grandparents. How's Teresa doing?"

"She's fine now. We were a little scared, though, when the docs admitted her to the hospital last week for a couple of days. But, like I told Mom over the phone, they said that everything seems to be okay now. We're back on track for an October delivery."

"I'm glad to hear it. How's my munchkin?"

"As feisty as ever. I think Mary Clare's a cinch for the terrible-twos' hall of fame."

The grandfather laughed. "That's my girl. She's got a good Irish temper. Got it from your mother, of course."

Kevin chuckled, "Sure, Dad. Whatever you say. Is that why Mom's graduating with honors?"

"Probably," his father said, grinning. "Seriously, she's tickled to death that you could come up for her graduation tomorrow."

"I wouldn't have missed it. Will Sean be able to make it?"

"No. It's graduation weekend at his prep school too. Since he's the junior guy on the faculty, they're keeping him pretty busy."

"Caps and gowns everywhere this weekend."

"Yeah, I was really surprised when your mother wanted got go back to college to get her degree. She's really loved doing it. And, despite all that education, the woman can still cook. She's putting on a real production for dinner tonight."

"Good. All this flying's given me an appetite."

"What're you doing tomorrow night?"

"I called up a classmate of mine who's stationed out at Andrews. We were in the same cadet squadron at the Academy. He's going to law school at night at Georgetown, and we're going out to dinner to catch up. Before that, though, we're going to have a drink with one of the guys in his class. I think the guy works for the State Department. Some kind of Asia expert I'm told."

"Well, that'll probably be a waste of time. State's pretty much playing second fiddle to Defense on Asia, now that there's a war on."

They fell silent for a while, and Kevin admired the view through the windshield. The Lincoln Memorial, its white marble gleaming in its evening flood lights, stood out from the yellow lamps of Virginia across the Potomac.

* * *

Paul Fortuna, Kevin's classmate, sat in a booth in the back of a Georgetown pub nursing a beer. An enlisted man before becoming a cadet, and the oldest man in the Class of '63, Fortuna had always seemed to march to his own drummer. While the great majority of the class had gone off to pilot training after graduation, Fortuna had become a contracting officer, eventually negotiating contracts for military hardware valued in the millions.

Fortuna stood up as Kevin came past the bar toward him and extended his hand. "Long time, no see. How's the Texas jet jock?"

"Hey, Paul. Doing well. How's the almost Perry Mason? Or is it F. Lee Bailey?"

Paul laughed as they sat down on opposite sides of the table. "Mostly driven to drink," he quipped. "Unlike me, Perry and F. Lee don't spend the better parts of their weekends in the law library."

"Are you still in class?"

"No, we're done for a while. I'm starting a summer research project for one of my professors. Federal-contracts law."

"Makes my pulse race just hearing about it."

"Yeah. It's a little dry, but there's a payoff down the road. After I become a civilian."

"You're getting out?"

"Yeah. That was always the plan. After I finish law school."

"I'm sorry to hear it."

"Well, eleven years in uniform's enough for me. And I've paid Uncle Sam back by saving him a lot of bucks in contract negotiations over the last few years. We all have to become civilians again sometime."

"Yeah. I guess so. Who's this guy who's going to join us?"

"Like I told you, he's in my law-school class, but I don't know all that much about him. I got teamed up with him for this research project by my prof. I thought a drink together might help us break the ice, and I thought you might get some inside scoop on the way the war's going, especially now that you've gotten your new assignment. He went to Yale and works in an office at State that sifts intelligence reports for foreign-policy stuff on Asia. That's about all I know. We really haven't talked much about anything other than the project."

"This should be interesting. From what I've been reading in the news magazines, we're going after more of the targets up north that were off-limits before. It looks like the war's entered a new phase. At the same time, they're printing rumors about McNamara having doubts about the bombing campaign. It's all pretty confusing to the reader in west Texas."

Paul looked up, glancing over Kevin's shoulder, and said, "Here he is now."

"Sorry I'm late, Paul," the newcomer said as he slipped easily into the booth beside his law-school classmate. "I had to run down one more citation after you left to hold up my end of our joint enterprise." Taking on a relaxed smile, he extended his hand to Kevin and said, "I'm Win Sexton."

"Kevin O'Dea." He shook hands and read the signals: *Four or five years older; long sandy hair, but not too long; pin-striped shirt, old but not quite shabby; signet ring. Ivy-league casual. But weary in the eyes.* "Good to meet you."

A waitress came over from the bar. "What can I get for you two?"

"Guinness for me," Sexton said.

"Miller draft," Kevin added.

"Another Bud?" she asked Paul.

"No, thanks. I'm okay for now."

She left them and returned to the bar.

"Paul tells me that you're on your way to Vietnam next year."

"Well, the airplane that I'll be flying is based in Thailand."

"Really. I was posted to the embassy in Bangkok before my current stint at Foggy Bottom. What base?"

"Actually two. Korat and Takhli."

"You'll be flying the F-105 then."

"Yeah."

"Some of the military people I deal with call it the Thud, if I'm not mistaken."

"Yeah. It's a kind of gallows humor. That's supposed to be the sound it makes when it crashes after being shot down."

"Morbid."

"It's all part of keeping up the derring-do fighter-pilot image," Paul added. "Kevin pales in comparison to our wilder classmates, though. I'm thinking of one from Mississippi in particular," he said, grinning at Kevin.

The waitress returned with two glass mugs and left after setting them down.

"I can only imagine," Sexton said. "I go to meetings at the Pentagon fairly regularly, but the staff officers I deal with there are intelligence types, not pilots. So, when Paul proposed our getting together, I thought I might get another view on the war. Now that you're close to going, how do you see things?"

Kevin took a drink of his beer, then said, "Well, I was just telling Paul. It looks like we're in a new phase in the air war. We're hitting targets that we should have hit at the beginning. Gradual escalation, with bombing halts, is a bad way to run an air campaign. Anyway, it looks like air bases and industrial sites in Hanoi and Haiphong are finally fair game. Now that we're hitting them that heavily, I don't think the North Vietnamese can stand the punishment for very long."

With a trace of a smirk in his smile, Sexton said, "They'll quit if we bomb them back to the Stone Age, eh."

What the hell is this? Kevin wondered. He saw that Paul was taken by surprise too, putting his mug back down after raising it to his lips, but not drinking. He looked Sexton in the eyes as he debated with himself on how to answer. *I didn't come here for elitist bullshit like this,* he decided. "Win, I came here to listen to what you have to say, and maybe to learn something, since you're supposed to know more than the press about what's really going on. I'm a little out of practice at playing the Washington cute-repartee game. So, I'm not going to try to defend General LeMay's unfortunate statement about bombing North Vietnam back to the Stone Age," he said, referring to a sentence near the end of the controversial general's memoirs that had injected considerable heat into arguments over the war. "You see, I'm not some primitive who's blind to the moral part of what we're doing over there."

Sexton's easy smile faded as he put his beer down. "My apologies. It was a bit of a cheap shot. Momentary bad manners caused by long frustration, I'm afraid. You see, I've become something of a boat rocker at State by opposing the current orthodoxy on the war. All right, let's not prance around before we get to the point. It might even be refreshing for conversation in Washington. So, here it is, unvarnished. I believe that Lyndon Johnson's blundered badly by letting hawks in Congress spook him into sending American ground troops to Vietnam. He did it because he could see the Republicans taking over the White House in sixty-eight if the South Vietnamese had caved in in sixty-five. He could see his legacy, his Great Society programs, being dismantled by a Republican administration if the South Vietnamese were to implode on his watch. It would be another chapter of the who-lost-China-to-the-commies fight from the forties. I know that he was between a rock and a hard place politically with the hawks coming after him, but by trying to avoid being the president who lost Vietnam, he's lashed us to a corrupt regime in Saigon that's not going to survive."

I can't believe I'm hearing this. "I guess, then, you never bought the idea of pay any price, bear any burden, support any friend and oppose any foe," Kevin said, trying to hide his growing irritation.

"Ah, the Kennedy inaugural address. Wonderful sentiment. But I'm not in the sentiment business."

"What business are you in?"

"I'm in the reality business. Starting with the history of Asia, which I studied in college and graduate school, and then looking at the facts there straight on, without an ideological lens."

"I'm listening."

"The North Vietnamese will fight for a very long time to unite their country and to throw off foreign domination. They're now in the process of ridding themselves of what they see as the last vestiges of the French occupation, an illegitimate government in Saigon propped up by the United States. Whether we like it or not, the regime in Hanoi has succeeded in casting itself as the heir to independence movements that go back in time to near the birth of Christ. They're tough and they're patriotic. Americans don't have a monopoly on those virtues."

"You seem to have a high regard for the Communists."

Sexton's eyes narrowed. "Well, Kevin, I'd say we're about even on cheap shots now. Can we get beyond shallow rhetoric to get to the real issues?"

"Sure."

"Before I continue, though, let me put your mind at ease and show you my true-blue-American credentials. I'm not saying that the North Vietnamese are humanitarians. They're ruthless bastards who'll do whatever it takes to get what they want. After they succeed in uniting the two Vietnams, and I do believe they'll roll over the South Vietnamese eventually, they'll fail miserably when they actually try to govern the country with the claptrap ideas being exported by the Russians and Chinese. So, you see, I'm not some pinko who crept into State after the late, unlamented Joe McCarthy purified Foggy Bottom and then passed from the scene."

"I don't agree with you that the North Vietnamese will succeed. History's one thing, but they've never experienced warfare on this scale before. The price they'll have to pay is too high."

"Like I said before, they're tough and patriotic. So, do you think we should target their population as the next step? Should we use atomic weapons on them after that?"

"No."

"Well, that's what it took to get Japan to quit. Would it surprise you to learn that there's some low-level work going on at Defense, looking at flooding the most-populated, agricultural areas of North Vietnam by hitting the dikes on the Red River? I also hear from my Pentagon contacts that there's a small group closeted away over there, conjuring up scenarios for the use of tactical nukes."

"Neither of those things will happen."

"I agree with you. We're at the end of our rope. The work at the Pentagon is a sign of desperation. There's no stomach in this country for going after the population of North Vietnam by drowning them, starving them or nuking them—or bombing them back to the Stone Age. That kind of thing was okay in World War II, but not any longer. So, we're caught in a bind. We're having to play under a new set of rules where bombing is concerned, but what we're doing isn't painful enough to make them want to quit."

"They'll end up losing everything they've invested in—railroads, bridges, industry. All of it."

"They didn't have that much to begin with, and they don't need it. They can import whatever they need from willing suppliers like the Soviet Union and its satellites, and they can use makeshift transportation systems until the war's over. After that, they can rebuild easily. We started bombing industrial targets because nothing else was working. We couldn't cut off the supply line to the Viet Cong guerillas in the South by bombing, because they can keep fighting even if they get only a trickle out of what starts down the Ho Chi Minh trail from the North. I won't bore you with the numbers, but the systems-analysis types at Defense have modeled the trail in detail. We simply can't shut off the supply of men, equipment and ammunition coming down it nearly enough to make a difference in the South. That's what's discouraged Mister McNamara and started rumors all over town that he's gone soft on the war. Meanwhile, we're taking casualties. We've lost over five hundred airplanes over North Vietnam, and more important, we've just passed the ten-thousand mark in Americans killed in the war. We're now losing two hundred men a week."

Paul intervened. "Look, Win. Then tell me why your boss, the unflappable Secretary Rusk, is so much of a hawk. He's the most pro-bombing guy in town."

"For openers, he thinks it's the only way to get the North Vietnamese into serious negotiations to end the war. It's the usual, unimaginative State Department solution. Everything has to end through negotiations."

Paul pressed Sexton. "What's wrong with negotiations?"

"They can be a trap. The North Vietnamese might eventually enter into negotiations to get relief from the bombing, although they've shown no willingness to talk so far. But negotiations don't guarantee a final settlement to our liking any time soon. The regime in Hanoi is simply not going to let go of its goal of conquering the South to unify the country. Once we're into negotiations, domestic politics will demand that we stay with them to the bitter end. So, negotiations would likely drag on while American casualties mount by the thousands."

"Is there anything else?"

"Yes. The root of everything we're doing in Vietnam is this mistaken belief in a Communist juggernaut threatening to roll over all of Asia. It's this vision of China on the march, fed by the rice fields of a united Vietnam, with North Korea thrown in for good measure."

"Mistaken belief?"

"The entire history of Vietnam is a story about resisting control by the Chinese. Why would they want to help strengthen China? Plus, now that China is eating its young in this latest convulsion, this so-called Great Cultural Revolution that Mao Tse-tung launched last year, China's going to be in turmoil for a long time to come. They're not going anywhere any time soon."

"So, what's your solution?" Kevin asked, starting to show his irritation and impatience.

"In the end, this is going to come down to who wins the war on the ground, the North or the South. This is a fight to the finish between one autocratic regime, the one in Hanoi, and another, the one in Saigon. This stuff about the fighting in the South being a civil war between the Viet Cong guerillas and the government in Saigon, that's being put out by the American doves, is pure hogwash. I think we should put the South Vietnamese on notice now that it's up to them to finish the fight, after we saved them from defeat by intervening two years ago. We can truthfully say that we did our job by pulling their chestnuts out of the fire. We keep giving lip service to the notion that, ultimately, they'll have to decide their own fate, but we never quite seem to act like we believe it."

"What precisely does that mean, Win?" Paul asked.

"It means that we should move American ground-combat units into defensible enclaves on the coast and then withdraw them. If the South Vietnamese can't cover our withdrawal adequately, we should concentrate air strikes from aircraft carriers and from bases in Thailand around the enclaves' perimeters where they can do some good. But I think the North Vietnamese would actually be quite happy to see us gone and would do very little to hinder our withdrawal. After that, we can show our solidarity with Saigon with an occasional air strike by B-52s, to hit troop concentrations from a safe distance away, to try to prevent any outright invasion by the North."

In lawyerly fashion, Paul went after the weakest part of Sexton's argument. "If what you say is true, Win, why are you such a lonely voice at State. Is everyone there a fool but you?"

Sexton smiled ironically. "No. They're afraid of being inconvenient."

"Inconvenient?"

"Tell me, has either of you seen the film, *A Man for All Seasons?"*

"Last month," Kevin replied.

"Sure," Paul added. "Had to. Movies about lawyers with high principles don't come along all that often. Seriously, it's a great flick. It deserves the awards it got. What about it?"

"Although it portrays the founder of my church in a bit of a bad light, even an Anglican like me can find a lot in it," Sexton said, his smile becoming more genuine with self-effacement. Then, growing thoughtful, he said, "There's one scene that gets at what you asked. The villain of the piece, Cromwell, is tutoring his protégé, Richard Rich, at the inn. Do you remember?"

Paul said, "I don't remember that one as well as the courtroom scene."

"Then let me refresh your memory. He tells Rich that the real job of government officials is to 'minimize inconvenience.' In this case, for their master, Henry the Eighth. Well, our own monarch, Lyndon the First, has let it be known that he's not interested in any ideas that could let that little pissant, as he calls Ho Chi Minh these days, appear to get the better of him before the election next year. So, those of us urging an American withdrawal as making the most sense for our long-term interests, given the history and realities of Asia, as well as the losses we're taking in lives and money, have become inconvenient to our sovereign and his lord chancellor, Dean Rusk. For Lyndon, I'm afraid, the long term doesn't extend beyond November of next year. If negotiations start before then, so much the better for his prospects in the election. As a result of all this, the lesser nobility at State, men with mortgages on their big houses and tuition bills from their children's expensive colleges, have converted to the Cromwellian school of government service, and fast. They've stopped being inconvenient to our liege lord and his chancellor, and they, in turn, don't want to be inconvenienced by knaves like me. Does that answer your question?"

"A loss of backbone that epidemic seems a little far out to me, Win. Even for the State Department."

"Your bosses at State seem to be agreeing with the rest of the country," Kevin added. "I read an article in *Time* magazine this week that said that seventy percent support the war and that something like sixty percent think that bombing should be expanded."

"Oh, yes. The jingo press. They're awfully good at reporting polls, but they're not terribly good at accurate forecasts. The one thing you can be sure about, though, where today's supporters of the war are concerned, is the thinning of their ranks as time goes on. *Time* has also reported, quite accurately by the way according to my contacts, that Mister McNamara has become disillusioned with bombing. It's not working. Even so, I predict that the list of targets will be expanded over the next few months, but that won't work either. And we'll lose more pilots and airplanes. On top of that, his close friend, Bobby Kennedy, who's hated by Lyndon, has gone over to the anti-war side. I believe that Mister McNamara has now become terminally inconvenient. Chancellor Rusk and the other hawks have King Lyndon's ear now. I also predict that you'll soon see support for the war start to erode rather precipitously. Kennedy's no fool. He's got a good sense of where the mood of the country is going, and he's given the anti-war types legitimacy."

"I think you're going way out on a limb now, Win," Paul said.

"That's nothing new for me, old man. I'll even crawl out to the far branches for you. I predict further that Lyndon will be in real trouble over the war by the time the primaries start in New Hampshire next year. Peace candidates will be perfectly respectable by then and will be popping out everywhere. I can't take credit for this particular insight. I got it from a friend of mine, a very smart guy on Kennedy's staff who knows the domestic politics a lot better than I do."

The waitress returned to their booth. "Another round, gentlemen?"

"Not for me. I've really got to go," Sexton said, starting to reach into his pocket.

"Just the check then," Paul said. "This is my treat, gentlemen. I insist. Keep your money in your wallets."

The waitress walked away after leaving the check, and Sexton stood up to go. "Thanks, Paul. My turn next time then." He paused for a moment and then looked at Kevin. "Kevin, I'm sure this wasn't entirely what you expected—or find pleasant, for that matter. I genuinely hope that I haven't offended you. I respect the fact that you're putting yourself on the line for what you believe, and for what it's worth, I've done that too. But not with nearly the same risks. All I've done is wreck my career. The handwriting's on the wall for me because of my boat rocking. That's why I'm in Paul's company at Georgetown these days, trying to hang on at State long enough to graduate. I hope to see you again sometime, so take care of yourself." Sexton offered his hand.

"You too," Kevin said as he took it reluctantly.

Sexton turned to go. "See you Monday night, Paul."

"Right, Win."

Kevin composed his thoughts for a moment after Sexton left and then said, "Well, Paul, you really know how to put on a great ambush."

"I'm as surprised as you are, classmate, and I would never have arranged this little get-together if I'd even suspected where Win's coming from. I thought he'd be on-board with his boss, Mister Rusk. Another illustration of that great law-school truism, never presume anything."

"That's okay. It wasn't a total loss. I did learn something about Kennedy and McNamara. I still don't think Sexton's right, though, about the North Vietnamese not cracking under stepped-up bombing. Even if he is, we've got guys on the ground over there who've got to be defended. Maybe I can keep some of them from getting killed."

"Look, let me make this up to you by buying dinner."

"Naah. That's okay. I've got all that flight pay to burn up."

Paul covered the check with several bills from his wallet, and the two of them left the booth, walking toward the door to M Street.

Chapter 9

Sunday, 28 May 1967

Sunday-morning traffic was light as Kevin drove across Memorial Bridge into Washington to pick up Rob Johnson. The exchange with Sexton the night before still gnawed at him. Up to then, he had ignored those who opposed the war as ignorant college kids, high on pot, looking for any excuse to raise hell, and he remembered television coverage of an anti-war rally in New York a month before that turned out over 100,000 demonstrators. "A convention of fringe lunatics," he had said to Teresa as they watched the antics of shaggy dissidents on the evening news. He had been mystified, he remembered, at the end when Martin Luther King appeared on the screen to denounce the bombing of North Vietnam. *What the hell does this have to do with civil rights?* he had wondered at the time.

Sexton's coldly analytical case came at Vietnam from a completely different direction, and it wasn't so easily dismissed. Paul had tried to reassure him later at dinner that they'd held their own in the debate. "Well, Kev," he had said, "I think you made good points when you said that history only goes so far and that the North Vietnamese haven't seen anything like Rolling Thunder before. And I think that Win was really reaching when tried to connect Vietnam and Japan, when he said that the Japanese resisted air attack until Hiroshima and Nagasaki. Win's analogy is pretty shaky. The Japanese held out because we were demanding unconditional surrender. We're not doing that in Vietnam."

He passed the Jefferson Memorial as he drove on. *I could have used your keen mind last night, Mister Jefferson,* he said to himself, as points he might have made, but hadn't, came to him too late to use.

Ten minutes later, he pulled up in front of the row house on Fourth Street and looked at his watch. *Five minutes early*. He was about to turn off the ignition and get out to go to the front door when he saw it open after the curtain at a front window moved.

Rob stepped out onto the stoop and waved. He turned and embraced his mother, who was dressed in a bathrobe and who stayed just inside the door. She handed him his clothing bag and closed the door as he walked down the steps to the car.

"Morning, Rob."

Rob put his bag onto the rear seat and got in. "Morning, sir. I thought your dad might be driving us back to Andrews."

"No, he's sleeping in," Kevin said as he pulled away. "Our routine when I'm in town is for me to take the clunker Buick back to Andrews. He and my mother go out to Annapolis for seafood on Sunday nights, and they swing by base ops to pick it up on their way home."

"I enjoyed meeting him."

"Well, you were lucky. You got him started on baseball. Otherwise, he might have gone into his recruit-the-young-officer-for-SAC number."

"Not for me, sir. If I get a chance at a fighter, I'll take it in a flash."

"Good man. Maybe we'll fly together again then. I've just gotten an assignment to Thuds."

"No kidding. That's great, sir."

"I report for gunnery school in January. I've got to finish up your class and go to a couple of survival schools before then."

"Will you be going to Nellis, sir?" Rob asked, referring to the air base near Las Vegas, Nevada.

"No. That's where they have the long course for guys coming right out of UPT. If you get a Thud assignment, that's where you'll go to get checked out. Guys who've flown fighter-type airplanes after UPT, like the T-38, go to the short course at McConnell in Kansas. It lasts about seven months."

"Do you think the war'll be over by then?"

"I don't know. My track record on forecasting Vietnam is pretty bad. Two years ago, I told my wife that we'd clean up on North Vietnam way before our tour at Laughlin was over. A prophet I'm not."

"Well, last night, we had a big gathering of the relatives. The women were against the war, and the men were on the other side."

"Is your mother worried about your going?"

"Yes, sir. You know how mothers are. She even tried to talk me out of going to UPT. Last night, she came up with a new thing. She and the other women said I shouldn't go to Vietnam because Martin Luther King's against the war."

"And you said?"

"Well, I said that Doctor King's a great man, but even a guy with the Nobel Peace Prize can go too far."

"I'm not sure I understand."

"Sir, I mean that I support what we're doing in Vietnam. We're fighting the bad guys there. And one of my uncles said that Doctor King's anti-war stuff could hurt the civil-rights movement here at home. He said that President Johnson's not going to keep working hard for civil rights if people like Doctor King give him a bad time on the war."

"I see." *Yet another level of complexity with this war,* he thought. *We barely scratched the surface last night.* The previous night's exchange came back to him again. He couldn't let go of it.

After an extended, uncomfortable silence Rob said, "Good music this morning, sir."

"What?"

"The radio, sir. The Four Tops."

"Oh, yeah," he said as he became aware of the music. "Reach Out, I'll Be There" was ending.

"A blast from the recent past to go with "Bernadette" at number thirty-eight," the disc jockey said, returning to playing the top-forty hits. "Now, at number thirty-seven, the Beatles with "Penny Lane."

"My little girl loves this one," Kevin said. "She calls it Pen Lay. Whenever she hears it, she screams, 'Pen Lay!' and starts dancing around the living room with one of her dolls."

Rob chuckled at the image. "Yes, sir. Kids are great. One of these days, after I meet the right woman, I'd like to have kids. They'll have to like that Motown sound, though."

They talked about music as they left Washington and drove into Maryland. They were a half mile from the main gate at Andrews when Kevin said warily, "Damn! Look at that up ahead."

A red muscle car, its front painted in orange flames, had turned at the light in front of the main gate. It fishtailed as it accelerated toward them, and Kevin eased to the right side of the road to give it plenty of room to pass.

"Shit!" Kevin blurted out when the oncoming car turned directly in front of them. He jerked his steering wheel to the left by reflex. The big Buick swerved, but hit the red car with a glancing blow to its rear. It began to spin as they went past. Kevin got his heavy car under control, moving out of the left lane and back to the right side of the road, braking to a stop. "Son of a bitch! That stupid bastard almost killed us."

Rob looked back at the red car as they stopped. "He's hit another car in a parking lot next to that diner."

"Okay, let's see what the damage is," Kevin said. They got out and walked to the front of the Buick. A slightly bent front fender and a scratched bumper were all that they saw. "We're lucky. Just a scrape. I guess we'd better go see what happened to the people in the other car."

They walked back toward a gravel parking lot enclosing a diner where the red car had come to an incongruous, abrupt stop, with its rear end smashed into the back of parked car. As they got to the edge of the lot, the doors of the red car opened, and three men dressed in jeans and T shirts got out unsteadily. Two of them were carrying baseball bats. Kevin and Rob stopped.

"Shit, sir. Let's get out of here," Rob whispered as the men began walking toward them.

"Too late. I don't want to turn my back on guys with baseball bats." Kevin looked the three of them over quickly. "They're probably drunk. I don't think they'll start anything. Let me do the talking."

"Yes, sir."

The three men walked across the parking lot and stopped three yards away. The heavyset driver, with DIXIE emblazoned in orange across his chest atop a Confederate battle flag, slapped the heavy part of his bat repeatedly into his left palm and said in a slurred voice, "Well, lookee what we got here, boys. I'll be damned if it ain't Joe Jet and Nick Nigger. How come you hit my car, Joe?"

Kevin answered, "Let's just call the police to sort this out."

"We don't need the cops. We know how to take care of assholes and niggers." The two other men sniggered in agreement.

"Look, you're in big enough trouble as it is."

"You're the one in big trouble, asshole. You totaled my car, and I'm gonna kick your ass. Do you think this nigger's gonna help you? You're a dumb shit. You don't know shit about anything."

Kevin felt something snap. Something stretched taut from the night before let go completely. "Yes," he said coldly, "I expect him to help me. Because he's a good man. A man I've known for a long time. In fact, he's twice the man you are."

The bat started up across the driver's right shoulder, but went no further. A short siren blast and a crunch of tires on gravel drew his eyes to his left as he stopped.

"All right, boys. Put the bats down on the ground," a loud voice ordered. "Don't give me an excuse to shoot your sorry asses."

The two men threw their bats down angrily. Kevin stepped back, looked to his right and saw a county policeman advancing slowly from his squad car with his revolver leveled at the driver's chest.

"Well, well. It's Jimmy boy. I thought it might be you again. You look like you really stepped in it this time, Jimmy," the officer said when he reached them, his pistol still pointed at the driver. "What happened, Captain?"

"They were speeding and cut in front of me. I tried to miss them, but I hit the back of their car. They lost control and spun into that parked car over there. We came over to help, but then they got out of their car with baseball bats."

"That's pretty much the same story our dispatcher got from guy in the diner who called us. So you boys are really in deep shit now. Get down on the ground, face down, all three of you."

The man in the middle protested, "I didn't do anything."

"Shut up, you punk. How about drunk and disorderly and disturbing the peace? I said, get down on the ground. Now!"

The three men complied, and the officer moved behind the driver. "Put your hands behind your back, Jimmy." The driver refused silently, keeping his arms at his side. "Do it, you moron, or I'm going to give you a shot of Mace right in your ugly face." The man snarled, but then did as he was told. The policeman put hand cuffs on him. Another police cruiser with two more patrolmen arrived, and the other two men were cuffed and led away with the driver. Kevin and Rob walked away to the other cruiser.

The first officer returned to his car and reached inside for a clipboard. "Sorry you were bothered by some of our local trash, Captain, but we've finally got Jimmy on something that'll stick. He'll do some jail time for this one. I'll need to take your statements."

"Sure," Kevin said, looking at the policeman's metal name plate. "Officer Maddox, we're supposed to be flying back to Texas this morning. Will we be delayed long?"

"Not long. I'll take down the preliminary information now, and we can reach you by phone or mail if we need to later. We've got witnesses in the diner too, so this shouldn't take up too much of your time down the road either." Maddox began writing, glancing at Kevin's leather name tag. "Last name, O'Dea; first name Kevin. I knew a Major O'Dea once. In Grand Forks when I was in the Air Force," Maddox said, naming the SAC base in North Dakota. "Any relation?"

"He's my father."

"It's a small world. Well, Captain O'Dea, your dad was a good guy. I was in the security police at Grand Forks, and sometimes when we were freezing our butts off out on the ramp, guarding B-52s at night in the middle of winter, your dad would come out with coffee to shoot the breeze for a while. It wasn't the coffee. We always had some in the guard shack. He didn't do it all the time either. But none of the other officers did it as often he did. It meant a lot to the troops."

"I didn't know about that."

"A good thing for you to remember. Okay, what's your address in Texas?"

Kevin and Rob answered Maddox's questions, then signed their statements. The officer shook hands with them and said, "Well, have a good flight back to Texas, gentlemen. When do you get your wings, Lieutenant Johnson?"

"In August, sir."

"You're a lucky guy. A lot of us wish we could have flown airplanes for a living."

"Yes, sir."

They walked back to the Buick and got in. Rob, elated at the outcome, said, "Well, sir, the good guys win again."

"No thanks to me. After I lost it out there with good old Jimmy Dixie." *What the hell came over me?*

"No, sir," Rob continued in high spirits. "You were great. I'm going to have to put you in for membership in the N, double A, C, P."

"Well, it wasn't that so much. I guess I just get pissed when some low-life jerk thinks he can mess with the troops."

"Yes, sir."

"Now I guess we'd better get back to the duller world of jet airplanes," Kevin said as he started the engine.

"Yes, sir."

* * *

Kevin was glad to see the runway at Laughlin approaching. He felt drained. *I can't wait to get home to Teresa and Mary Clare.*

Rob flew another excellent approach, this time with a simulated failure of one engine and partial failure of his ILS instruments. "Decision height, sir."

"Okay, my airplane."

"Your airplane, sir."

"Come on out from under. Beautiful approach, Rob. I think you've got ILSs pretty well nailed."

"Thanks, sir."

He didn't like the landing, with one gear touching down before the other, but it felt good to be on the ground again. "Okay, Rob, same drill on the intercom," he said as they taxied off the runway.

"Yes, sir."

He turned off his interphone, opened his canopy, and unfastened his oxygen mask after closing out their flight plan with Laughlin ground. The warm Texas breeze felt good to him as it flowed over his face. Peering at a shaded area under a tree next to the base-operations building, he looked for Teresa and Mary Clare in their usual waiting place. He didn't see them. *Maybe the guy in base ops gave her the wrong arrival time.*

He taxied to the parking ramp. As he turned the jet toward its crew chief, he saw Josh Pemberton in civilian clothes walking toward them from his car parked on the edge of the ramp. *What's this?* "See you on the ground, Rob," he said after stopping and shutting down the engines. Not waiting for a reply, feeling apprehensive, he shut his cockpit down quicky.

Josh climbed a ladder to his cockpit after the crew chief attached it to the side of the airplane. "Hi, Kev. Let me help you with your stuff. I'll give you a lift back up the hill."

"Okay, but where's Teresa?"

"She's in the hospital," Josh said in a low voice so the others couldn't hear. He took Kevin's gear from the cockpit and descended the ladder. Kevin unstrapped quickly and followed him down.

Rob was still in his cockpit. Kevin looked up at him and said, "Rob, we'll debrief tomorrow. You did a great job on the whole trip. Something's come up, and I've got to go now. Would you finish up here?"

"Yes, sir. Sure. I'll see you tomorrow."

As they walked to his car, Josh said, "It happened this morning when Elena and I were visiting after church. I drove Teresa to the hospital. We tried to reach you at Little Rock after we found out where you'd stopped to refuel, but you'd already taken off by the time we tracked you down."

"Is she okay?" His stomach knotted and his arms felt weak.

"Kev, I don't know. I came down here right after I got her to the hospital, to make sure I didn't miss you when you landed."

Josh drove the short distance to the hospital and let him out. "I'll take your stuff home, and Elena and I'll stay with Mary Clare until you get back. Give me a call, and I'll pick you up when you're ready." He paused for a moment, trying to find the right words. "Kev, I hope everything's okay with Teresa. I think she's the absolute finest."

"Thanks, Josh." He walked quickly inside to the reception desk and asked the airman on duty, "Could you tell me where Mrs. O'Dea's room is, please?"

"Yes, sir. But Doctor Ward asked me to have you talk to him first when you got here. I'll go get him for you."

"Okay. Thanks."

The airman left the desk and returned with George Ward, a neighbor from across the street.

"Hi, George."

"Hi, Kev. Let's go to my office for a minute." They walked down a corridor to a room with Dr. Ward on the name plate on the door. They went inside, and he closed the door. "Let's sit down," he said, gesturing toward two chairs in the crowded cubicle. "Teresa's resting now. She's doing fine, but I'm afraid we lost the baby. I'm truly sorry, Kevin."

"But after last week, I thought everything was okay."

"Things looked better after the initial bleeding stopped, Kev, but no one can predict what might happen later. Teresa just wasn't able to take this pregnancy to term."

He didn't reply immediately, but then, resigned to what he had heard, he said, "I understand. I want to see Teresa now."

"Sure. She was pretty upset, so we gave her something to calm her down and get her to sleep. You can stay with her as long as you want." Ward led Kevin to her room and closed the door behind him after he went in to leave them alone.

He felt overwhelmed as he watched her in her sad sleep. He pulled a chair close to her bed and sat down, taking her hand in his. He pressed her hand to his cheek, and the last of his strength seemed to ebb away as a strange, new sense of vulnerability came over him.

Chapter 10

Monday, 23 October 1967

"Breakfast's ready, Kevin," Teresa called from the kitchen.

"Be right there, love." He finished putting on his uniform in the bedroom and walked out to the table in the dining area to sit down.

Mary Clare was in her high chair next to the table, finger-painting on its tray with the last of a dish of oatmeal. "Daddy home."

"Did you miss Daddy while he was in Florida, Mary Clare?"

"Daddy stay home."

"Both of us missed Daddy," Teresa said as she brought a pot of coffee to the table and sat down with him. "We're glad you're back."

He poured a cup of Teresa's strong coffee and took a sip. "That's really good. I missed it last week. Rotten coffee at Homestead," he said, referring to the air base near Miami where the Air Force conducted a one-week course in survival and rescue at sea.

"What are you doing today, now that you're finished flying with students?"

"I've got to go to the finance office to get reimbursed for last week's travel, and then I'll start clearing the base. I'll try to get the movers scheduled today, and I've got to run around to some other places to make sure records are up to date before I go to Fairchild next week," he said, naming the air base near Spokane, Washington where the Air Force conducted a two-week course in survival, escape, resistance and evasion for crews of combat aircraft.

"Will you be home for lunch?"

"Uh huh. About noon," he said as he became distracted by the image of the Lincoln Memorial on the television set in the living room. He got up and walked over to turn up the volume.

"Saturday's march started at the Lincoln Memorial," an off-screen newscaster said as Kevin returned to the table. "Some fifty-thousand demonstrators assembled there to hear leaders of the anti-war movement denounce the Johnson Administration for the war in Vietnam. Later, many of them made their way across Memorial Bridge to the Pentagon where about thirty thousand gathered." The picture changed to show an angry confrontation between taunting demonstrators and helmeted soldiers in tight, shoulder-to-shoulder ranks, standing with rifles held forward to keep the crowd at bay. Two sides of the five-sided building on the Virginia side of the Potomac were visible in the background. "A number of the marchers tried to get past federal marshals and military policemen who were guarding the building, and a few made it inside before being arrested. All together, more than two hundred were taken into custody." The newscaster, behind a desk in a studio, appeared on the screen. "This demonstration climaxed a week of rallies against the war across the country. Their organizers hope to put even more pressure on an embattled President. With frustration over the war growing among both supporters and opponents, and with a summer of race riots in northern cities that killed and injured more than seventeen hundred in Newark and Detroit alone in July, the President's approval rating, already below fifty percent, continues downward."

"Down!" Mary Clare shouted, responding to the television.

As he took her out of the high chair, Sexton's prediction hammered at him again. *You'll soon see support for the war start to erode rather precipitously.* "Well, the latest tantrums of sign-carrying college kids ought to interest and encourage the viewers in Hanoi," he said in disgust.

"I understand how you feel, love, but even ordinary people are very torn. While you were away in Florida, there was a series on TV about how Vietnam is affecting the country. Even people who support the war can't understand the lack of progress, and they're shocked at our own losses. One man they interviewed, who fought in World War II, said that by the third year of that war, the invasion at Normandy had taken place and the Nazis were all but finished."

The phone rang, and Teresa went into the kitchen to answer it. "Kevin, it's Major Jenkins at the squadron for you."

He went to the kitchen and took the phone. "Thanks, love. Good morning, sir."

"Morning, Kevin. How was sea survival?"

"I swallowed a little salt water, but I made it back alive."

"Good. Listen, I've got a one-time good deal for you. An airplane broke at Colorado Springs on a cross-country this weekend, and we need to fly a part up there to get it fixed. Since we're night flying tonight, I can't really spare one of the IPs to go. So I thought you might like to take a solo hop to end your career in the White Rocket in style."

"Sounds good, sir. When would I take off?"

"Well, we can't spare an airplane until this afternoon. You'd get back after dark, but not too late."

"Okay, sir, I'll take it."

"Great. I appreciate the help. See you this afternoon."

"Yes, sir. Thank you," he said as he hung up. "Well, love, they're going to give me a swan-song flight. It's a solo out-and-back to Colorado Springs."

"When will you be back?"

"This evening. I don't take off until after lunch. I'll still have time to do my errands."

* * *

Kevin taxied his T-38 up to yellow lines painted on the taxiway and stopped short of the takeoff runway. *I'm going to forget about the war, war protests, race riots and everything else. Nothing but flying for two hours.* "Laughlin tower, Speedy four zero is number one for takeoff, runway three one center."

"Roger, Speedy four zero," the tower controller acknowledged, "cleared into position and hold."

"Speedy four zero, roger. Position and hold." He advanced the throttles slightly and moved the jet onto the runway, swinging its nose around with its rudder pedals to line up with the mile and a half of pavement that stretched away from him to the northwest. Braking to an easy stop on the runway's white center line, he felt impatient to get into the air.

"Speedy four zero, change to departure control," the controller said. "Cleared for takeoff."

"Speedy four zero, roger. Cleared for takeoff." He changed the radio frequency and moved the trainer's throttles to full power, holding its brakes. The jet seemed eager. He had to bear down hard with his feet on its brakes to keep it from creeping forward. He scanned its engine instruments. *Perfect. Okay, let's fly.*

Releasing brakes, he moved the jet's throttles forward to light its afterburners, and the airplane rushed ahead smoothly, as thrust from its engines surged from raw fuel being sprayed into their tailpipes. Speed came quickly, and he covered thousands of feet of runway in seconds. He moved the stick gently back, and the nose lifted up. Not hesitating, the accelerating jet flew effortlessly into the air. With the airspeed indicator showing nearly 200 knots, he moved the gear handle firmly upward and raised the jet's flaps. Fully streamlined, with its appendages folded away, the airplane rapidly gained another hundred knots of speed and continued to accelerate. As the needle on the airspeed indicator approached 400, he pulled the trainer's nose smoothly upward and closed rapidly on a rain shower ahead of him. "Del Rio departure, this is Speedy four zero, airborne and passing three thousand."

"Roger, Speedy four zero. Radar contact. Call passing ten thousand."

"Speedy four zero, roger." Everything around him went white in a misty baptism as the jet streaked into low clouds in its flight path. Seconds later, he roared out the top, into bright sunshine again. With the jet's nose well above the horizon to hold 400 knots in an afterburner climb, he glanced at the spinning hands of the altimeter. "Speedy four zero is passing ten thousand."

"Speedy four zero, contact Fort Worth Center now on two, seventy-nine, point four."

"Roger, Fort Worth on two, seventy-nine, point four." He dialed in the new frequency. "Fort Worth, this is Speedy four zero, passing thirteen thousand for flight level four one zero," he said, meaning 41,000 feet of altitude.

"Roger, Speedy four zero," the new controller replied in a lazy Texas accent. "Squawk ident."

"Speedy four zero, ident."

"Speedy four zero, radar contact. Continue climb to flight level four one zero. Say your passing altitude."

"Speedy four zero's passing seventeen thousand," Kevin replied as the jet continued its rapid climb.

"Roger, Speedy four zero. Looks like you got the express elevator today. Okay, call level at four one zero."

"Speedy four zero, roger. Yes, sir. The White Rocket loves to climb." At 25,000 feet he punched through a thin cloud layer as the airplane kept streaking heavenward. *God, this is beautiful. Just absolutely beautiful.*

Less than a minute later, he disengaged the jet's afterburners as he approached his assigned altitude. "Speedy four zero is level, flight level four one zero."

"Roger, Speedy four zero. I just won five bucks from the new guy next to me on your climb time. He's a believer now."

"Yes, sir. Glad to be of service." Cruising now, he surveyed the parched-earth horizon of west Texas. Below him, contrails hanging in the wakes of long-gone airliners billowed outward, gradually losing definition. Alone in a silent cockpit, he welcomed the fleeting serenity of the high atmosphere, as the DME registered miles traveled and fewer left to go.

Turning northwest over San Angelo, he called, "Fort Worth, Speedy four zero."

"Go ahead, four zero."

"Speedy four zero requests a block altitude from flight level four one zero to flight level four five zero."

"Okay, four zero, it's all yours. You're the only one up that high."

"Speedy four zero, roger. Thanks. It's mighty pretty up here." He eased the throttles forward, letting the jet creep slowly upward toward 45,000 feet as it became lighter in consuming its fuel load.

Looking outside his canopy, seeing the earth's curvature faintly, he became reflective as he headed toward north Texas and Colorado beyond. *Three years after pilot training and another chapter is closing, The tour at Laughlin has worked out well,* he thought. He was glad he had followed Sherman's advice, despite his father's misgivings about an assignment that wasn't front-line. It had given him and Teresa, he realized, time they needed to put strength into their marriage, and they had called on all of it when they lost a child five months earlier.

He remembered Karin's visit soon afterwards and Juan's later that helped close a gaping wound. Clare, too pregnant to travel, had called Teresa every day for over a month. And there was Mary Clare, who bound them together with cords only a child could tie.

He thought about some of his classmates who hadn't fared so well. For them, fantasies about the glamor of a military marriage had come up against the hard realities of long absences from home in assignments to other cockpits, and divorces had started to take their toll. He suspected that the marital casualties were only just beginning, as combat tours in Vietnam increased pressures on frail unions. *Not for Ed and Clare, The Pair, though,* he mused, as he thought about Ed, now in Thailand flying combat missions in B-52s. *Or Josh and Elena either, I hope,* he said to himself as he recalled their wedding four months earlier in Del Rio.

Del Rio. The skies of Del Rio. Over twelve hundred hours of flying time since UPT, he considered as his thoughts continued to wander. He had done a good job in making pilots of his students, and his fitness reports reflected the confidence of his commanders. As Sherman had predicted, his tour as an IP had made him expert in a wide range of fundamental flying skills, and he was ready now to move on. He would have welcomed a fighter assignment immediately after UPT, but he was glad now that it was coming later, he admitted to himself, after he had mastered the basics.

His thoughts drifted to his students as his jet ate up distance at nine miles a minute. He had washed out only one, a foreign student, an Iranian, who hadn't been able to make the jump from the T-37 to the more demanding tempo of the T-38. The others were wearing their wings now. *And two of them were buried wearing them,* he reflected, remembering the crashes that had brought jarring ends to young lives. *But the best of them are doing well.* Rob Johnson, now checking out in Thuds at Nellis, came to mind, and he remembered the incident near Andrews. He wondered again if he had done the right thing in not telling Teresa about it or about the exchange with Sexton. He convinced himself again that he had. *She didn't need any of that while she struggled with the loss of a child, and that weekend in May is ancient history now anyway.*

After a long silence, a radio call interrupted his reverie. "Speedy four zero, contact Denver Center now on three, one zero, point eight. Good day, sir."

"Speedy four zero, roger. Denver on three, one zero, point eight. Good day to you, sir. I enjoyed it." He changed frequencies and called, "Denver Center, this is Speedy four zero in the block, flight level four one zero to four five zero."

"Roger, Speedy four zero. Squawk ident."

"Speedy four zero, ident."

"Roger, Speedy four zero. Radar contact."

He was surprised at how quickly the flight seemed to be going. *Too fast. Nearly out of Texas already.* Reaching down, he changed TACAN channels, and the receiver locked onto Tobe, the station near the town of Trinidad in southern Colorado.

To his left, the mountains of New Mexico took clearer shape as he angled northwest toward them. *I really miss the mountains,* he said to himself as the strong memories they were a part of came to him again. He could see Teresa waiting for him in the shade of pines as if it were yesterday. *And graduation day. Things have gotten a lot more complicated since then.*

"Speedy four zero," the Denver controller called. "Say your request for descent into Peterson," he said, using the name of the destination air base near Colorado Springs.

"Speedy four zero requests an en-route descent direct Peterson," he replied, asking to avoid a more-complex arrival through a formal instrument approach to the airfield.

"Roger, Speedy four zero. After Tobe, proceed direct Peterson. At pilot's discretion, descend and maintain flight level two one zero. Call departing present altitude."

"Speedy four zero, roger." He looked at the DME. *Ten miles to Tobe.*

"Speedy four zero is departing flight level four five zero for flight level two one zero," he radioed sixty miles later as he pulled the jet's throttles back to enter a long, fuel-saving glide.

"Roger, Speedy four zero."

Pueblo was ahead of him, beyond isolated patches of flat clouds when he leveled the airplane at 21,000 feet, headed toward the TACAN at Colorado Springs. "Speedy four zero is level, flight level two one zero."

"Roger, Speedy four zero, continue descent now to one seven thousand. Colorado Springs altimeter is three zero point zero two."

"Speedy four zero, roger. Out of two one zero for one seven thousand. Altimeter three zero, zero two."

The descent placed him on top of a cloud patch as he leveled off again. "Speedy four zero is level, one seven thousand."

"Roger, Speedy four zero."

He couldn't resist the urge. He pushed the throttles forward to increase speed, to race along the cloud layer, punching through its wispy mounds for five miles before it ended. Once clear, he called the controller. "Denver, Speedy four zero."

"Roger, four zero. Go ahead."

"Speedy four zero has the airfield in sight. Cancel IFR," he said, meaning instrument flight rules, rules that governed flight in weather and at altitudes above 18,000 feet where radar control was mandatory.

"Roger, Speedy four zero. IFR cancellation received. Contact Peterson tower on two, ninety-four, point three. Squawk VFR," the controller directed, telling him to change the code in the airplane's transponder to one designated for flight under visual flight rules.

"Speedy four zero, roger. So long." He banked the jet steeply to the west away from the airfield, heading for the mountains, losing altitude gradually.

He flew westward, skirting Pikes Peak, flying below its snow-capped crest, and turned north again to parallel the spine of the mountains, continuing to let down to a comfortable altitude. The rolling forest west of the front range, where he had spent so many hours, came hurrying toward him, and he felt a lightness in its welcome. Flying over it, the pleasure of its many memories found him again, and he felt renewed.

Then, looking eastward, he saw a familiar notch in the ridge line, and he eased the jet into a lazy right turn to fly north of it. Tightening the turn as he approached the crests, he saw the first of the Air Force Academy's white-granite buildings on the mountains' eastern foothills, its brighter half lying just outside the mountain shadow cast by the setting sun behind him. Its companions in the shade of the mountains came quickly into view as he completed his turn, heading south, just east of the peaks that were now slightly above him, to his right. Ahead, he could see cadets moving from green, rectangular fields toward the gym with another afternoon of athletic combat over. When he reached them, he lit the jet's afterburners to dramatize its presence with trailing fire for its young spectators, and pulling away from them in a rolling climb, he disappeared from their sight to the west, behind the summits of the Rampart Range.

Continuing south behind the ridge line, he pulled the jet's nose up a minute later to gain altitude. The arrowhead on the compass locked onto the TACAN at Colorado Springs again, and he turned to put the sun on his tail as he dialed the frequency for Peterson tower into the radio. *A great ride, but it's time to land,* he decided reluctantly. *Let's get refueled and turned around to get home.*

Chapter 11

Wednesday, 27 December 1967

Teresa's breathing was soft and deep as she slept. *Christmas in Durango is just what she needed,* Kevin thought as the moonlight coming through the bedroom window bathed her face faintly on the pillow next to his. His stomach grumbled again. *That's what I get for making a pig of myself at Karin's tonight. Maybe a glass of milk will settle me down so I can get some sleep.* Moving slowly from under her arm on his chest, trying not to disturb her, he eased out of bed, put on his bathrobe and made his way to the kitchen. He was surprised to see Juan up late, reading at the kitchen table.

"Getting an early start on Sunday's sermon, Father Juan?"

Surprised, Juan looked up from the papers that absorbed him. "What? Oh, it's you, Kevin. No, I'm trying to finish up grading some essays that I have to hand back when school starts again next week." He looked at his watch. "One o'clock. I'd lost track of the time."

Kevin opened the refrigerator and took out a carton of milk. "I'm going to try some milk to help me get to sleep. Like a glass?"

"No, thanks. I think reading a few more pages from the pens of high-school seniors will do the trick for me."

Kevin poured a glass and sat down at the table. "What did they write about?"

Juan paused for a moment, hesitant to tell him, but then said, "Morality and warfare."

"Whew. Pretty heavy stuff for high school."

"Now that they're seniors, trying to figure out what to do about the draft with a war on, their interest in the topic is fairly intense. A number of them did a good job with the assignment. Some of the papers are quite thoughtful."

"Really."

"Several of my students asked me to sponsor and moderate a debate on the war in Vietnam next semester. I agreed to do it if they could meet Jebbie standards of intellectual rigor and rise above emotionalism in dealing with the issues, and I assigned these essays to get a sense of how well they understood the material we covered at the end of last semester."

"I've seen enough emotionalism on television this year to last me."

"I guess you mean the anti-war rallies. To some extent, I suppose, they were the catalyst behind the debate idea, but not all of my students are anti-war. In fact, the best-written of the essays supports American involvement in Vietnam. Does that surprise you?"

"No."

"The boy who wrote it comes from a military family. He's thought about the war fairly deeply."

"What did he have to say?"

"This is fairly academic stuff for this late hour, Kevin."

"That's okay. I might learn something. Like your students, I have a fairly intense level of interest."

"Well, okay. I'll try not to be too abstract. In the classroom, I covered what the moral theologians call the theory of the just war. First, there's the right of a state, along with its allies, to defend itself against aggression, and second, there's the principle of discrimination. That's what the moralists call the right conduct of war. It means conducting warfare in a way that distinguishes between military combatants and non-combatant civilians."

"Not always an easy thing to do. I remember some discussion about that in this house four years ago."

"Yes. I remember it too. A paradox. Trying to reconcile a clear case of a just war against aggression with saturation bombing of German and Japanese cities. The contradiction made for lively discussion in my classroom last semester. In their essays, a number of my students argued that the American use of massive firepower in Vietnam is indiscriminate."

"Well, I think that the air campaign over North Vietnam's been a model of what you call discrimination. We're not carpet bombing Hanoi with B-52s. We've gone out of our way to limit civilian casualties in hitting targets near populated areas. If anything, we've been too restrained."

"What do you mean?"

"An air campaign that hit legitimate targets heavily from the beginning might have shocked the North Vietnamese into coming to terms by now. Instead, we had this gradual escalation of the bombing. I think they'll knuckle under eventually, but it'll take a lot longer and be a lot tougher than it might have been."

"I see. I've been reading recently that there's quite a difference of opinion about that."

"Yes. In fact, I ran up against it earlier this year." He told Juan about the encounter with Sexton. "I don't agree with him, but there's this problem with his predictions coming true. He said that Johnson would be in political trouble over the war about now, and he is. He also said that the Defense Secretary, McNamara, had become, as he put it, inconvenient to Johnson by saying that bombing North Vietnam is ineffective. McNamara announced his resignation a few weeks ago."

"Well, Kevin, if your adversary is right, before long, there'll be a lot more trouble with the moralists. They'll say that what we're doing in Vietnam isn't proportional. Proportionality is the third just-war principle. It requires that the evil of war be outweighed by the evil it avoids."

"I'm not following you."

"It means, for example, that the fight against the Nazis was just because it avoided the greater evil that they would have inflicted on an occupied Europe over, perhaps, decades. If our involvement in Vietnam has resulted in an inconclusive war that's causing more death, pain and suffering than a takeover of the South by the Communists would bring, more and more church leaders in this country will start coming out against the war. My students who took the anti-war position in their essays argued strongly that what we're doing in Vietnam isn't proportional."

"That's not an easy thing to measure, it seems to me. Will the church leaders factor into their calculations what could happen if the South falls, if the regime in Hanoi decides to move on to other places like Cambodia and Thailand?"

"Some may. The student from the military family made the same point in his essay. He made it quite passionately, in fact."

Kevin smiled. "I don't remember the Jebbies at Gonzaga giving out too many points for passion when I was in high school. What did you call it a minute ago? Intellectual rigor? Well, they really lived up to their nickname, God's marines of the mind."

"Well, at Regis High, the same standard applies academically," Juan said with a slight smile. Then, sighing lightly, he added, "It doesn't, though, at the personal level."

"You've lost me, Juan."

"I have the feeling that I'm getting in too deep here, Kevin. I should probably stop now, but somehow, I can't. The boy's father is a prisoner of war in North Vietnam. He was shot down and captured six months ago, and I've been counseling his son since then. It's been very rough, especially right before Christmas," Juan said quietly.

Kevin felt almost immobilized as he groped for something to say. *And who comforts the comforters?* Struggling, he said, "Juan, I'm sorry I pushed you into talking about this."

"Maybe I needed to talk with you about it, and maybe that's why we're here now. Things don't happen without a reason."

"If I can help, I'll talk as long as you want."

"Maybe if I knew more than I do now about what his father's facing, I could help to his son more. The boy keeps dwelling on something that happened last March, when the North Vietnamese displayed a captured Navy pilot to photographers. Do you remember? He kept bowing at them with a vacant expression on his face and said nothing. It looked like he'd lost his mind."

"I remember seeing it on TV. Juan, I don't know, but maybe I've learned some things that might help. Last month, I went through the Air Force's basic survival school for two weeks. Part of the course is about how to deal with becoming a prisoner of war, and we got some information on the POWs in Vietnam in the classroom sessions. I can't give you details or tell you how we know what we know, because it's classified."

"I understand. I'd be grateful for anything more than what I know now."

"They're being tortured and they're being kept in solitary confinement, but they are resisting. In fact, we think that the incident in March was a shrewd form of resistance that made the session with the photographers backfire on the North Vietnamese. The POWs are communicating with one another and supporting one another, and they're holding on to the hope of coming home one day. You can tell the boy that his father isn't all alone in what he's going through. Tell him that he can't lose hope, because his father hasn't."

"That's very helpful, Kevin."

"I hope it does some good."

"Talking with the boy has made this war a lot less of an abstraction for me, Kevin. Our sessions have made me think about you quite a lot."

"I understand what you're saying, Juan. I'm not doing this blindly, and I'm not doing it because I think I'm John Wayne. I'm not a reckless guy, and the odds are very high that I'll finish my tour and come home like the vast majority of the other pilots have."

"I'll be praying for you anyway."

"I'm glad, and I'm very grateful. Could you do something else for me?"

"Certainly."

"Teresa's decided to stay here at the ranch while I'm overseas. It would mean a lot to both of us if you could come down from Denver to see her and Mary Clare as often as you reasonably can."

"Of course. The ranch is a source of strength for both of us, Teresa and me. Actually, I'm glad that I'm able to be here now. I feel like I'm almost ready to go back to Regis for another semester."

Kevin got up to put his glass in the sink. Pausing, he put his hand on Juan's shoulder. "Juan, you're a great guy. That young man's lucky to have you to help him."

"Before I went into the seminary, the idea of helping people get through their bad times held a great attraction for me. I didn't understand then how people in general become individuals in particular, and then the trying to help gets a lot harder."

"I can't imagine anybody being any better at it. Good night, Juan."

"Good night, Kevin. And thank you."

Chapter 12

Tuesday, 23 January 1968

The instruments glowed faintly in Kevin's dimly lit cockpit. In the center of the instrument panel, the compass dial turned slowly counter-clockwise, indicating a shallow right turn onto the final-approach course at McConnell. His eyes scanned quickly from one instrument to another as he cross-checked altitude and airspeed to hold them steady in the turn. Five degrees before the final heading, leading it, he began a slow rollout to wings level, reducing power with the throttle to slow to a final-approach speed of 190 knots. *Everything looks good. On course; gear down; flaps down; airspeed 210 and coming down; begin descent in two miles.*

A bright-orange light at the top of the instrument panel lit up. It was labeled MASTER CAUTION by a small placard above it, and it got his attention instantly. He pressed the light to extinguish it, and his eyes darted quickly to its companions, 20 smaller warning lights stacked below it in a compact rectangle. One of them was illuminated. It read OIL LOW PRESS. Looking quickly at the oil-pressure gauge, he saw its needle dropping steadily, passing the red line for minimum pressure on its way to zero. He pushed the mike button on his throttle and called, "Wichita Approach, Jayhawk two one is declaring an emergency. I'm ten miles on final at McConnell."

"Roger, Jayhawk two one. Understand you're declarin' an emergency. We're scramblin' fire and rescue. You're cleared to land," an answering voice said lazily.

"Jayhawk two one, roger. Cleared to land." *Not much I can do now. Just continue the approach.* Over the outer marker, he reduced power slightly to enter the glide path. Thirty seconds later, the instruments announced a dying engine as, unbidden, they began unwinding. *Flameout. Too low. Can't restart. Got to punch out.* He yanked the control stick back to stop his descent momentarily, then he grabbed both ejection handles at the sides of his seat, raised them and pulled the triggers.

The instruments froze, and the florescent light of a large room entered the cockpit as Sam Prentiss raised the canopy on the flight simulator. "I am the simulated rescue helicopter comin' out to pick your ass up and get you back home to Teresa."

"Good. Ten emergencies in an hour are enough for anybody."

"Well, that completes the list. You made the right decision to eject on the last one, Kev. Believe it or not, some guys actually try to restart the engine that low to the ground. Naturally, they never make it. The Thud definitely ain't a glider. Okay, that wraps it for today. How about a beer at the club before we head home?"

"You got it. I'm glad this one's over. If there's a hell for pilots, I'll bet it's having to fly a simulator for eternity."

"You could be right, but we Baptist aviators believe it's flyin' some multi-engine air-barge forever as Satan's co-pilot. I don't know what's worse."

Kevin chuckled as he stood up and crawled out of the earth-bound replica of the F-105's cockpit. "Well, now that we've come this far, I suppose I can put up with another week in the classroom and the simulator before we start flying."

"Hell, we'll be out on the range droppin' bombs and strafin' before you know it. See ya at the club," Sam said as he headed for the door.

"Right. See you there, Sam."

Sam's mood had changed when Kevin saw him again at the bar. "Son of a bitch!" he said angrily, responding to something he had been told by two other men in flight suits drinking with him. Both were students in Kevin's training class. The older of the two, recognizable from the back by hair that was prematurely gray, was the class's senior ranking officer, Lieutenant Colonel John Reynolds. The other's red hair screamed his identity. It was Charlie Rasmussen.

"Afternoon, sir. Hey, Charlie," Kevin said as he joined them. "Draft, please," he called to the bartender.

"Hello, Kevin. We were just bringing Sam up to speed on world events," Reynolds replied.

"What's going on, sir? I missed the news this morning."

"The North Koreans grabbed one of our ships last night. It happened around midnight Washington time. A lot of people back east didn't get much sleep, and I would've been one of them if I were still at the Pentagon."

"What kind of ship, sir?"

"A Navy intelligence gatherer, apparently disguised as a fishing trawler. Called the *Pueblo*."

"And, sir, you're really sayin' that we let the Koreans take the ship without a fight?" Prentiss asked incredulously.

"Apparently so. I guess the Navy still hasn't learned how to protect its snoop ships when they're out on station. After they let the Israelis shoot up that other ship, the *Liberty*, off the coast of Egypt last June, you'd think they'd figure out how to get things right."

"Well, sir," Sam said, "the Israelis might have trouble identifyin' ships, but they know how to run a war. Winnin' in six days last June sounds about right to me."

Charlie said, "This has got to be a political disaster for the President."

"Well, it sure as hell can't help him much," Reynolds agreed as he put his empty glass on the bar. "On that happy note, gentlemen, I've got to go. See you at class in the morning."

"Yes, sir."

The bartender returned with Kevin's beer as Reynolds left. "Fifty cents, please, sir."

Kevin found two quarters in the cigarette pocket on the left sleeve of his flying suit and put them on the bar. "Thanks," he said, picking up the glass.

"Man, somethin' bad has happened to this country," Sam said angrily. "First, we won't show Uncle Ho we really mean business, and now we let the goddam North Koreans kick us in the balls. We've got to git rid of that sorry excuse for a president and git somebody who'll fight."

"Well," Charlie replied, "this *Pueblo* thing might really rip it for Johnson. His approval rating is in the dirt, and that nobody senator from Minnesota is going after him in the primary in New Hampshire. That guy, Eugene McCarthy."

"Mister dove, himself," Sam muttered.

"I read somewhere," Kevin said, "that McCarthy could be a stalking horse for Bobby Kennedy."

"Oh, terrific," Sam groaned. "That's just what we need. Mister superdove as president." He looked at his watch. "This's really depressin' me. I've got to go make a phone call to a lady to lift my spirits."

As Sam left, Charlie said, "Yeah, Kev, I've read the same thing. It's plausible."

Sexton's words came back to him. *Peace candidates will be perfectly respectable by then and will be popping out everywhere.* "I just can't believe that a sitting president, *Time* magazine's Man of the Year, could get knocked off by someone in his own party."

"Well, we're in strange times, my friend."

"Maybe so."

"Strange at the local level too."

"How do you mean?"

"Our class commander. A lieutenant colonel in the land of captains and majors who flew bombers, B-58s, the last time he was in a cockpit."

"I didn't know about that. I'd figured out that he's a fast burner after seeing his West Point ring. Class of fifty-six and wearing silver leaves already."

"Yeah, that piqued my curiosity. I called one of the guys from my Georgetown class who's at the Pentagon now. He said that Reynolds worked for the three-star there who heads up the operations shop. They're obviously grooming him for bigger things. Instead of sending him back to SAC after his Pentagon tour was over, they sent him out here to broaden him with some fighter experience. I'd bet that he'll get command of a squadron while he's in Thailand."

"Interesting. What kind of guy is he."

"The guy I talked to said he's smart and really sharp. A straight-shooter who knows how to work the system."

"Someone good to know then," Kevin said before finishing his beer.

"Yeah."

"Well, Charlie, I'd better saddle up and get on home. Say, why don't we get together with our brides for dinner and a movie sometime soon."

"Sure. We can't do it this weekend, but how about the weekend after, if the wives say okay? Kelley's dying to see *Cool Hand Luke* before it closes. Anything with Newman in it gets her excited."

"And there's that new one. *Guess Who's Coming to Dinner.* Great cast. Hepburn, Tracy and Poitier."

"Oh, yeah. Nothing like a little miscegenation controversy to liven up an evening."

"Well, either one would be good."

"Okay, let's figure it out after we talk to the women folk."

"Good. See you tomorrow, Charlie."

Chapter 13

Saturday, 3 February 1968

"Just give me a few more minutes and I'll be ready," Teresa called from the bedroom.

"No hurry, love. We've got plenty of time before the movie starts." Sitting on the living-room floor with his daughter, Kevin picked up another piece of a wooden puzzle and asked, "What's this one, Mary Clare?"

"Bear, Daddy."

"That's right. Where does it go?"

"Right here," she said, taking it from him and putting it in its place.

"You're very smart."

"Smart!" she repeated, and she began taking loose pieces from a pile and placing them in the puzzle's frame without his help.

His attention wandered to the television as she worked her way steadily through the pile of puzzle pieces. The evening news was nearly over when an anchor man returned to the screen after a commercial break. "We conclude our broadcast this evening with another report from South Vietnam on this, the fourth day of massive, country-wide attacks by the Viet Cong, now being called the Tet offensive, marking the Buddhist religious holiday going on when it began. This report comes from the northern city of Hue."

A familiar face appeared on the screen. "This is Peter Holmes on the outskirts of Hue, the ancient imperial capital of Vietnam. I am accompanying a battalion of U.S. Marines who are fighting to retake this city that was overrun by the Viet Cong in the pre-dawn hours of

Wednesday morning when the Tet offensive began. To many Vietnamese, Hue is also the cultural capital of their country, and its capture by the enemy is intolerable." Holmes was huddled against a crumbling stone wall, his trademark bush hat replaced by a helmet covered with cloth camouflage, and a flak vest over his bush jacket. "I've just arrived here from the outpost of Khesanh where other marines continue to hold off an encircling enemy with the support of massive air strikes from B-52 bombers."

Ed's probably part of that, he thought. Seeing that Mary Clare had finished, he said, "Very good, sweetheart. Let's see you do it again, all by yourself."

"Again!" she said emphatically, dumping the puzzle. She mixed up the pieces and then began placing them methodically into the frame a second time.

Crouching as he went, Holmes moved alongside a marine firing his M-16 rifle around a corner of the wall on full automatic, on rock and roll as the foot soldiers called it. "How's it going?" Holmes shouted to him above the staccato sound of small-arms fire.

Pausing from the firefight, the marine said, "It's going slow. It's gonna be a house-to-house duke-out with the VC this time. The gooks are dug in, and they're not giving up. We're gonna be here awhile." The marine put another clip of ammunition into his weapon and started firing again.

Holmes turned to face the camera. "These marines, used to fighting the VC in the bush, are having to adapt quickly to a new style of combat in city streets. The enemy appears to be well-placed and well-supplied in trying to hold out, and it looks like we're in for a lengthy siege here. This is Peter Holmes reporting from the combat zone."

The anchor man returned to the screen. Slowly, he removed his glasses and said, "We conclude our broadcast sadly tonight with that report from a reporter who was one of the best any of us has ever seen." A picture of a smiling Holmes in his bush hat and jacket appeared on the screen. Superimposed over it, at the bottom, appeared: 1933-1968. "Peter Holmes was struck down by a sniper's bullet an hour after filming that report. We will remember him as a combat journalist who always wanted to be where the action was. He respected the troops in the field as much as he despised the brass in Saigon who, he believed, couldn't be trusted to tell the truth. The troops, the grunts of this war, returned that respect. We will all miss Peter terribly. Good night from New York."

Kevin stood up, walked over to the TV set and turned it off. *You were a good guy, Peter.*

"I'm ready," Teresa said as she entered the room.

He turned around. "Wow! You look fantastic."

"I've used all my make-up tricks. I don't want you to stare and drool over Kelley all night the way the rest of the guys in your class do."

"Not a chance. She's not my type. I don't have a thing for blondes. I go for that smoky Iberian-mystery look." He picked up his daughter's jacket from a chair. "Okay, Mary Clare, let's put your coat on and go meet baby Heather."

Mary Clare jumped up and ran to him. "Feather!" she shouted as she put her arms in the jacket's sleeves.

"No, Mary Clare. HEA-ther," he repeated, putting emphasis on the first syllable of the name, as he zipped her jacket.

"Feather!" she shouted again and started laughing.

"Are you being funny, Mary Clare?"

"Funny!"

"I'll show you funny, tiger lily," he said as he picked her up and began tickling her. She squealed with laughter.

"All right, you two," Teresa said, putting on her coat. "It was nice of Kelley to let us share their baby sitter after ours canceled at the last minute. I like her. In some ways, she reminds me of Clare. By the way, I called Clare this afternoon while you were at the gym. She's leaving for Hawaii next week to meet Ed for R and R," she said, meaning rest and recreation, a five-day leave out of the combat zone authorized once during a tour of duty in Southeast Asia.

He put Mary Clare down and put on his jacket. "We'd better start saving for our own R and R. I'll be ready to blow a wad of money when we meet in Hawaii. Okay, you lovely ladies, let's go meet baby Heather."

"HEA-ther!" Mary Clare said, mimicking him, emphasizing the first syllable.

* * *

Their waiter served them their main course and asked, "Will there be anything else, folks?"

"No, thanks. We're fine for now," Charlie answered.

"Okay then. Enjoy."

"So, Kelley, you were saying that the movie had a little too much violence," Kevin said to resume their conversation.

"Physical violence. Psychological violence is much more interesting. My favorite Newman movie is *The Long Hot Summer.* Orson Welles plays such a great emotional bully."

"My wife, the psych major," Charlie explained. "She likes the physical part, though, when Paul takes off his shirt."

"What woman wouldn't?" Teresa responded.

"You see, Charlie? It's not just me. Thank you, Teresa. I knew from the beginning that I'd like you."

"Well, I thought there was a fairly even mixture of the two," Charlie said. "Like when the prison warden says, 'What we've got here is failure to communicate,' just after he whacks Newman. And then there were the guards. Did the guy who played the head guard, Honeycutt, remind you of anyone, Kev?"

"Yeah. He looked a little like Kale. Acted a little like him too."

"Who's that?" Teresa asked.

"He's my IP," Charlie said. "I've had the pleasure of his instruction during our sessions in the simulator. Not the most fun I've ever had. The guy always seems to have this sneer in his voice. He really enjoyed pointing out my screw-ups. I don't know where he found out about it, but lately he's started calling me Georgetown when he wants to grind it in."

"I've tried to tell you, honey," Kelley said. "The little man is just insecure."

"I keep trying to remember that," Charlie said. "Well, I guess that's just minor-league insecurity. Nothing compared to what Lyndon Johnson must be feeling right now. The stuff on TV during the last few days has just been mind-boggling. Like the Viet Cong fighting inside our embassy in Saigon."

"Or that policeman executing that Viet Cong prisoner with his pistol in the middle of the street. Grisly," Kelley said.

"It looks like the VC have really taken some pretty heavy hits," Kevin said. "They rolled the dice on a big offensive and lost."

"Somehow," Teresa said quietly, "this doesn't feel like a victory for us."

"I think Teresa's right," Kelley said. "I think we've been lied to all along. All we've been hearing from Washington is that the tide has turned in Vietnam, and then there's this massive surprise attack."

"The irony is," Charlie said, "that everybody might be right. Kev's probably right in saying that the bad guys have taken some big losses by coming out of hiding to mount this major offensive that didn't work, but the military message'll probably get drowned out by the politics. Johnson had rock-bottom credibility before all this happened, and I think that this and the *Pueblo* thing could really sink him. The ladies are on to something here, Kev."

"Well, Charlie," Kevin replied, "I think that's a little premature. It's a long way to the election. A lot can happen between now and then."

"I hope an end to this war happens," Kelley said, her voice rising in anger.

"Kel-ley," Charlie said, whispering, trying to stop her.

"No, Charlie," she shot back. "Those bastards in Washington are perfectly willing to send you to Vietnam, while they lie to you about what's really happening there. Meanwhile, they're keeping their own sons safe at home with draft deferments and whatever else they can find."

"Kelley, people are starting to stare at us," Charlie whispered.

"I'm sorry, honey," she replied, lowering her voice. "I don't want to embarrass anyone, but sometimes, things can't be held back."

Continuing to whisper, Charlie said, "Kelley, you come from a military family. Your dad served in Korea. You know that career officers see duty differently than other people do."

Seeing that conversations at other tables had halted, they stopped talking. Teresa waited until the noise around them resumed and then said in a low voice, "Charlie, let me try to tell you how we wives feel. When you men can be dragged into talking about why you're here, you talk about things like duty and how a combat tour will help your careers. We know that there's more to it than that, something that you'd never admit to. It's a huge part of what we love about you. There's a selflessness in your volunteering to fight in this war. I believe, and I think Kelley does too, that those responsible for what's going on in Vietnam are taking advantage of that by lying to you. It's the lowest form of disrespect."

"That's it exactly," Kelley said, putting her hand on Teresa's.

Chapter 14

Sunday, 31 March 1968

"Good night, angel," Kevin heard Teresa say from the hallway as she turned off the light in Mary Clare's room. He re-read a paragraph on radar systems in the F-105 flight manual he was studying, half-listening to Lyndon Johnson on the television beginning an address to the nation on the war in Vietnam. Returning to the living room, Teresa sat down with him on the couch and began working on a woven piece she was finishing with hand sewing.

After lamenting the failure of the North Vietnamese to respond to his earlier overtures to begin peace negotiations, LBJ started talking about the Tet offensive two months earlier. Putting down his thick book, Kevin listened more closely:

> Their attack—during the Tet holidays—failed to achieve its principal objectives.
>
> It did not collapse the elected government of South Vietnam or shatter its army—as the Communists had hoped.
>
> It did not produce a "general uprising" among the people of the cities as they had predicted.
>
> The Communists were unable to maintain control of the more than thirty cities that they attacked. And they took very heavy casualties.

True, Kevin thought, remembering the news coverage since Tet, *but it looks like Charlie was right. That message got lost.* He concentrated again on the television:

> The Communists may renew their attack any day.
>
> They are, it appears, trying to make 1968 the year of decision in South Vietnam—the year that brings, if not final victory or defeat, at least a turning point in the struggle.

And how many turning points have we had? Kevin wondered, as he remembered his all-too-wrong predictions about the North Vietnamese cracking as the bombing of the North intensified in stages. His attention wandered back to LBJ:

> We are prepared to move immediately toward peace through negotiations.
>
> So, tonight, in the hopes that this action will lead to early talks, I am taking the first step to de-escalate the conflict. We are reducing—substantially reducing—the present level of hostilities.
>
> And we are doing so unilaterally, and at once.
>
> Tonight, I have ordered our aircraft and our naval vessels to make no attacks on North Vietnam, except in the area north of the demilitarized zone where the continuing enemy buildup directly threatens allied forward positions and where the movements of their troops and supplies are clearly related to that threat.
>
> The area in which we are stopping our attacks includes almost ninety percent of North Vietnam's population, and most of its territory. Thus there will be no attacks around the principal populated areas, or in the food-producing areas of North Vietnam.
>
> Even this very limited bombing of the North could come to an early end—if our restraint is matched by restraint in Hanoi. But I cannot in good conscience stop all bombing so long as to do so would immediately and directly endanger the lives of our men and our allies. Whether a complete bombing halt becomes possible in the future will be determined by events.

"This sounds like the beginning of the end," Teresa said as she put down her sewing.

"Well, we've had bombing halts before."

"Those were always announced with a time limit, like a month or two weeks. This feels very different to me."

They listened for nearly an hour more as LBJ elaborated on his initiative, ambivalently alternating between offering Hanoi the olive branch and brandishing the sword, as he tried to reconcile retreat with continued allegiance to South Vietnam. Along the way, he wandered into strange digressions, international finance, budget politics and swipes at Congress, that revealed a man under enormous pressure, unable to focus clearly on the essential. Near the end, he became wistful:

> Fifty-two months and ten days ago, in a moment of tragedy and trauma, the duties of this office fell upon me. I asked then for your help and God's, that we might continue America on its course, binding up our wounds, healing our history, moving forward in a new unity, to clear the American agenda and to keep the American commitment for all of our people.

Kevin felt the stirring of a curious sympathy for the man for the first time as he considered what had happened since that November day in Dallas four years earlier. *But you're responsible for a lot of it,* he thought, unable to get past his feeling that the President had been found wanting as commander-in-chief. Even as his attention wandered, LBJ's closing words rang in his ears:

> Accordingly, I shall not seek, and I will not accept, the nomination of my party for another term as your President.

He didn't listen to the rest. "Incredible," he murmured, not quite believing what he had heard.

"He's not the first casualty of this war," Teresa said. "But he's not one of the fatalities either. I won't be missing him."

"Not many will, by all accounts. Do you want to hear any more?"

"No."

"Okay," he said as he got up and collapsed the light of the television screen into a bright dot at its center. "I need to get to bed. I've got the first flight in the morning."

* * *

Early the next morning, a flight of four Thuds was making the last of its three strafing passes on the Smoky Hill gunnery range, northwest of Wichita. Kevin watched as the flight's number-three jet, one ahead of him, rolled out of a descending turn and lined up on a strafe target in a shallow dive. A short trail of gray gun smoke appeared behind the airplane as Sam Prentiss fired the last of his hundred rounds for the training mission, and dust rose around the target, a white, square panel, twenty feet on a side, when the volley tore through it and hit the soft earth behind.

Kevin began a ninety-degree turn to line up on his target as Prentiss pulled the nose of his jet sharply upward and rolled left to avoid ricochets and to exit the range. "Four's in," he called over the radio.

"Four's cleared in hot," the range controller answered, telling him that he was cleared to open fire.

In the last part of the turn, he shallowed his bank angle to ease the jet's gun sight around to the target. On a heavy glass rectangle in front of him, just inside the windscreen, the two concentric circles of the sight reticle shone brightly in orange light. In the center of the reticle was a bright-orange dot, the pipper. With light pressure on the stick, he rolled out of the turn and coaxed the pipper up to the top center of his target, the end panel in a row of four. He hesitated, letting the pipper stabilize momentarily. More out of instinct now, no longer mechanically as he done on his first range missions, he pulled the trigger at the top of the stick grip when he saw the right picture, telling him he was in range. The six-barrel gun on the left side of his airplane gave out a muffled roar as he fired the last of his 20-millimeter rounds. With light, forward pressure on the stick, he eased the pipper down through the target as he closed on it to concentrate the burst.

His firing pass done, he pulled firmly on the control stick, back and left, climbing and turning, tightening the turn as he gained altitude, searching ahead for the three other jets in his flight as they maneuvered to rejoin before returning to McConnell. Seeing the leader three miles away, he let his airspeed build to close the distance quickly, giving the Thud its head. He turned off the jet's master-armament switch to safety its weapons circuits, putting off a more elaborate safety check until after the rejoin.

With half a mile to go, he glanced at his airspeed indicator. It read 450, giving him a hundred knots of overtake on the other jets, and his eyes confirmed a high rate of closure. At a quarter of a mile, he brought the throttle back to slow the big jet down, and closer, he opened a switch on the throttle with his left thumb to extend the airplane's speed brakes, four large panels on the Thud's tail that encased its engine's exhaust. He felt rapid deceleration as the four metal boards, twenty-five square feet of them, forced their way into the airstream, sharply increasing drag. Fifty yards away, feeling the right rate of final closure, he retracted the boards, before they killed off the slight speed margin that eased him forward, toward his assigned position in a loose spread formation. Once stabilized, five wingspans away from Prentiss on the outside of the flight, he turned off other switches that activated the airplane's bomb rack and gun. Rejoined, the four of them streaked southeast over the barren wheat fields of Kansas, looking like a pack of winged wolves in their dark, mottled paint.

Major Kale, the flight leader, called over the radio for weapons status and fuel remaining. "Saber lead has armament safety check complete; six thousand."

"Two complete; five thousand," Rasmussen answered.

"Three complete; six thousand," Prentiss called.

"Four complete; five thousand," he responded when his turn came, rechecking the master-armament switch off by touch and the rest of the weapons switches safe by sight, then glancing at the large, round fuel gauge that showed what remained of the 15,000 pounds of starting fuel that his Thud had gulped in an hour.

He relaxed for a moment, taking stock of the mission, as he scanned his quadrant of the sky, looking out to keep the flight clear of other airplanes. *Dive bombing isn't there yet, but the strafe passes felt pretty good.* As he glanced momentarily inside the cockpit, the master-caution light came on. He pressed it to turn it off and looked at the stack of warning lights below it. The message, AC GEN, glowed up at him, telling him that the airplane's alternating-current generator had gone off the line. He tried to reset it with a toggle switch, but the warning light stayed lit. After several more unsuccessful attempts, he called the flight leader. "Saber lead, Saber four. I've lost my AC generator."

"Roger," Kale replied. "Try reset."

"It won't reset."

"Roger," Kale said. Calling for a change in radio frequency he added, "Saber flight, go channel six."

"Two."

"Three."

"Four." He dialed in one of the twenty often-used frequencies preset in the radio.

Kale called again on the new frequency, "Saber flight, check."

"Two."

"Three."

"Four."

"Wichita Approach," Kale transmitted, "Saber flight of four is thirty miles northwest of McConnell at five thousand."

"Saber flight, roger. This is Wichita Approach. Squawk ident."

"Saber's ident."

"Radar contact. McConnell is landing runway one nine," the controller said, meaning the runway oriented to the south. "Ceiling is four hundred feet overcast; visibility two miles. Winds are light and variable. Altimeter two niner point eight six. Say your request."

"Roger. Two nine, eight six. Saber requests recovery in elements to the ILS final," Kale answered, meaning dividing the four-ship flight into two flights of two aircraft for separate ILS approaches. "Three and four will land first."

"Roger. Saber three and four, continue present heading. Saber lead and two, take up heading zero four zero. Descend and maintain four thousand. Change frequency to two, fifty-six, point eight."

"Roger. Zero four zero and four thousand. Two, fifty-six, point eight," Kale confirmed as he began a shallow, descending turn to the northeast, slicing away with Rasmussen in tow. "Saber two, go channel seven."

"Two."

Kevin tried to reset the generator once more without success. He glanced at his compass dial and saw the TACAN arrowhead circling aimlessly around it, unable to lock on after the loss of AC power. He remembered from his classroom lectures that all his navigation instruments would be useless without a functioning AC generator. Orienting himself by landmarks, he saw that they were north of Wichita, its southern half covered by a cloud layer that had moved in since their takeoff. McConnell lay under the weather, somewhere to the southeast.

"Saber three and four, descend and maintain three thousand," the controller directed. "You're on course to intercept the ILS final, runway one nine right at McConnell. Say type of landing."

"Saber three and four will land together out o' this approach. Leavin' five for three thousand," Prentiss answered.

"Roger. Saber three and four are cleared for the approach. Call intercepting final approach course."

"Roger. Cleared for the approach." Prentiss rocked the wings of his airplane slightly and began a lazy right turn.

Responding to the signal, Kevin moved in to close formation on Sam's wing.

"Saber three's on a twelve-mile final," Sam called when they rolled out of the turn.

"Roger. Report wheels down."

"Saber three, roger." Looking back at his wingman, Sam put his fist to the top of his canopy, thumb down. Getting a head nod in reply from Kevin, he looked forward again and nodded sharply once, calling for the lowering of gear and flaps with a visual signal.

Kevin lowered the gear and flap handles quickly with his left hand, keeping his eyes on the lead airplane. His heavy jet barely reacted to the change in configuration. Ready to land on Sam's wing, he eased his Thud forward to final-approach position with a slight increase in power. The green light on the leader's right wingtip appeared to slide backward as he moved forward, until it reached the center of the white star in the insignia painted on the lead airplane's rear fuselage. *Light on the star,* he said to himself as the simplicity of the formation reference struck him. *Not in the corner of the star; not near it; but directly over it. Like I'm finally there,* he mused.

"Saber three and four have gear down," Sam transmitted after looking back at his wingman.

"Roger, Saber three and four are cleared to land, runway one nine right."

"Roger. Cleared to land."

The cloud tops moved up toward them as they began descending on the glide path. He checked for three green lights above the gear handle, and seeing them, he focused his full attention outside the cockpit, on Prentiss, readying himself for a ride of nearly two hundred knots through the weather to a landing on Sam's wing. He raised the sun visor on his flight helmet, getting ready for things to happen fast. *Okay, O'Dea. You're in the big leagues now. Let's see your stuff.*

The cloud layer was thin, and the big jets seemed to tear through it. When they dropped into the clear, he picked up the runway, his eyes darting between it and the leader as he worked the stick and throttle in small, rapid movements to hold position on the wing, to keep the light on the star. They ripped across the runway's threshold, and he brought the stick well back as he pulled the throttle toward idle, matching Sam's control movements, staying in position as the lead jet's nose rotated up in the last part of the flare, just above the runway. *Touchdown*. Keeping his eyes on the leader, Kevin reached immediately for the drag-chute handle at the top of his instrument panel and gave it a hard pull.

He jerked forward into his shoulder harness as his drag chute bit into the air. "Good chute," he called over the radio.

A second later, a small door popped open behind the rudder of the lead jet, and the leader's drag chute streamed into the air and snapped into full deployment. The two airplanes decelerated smoothly, one dropping behind the other as Kevin began light braking to get separation between them. He felt good as he began to relax, his breathing slowing and shallowing. *Not bad for my first wing landing in the Thud,* he thought.

The debriefing after all four of them landed didn't go nearly as well. The three wingmen from Saber flight were sitting at a metal table in a small briefing room, one of four cubicles off the lobby of the squadron, listening to Kale. He finished marking up the plexiglass covering a diagram of the gunnery range on the wall behind him and put down his grease pencil. "So, in the future, I want to see better flying in the pattern around the range. You two," he said, looking at Kevin and Charlie, "took too long to get back to altitude after your dive-bomb passes, and that's why the pattern got so wide. Plus, you didn't compensate enough for the wind at altitude, and that's why your bombing was dog shit. All right, that's it for the range work. Recovery from the range was standard, except for O'Dea's generator problem. You want to say anything about that?"

"No, sir. Just the breaks of single-engine flying," Kevin replied, trying to appear nonchalant about the incident.

"You worried about flying with just one motor, O'Dea?" Kale jabbed, a belittling tone in his voice.

"No, sir."

"We could transfer you to something with four, maybe eight, engines if it's a problem."

"No, sir. It's not a problem." *Charlie's right. You really are an asshole.*

"Okay then. That's all I've got. You got anything, Sam?"

"No, sir. That pretty much covers it. The strafe scores should be in from the range by now."

"Yeah. Okay, we're done." Kale got up and left the cubicle first.

"Well, gents, y'all remember the three answers we used to give when we were doolies?" Sam asked in a low voice, using the term for freshmen at the Air Force Academy. "Yes sir, no sir and no excuse sir? Well, Major Kale kind o' thinks students are like doolies. I'd keep the answers kind o' short with him next time, if I were you."

"Good advice, Sam," Kevin said. "Why don't we take a look at the strafe scores and get some coffee?"

They got up and left the cubicle together, making their way to the operations counter that took up one wall of the lobby. Behind the counter, a large scheduling board, covered with plexiglass and marked with various colors of grease pencil, showed the information that kept the squadron running. Pilots' names, aircraft tail numbers and takeoff times took prominence in the center of the board, and other data were displayed in sections around its periphery. They had gotten their dive-bombing scores on the range, immediately after each pass, with the range officer calling out distance and clock position from the target when their blue, foot-long practice bomblets hit with a puff of white smoke. The holes in the strafe targets, though, had to be counted by the range crew by hand after the flight had finished firing and had gone home. The squadron clerk, Airman Stanislavsky, was posting their strafe scores on the big board when they reached the counter.

"Hey, Stan," Sam asked, "who got the money today?"

"Well, sir, it looks like you get free beer again today. You're the winner, but the take is getting smaller. You shot seventy-one percent. Captain O'Dea got sixty-two, and Captain Rasmussen got thirty-one."

"Okay, gents, pay up. Let's see. At a nickel a hole, you owe me two bucks, Charlie, and Kev owes forty-five cents. Yeah, you're right, Stan. They're gettin' better. The pickin's ain't as easy as they used to be."

"I guess it's a worthy cause," Charlie said as he handed over two bills from his wallet. "With Mississippi being the most poverty-stricken state in the country and all."

"I just love takin' that Yankee money. Boys, I tell you what. After gettin' so much money off you, it's only right that I buy the coffee."

"This's what's known as southern hospitality," Charlie said to Kevin as they followed Sam to the coffee bar in the next room.

After they'd each poured a cup, Charlie asked, "Well, Sam, what did you think of Johnson's speech last night?"

"I didn't listen to it. I was, shall we say, otherwise engaged last night. So, was it the usual bullshit? An hour o' we're ready to talk peace anywhere, anytime, if only Uncle Ho would see the light?"

"Well," Charlie said, "there was some of that, but the big news is that Johnson isn't going to run for president again and that we're scaling back the bombing of North Vietnam. It looks like we won't be going downtown to Hanoi any more."

"What? You got to be shittin' me."

"Yeah," Kevin added. "Johnson wasn't specific in his speech, but one of the news guys this morning said that we've stopped bombing north of the twentieth parallel."

Kale entered the room and, overhearing Kevin, said, "We shouldn't be stopping the bombing. We should be nuking the fuckers. Right, Georgetown?" he asked, pouring a cup of coffee.

Surprised, Charlie looked nervously at Sam and then at Kevin. "Well, sir, after last night, it looks like we're de-escalating."

"I didn't ask you what we're doing. I asked you what we ought to be doing. What about you, O'Dea? How about making the slant-eyed bastards glow in the dark?"

You're a pig, Kale. "No, Major," Kevin said, using a less-deferential form of address than sir, "we shouldn't be nuking them."

Kale, reacting to the slight, kept up the pursuit. "So, O'Dea, are you telling me that you wouldn't drop a nuke on Hanoi if you were ordered to do it?"

Kevin saw the clumsily laid trap. Kale wanted him to say that he would disobey an order. He took a long drink of his coffee to buy time and then said, "Major, I'm not going to get into twilight-zone stuff about hypothetical orders from some hypothetical president. The one who gave the speech last night told us what we're going to do in the real world."

Kale was enraged at the second slight and putdown. "So, all the guys we've lost up north don't mean anything to you, O'Dea?" he asked in a rising voice.

It was the ultimate cheap shot. Kevin's anger burst from its cage and was forming a stinging reply when Colonel Reynolds appeared at the door. "It's awfully loud in here for this time of the morning. Has the coffee gone bad again?"

Charlie jumped quickly into the breach. "No, sir. We were just going over the President's speech last night."

"I guess maybe that's something harder to digest than bad coffee," Reynolds said. Sizing up the situation quickly, he asked Kale, "Ray, could we go to one of the briefing rooms for a minute? I need some help with something on dive bombing that's been bothering me. I'll need to sketch it out for you."

"Yes, sir. Sure," Kale replied, glaring at Kevin before he left with Reynolds.

After they were gone, Prentiss asked, "Well, Kev, when did you become such a fuckin' boy scout? Would it have killed you to let him blow off a little steam and rant and rave some? The guy flew a hundred missions up north and got shot down. Now Johnson's cuttin' and runnin' and tellin' him, and me too, that what we did don't count for shit. We didn't do what we did to lose to a bunch of raggedy-assed rice pickers in Hanoi."

"Sam, no one's going to get away with saying that I don't care about the guys we've lost. Some of them are our classmates, for Christ's sake."

"Yeah? How about the other part? The part about stoppin' the bombin'."

"Look, Sam, I'm here because I thought hitting North Vietnam would end this war. Maybe I was wrong. I don't know. But that doesn't mean that we should start killing people now just to lash out and kill people. That's what Kale really meant. Words mean something, Sam."

"Yeah? Then you'd better start watchin' yours, Kev," Sam said angrily and left the room.

"Damn!" Charlie said in a low voice after Prentiss left. "Emotions are running pretty high today."

"Yeah. I guess so."

"I'd listen to what Sam just said about being careful, Kev. It looks like I've just been replaced as the number-one guy on Kale's shit list."

Chapter 15

Friday, 5 April 1968

Two Thuds from Nellis taxied to the transient ramp at McConnell after turning off the runway. Kevin waited on the sidewalk that led from base ops to the ramp until he heard the distinctive whine of engines shutting down, and he started walking toward the wingman's jet. Its pilot took off his helmet and, smiling broadly, waved casually from his high cockpit.

Kevin waved back as he approached the airplane and called out over the noise of the ramp, "Hey, Rob. Welcome to McConnell."

"Thanks, sir," Rob Johnson yelled back. "Be right down."

As Kevin waited, a man in white coveralls from transient alert attached a yellow ladder to the jet's canopy rail and climbed up to help Rob unstrap. The flight leader from the other Thud descended his ladder, gathered his gear and began walking toward his wingman's airplane. He wore the same patch at the top of the left sleeve of his flight suit that distinguished instructors from students at McConnell. Shaped as a shield, the patch was predominately blue with a small red field at the top. In the red portion, written in white, were the words, NORTH VIETNAM. Below, in larger white letters over the blue background, was the patch's main message:

100
MISSIONS
F-105

"Hi. I'm Joe Steele," the flight leader, a captain, said as he offered his free hand.

"Hi, Joe. I'm Kevin O'Dea," he said, shaking hands.

"Rob says that you were his IP in UPT."

"Yeah. How's he doing at Nellis?"

"He's solid. You did a good job getting him ready."

"Well, it was more Rob than me."

Rob followed the man in white coveralls down the ladder and joined the other two pilots. "Afternoon, sir. It's good to see you again," he said as he extended his hand.

"Likewise, Rob. How was the flight?" he asked, returning Rob's firm grip.

"Good trip, sir."

"Good. Well, my car's parked behind base ops. Let's meet back there after you're done buttoning up, and I'll give you a lift to the Q," he said, meaning the VOQ, shorthand for visiting officers' quarters, lodgings for transient pilots.

"Thanks," Steele said. "See you in a few minutes."

After they met again in the parking lot, Rob and his IP put their gear in the back of Kevin's station wagon and got in. As they drove away, Steele asked, "How's your checkout going?"

"Good so far. We've been on the range a little over a month now."

"That's about where Rob's class is at Nellis," Steele said. "We give the guys straight out of UPT a lot of extra time at altitude, to learn how to maneuver a heavier jet, before we let them on the range."

"To me," Rob said, "the Thud seems to handle like a big T-38. You just fly everything fifty knots faster."

"Well," Steele said, "as they say, speed is life for a fighter pilot. Especially in the target area."

"Yes, sir."

After a short drive from the flight line, they arrived at the VOQ, a two-story, wood-frame building. Before his two passengers got out, Kevin said, "Joe, I'll be coming back to pick Rob up after you guys get settled in. Do you need a lift anywhere?"

"Thanks, but I'm going to meet a guy at the bar I flew with at Takhli. After that, we're going to hit all the hot spots in Wichita. Both of them," he said with a grin. "Do you know him? Sam Prentiss?"

"Yeah. We've known each other a long time. If anyone can find the action, Sam can."

"That's definitely the same man," Steele said, extending his hand. "Well, Kevin, good luck with the rest of training and your tour in Thailand."

"Thanks," he said, shaking hands. "Rob, how about if I come back for you in half an hour? Will that give you enough time to get civilianized?"

"Sure, sir. See you then," Rob said as he got out with Steele to get his gear.

When Kevin drove back, Rob was waiting for him at the curb in front of the VOQ. "Ever been to Kansas before, Rob?" he asked after his former student got in and they drove off.

"No, sir. First time. It looks a little sparse to a guy from the East Coast. Not many trees. A little like Nellis."

"Yeah. But maybe a little less crazy. This's been a tough week for news from back east."

"Yes, sir. I remember when we were driving back to Andrews when we were in DC on our cross-country. We were talking about Martin Luther King and the war, and now he's dead. I just can't believe it."

"My wife tells me that we're living in a bad time. She seems to have this sixth sense about things like that. Whatever's going on, it sure as hell ain't the fifties any more. Not with political killings, a war turning bad and college kids on dope raising hell in the streets."

"They're not the only ones, sir. Did you see the news this morning?"

"Yeah. Riots and looting in downtown DC, not far from Gonzaga. They said something like two-hundred people were arrested."

"Yes, sir. I called my mother at work right after I saw it. She said that the cops had things back under control by early this morning."

"I suppose it could've been a lot worse. There has to be a lot of anger out there."

"Yes, sir. No question about it."

And how much anger are you feeling, Rob? he wondered. Not knowing what to say next about King's assassination the night before, he turned up the volume on the radio to change the subject. Otis Redding was beginning "The Dock of the Bay," the number-two song on the pop chart. "I really like this one. It's kind of a blend of folk and Motown."

"Yes, sir. Otis was really good. He died too soon."

"Yeah, he did."

The song's soulful lyrics filled in the rest of the time it took to make the short trip from McConnell to the house Kevin was renting. "Well, this is it," he said as they pulled up in front of a nondescript, brick one-story. "Not the biggest place in the world, but my little girl likes the park down the street."

"Yes, sir. Well, the neighborhood seems to be nice and quiet."

"Yeah. We wanted something away from a lot of traffic, so this was the compromise."

"Yes, sir. I guess almost everything these days is a compromise."

They got out and walked up a short walk to the front door. As Kevin opened it and walked inside, Mary Clare saw him and shouted, "Daddy!" She ran toward him, and catching her, he pulled her up into his arms.

"Hi, tiger lily. Where's my kiss?"

"Mwah!" she said as she kissed him hard on the cheek.

"Mary Clare, this is Rob. Can you say, hi, Rob?"

"Hi, Wob."

"No, Mary Clare. Rob," he repeated, emphasizing the first letter of the name.

Smiling impishly, she said, "Wob Rob."

"That's close enough," Rob said with a smile. "Hi, Mary Clare."

Teresa appeared from the back of the house, and gave her husband a welcoming kiss on the cheek. "Hi, love." Looking past him, she said, "Hello, Rob. It's nice to see you again. We're glad you could join us for dinner."

"I've been looking forward to it, ma'am."

"Now, Rob. At Laughlin, you promised you'd call me Teresa."

"Sorry. I forgot . . . Teresa."

Kevin sensed something beneath his wife's hostess' charm. He saw uneasiness below a thin cover of lightness.

"That's better," she said. "Come with me, you good-looking jet jocks, and I'll get you both something to drink."

Kevin put Mary Clare down, and the two men followed Teresa into the kitchen. She opened the refrigerator and got them both a bottle of beer, asking, "Would you like a glass, Rob?"

"No, thanks. Real fighter pilots are bottle guys."

Kevin took his bottle from her after she opened it and said, "I agree. Well, now that I'm properly equipped for Friday afternoon, I'm going to duck into the bedroom for a minute to change."

Taking her cue, Teresa said, "Rob, I need to do something in the bedroom too. Would you mind terribly entertaining Mary Clare for just a minute?"

"Not at all. Want to play, Mary Clare?"

"Play!" Mary Clare said with delight as she crawled up into a chair to resume work on a half-completed puzzle on the kitchen table.

When they reached the bedroom, after he closed the door, Kevin asked, "What's wrong, love?"

"It's been on TV all afternoon, Kevin. Huge riots are going on in Washington. Fires have broken out, and troops have been called in. I didn't want to say anything in front of Rob. For some reason, I feel so incredibly uncomfortable."

"Okay. Let me call my folks first to find out what's going on. I'll be out in a few minutes, and we can tell Rob then."

"All right," she said as she opened the door to return to the kitchen.

He dialed the number, and his mother answered, "Hello?"

"Hi, Mom. It's Kevin."

"Hi. How are you?"

"I'm fine. I've just gotten home, and Teresa said that the TV news is wall-to-wall reports about rioting in DC."

"Yes, that's the only thing on television here too. It looks like, though, that most of it's confined to a few areas in the northwest part of the city."

"She said that troops have been called in."

"That's what's being reported. Let me put your father on. He's just gotten home from Capitol Hill, and he may have seen something."

"Okay. Bye, Mom."

"Hello, Kevin."

"Hi, Dad. What's going on there?"

"Well, everybody thought that things were back to normal this morning, but it started up again around nine o'clock and just kept getting worse. When I left the Hill about an hour ago, you could see fires in a couple of different places to the north. It was a real bitch getting home through all the traffic jams. Johnson's called out the National Guard, and he's bringing in regular troops from Fort Meade in Maryland. The local news showed some of them taking up positions around the Capitol Building with machine guns a few minutes ago. The place looks like a goddam war zone."

"Are you and Mom going to be okay?"

"Oh, sure. We'll be fine here in Virginia."

"Do you remember giving a lift to one of my UPT students when I came home on a cross-country for Mom's graduation last year?"

"Sure. The Negro kid. The baseball player from Gonzaga."

"That's right. Rob Johnson. He's here at the house for dinner tonight. He just flew in from Nellis, and I need to tell him what's happening. Is there anything going on south of Capitol Hill?"

"I don't think so. Not that I can tell, anyway. I didn't see anything on my way home."

"Okay. Thanks, Dad. I'm going to have to go now. I'll give you a call later tonight."

"All right. You'll be able to talk to Sean then. He's home from New Hampshire for spring break, but he's not here now. Don't worry about us. We're fine. We'll talk to you later."

"Okay. Bye, Dad."

"Bye, Kevin."

He put the phone down and walked out of the bedroom to the living room to turn on the television. When the picture stabilized, it showed an exhausted man with a blackened face sitting on the running board of a fire truck, quickly downing a soft drink. His heavy, water-repellant coat was open, and his fire helmet was resting on his knee. In the background, beyond a pair of soldiers in battle dress, a row of buildings was on fire. All of their show windows were shattered.

Kevin walked to the kitchen and said, "Rob, I think you need to see what's on television."

"Okay, sir," Rob replied, a puzzled tone in his voice.

He followed Kevin to the living room, and they heard a news commentator say, " . . . firefighters are still struggling to contain blazes set by arsonists following a wave of looting that swept over these small-business establishments earlier this afternoon. Now under the protection of armed troops, they hope to make better progress as evening wears on."

"Where is this, sir?"

"It's downtown DC."

"Sweet Jesus!"

"Rob, I've just talked to my folks. They say that it's apparently confined to a couple of areas north of Capitol Hill. Do you want to call your mother anyway?"

"Yes, sir. Please."

"Go ahead and use the phone in the bedroom. I hope everything's okay."

"Thanks, sir," Rob said, the concern in his voice registering as he turned toward the hallway.

Rob returned to the kitchen a few minutes later looking subdued. "Sir, you were right. It's all north of Capitol Hill. My mom's okay, and one of my uncles is at her house in case anything happens."

"I'm glad."

There was awkward silence for a moment, until Teresa said, "Rob, this is heartbreaking. Hatred's murdered a good man, and this rage and destruction are just tragic."

Rob didn't reply at first and then said quietly, "I swear to god, sometimes I feel like I'm being torn in two. I didn't agree with everything that Doctor King said, but he was a beacon for a lot of black people. Yeah, I felt real rage last night when I heard he'd been killed, but this morning, I went back to swallowing it, like I've done all my life. This burn-baby-burn thing that's going on in DC isn't the answer, but I don't know what is. Sometimes I wonder if what I'm doing isn't completely phony. Some people I know call it being an oreo, being black on the outside and white on the inside."

Kevin said, "Rob, you're one of the best guys I know. I can't even begin to imagine what it's like to be a black man trying to make it in this country, but you are making it. And it's not because anybody's giving it to you. You're that good. I know it from first-hand experience."

"Thanks, sir."

"Rob, with everything we've been through together, you should call me Kevin."

"Okay, sir. I mean Kevin."

Mary Clare looked up from her puzzle and said, "Wob Rob sad."

"Not when I'm around you, sugar pie," Rob said as he walked over and sat down beside her to help her put the pieces together.

Chapter 16

Monday, 15 July 1968

Kevin scanned the afternoon flight schedule posted on the large plexiglass board behind the ops counter after he came back from lunch. His three-month run of luck had ended. He was scheduled to fly in Kale's flight. "Hey, Stan," he said to the squadron's clerk working behind the counter, "what's the story on the changes to the afternoon flights?"

"Major Barnes went home sick just before lunch, sir, so we had to juggle the schedule."

"I see."

His assigned IP, Ralph Barnes, had come back from leave a few days after the confrontation with Kale in the coffee room, the morning after LBJ announced his decision to abdicate his presidency in slow motion. Barnes' return had reduced his chances of flying with Kale again, but scheduling wasn't rigid, and students didn't fly with their assigned IPs exclusively.

I wonder if something else might have been going on. Maybe Colonel Reynolds had something to do with keeping me away from Kale, he mused, imagining a quiet conversation that might have taken place between Reynolds and the squadron commander. *Who knows what two lieutenant colonels might talk about in private.* He saw that Reynolds was also in the flight, along with Kale and Prentiss, and looking at the details of the schedule, he spotted the word, Snakeye, in parentheses, next to the flight's call sign, Jaguar.

The Snakeye bomb, designed to be delivered in level flight at low altitude and at high speed, combined the front end of a standard five-hundred-pound bomb with a unique tail assembly. The bomb's rear end consisted of four metal petals, folded to keep the weapon streamlined while it was being carried, that snapped open into the airstream after the Snakeye was dropped. The resulting increase in drag on the bomb made it fall well behind the airplane delivering it, to explode at a safe distance to the rear.

To give a pilot the option to dive bomb from high altitude with the Snakeye, its designers had provided the bomb a second mode of operation, one in which its tail petals remained folded after it was dropped to keep it streamlined. But options increased risks. If a pilot weren't careful, and inadvertently selected the slick mode for the weapon at low altitude, the mistake could be deadly. The bomb would explode directly under his airplane, since it wouldn't slow down after it was dropped and would match speed with the airplane until it hit the ground. Malfunctions of the tail assembly could give the same result, but the Snakeye's designers were quick to point out that such things happened only rarely.

"So, it's Snakeyes today, Stan."

"Yes, sir. This's what the IPs call junk month. At the end of training, we schedule all these odd-ball things that headquarters thinks students should do, that you'll probably never do again. Like Snakeyes. The IPs say that none of them ever saw one in combat, but headquarters thinks you should learn to drop them in training anyway."

"Well, we have to fill all those squares. Right, Stan?"

"Yes, sir," Stanislavsky agreed. He pointed to an area at the bottom of the giant board where students' names formed the vertical side of a matrix, with the much-longer horizontal side showing each training requirement a student had to accomplish to complete the check-out course. Most of the cells of the matrix were filled with black grease-pencil Xs. "This flight's a two-fer. You'll get the last aerial-refueling X today and the Snakeye X," he said, tapping on two empty cells opposite the name O'Dea.

Taking a blank mission card from a stack on the counter, Kevin filled in preliminary information for the flight: call sign; pilots' names; aircraft tail numbers. *Fifteen minutes until briefing,* he calculated, subtracting an hour and a half from the takeoff time he copied onto the card from the board. "I'll be in here, Stan, if anyone wants me," he said as he walked away from the counter toward the empty briefing room where he had left his briefcase before lunch.

"Okay, sir."

Inside, he slid the door almost closed, leaving a small opening to listen for the others in the flight, then sat down and pulled out a booklet with Ground Attack—Weapons and Tactics written on its cover. Turning to a dog-eared page, he began reviewing the material on the Snakeye that he had read and underlined the night before, testing his memory for the two different settings of the Thud's weapons switches in the cockpit, one for its high-drag mode and another to release it slick. A few minutes later, he heard Kale through the door opening.

"Fucking SAC. What's this change in fuel offload from the tanker, Stan? We asked them for the standard five-thousand pounds of gas for each jet. Now they're saying that they're only going to give us three thousand?"

"Yes, sir," Stanislavsky explained, "SAC's apparently just started a big no-notice exercise, and they pulled back some of our fuel for their bombers. I tried to get you more, sir, but they just wouldn't do it. Since SAC owns the tankers, sir, there isn't much we can do about it."

"Great. Just fucking great," Kale said as he made his way to another briefing room across the lobby from the one Kevin occupied, leaving Sam Prentiss at the counter to fill out his mission card.

Kevin joined Prentiss at the counter after Kale left. "What's the problem with a little less gas, Sam? Can't we just take off a little later?"

"'Fraid not. We have to hit the tanker at a fixed time, and our slot time on the range is firm. So, there's no flex in the schedule. We're gonna be light on gas gettin' back."

Reynolds walked to the counter from the coffee room, joined them and began filling out his mission card. "Afternoon, gentlemen. What's that about being light on gas, Sam?"

"Yes, sir. The SAC guys shorted us two-thousand pounds apiece on the tanker. Seems they got some kind o' surprise exercise goin' on."

"I see. Well, some full colonel, probably a wing commander, is covering his ass. They won't risk flunking their exercise to be kind to some fighter guys in training. It's the golden rule. The guys who own the gold, tankers in this case, make the rules."

"Yes, sir. Well, we're all here. Major Kale's in the briefin' room over there."

The two captains trailed Reynolds to the briefing room, and Kale rose when he entered.

"Afternoon, Ray," Reynolds said as he took his seat, followed by the others.

"Good afternoon, sir. All right, we're Jaguar flight for this mission," Kale began. For the next twenty minutes he covered details of the flight, from engine start and takeoff, through refueling procedures on the tanker and then the descent to the range at Smoky Hill. "We won't make the usual entry to the range where we separate, then attack as single ships and then rejoin after we're done. Instead, when we get ten miles from the range boundary," Kale briefed, pointing to a diagram of the range on the wall, "after we get cleared on, the second element will drop back to a mile in trail. Then, each element will make one pass, in route formation, on the simulated missile site—here. I'll call ready, ready, drop over the radio, and lead and two will release bombs together."

Strange, Kevin thought, looking past Kale. *Would we really do that in combat? Where a switch screw-up or a bad bomb could take out two airplanes flying next to each other?* Becoming aware that Kale had stopped talking, he looked back at the flight leader who was staring directly at him.

"Did you get that, O'Dea? You seemed to be off in your own little world there."

"Yes, sir. I got it."

"Then what's your problem? You look confused," Kale pressed.

"I was just thinking about the possibility of fratricide if, for some reason, a bomb came off slick with two airplanes that close together."

Anger, banked for three months, leaped up in Kale's eyes. "Who's the IP here, O'Dea? Me or you?" he asked, dropping his voice to a low, menacing tone.

"You are, sir."

"Right. And all I want out of you, O'Dea, is three things. Your boots shined, your mouth shut and the light on the goddammed star. You got that?"

You lousy bastard. "Yes, sir."

"Okay," Kale continued, regaining his composure. "After the first element drops, we'll exit the range in the standard left turn and head directly for McConnell. The second element will drop next, using the same command over the radio, then exit the range and rejoin. The lead element will hold three hundred and fifty knots until we're joined up.

After that, we'll get the armament safety check and enter the landing pattern with a standard four-ship entry. Any questions?"

Prentiss and Reynolds shook their heads.

Kale stood up. "All right. I'm going to check the weather again. We'll meet in the flight-line van in twenty minutes." He walked out of the room.

Reynolds stood next. "Kevin, how about I buy you a cup of coffee before the mission?"

"Okay, sir."

As Reynolds left, Prentiss turned in his chair toward Kevin and said in a lowered voice, "Way to fuckin' go, Kev. When're you gonna learn to keep your mouth shut?" Not waiting for an answer, he got up and walked out.

Kevin walked to the coffee room and joined Reynolds who was pouring a fresh pot into two mugs. Taking his, he said, "Thank you, sir."

"You and Major Kale don't seem to be the best of friends."

"No, sir."

"Do you know what's going on?"

"Well, sir, I guess no one likes to be second-guessed."

"That's true. But, of course, you were right on the merits."

"How do you mean, sir?"

"Well, it would be risky for two airplanes in formation to drop live Snakeyes—for the reason you pointed out. Since we'll be dropping sand-filled training bombs, not the real things, Kale's not worried about the blast effects of actual weapons. And, he had to find a way to make up for the two-thousand pounds of gas that SAC shorted us on the refueling. So, he improvised. He decided to do this artificial delivery on the range to save fuel. Actually, none of these IPs have ever delivered a Snakeye for real."

"Yes, sir. That's what I've been told."

"Basically, he sees this mission as a meaningless square-filler, and that's how he's rationalized everything."

"Yes, sir."

"If this were a mission with live ordnance, I would've objected to the formation attack he briefed. Since it's not, I didn't want to embarrass a flight leader in front of junior officers. Even though I outrank him, I'm still a student, and I've only got a limited number of chips I can play. I didn't want to burn one up in the briefing, but I wanted you to know that what Kale briefed isn't real-world."

"Thank you, sir."

"That's just the tip of the iceberg, though, Kevin."

"Sir?"

"There's a lot going on under the surface. Did you know that Kale's not a college graduate?"

"No, sir."

"Well, back in the early fifties, when the Korean war came along, a lot of high-school graduates became pilots under the aviation-cadet program. The best of them took advantage of opportunities the Air Force offered later to get their college degrees. People like Kale didn't. For some reason, he thought that being a good stick-and-rudder guy was enough. Now it's too late for him, and he knows it. A major's rank and twenty years of service are all he's going to get before he's forced to retire. He looks at you young guys, with very bright futures, and it just eats at him. You have fine careers ahead of you, and he'll be out selling used cars in a few years."

"I see, sir."

"But that doesn't excuse what he did in the briefing. After the flight, I'm going to take him aside and tell him to knock it off. I may take it up with the squadron commander too." Reynolds finished his coffee with a long swallow. "So, let's go ahead and fly the mission the way he briefed it, and things will get better afterward. Okay?"

"Okay, sir."

"Good," Reynolds said, putting his mug on the bar and looking at his watch. "Well, there's just enough time to hit the head and to suit up."

"Yes, sir."

* * *

Well into the mission, Kevin flew in formation below a tanker, its refueling boom connected to the nose of his Thud. As jet fuel flowed through the telescoping pipe that joined the two airplanes, he watched signal lights on the tanker's belly to stay in proper position, to keep the boom at the right angle down and at the right extension.

"Jaguar four, you've received three-thousand pounds," the boom operator called over the radio from the big airplane above.

"Roger. Jaguar four's disconnect," Kevin answered, pushing a button on top of his throttle to deactivate the latches in the refueling receptacle on his Thud's nose. The boom separated, spraying his windscreen with a trace of fuel that quickly vaporized in the onrushing air, as its operator in the tanker swung the winged pipe upward to stow it under the big airplane's tail. With slight pressure on the stick, Kevin slid his Thud down and right and then, advancing the throttle, moved up and forward to join on Prentiss, who held formation on the tanker's right wing.

The tanker's pilot called on the radio, "Jaguar flight, you've received your scheduled offload of twelve-thousand pounds total. Sorry we couldn't give you more, guys."

"Roger," Kale responded tersely, skipping the informal, customary thanks that flight leads normally gave tanker crews after refueling. "Jaguar flight will be separating down and left."

"Roger."

The four jets dropped off the tanker's wings, and turning away from northern Nebraska, began the last leg of their flight to the range at Smoky Hill. Kevin surveyed the three other jets as they leveled off and took up a southerly heading in spread formation. Not carrying the innocent-looking white cylinders usually attached to their bellies that housed miniature training bomblets, the Thuds took on a deadlier appearance. *We look like the real thing,* he mused, as he concentrated on the dark-green bombs hung on the two outboard stations of each jet's wings. Only a thin ring of blue paint on the nose of each Snakeye revealed the weapon for what it was, another training round, although full-size, filled with sand.

Thirty miles from Smoky Hill in a descent, Kale called, "Jaguars, go channel five."

"Two."

"Three."

"Four."

Kevin changed the radio channel to the range frequency and waited.

"Jaguars, check."

"Two."

"Three."

"Four."

Kale waited for a break in the radio calls being made by a flight ahead of them on the range, then transmitted, "Jaguar flight of four is thirty miles east for entry to the tactical range," meaning the part of the range used for advanced training. There, targets approximated real ones in appearance and were partially camouflaged, unlike those on the controlled part of the range, used in early training, that were well-marked with white approach lines and boundaries.

The range controller replied, "Jaguar flight, roger. Hold twelve miles east of Smoky Hill until cleared on. We have a flight on the range finishing up."

Irritated, Kale replied, "Roger. It's our range time now, and we're skosh on fuel."

"Roger, Jaguar. We'll clear you on shortly."

"Roger."

Listening to the radio calls from the flight ahead of them, Kevin recognized one of the student pilots from the class behind his, which was just beginning the last phase of range training. *If these guys are as screwed up as we were when we first got on the tactical range, they won't be gone shortly.*

At twelve miles away, Kale began a shallow turn away from the range to enter a holding orbit. With increased irritation in his voice, he called, "Jaguar flight's holding at twelve miles out. Fuel is close to bingo," he added, meaning the fuel level at which they would have to return to McConnell, if they couldn't rid themselves of the extra weight and drag of the Snakeyes.

"Roger, Jaguar. Hold tight. You'll be cleared on momentarily."

"After completing one orbit, Kale brought the flight to within five miles of the range, gambling that he wouldn't need to hold a second time. Not getting clearance, he turned eastward again. "Jaguar flight's turning out again. We're at bingo. We're going to have to go back to McConnell," he called, anger rising in his voice at the delay.

"Okay, Jaguar flight, you're cleared on now. Say your intentions."

Kale tightened his turn to head west to the range again. As Prentiss shallowed his turn to take spacing behind Kale and his wingman, it became clear that the first element's attack would be rushed. Kale replied quickly, trying to get a required radio call out of the way to concentrate on the run-in to the target, "Jaguar flight will attack the simulated SAM site in two elements. We'll be dropping two Snakeyes apiece. Each element will make one pass and then exit the range. Jaguar flight, green 'em up," he ordered, telling each pilot in the flight to arm his Thud's weapons circuits.

Flying loose formation on Prentiss, Kevin glanced inside the cockpit and turned the master-armament switch on. Two small lights on the selector buttons for the two outboard stations on the wings glowed green back at him, telling him that the release circuits to the Snakeyes were hot, confirming that the weapons would drop when he pressed the bomb-release button on the top of his stick grip. After looking quickly out at Prentiss's Thud again, to hold position as his element leader tightened his turn to follow a mile in trail behind Kale and Reynolds, Kevin looked back inside the cockpit quickly, focusing on one rotary switch. It controlled the petals on tails of the Snakeyes. Set one way, the switch signaled the petals to snap open for the bomb's high-drag mode. Set in another position, it kept them closed for dive bombing. He cycled the switch once to make sure it was set properly for a low-altitude, high-drag delivery.

He looked out at Prentiss's jet again as they accelerated out of the turn and dropped to attack altitude, a hundred feet above the ground. A quick glance at the airspeed indicator showed them at attack speed. *500 knots. More power. Stay in position.*

"Ready, ready, drop," Kale called.

Getting ready to drop on Prentiss's call, Kevin felt the adrenaline rush of the dash to the target, visible now, less than a mile ahead in his windscreen. He moved his thumb lightly over the bomb-release button as he looked out at Prentiss's Thud to hold position on the wing.

"Bail out! Bail out!" the range controller screamed over the radio. "Second element, abort! Abort!"

Startled, Kevin looked ahead. Reynolds' Thud had snapped over on its back. A huge piece of it flew upward. Before he could yell in protest, Jaguar two hit the ground, igniting in a streak of flame, scarring the earth with a long, black trench, breaking up into a fan of debris.

Prentiss pulled his Thud up, and Jaguar four followed. Still not believing his eyes, Kevin looked down at the crash, the afternoon sun glinting on a thousand shards of metal that had once been Jaguar two.

Sounding shaken over the radio, Kale asked the range controller, "Smoky Hill, what . . . what happened?"

"It looked like lead's bombs came off slick, and one of them skipped up into the wingman. It tore his right wing off."

Oh, my god, Kevin thought, *I never thought about that. With no explosion, the bomb stayed intact and ricocheted off the ground. A 500-pound missile going 500 knots. Oh, my god. He never had a chance.*

Kale didn't reply as he began a shallow left turn toward McConnell. Prentiss turned inside Kale, using cutoff geometry to make a slow rejoin, keeping the throttle back to save fuel.

Jaguar flight was given priority in the landing pattern after Jaguar four declared minimum fuel on initial. After landing, twenty minutes after the crash, Kevin taxied his Thud into a parking space next to Prentiss's jet. He shut his engine down and sat motionless in the cockpit until a crew chief came up the ladder.

"Sir?" the enlisted man asked, seeing that the pilot had made no attempt to finish shutting down and to get free of the straps that held him to his ejection seat. "Sir, are you okay?"

"Yeah, chief. I'm okay," he said, beginning to take off his helmet, and then handing it to the man on the ladder.

"What happened to the other airplane, sir? Only three came back."

"It crashed on the range."

"Oh!" the crew chief said awkwardly. "I'm sorry, sir," he added, and dismounted the ladder quickly.

Kevin finished in the cockpit and descended the ladder slowly as Prentiss walked toward him from the other Thud.

"Colonel Reynolds was a fine officer, Kev."

"Yeah, he was." He felt something inside burst. "And he didn't have to die today," he said in a rising, angry voice.

"Accidents happen in this business, Kev," Prentiss said quietly, aware that enlisted men were watching.

"This was no accident. This was a fuck-up by an incompetent flight lead. That's what I'm going to tell the accident-investigation board."

"What? That's bullshit, Kev."

"Is it, Sam? I warned him about fratricide."

"More bullshit, Kev," Prentiss said, getting angry. "You were talkin' about live bombs, and you wouldn't've said shit if he hadn't dragged it out of you."

"That's what you say. I remember exactly what I said. I didn't make any distinction between live bombs and what killed Colonel Reynolds."

"I'll just tell the board that you're full o' shit. Who're they gonna believe? An instructor or a student?"

"They're going to believe me. You're just not seeing it, are you?"

"Seein' what?"

"Colonel Reynolds was a three-star's fair-haired guy. Somebody's going to hang for this, and I'm going to supply the rope."

"Ray Kale's a good guy. He risked his ass to fly a hundred up north. What've you ever done?"

"I've never killed any of my students. Sam, don't give me any more of this stuff about a hundred missions justifying everything."

"When did you get to be ruthless, Kev? I never saw that before."

"Now I'm ruthless. Three months ago, I was a boy scout. Which is it, Sam?"

"I don't know. I don't know who you are anymore." Prentiss saw the van to the squadron approaching and turned away to meet it.

Seeing Kale already inside the truck as it rolled to a stop, Kevin said to Prentiss, "I'm walking back to the squadron. I don't want to be anywhere near that bastard ever again."

* * *

Later in the afternoon, Kevin pulled to a stop in front of his house and waited for the haunting voice of Roy Orbison to finish "Only the Lonely," resurrected by a disc jockey from a simpler time, eight years earlier. He turned off the engine. Some part of him wanted to scream out, but the rest of him felt just too beaten down.

After he came through the front door, Mary Clare ran to him, and he picked her up. "Hi, tiger lily," he said in a flat voice, not nuzzling her or tickling her as he usually did.

"Daddy sad."

"Well, maybe a little, but I love you."

"Love you. Mwah!"

He kissed her lightly on the cheek and put her down. She ran to the door to the back yard and called, "Mommy! Mommy! Daddy home."

Teresa came inside carrying wildflowers from her garden and put them on a kitchen counter. "You're home early. You look worn out," she said before kissing him on the cheek.

"Colonel Buford sent me home to get some rest," he said, deciding not to say anything more about the hour alone with the squadron commander in his office for a casual, but pointed, interrogation.

"What's the matter, love?"

For an instant, the words caught in his throat. Then he said, "John Reynolds was killed on the gunnery range this afternoon. He was in my flight."

"Oh, no!" she blurted out, as her eyes widened and her hands went upward involuntarily to cover her mouth. "Oh, no! No! No!" She came to him and embraced him, and he held on to her tightly. "Oh, my god! Ginny and their two boys," she whispered.

He held her for what seemed like a very long time, like a man about to drown finding a life preserver.

"Daddy? Mommy?"

Relaxing his arms from around Teresa, he knelt down on one knee and put his hand on his daughter's cheek. "It'll be okay, Mary Clare."

"Mommy sad too."

"Yes. But she'll be okay."

Teresa quickly wiped the tears from her eyes. "Yes, angel. Mommy will be fine. Let's go outside and finish picking some pretty flowers for Daddy."

Kevin picked Mary Clare up and handed her to Teresa. "I've got to phone my dad. I'll come outside in a few minutes."

She nodded silently, and then turned toward the back door, carrying Mary Clare with her.

Kevin walked to their bedroom and closed the door. He looked up his father's office number and dialed it.

"Hello. Mister O'Dea's office," the receptionist answered.

"May I speak to Mister O'Dea, please. I'm his son, Kevin."

"Of course, Captain O'Dea. Just a moment, please."

"Hi, Kevin. What's up?"

"Hi, Dad. Sorry to bother you at work, but something's happened out here, and I need your advice."

"Are Teresa and Mary Clare all right?"

"Yes. They're fine. Something happened during a flight I was on today."

"What happened?"

"One of the guys in the formation was killed. I think you may have known him."

"Who was it?"

"Lieutenant Colonel John Reynolds."

"Yes, I did know him. When we were working with the Air Staff in the Pentagon to put our story together on the need for a new bomber to replace the B-52, Reynolds was in the group that sharpened up our message for the Hill. He was an exceptional officer. What happened?"

Kevin recounted the briefing, the flight and the conversations with Reynolds before and with Prentiss and Buford afterward.

"You're right about people hanging for this one. The flight lead for sure. Maybe the squadron commander and possibly even the wing commander for lack of proper supervision. The important thing is that you tell the complete truth when you're questioned, including the part about the bad blood between you and the flight lead if that comes out. Otherwise, you'll compromise yourself as a witness. I'm talking to you as your lawyer now as well as your father, Kevin. Forget about settling your personal scores. There're much bigger things going on."

"Okay, Dad."

"I know General Gordon pretty well. He's the three-star in ops who looked out after Reynolds. I'll talk to him, and I'll get back to you with what I find out."

"Okay, Dad. Thanks."

"Give my love to Teresa and Mary Clare."

"I will, Dad. Bye."

"Bye, Kevin."

He hung up and sat on the edge of the bed, trying to summon up the energy to get out of his flight suit. He began unlacing his boots when the phone rang. He picked it up. "Hello?"

"Hi, Kev. It's Sean. I didn't know if you'd be home this early, but I had to try to talk to you."

It didn't sound like easygoing Sean. The voice on the other end was tense and halting. "What's going on, Sean? Where are you?"

There was a long pause. "I'm at my place in New Hampshire. I've gotten into some trouble."

"What's happened?"

"My draft deferment's been revoked, and . . . I've gotten a notice to report for induction."

"Tell me what happened."

"It was just so damned stupid. After one of the prep school's hockey games in March, a couple of friends of mine in town and I went out to a bar. We got a little wasted, you know, and one of the guys I was with says he's going to burn his draft card. He got a little loud about it, so the owner of the place told us to take it outside. Well, we went outside, and some of the other people in the bar came out with us. So, on the sidewalk outside . . . this guy I was with torches his draft card. I mean, shit, it wasn't a big protest or anything. You know? Kev, you know that I've never been interested in politics. All I ever wanted to do is be a good teacher and make a decent living. I mean we were just tanked up, and the people outside egged the guy on. Well, there was this guy with a camera, and he took a picture of us. I mean, it was no big deal, but this guy takes a fucking picture. Two days later . . . the picture shows up in the local paper. The next thing I know, I get a letter from my draft board telling me to report for a hearing on the status of my teaching deferment."

"Wait a minute, Sean. Your draft board's in Virginia, not New Hampshire."

"The guys on these draft boards talk to each other, Kev. Someone on the draft board in New Hampshire sent the paper to the board in Virginia. I went to the hearing while I was home at Mom and Dad's over spring break. I even hired a lawyer, . . . and he tried to tell them it was no big deal and that I was just watching. But I was laughing in the picture, and they seemed to get really pissed during the hearing. They really grilled me. After I got back to New Hampshire, I got this letter telling me that the bastards had revoked my deferment. Then I got this next letter . . . to report for induction."

"Have you told Dad about this?"

"No. Kev, you know what a hard-ass he is about things like this. He just wouldn't understand."

"Maybe he can help you fight it."

"That's over, Kev. I've found out that these local draft boards can do basically whatever they want with deferments."

"What're you going to do now?"

There was a long pause. "I'm not going to report for induction. I'm going to Canada."

"Oh, Jesus, Sean! You can't do that! You'll be a criminal. You'll never be able to come home again."

"I don't have any other choice, Kev. I'm not going to go to Vietnam to get killed in the fucking jungle."

"Look, Sean. Just because you've been drafted doesn't mean that you're going to end up carrying a rifle in Vietnam. You've got a college education, for Christ's sake. You're smart. You can find a way to get some kind of duty in a support unit."

"I don't think so, Kev. After the picture in the paper, I'm a marked man. The draft board in Virginia showed me that."

"That's not true, Sean. You're not thinking clearly. There've got to be some alternatives here. You've got to call Dad."

"I can't, Kev. I just can't. I tried to call Mom, but she wasn't home. I'm sorry to put this on you, but I had to talk to someone before I left. I've got to go. My ride's here. Bye, Kev."

"Sean, wait—" The line went dead after his brother hung up. He put the phone down and put his head in his hands, trying to fight back against a wave of helplessness he felt beginning to wash over him.

He heard a soft knock on the door. Teresa came in with a vase of flowers. When she saw his face, she put the flowers down, sat beside him on the bed and put her arms around him. "I'm so sorry, love."

In a hoarse, barely audible voice, he said, "Sean just called. He's been drafted, and he's running away to Canada."

She tightened her embrace. "Oh, my god, Kevin," she whispered.

"I feel like my heart's been ripped out."

"No matter what happens, I love you."

"I think I need to lie down for a while."

"Just rest, love. I'll be back in a little while," she said as she got up. She turned off the light and closed the door softly behind her.

Chapter 17

Wednesday, 28 August 1968

A black man in a blue uniform sat at the bar in a nearly empty airport lounge, sipping a beer and watching a baseball game on a television above shelves of bottles in front of him. Kevin worked his way around the bar to surprise him from the rear.

"Check six, Thud jock," Kevin said, grabbing Rob Johnson by the shoulders, using a pilot's call to warn about threats behind the tail, in the six o'clock position.

Rob turned around and smiled broadly at his former IP. He stood up and extended his hand. "Damn, sir. I never expected to see you here."

"No more of that sir stuff," he said, shaking Rob's hand. "It's Kevin, Rob. Remember?"

"Okay, sir. I mean Kevin. It's hard to forget all that conditioning."

"What flight are you on?"

"TWA at three forty-five."

"Me too."

The bartender came over. He was a short, slightly overweight man in his late forties with a blond crewcut. "What'll you have, Captain?" he asked with a slight accent that sounded vaguely European.

"Miller draft, please."

"Right. Coming right up." He filled a glass quickly, put it on the bar in front of Kevin and moved on to another customer. Kevin sat down on an empty bar stool next to Rob.

Rob asked, "Where're you coming in from?"

"Durango by way of Denver. Teresa and Mary Clare are staying at the family ranch while I'm in Thailand. How about you? Did you come in from DC?"

"No. I went back home for a few days after I finished at Nellis. Then it was off to survival training at Fairchild, and then directly here. Too bad I won't get to see any of the city before we have to catch our plane out. I've never seen San Francisco."

"Well, maybe on your return trip," Kevin said, after taking a long drink of his beer. "So, what did you think of Fairchild?"

"Well, one of the guys in my class put it pretty well after it was all over, when we were on the bus coming back from the woods. This survival instructor, a senior sergeant, was shooting the breeze with us, and he asked us what we thought about the evasion part of the course. We were pretty surly by that point, and the guy said, 'Well, sarge, I learned three important things: if you don't eat, you get hungry; if you walk a long way, you get tired; and, if you cut yourself, you bleed.' It cracked us all up."

"That about sums it up, all right."

"Aren't you a little late going to Thailand? I thought you said in April that you'd be over there by now."

"Yeah. Something happened. I got caught up in an accident investigation, and that delayed things."

"Was that the one with the Snakeye skipping up into the Thud on the range?"

"Yeah."

"Man, that was creepy. I read the preliminary accident report on that one. Talk about bad luck."

"Well, the accident board thought it was a little more than bad luck. They fried the flight lead. It was his bomb that hit the other airplane."

"What happened to him?"

"They didn't ground him outright, but he was reassigned to ground duty at a base in North Africa. He'll be there until he retires."

"Talk about exile."

"They exiled the element leader too. He was told quietly that he should volunteer for a second combat tour."

"Why did they go after the element lead?"

"It's a little complicated. My dad gave me the inside story after it was all over. He knows some of the people involved. The guy who was killed was a fast-burner lieutenant colonel who came up in SAC. After the accident, the bomber generals, including one in particular at the Pentagon, wanted heads to roll. They went after the flight lead and the squadron commander, but the fighter generals closed ranks around the squadron commander. It turns out that he has a four-star sponsor. So, a deal was cut, and they burned the two leaders in the flight. The accident board ended up saying that the element lead, being a fully qualified instructor, should have warned the flight lead about what they called an inherently dangerous tactic."

"I don't remember any element leader ever questioning a flight lead when I was at Nellis."

"Yeah. The element lead got screwed. He's a classmate of mine too. But as unfair as it was, it's nothing compared with this particular guy getting killed."

"It sounds like he was a good guy."

"One of the best." Kevin felt something he had pushed far down inside trying to claw its way to the surface. He abruptly changed the subject. "So, who's ahead?" he asked, looking up at the television.

"I don't know. I was daydreaming when you bounced me a minute ago."

"Does the daydream have a name?"

"Uh huh. Sandra. She's a nurse I met at Nellis."

"And how serious are things?"

"Well, if I weren't going off to war, I would've done the guy-on-one-knee thing. That'll have to wait for a while."

"When you do, put Teresa and me at the top of the list of well-wishers."

"You're already there."

Above them, the words, SPECIAL REPORT, appeared on the television screen. An announcer's voice said, "Now, at the top of the hour, we bring you this live update from the Democratic National Convention in Chicago."

The picture changed to show police in riot gear facing a throng of young, angry protestors. Among the signs they were carrying, several red-and-blue flags, imprinted with the gold star of the Viet Cong, waved back and forth. "After two days of escalating confrontations between anti-war demonstrators and law-enforcement authorities, city police and National Guard troops from Illinois, tensions continue to build here in Chicago. Within sight of the Democratic convention's headquarters at the Hilton Hotel, dissidents are gathering here in Grant Park for a march that could lead to the biggest clash yet between the two sides."

Mutual hatred leaped off the screen. The protesters, mostly college age, were taunting those they considered to be the guardians of a rotten-to-the-core political system. They were chanting an incendiary refrain, shouting, "Ho, Ho, Ho Chi Minh. The NLF is going to win," taking sides with the National Liberation Front, more commonly known as the Viet Cong. The working-class police, barely containing their rage, seethed at those they considered to be the pampered offspring of America's well-to-do, liberal elite, rich punks tearing down America, while they waited for the cover of darkness and the absence of TV cameras to deliver payback. Individual scuffles broke out as a few of the demonstrators entered the no man's land between the two sides, raised middle fingers at the cops, shouted obscenities and were beaten back with police batons.

"The convention is poised to nominate Hubert Humphrey tonight as the Democratic Party's standard bearer to contest Richard Nixon and George Wallace for the presidency, after Senator Edward Kennedy this morning refused to be drafted as the party's nominee. Eugene McCarthy, the early anti-war candidate who was eclipsed in the primaries by Robert Kennedy, has not yet indicated whether he'll endorse Humphrey. Clearly, the martyred Robert Kennedy, who galvanized the anti-war movement, and who was assassinated in June, has cast a long shadow over this convention. Now back to our scheduled programming."

"Well, what did you think of that, Captain?" the bartender asked as he took away Rob's empty glass.

"Pretty ugly."

"I can't believe it. A week ago, goddammed Russian tanks rolled into the country where I was born, and these college kids in Chicago are raising hell, supporting the Communists. When I was growing up in Prague, I dreamed about getting to America one day. In Czechoslovakia, America's a lighthouse. These goddammed kids are trying to turn it into an outhouse."

"I never thought I'd ever see anything like this," Kevin said. "I just hope the country can come out through the other side of this war without being completely ripped apart. Well," he said, looking at his watch, "it looks like it's time to get to the gate to catch our plane. How much do we owe you?"

"Where're you headed, Captain?"

"My friend here and I are on our way to a fighter wing in Thailand. We're going to give Ho Chi Minh another kind of greeting."

"In that case, these are on the house. Take care of yourselves."

"Thanks. We appreciate it."

Chapter 18

Saturday, 5 October 1968

The weatherman was ending his portion of the briefing for the early-afternoon flights in the auditorium of the wing's headquarters building. "So, it'll be clear over the southern portions of North Vietnam. On the way back, you may encounter some build-ups to forty thousand, but they'll be isolated, and you'll be able to get around them easily. Any questions? No? Okay, have good missions," he said as he turned off the light to the overhead projector, blanking the screen in front of the twenty officers in flight suits.

"Okay, let's go inside and brief," Major Rod Burke said to the three other pilots in his flight as he stood up when the auditorium lights came on. A veteran fighter pilot, Burke had flown Thuds from the time they were first operational. Before that, growing up in the mountains of southwestern Virginia, he had learned how to mask the wildness of his Scottish ancestors with the coal miner's stoicism handed down from his father and grandfather. At other times, he had given it free rein at high speed on a motorcycle, slaloming along twisting, narrow mountain roads.

Burke's three wingmen followed him through a side door into a restricted area where large, classified maps of portions of North Vietnam and Laos covered the walls. Adorned with various symbols and circles to show effective range, they depicted the latest intelligence about anti-aircraft guns and surface-to-air missiles that the pilots might encounter later that afternoon.

They sat down around the table in an empty briefing cubicle, and Burke distributed target folders put together by the wing's intelligence staff on orders from Seventh Air Force Headquarters in Saigon. Next, he gave out xerox copies of the mission card he had worked up that morning. "All right, guys, time hack. It'll be twelve-thirty in five seconds. . . . Hack. We're Shark flight today, and we'll be starting engines at thirteen-thirty," he said, meaning 1330 hours, or one thirty p.m. He moved quickly through the sequence of mission events that had become routine—taxi, takeoff, flight to rendezvous with a tanker, refueling and flight to the target area.

"We may be working with a FAC," he continued, meaning a forward air controller, a pilot in a spotter plane who patrolled a sector of the enemy's territory, who directed bomb-laden fighters from far-off bases to the most lucrative targets available. "If not, we'll hit this target," he said, opening his target folder. Inside each of the four folders was a reconnaissance photo of the target paired with a section of a map with the target's location circled in red. "Even though it looks like just another bunch of trees, the intell' wizards think it's a new staging area for supplies and ammunition, near the coast here, south of Dong Hoi, in Route Pack One," he said, shortening the formal designation of Route Package 1, one of the areas into which target planners at Seventh Air Force had subdivided all of North Vietnam. The numbers of the route packages got higher with increasing distance northward from South Vietnam to Hanoi.

"We've got the standard load of eight, seven fifties each," he continued, meaning eight, seven-hundred-and-fifty-pound bombs that the Thud carried, one under each wing and six on a bomb rack under its belly. It was the same bomb load carried by a four-engine B-17 flown by a ten-man crew two decades earlier. Even though airplanes carrying the 750 had changed radically in design and capability over the years, the bomb itself hadn't.

"Let's plan on using dive angles of forty-five degrees, with five hundred knots at bomb release. Since we'll be hitting an area target, east of this road and north of this river, I want you to spread your bombs out to maximize coverage of the target. Two will drop north of my bombs, three north of two's and so on. It'll be one pass and haul ass, unless we get something better than trees to attack. If we do, we'll make one strafe pass after we drop the bombs. So, make it count. We're not going to hang it out with multiple gun passes. I'm planning on attacking from west to east, so that the pullouts are headed toward the beach, in case any of us gets hit and has to bail out."

"The radio frequencies for SAR," Burke said, meaning search and rescue, "are on the mission card. Try to get as far out into the Gulf of Tonkin as you can before you punch. The rest of the flight will orbit the guy in the water in a standard strafe pattern until the rescue chopper arrives, and we'll shoot anything that looks North Vietnamese headed toward the guy who's down. If one of us gets heavy battle damage, or gets low on fuel because of a SAR, the whole flight will divert into Danang," he said, referring to the air base in northern South Vietnam.

Burke neared the end of the briefing. "Remember that the bad guys will be shooting at us with everything they've got, so keep your speed up in the target area, and move your airplane around so that they can't track you. We'll do a straight-ahead rejoin after we drop, heading west, and I'll hold three hundred and fifty knots until we're all joined up. Then it'll be the usual trip home. Bingo fuel will be seven thousand pounds, and I'll try to get a post-strike tanker if any of us gets light on gas on the way back. If I can't, the element with the low-gas jet will divert into Udorn," he said, naming an air base in northeastern Thailand between theirs at Takhli and the target in North Vietnam. "All right, that's it. Any questions?"

Kevin shook his head along with the two other pilots.

"Okay, let's go back to the squadron and suit up."

They stood up and put their folders into strap-handled bags that they all carried to lug mission documents, navigation charts and check lists to their airplanes. Beyond anyone's memory, someone had started calling the bags purses. Despite its feminine overtones, the irony had for some reason appealed to the pilots, and the name had stuck. They walked outside into muggy tropical heat and put on Australian-style bush hats, one side of the brim attached to the crown. On the hatbands, in ink strokes in groups of five, they kept a running count of the missions they'd flown.

They piled into a blue pickup truck with a double-size cab. Wooden side-boards atop its bed walls in back were painted yellow-gold, their squadron's color, and black lettering proclaimed the truck to belong to the 357th TFS, short for tactical fighter squadron. A large version of the squadron's patch insignia, featuring a red-tongued dragon's head, completed the side-boards' decorations.

Burke took the wheel on the American left in the cab and drove off into the left lane of the roadway, complying with Thai traffic laws.

"When I get back to the States, I'll probably have a head-on with somebody after driving on the wrong side of the road like this for the last four months."

After a short drive, he pulled up in front of the 357th's building, and the four of them got out and went inside, through an entrance designated by a sign as the door to Personal Equipment and Life Support. They walked to the places where their parachutes, combat vests and g suits hung from pipes extending from two walls of the room, beneath locked wooden cabinets. Their flight helmets sat on top of the wooden boxes.

Like the others, Kevin began the quiet ritual of removing the things that connected him to the outside world. He unlocked the combination padlock securing his box, and after taking his Air Force identification card out of his wallet, along with a twenty-dollar bill, he put the billfold inside. He put the bill and his ID card into a plastic tobacco pouch he stored in the cabinet when he wasn't flying, placing them next to a second card already inside the pouch, one that complied with the requirements of the Geneva Convention on the treatment of prisoners of war. It identified him as a member of the armed forces of the United States. He put the pouch into the breast pocket of his flight suit. Next, he took off his Academy class ring and his wedding band, and securing them inside, he locked the box again.

Carrying only the essentials of his identity, he began dressing for the mission. He zipped himself into his g suit and then put on his survival vest. Zippered compartments that protruded from the front of the vest held the things he would need immediately if he were forced down—survival radios, smoke flares, a first aid kit, and other bits and pieces of gear, all crammed into zippered, cloth bulges that could make the difference between rescue and capture.

And water. He carried water in two plastic flasks that he had bought and put inside the ankle pockets of his g suit. On their way to Thailand, he and Rob had stopped at Clark Air Force Base in the Philippines to attend a one-week school on survival in the jungle. The school's instructors had relayed stories from pilots who had been rescued, tales about the powerful thirst that shock, fear, being hunted and evading through the jungle inflicted. Knowing this, the enemy who had hunted them had staked out sources of water, waiting for their dehydrated prey to come out of hiding to satisfy a maddening craving.

One last thing, he said to himself as he walked to a circular metal rack in the center of the room that held their pistols. He took the .38-caliber revolver assigned to him, put six tracer bullets into its cylinder, and shoved the weapon into a leather holster sewn to his survival vest, under his left armpit. Its manufacturer called it the Combat Masterpiece. Pilots had few illusions about shooting it out with an enemy armed with automatic weapons, but the pistol could fire tracer rounds that might attract a rescue helicopter above a triple-layer jungle canopy. Like most of the other pilots, Kevin carried extra ammunition in plastic bags in his g suit pockets, along with extra batteries for his survival radios.

Returning to his locker, he pulled on his parachute, put his helmet into its carrying bag and picked up his purse. *Ready*. He walked outside and got into the squadron's van that transported pilots laden with equipment to the flight line. The Thai driver they called Ting relaxed at the wheel, waiting for the last of the pilots in the flight to come out of the building. Burke and Rob were already inside.

"What mission's this for you, Kevin?" Burke asked.

"Ten total and seven over the North, sir," he replied, differentiating between his warm-up missions in Laos and the seven with the varsity.

"How about you, Rob?"

"Nine and five, sir."

"Well then, you guys are old hands by now."

"Yes, sir."

Captain Joe England hurried through the door and got into the van. "Sorry to hold you up, guys. The valve in my mask was sticking. I had to have a new one put in."

Ting pulled away and drove the van onto the flight line, between rows of revetments that corralled the wing's Thuds. Filled with sand between its metal walls, each revetment enclosed one jet and protected against the loss of multiple airplanes parked next to one another from an accidental explosion of the weapons they carried. Ting dropped Burke off at his jet first and stopped at Kevin's next.

"Have good flight, sir," Ting said as the second pilot stepped out of the van.

"Thanks, Ting." He walked over to his jet and greeted its crew chief, a blond, muscular man, about the same age, stripped to the waist and wearing green fatigue trousers and combat boots. "Afternoon, chief. How's the bird?"

"It's in great shape, sir. All ready for you to send eight, seven-fifties right up Uncle Ho's ass."

"Good. Let me put my stuff up in the cockpit, and then I'll give it a quick walkaround. How's the tan coming along?"

The crew chief laughed. "Well, sir, it's just another great day at the beach."

Kevin climbed the ladder to the cockpit, feeling the weight of the equipment he was carrying. He stowed his gear, putting his parachute on the airplane's ejection seat and his helmet on top of the jet's windscreen. Unburdened, he descended the ladder to look at the airplane's exterior.

As he walked around the jet, he saw the telltale marks of a veteran that had flown to Route Package 6, to Hanoi. Looking closely, he saw several access panels that didn't fit quite flush the way they should and small cracks around some of the panels' fasteners, blemishes caused by many pilots before him putting g's on the airplane under fire, pulling on the stick for all they were worth, to escape guns and missiles trying to bring them down. Jinking, the pilots called it—random, high-g maneuvering inside the lethal range of guns and missiles to throw off a gunner's aim. Several odd-shaped skin patches on the Thud's tail surfaces showed that a few of the gunners, firing small-caliber weapons or exploding flak shells, had nicked their target. Two 450-gallon fuel tanks attached to the inboard pylons on the wings looked new in fresh paint. *Maybe the guy on the last mission jettisoned his tanks when they were shooting at him.*

He made one last check before ascending the ladder again. He looked closely at each of the six 750s on the jet's belly, examining the two fuses on each bomb and arming wires that ran through them. A ring of yellow paint on the nose of each bomb declared it to be the real thing, and he didn't want an arming wire to come loose in flight, allowing a fuse to arm a bomb while it sat on the rack under his cockpit. The name the jet's pilot had painted on its belly above the bomb rack caught his eye. *The Iron Banshee. I wonder what I'll name mine when I get one,* he thought for a moment, musing about the day when he would rise into the group of veteran pilots in the squadron, those assigned a Thud they could call their own for a few months, when others ahead of him completed their tours and went home.

Satisfied with the load he was carrying, he went up the ladder again, strapped in and got the cockpit ready for engine start.

He looked at his watch and adjusted the jet's cockpit clock to the same time. At 1330, he saw black smoke rise behind Burke's Thud over steel walls, two revetments away. He pressed the start button in his own cockpit, and the jet's engine began turning over as a black-powder start cartridge began burning in a cylinder latched to a housing over the engine's turbine blades. Watching the engine rpm gauge, he brought the throttle from off to idle, letting jet fuel begin to flow into the engine. Dormant systems, and the cockpit instruments that awakened with them, oil, electrical and hydraulic, began stirring to life as fuel ignited in the engine, spooling it up rapidly to idle speed.

He went through the post-start checks quickly, wanting to be ready when Burke called.

"Shark flight, check."

"Two," Kevin answered.

"Three," England replied.

"Four," Rob transmitted last.

"Takhli ground, this is Shark flight. Taxi four."

"Roger, Sharks. The active is runway one eight," ground control responded, meaning the runway oriented to the south. "Altimeter, three zero, zero one. Cleared to the arming area."

"Sharks, roger."

Kevin saw the tail on Burke's Thud begin to move forward, and he held up his fists and jerked his thumbs outward, signaling his crew chief to remove the wooden chock that immobilized his jet. The bare-chested airman sprinted under the airplane, kicked a wooden block away from the tire of the left gear and ran back in front of the Thud he had sweated over for hours, to get it ready for a second go that day after an early-morning mission. Visible to Kevin again, he began motioning with upraised arms for a new pilot to start another sortie.

Kevin advanced the throttle, and the husky, weighted-down airplane rolled forward. In almost one motion, he tapped his brakes to check them and then turned the jet out of the revetment. The crew chief came to attention and saluted as the airplane made the turn, and Kevin snapped his hand to his helmet in reply. In line behind Burke, he selected pure oxygen on the cockpit regulator to keep from breathing the exhaust fumes of the lead airplane.

The four jets came out of the revetments onto the main taxiway, waddling with the load of fuel and bombs they carried under their wings and bellies, taking proper sequence behind the leader. After nearly a mile of slow taxiing, they turned onto an expanded section of taxiway, adjacent to the takeoff end of the runway. Resting near two trucks parked at the edge the pavement, a group of men in noise-suppressing ear muffs, the younger ones barechested and the older ones wearing fatigue shirts with five or six stripes on the sleeves, waited to swarm the jets when they stopped. Taxiing their Thuds into positions next to one another by following lines painted on the taxiway, the four pilots halted their procession and raised their hands out of the cockpit, away from cockpit switches, where the arming crews could see them.

One of them plugged a microphone and headset into Kevin's jet. "Afternoon, sir."

"Afternoon, chief."

"We'll be done in a jiffy, sir. Your jet looks good. No fuel or hydraulic leaks. We're taking the pins out now," the enlisted man advised, telling the pilot that ground-safety devices, attached to red cloth streamers, were being removed from explosive charges in the jet's bomb rack and wing pylons. "Okay, sir, you're ready to go. I'm going to unplug now and hand you over to the padre. Have a good mission, sir."

"Thanks, chief." He was sweating heavily in the afternoon heat under his flight gear and was anxious to be airborne.

Kevin's interphone went dead when the armorer unplugged, and an officer in a fatigue uniform walked casually down the row of Thuds, waving to each pilot as he went. An embroidered blue cross above the left pocket of his shirt identified him as one of the wing's chaplains. Kevin recognized Major Ben Edwards, the ranking man among the three Protestant ministers at Takhli, a Methodist, who was an honorary member of the 357th. He had drawn the afternoon's arming-area duty that rotated among the chaplains. Kevin waved back.

The enlisted men returned to their trucks to await the next flight to be armed, and Burke moved his Thud forward into a turn toward the runway, lowering his canopy and then calling for a channel change on the radio. He checked them in. "Shark flight, check."

"Two."

"Three."

"Four."

"Takhli tower, Shark flight's number one with four.

"Roger, Shark flight. Winds are two zero zero at ten. Change to departure control. Cleared for takeoff."

"Sharks, roger." Burke taxied the lead Thud onto the runway and stopped near the left edge of the pavement. The other pilots lined up on him, in echelon, taking up the rest of the runway's width. After he put them on the frequency for departure control, he advanced his throttle to full r.p.m. His wingmen moved theirs forward in response, as the nose on Burke's jet lowered from the jump in engine thrust, as black smoke rose behind him.

Kevin looked at his engine instruments. *Everything's okay.* He turned his head to look at England, who was turned looking at Rob. In a succession of head nods, from four to lead, each man signaled his readiness for takeoff. After Kevin nodded to him, Burke released brakes, and the bang of his afterburner was audible to the others, as flame leaped from the tail of the lead airplane. Kevin pressed a knob on the cockpit's clock that started the second hand moving.

At ten seconds, he released brakes and moved his throttle outboard to light the jet's burner. A fraction of a second later, he heard a muffled bang and felt a surge in thrust come through the ejection seat into his back. The Thud picked up speed, 50,000 pounds of airplane, fuel and weapons beginning to rumble down the runway like a heavily loaded freight train.

Kevin glanced back and forth from the runway ahead to his engine instruments, looking for abnormal indications and warning lights, ready to yank the throttle back and jerk the drag-chute handle to abort the takeoff. After lumbering down the runway for over a mile, he started easing the Thud's nose up when the airspeed indicator showed that he was approaching flying speed. The airplane rolled for another thousand feet before it lifted off sluggishly with the weight it was carrying in the tropical heat. It accelerated slowly above the runway, almost reluctantly, and Kevin raised the gear. He breathed easier as the Thud awakened to the air and consented to gallop. Bringing its flaps up as it thundered on, he waited for the airplane to reach 300 knots, and he brought the throttle inboard to turn off its fuel-gulping afterburner. He picked up Burke's jet above him and left, in a turn, and he rolled left to join the leader in formation.

Forty-five minutes later, refueling completed, the four Thuds dropped off their tanker and turned east. Burke took up a heading to a rendezvous point off the TACAN at Danang given to him by the A,B, triple-C, or ABCCC, meaning the Airborne Command and Control Center with the call sign, Hillsboro. A colonel and his staff aboard Hillsboro, a C-130 transport plane jammed with communications gear, controlled the daylight air war, deciding whether a flight would strike its pre-assigned target or be diverted to a target of opportunity. For targets of opportunity, Hillsboro matched up FACs calling in for fighters with strike flights checking in during dead time on their tankers while refueling.

Shark flight glided across the afternoon sky in spread formation. Burke called for a new radio frequency and Kevin began setting his armament switches after they checked in, during the en route lull before they attacked.

"Misty four two, Misty four two," Burke called for the FAC he had been assigned. "This is Shark flight on your freq."

"Shark flight, roger. This is Misty four two. Go ahead."

"Shark flight's about forty miles out from the rendezvous point at fifteen thousand."

"Roger. Give me your lineup."

"Roger. Shark's a flight of four Thuds, with eight, seven-fifties and a thousand rounds of twenty mike mike apiece."

"Okay, Shark flight. That's a good load for this target. Keep heading east. I've got a good bearing on you. I'll join up on you and lead you in to the target."

"Roger," Burke replied. "Sharks, green 'em up."

Kevin set the last of the armament switches for his bomb rack and gun, and faint green lights in the selector buttons for the wing and belly stations came on. He uncaged his sight, and dialed in a dive-bomb setting he got from a table in his weapons checklist. The sight reticle, the pipper and the bright-orange rings around it, moved downward in his windscreen.

The coast of Vietnam became visible as they flew eastward, and as the weatherman had predicted, no clouds obscured Route Pack One. Feeling thirsty in anticipation, Kevin reached behind him, to the right side of his head rest, and pulled a plastic tube out of its clamp holder. He unfastened his oxygen mask and put the tube in his mouth, sucking a mouthful of ice water from a steel bottle mounted behind the head rest, once more silently thanking the genius who had designed this feature into the Thud.

Scanning past Burke's jet, he saw a single swept-wing airplane in the distance above them, about five miles away, going in the opposite direction. It began a hard turn toward them, losing altitude as its nose came around. He stowed the drinking tube and reconnected his mask.

"Misty four two has Shark flight in sight. I'm at your two o'clock, high, in a descending right turn. I'll join on your number-two jet."

"Roger," Burke replied. "Shark lead has a visual on Misty four two. Cleared to join."

Craning his neck rearward, Kevin followed the solo jet as it swept behind Shark flight. Its pilot dove below them, picking up overtake speed, and then pulled his airplane up, gaining altitude and sliding into loose formation on Kevin's left wing. It was an F-100, the same type flown by the Thunderbirds, but this one had a working-class look in drab camouflage paint, with fuel tanks and rockets hung under its wings and with two seats for a pilot and an observer.

"We're about thirty miles out from the target," Misty 42 radioed. "You guys drop back on me about a mile in trail, and I'll mark the target with a smoke rocket. I'll set you up for west-to-east attack runs out of right turns."

"Roger," Burke replied. "Sharks, take spacing."

"We'll be hitting the south bank of a river. We saw signs of activity there a few hours ago," Misty 42 advised. "I want lead to hit my smoke, and then I want the rest of the flight to walk your bombs east, right along the river bank."

"Roger," Burke said. "Sharks acknowledge."

"Two."

"Three."

"Four."

Burke turned his jet left a few degrees in heading, keeping his airspeed up while sliding the flight slowly behind the FAC. England, with Rob in tow, made a more pronounced left turn, taking his element out left and behind Shark two. As they approached the target, Misty 42 led a loose chain of four other jets, in echelon off his left wing.

Kevin recognized the target area from the target folder he had studied earlier. Instead of hitting the pre-planned area north of the river, Misty 42 was calling for a strike on its south bank.

"Four two's in," the FAC called, as he rolled his jet inverted and pulled its nose earthward. Dropping quickly below the Thuds, the F-

100 rolled upright again, hesitated for a second and then fired a rocket at the ground. Its missile away, the spotter jet rolled right, the first in a series of jinking turns it made as it climbed back to altitude. A cloud of dense white smoke blossomed in the trees near the south bank of the river.

"Lead's in," Burke called, rolling his Thud into its attack dive.

Kevin delayed a few seconds and then began his attack. "Two's in." He rolled inverted and pulled on the stick to get the Thud's nose down quickly. Sensing his dive angle, plunging earthward nearly vertically, he rolled upright, placing the sight reticle's rings and pipper just west of the smoke. Below him, Burke began his pullout, rolling into a climbing right turn toward South Vietnam. A few seconds later, the leader's bombs exploded, engulfing the white smoke. The world below them silenced by closed cockpits and padded helmets, orange fireballs from the lead Thud's bombs blossomed soundlessly along the riverbank.

"Three's in."

Kevin looked at his attitude indicator to confirm his dive angle. *Fifty degrees and shallowing. Airspeed.* The indicator showed 450, and he brought his throttle to idle, leading a release speed of 500 knots. His sight reticle tracked eastward though the smoke of Burke's bombs and reached undisturbed jungle green next to the river on the other side.

"Four's in"

Kevin's altimeter showed 6,000 feet, and he mashed the bomb-release button on the stick, holding it down long enough for all eight bombs to release. The bombs gone, he released the button and rolled slightly left, jinking opposite to Burke's pull-off direction, and put five climbing g's on the Thud as he firewalled the throttle.

"Keep it moving, guys!" Misty 42 called as he orbited the strike at altitude, "I see ground fire! There's tracer from automatic weapons."

Relaxing the g's for a fraction of a second as the jet's nose swept up through the horizon, Kevin reversed direction, rolling right to follow Shark lead, before pulling the g's back on to continue climbing. Looking quickly behind him, he saw his bombs explode silently, followed by another larger, soundless explosion.

"Shit hot!" Misty 42 called. "Two's got a secondary."

England's bombs ignited another secondary explosion, and fires raged in the trees south of the river as the third Shark jinked hard, climbing to altitude. Rob's bombs hit beyond England's.

As the three wingmen climbed to rejoin their leader, Burke set up an wide orbit around the target. Misty 42 called, "Nice work, guys. Hold high while I get the BDA," he said, meaning the bomb-damage assessment to be reported to Seventh Air Force. The F-100 plunged earthward again in a series of jinking turns to inspect the target. As he completed his pass and pulled up, he called excitedly, "Four's bombs blew some camouflage off some sampans! Can you guys strafe along the south bank to get the boats?"

"That's affirm," Burke called as his orbit took him west of the target again. "Lead's in. Everybody keep your speed up, and keep it moving."

Kevin dialed in a new sight setting from memory. The pipper moved far upward in the windscreen, from a depressed setting for dive bombing to one calculated for gun ballistics. "Two's in." Taking close spacing on Burke's Thud, he rolled in behind the leader, but slightly offset to make the gunners divide their fire. He pushed on the throttle, making sure he had full power, and glanced at his airspeed. *Building to 500.* Closer to the ground in a slight turn, he saw two silent streams of tracer fire tear above his canopy as he worked the pipper up to the river bank. As Burke pulled off ahead of him, he picked up the sampans and eased the pipper slightly above them, closing the range. *Now!* He pulled the trigger and sent a long, roaring burst into the boats from his Thud's six-barrel gun. He pulled up hard, weaving through the ground fire in jinking turns to get back to altitude.

The sound jolted him. It was unmistakable—like the crack made by the end of a knife handle being rapped sharply against a wooden table. *I'm hit!* He pulled harder on the stick to gain altitude more quickly as his eyes locked onto his engine instruments. *Normal.* Calming himself before he pressed the mike button, he transmitted, "Two's hit."

"Roger, two," Burke replied quickly. "I'm at your two o'clock. Where're you hit?"

"Can't tell. But all the instruments look okay."

"Okay, expedite the join-up and I'll look you over."

There were no warning lights and no abnormal instrument readings. Relaxing slightly, he concentrated on the rejoin on Shark lead. Burke rolled out of his turn and took up a westerly heading. He looked back. England and Rob were climbing below him, closing on the leader.

Misty 42 transmitted, "Nice strafe job on the boats, guys. We counted six on our last pass, and it looks like you got them all. Just a shit-hot job all around, Sharks."

"Thanks," Burke replied. "It was good working with you, Misty. So long."

"Roger. So long."

"Sharks, go squadron common," Burke ordered.

"Two."

"Three."

"Four."

Kevin dialed 357.0 into his radio as he slid into position on Burke's left wing.

After he checked the flight in, Shark lead said, "All right, Sharks, let's look each other over for battle damage. Check two and four first." Burke pointed forward and then held up two fingers, telling Kevin he should take the lead of the first element temporarily. When Kevin nodded, Burke eased his Thud toward Shark two, sliding under his wingman's jet to look for belly damage, before he moved to Kevin's left wing and pulled up, to search for holes on top. "You look good underneath, Shark two, but check the left side of your canopy behind you. I think I see something."

Kevin twisted left in his seat to look behind and saw neat, round holes through both layers of the canopy's plexiglass. "Roger, it looks like a small-arms hit."

"Is everything still running okay?"

"Affirmative."

"Okay, we'll take it on home."

Burke resumed the lead, and Kevin checked his Thud for hits. Finding none, he moved back to his position on the left wing and called, "Shark lead looks clean."

"Four's clean," England reported when his turn came.

"Three's clean," Rob said a minute later.

As Shark flight settled into spread formation for the trip back of nearly 400 miles, Kevin began to relax and felt dryness in his throat for the first time. He unfastened his mask and pulled the drinking tube from the head rest to his mouth. *Nothing. Strange.* Letting go of the tube, reaching down, he unzipped one of his g-suit pockets, took out the plastic flask he found there, opened it and drank it dry.

* * *

The mission nearly over, Kevin flared his Thud to touchdown and pulled on the drag-chute handle. *Good chute.* As he lowered the jet's nosewheel to the runway, he glanced at the cockpit clock. *Two and a half hours.* He slowed to taxi speed near the end of the runway and turned onto the last taxiway, unlocking and raising his canopy after the turnoff. He unfastened his mask and jettisoned his drag chute on the grass infield between the runway and the taxiway, then headed for the de-arming area. Shark lead was pulling out as he rolled to a stop. In less than a minute, armorers put safety pins back in and motioned for him to start taxiing again. He made another turn to return to the revetments, taxiing parallel to the runway.

Ahead on the ramp, by themselves, sat five forlorn-looking F-111s. Once called the TFX, the swing-wing airplane had been a special project of former Secretary of Defense McNamara in his quest for economy in the Pentagon. He had wanted both the Navy and the Air Force to put large numbers of one type of aircraft into service to save money. The Navy, though, had managed to wriggle out of the program, but the Air Force had stayed with it, calling the operational version the F-111. Equipped with advanced radar and attack systems, it had promised major increases in capability.

The Air Force had rushed the F-111 into combat with disastrous results. Out of a combat test force of eight jets, three had crashed on solo missions at night out of Takhli, and the loss of another at Nellis had grounded the remaining five. *I guess this is what they mean by limbo,* Kevin thought as he taxied past the buttoned-up airplanes.

Reaching the revetments, Kevin taxied slowly into the one he had started from and shut down his engine on the crew chief's signal. Moving quickly from left to right around the cockpit from memory, he turned switches off to complete the shutdown.

"How's the airplane, sir?" the airman asked as he put a ladder on the jet's canopy rail and started up.

"Bad news, chief. I took a hit in the canopy."

The crew chief found the holes and looked at the back of the ejection seat. "Well, sir, there's more." Taking a screwdriver out of his pocket, he started prying behind the head rest. "Got it." He showed Kevin the misshapen slug he had retrieved. "It went through the water bottle and lodged in the head rest, sir."

"It's a good thing the guy who fired it didn't lead me by another foot. I'd have a real headache now."

"Yes, sir. Do you want to keep it for a souvenir?"

"Okay," Kevin said, accepting the slug and putting it into the sleeve pocket of his flight suit, wondering whether or not he was violating some fundamental rule of luck. "Sorry about the damage, chief, but we blew up a lot of ammo the bad guys were taking south, and we shot up some boats they were using to get it there. That's when I got hit. On the strafe pass. But maybe some grunts in South Vietnam won't die as a result."

"That's good, sir. Don't worry about the Banshee, sir. She's been hit a lot worse. At least this time there's no skin damage. We'll just pop in a new ejection seat and put on a new canopy, and she'll be ready to fly again. I'm glad you're okay, sir," the crew chief said as he began helping Kevin unstrap.

"Thanks, chief." Nothing else had to be said.

After getting out of the cockpit and collecting his gear, Kevin descended the ladder as Ting pulled up in front of the revetment in the squadron's van. "Thanks again for the loan of the Banshee, chief. I'd like to fly it again after it's fixed."

"Yes, sir. Anytime."

He got into the van and took the cold can of beer Ting handed him after taking it out of a cooler next to the driver's seat. "Major Burke say you got hit, sir."

He put his helmet bag and purse down, opened the beer and took a long chug. "Ah, that's good. Yeah, I did, but we hit them a lot harder than they hit me."

"Good, sir. I take you back to squadron first, then get rest of flight."

"Thanks, Ting."

Burke was stowing the last of his flight gear when Kevin walked through the door. "Hey, Kevin. Did they find whatever went through your canopy?"

"Yes, sir," he said, taking the slug out of his sleeve pocket. He showed it to his flight commander. "The crew chief found this in the back of my head rest."

"Looks like a rifle round. It's good that it wasn't from one of those bigger guns that were trying to put tracer on us."

"Yes, sir," he said after stowing his parachute.

"Well, you've taken your first hit. You need to shake it off. Don't worry about it. I've taken a few. I even had to punch out once, but as you can see, I got picked up and I'm still in the game."

"Yes, sir."

"Let's meet at the truck after the other two guys get back in. Say fifteen minutes. We'll do a quick debrief with the intell' guys at wing, and then we'll all go to the club for some drinks and dinner. You can tell everybody at the bar about the luck o' the Irish."

Kevin grinned. "Yes, sir. Sounds good."

Later at the bar, five officers, four in flying suits and one in fatigues, passed around the slug that Kevin had handed them.

"So, Kevin," Ben Edwards asked with a smile as he took the battered piece of metal from Rob Johnson, "when can I expect to see you, to start your conversion to Methodism, now that you've seen the power of our influence with the Lord?"

Kevin laughed. "Well, as grateful as I am for your send-off this afternoon, my brother-in-law's a Jesuit priest, and I'm sure he'd claim full credit."

Edwards put his empty glass on the bar as he got ready to leave, handing the slug back to Kevin. "Hmm, I didn't know about that. Yeah, on second thought, you might be too much trouble. Those Jebbies don't let go easily. Well, I've got to go make a sweep across the base to look for more wayward souls. But I'll be back here after you guys get a few more under your belts, after tomorrow's flight schedule gets posted. You may be more susceptible to my evangelizing then. See you later."

Joe England waited until the chaplain was out the door and said, "Now that Ben's gone, let me give you the rest of the story. We kicked their fucking asses today. It was shit hot, Charlie," he said to Charlie Rasmussen. "The FAC we worked with was outstanding. He put the smoke in right on top of the bastards. We got two major secondaries out of our bombs, and their shit was still burning after we pulled off from the strafe passes. Too bad you're in that brand-x squadron, instead of the Three Fifty-Seventh," he added with a grin, poking on the patch from one of the wing's other squadrons sewn on Charlie's flight suit. "You might have been with us on a real mission instead of dinking around in Barrel Roll today," he said, using the code name for northern Laos.

"Yeah," Charlie agreed. "All we did was bomb this mountain trail in the jungle. The FAC we worked with, this guy in an unmarked airplane with a Raven call sign, said we were attacking enemy pack animals."

"Barrel Roll's strange," Burke said. "Those pack animals could've belonged to opium runners or to the Pathet Lao," he said, meaning the Laotian Communists allied with the North Vietnamese. "There're all sorts of weird airplanes operating up there, a lot of them flown by guys working for the CIA. When I was here at Takhli on TDY for the first time," he said, meaning temporary duty away from home station, "when we were still going to Route Pack Six, a guy had to bail out over Barrel Roll on the way home after being shot up. He got picked up by some civilians in a helicopter with no markings. It was just painted gray. They flew him to Udorn after refueling at this dirt landing strip on top of some mountain. He had to help them pump gas into the helicopter out of some fuel drums that were hidden away there, and they didn't say much during the flight. They just dropped him off and took off again."

"Well, sir," Charlie said, "I'm glad we don't have to go up there all that often, since those sorties don't count toward a hundred missions."

"Yeah. Well, Charlie, why don't we continue this at dinner, so Joe can keep ragging on you."

Charlie grinned. "Okay, sir. I'm a glutton for punishment."

"Good. I'm going to duck around the corner for a minute to see if tomorrow's schedule's been posted in the stag bar. I'll join up with you guys at the table."

"Why don't you and Kev go find us some seats," England said. "I've got to hit the head first."

"Me too," Rob added.

Charlie and Kevin left the bar and walked through the club's dining room immediately adjacent to it. Tables with seating for four were closest to the bar and were occupied by officers in support units. Four round tables, each with seating for twelve, elevated on a platform, were at the far end of the room and were reserved for the wing's fighter pilots and their guests. Three of the tables were full, and the other was being vacated by a large group that was standing up to return to the bar. As the others left, Sam Prentiss stayed seated to continue his conversation with Nancy Pritchard, a nurse captain.

"Hi, guys," Charlie said. "Mind if we join you?"

"Hi, Charlie. Hi, Kevin. Please do," Nancy said with a smile, in her lilting Tennessee accent. "But I'm just about to leave."

"Don't let us scare you away."

"I'd love to stay, but I've got to get to the hospital. I promised one of the other nurses that I'd fill in for her for a few hours."

"Our loss then," Charlie said as he sat down.

Kevin took a seat next to Charlie. As a Thai waitresses began to clear away dirty dishes and as Nancy stood to leave, he retrieved a copy of the *Stars and Stripes,* the newspaper printed for troops in the Pacific theater, that had been left on the table.

"Bye, guys," Nancy said as she left, waving.

Kevin turned the paper over to look at the headlines. LeMay to Run With Wallace, it read in bold print. "Unbelievable," Kevin murmured as he started to read the story.

"What's unbelievable?" Charlie asked.

"General LeMay running on the same ticket with Wallace."

"What's wrong with that?" Sam asked.

Kevin looked at his classmate, not knowing what to say. Their long friendship had been badly damaged by the aftereffects of Reynolds' death, and he didn't want to destroy whatever was left of it.

"Well, Sam," Charlie intervened, "you'll have to admit that Wallace isn't exactly mainstream."

"That's why I'm goin' to vote for him. He's the only one o' the three who wants to win this war. You got happy Hubert Humphrey who'll git picked clean by Ho Chi Minh in Paris at the so-called peace talks, or you got tricky Dick Nixon with his secret plan to end the war. What complete bullshit. Look, I got to go too. See ya later," Sam said as he rose abruptly and walked away toward the bar.

"What the hell was that all about?" Charlie asked.

"It's me, I think. Sam and I had some pretty harsh words about the accident at McConnell, and he thinks I'm partially responsible for the screwing he got from the accident board."

"That's completely unfair."

"Yeah, I know it is, but this's one of those life-is-not-fair things. Have you read this article?"

"Yeah. Wallace introduced LeMay as his VP candidate at a news conference in Pittsburgh. The most interesting line in the article is LeMay saying that nukes are just like any other weapon in the arsenal."

"Oh, shit. You're kidding. Did he really say that?"

"Yeah, he did. It's all so simple. If iron bombs aren't working for you, just drop the big one, and everything will be just dandy. Well, I guess that's what passes for deep strategic thinking these days among LeMay's generation of generals. Anyway, he got a free ride in the *Stars and Stripes* article, but I can't wait to see how the rest of the press covers the story. All in all, this's not the best thing that's ever happened to the Air Force. A former chief of staff waving nukes around like they're no big deal and running on the same ticket with the number-one segregationist in the country."

Chapter 19

Thursday, 31 October 1968

The pilots of the 357th were in high spirits as they waited for a C-130 transport on final approach to Takhli to land. They stood just outside the covered-porch entrance of the base-ops building, wearing bright-yellow jump suits cut to resemble flying suits. Each was embroidered with an officer's rank on the shoulders and with pilot's wings over a script-stitched name on the left chest. Patches completed the suits' decorations—an American flag at the top of the left sleeve, the squadron's dragon's-head insignia on the right chest and a patch shaped like an arrowhead on the right sleeve, featuring a top-view rendering of the Thud and, below it, the jet's official designation, F-105 Thunderchief.

Other patches gave an individual flair. Many wore a black jolly-roger flag with the words YANKEE AIR PIRATE stitched under its skull and crossbones, mocking the epithet that the North Vietnamese used in their stilted propaganda diatribes, broadcast over Radio Hanoi, to denounce American pilots as war criminals. Production of these party suits, as the pilots called them, provided a thriving business for a Thai tailor who ran a shop in the middle of the base and who outfitted newly arrived pilots with the official garb for hell-raising in the stag bar at the officers' club. Like those in the 357th, pilots in the wing's two other fighter squadrons sported party suits in the colors of their units, blue for one and red for the other, when they wanted to blow off steam.

The C-130 completed its short landing roll and taxied off the runway, making its way to the ramp in front of base ops. Operating out of

Bangkok with the call sign Klong, the Thai word for canal, a small fleet of C-130s made two circuits a day to connect the airbases used by Americans in Thailand, carrying passengers and light cargo around the country.

Rod Burke walked out the door of the building and onto the porch, looking for Kevin and Rob. Seeing them on the edge of the crowd, he walked up behind them. "Hey, guys."

The two pilots turned around to greet their flight commander. "What did you find out, sir?" Kevin asked.

"What Charlie told you is the straight scoop, Kevin. The last strike flight to North Vietnam takes off at fourteen-thirty tomorrow, and after that, a permanent bombing halt goes into effect."

Sam Prentiss, standing a few feet away, heard Burke and walked over. "Sir, did I hear you say it's true?"

"Yeah, Sam. The duty officer at wing just got the confirmation message from Seventh Air Force. After tomorrow, there'll be no more strike flights over the North."

"This's bullshit, sir. It's pure politics. I didn't think Johnson could sink any lower, but he's doin' this right before the election to try to help Humphrey win."

"Well, Sam, who knows what's behind what happens in Washington, but I did read an article in the paper this morning about Humphrey closing on Nixon in the polls."

As the C-130 taxied toward them, the high-pitched noise from its four turbo-prop engines grew louder and drowned out further conversation. The airplane made a turn to present its side to its onlookers, and the fighter pilots began walking out toward it, led by Lieutenant Colonel Hank Wise, their squadron commander. As its engines shut down, a door at the rear of the transport lowered to discharge its passengers. When the door touched the pavement, Joe England walked down it and waved, and was greeted by hearty cheers of his squadron mates. His left arm was in a sling over his flying suit, and he had large bruises on his neck, under his jaw, from his ejection in southern Laos the previous day.

When he reached the airplane at the head of the welcoming throng, Wise thrust out his right hand and shook England's vigorously. To the raucous approval of the rest of the squadron, Wise yelled to his troops, "By god, dragons are tough to kill! You can shoot 'em down, but they come back to fight again!"

As the rest of the passengers disembarked, most of them new arrivals at Takhli, they moved around the knot of pilots, staring curiously at the strange yellow uniforms. England raised his fist and shouted, "Dragons are shit hot!" Another chorus of cheers went up from the pilots as they surrounded England and began walking with him to the squadron's trucks parked on the edge of the ramp. They jumped into the cabs and beds of the pickups, and assembling behind Wise's vehicle, they began a loud, horn-honking parade to the officers' club.

At the club, the pilots from the 357th moved noisily through the main bar and into the stag bar. One of them cranked the volume on the juke box all the way up to signal the beginning of hard drinking to celebrate the return of one of their own. Jose Feliciano belted out "Light My Fire" as the pilots crowded around the bar to place their orders. Wise was the last to enter. As he came through the door, he yelled, "Dead bug!"

The pilots threw themselves to the floor, rolled over on their backs and shot their arms and legs into the air. Wise surveyed the room, looking for the last man to make it to the floor. "Jensen!" he yelled, pointing at a recently arrived lieutenant who had the bad luck to fall on top of another pilot before he got his back onto the linoleum.

"Jen-sen! Jen-sen! Jen-sen!" the other pilots chanted as they got up, saluting their benefactor, the buyer the first round of drinks for the entire squadron. Two Thai bartenders hustled to meet a barrage of drink orders as the voices of Steppenwolf came out of the juke box next and captured the mood, singing, "Born to be wi-ild."

Burke waited until the initial frenzy of celebration was over, after the second dead-bug call, before he motioned for guest of honor England to join him and the other members of his flight, Kevin and Rob, in a corner of the room. His voice drowned out to others by the music, loud conversation and laughter at the bar behind them, Burke asked England casually, "What were you strafing when you got knocked down?"

"Well, sir, it was a suspected truck park. We'd already bombed it, but Major Sears called for strafe passes," England said, referring to another of the squadron's flight commanders. "I got hit on the third pass."

"So, you were making multiple gun passes, shooting at trees?"

"Yes, sir. I didn't think it was such a great idea, but the flight lead called for strafe, and there wasn't much I could do about it."

"Well, I might be doing something about it the next time one of you guys gets loaned out to fill a hole in another flight."

"Yes, sir."

Burke nodded toward the stag bar's entrance. "It looks like it's time for GCAs," he said, using the acronym for ground-controlled approach, a type of instrument approach to landing that was guided by radar instead of the electronic ILS cone.

A loud cheer went up from the bar as two of the squadron's lieutenants came through the door lugging a trash can filled with crushed ice from the kitchen. They tossed the ice onto the floor, covering a strip of light-colored linoleum that was cut into the darker flooring surrounding it, that stretched from the bar's entrance to an exit door about fifty feet away. Other pilots began placing lighted candles, inside glass bulbs and white plastic netting, around the strip on the floor.

With ice and candles in place and the exit door open, Wise declared, "The runway's active!"

The pilots lined up against the entrance wall of the bar. When his turn came, each man pushed off the wall, getting as much speed as he could before leaving his feet, trying not to hit the row of green-glass candles that stretched across the runway's threshold. Each contestant belly flopped onto the ice and slid toward the exit door, trying not to foul by touching any of the white-glass candles that served as runway lights down the length of the floor strip. Those not lucky enough to slide through the exit door, onto a porch outside, bought the rest of the squadron a round of drinks. Candle touchers also ponied up.

The party began winding down after the fifth round of GCAs. A guest flight surgeon, newly affiliated with the squadron and outfitted in a freshly made party suit, had not participated in the floor sliding, but had stayed late to observe the celebration rites of his new clients. Kevin, standing next to him at the bar near the end of the festivities, heard him dispensing sound medical advice to a soaked, bleary-eyed Lieutenant Jensen.

"Roy," the doctor said, "whenever you get as drunk as you are now, thousands of brain cells get destroyed, and they're never regenerated."

"Thass a lotta bullshit, doc," the lieutenant retorted, fixing his adversary with his best late-hour stare. "What happens is . . . it kills off the weak ones . . . so the tough ones can grow stronger."

Chapter 20

Tuesday, 19 November 1968

Kevin and his flight commander stood outside the entrance to wing headquarters, watching the last of the five surviving F-111s take off. After eight months at Takhli on TDY, the airplanes had been released from grounding to return home to Nellis, to end their ill-starred debut in combat.

"I once heard a three-star say some pretty negative things about the one-eleven when it was still called the TFX," Kevin said.

"Well, Kevin, it's no fighter pilot's dream, but it's got a lot of potential for the deep-strike mission. Even though it's big and not very agile, it's got long legs and a new radar system that'll let it operate right down on the deck, if they can get the bugs worked out. Right now, it's going through the same kind of growing pains that the Thud had in the early days. I had to jump out of one of the first models."

"What happened, sir?"

"At first, the airplane tended to blow up a lot. Eventually, the accident investigators found out that fuel pooled under the rear of the engine sometimes, and engine heat would make it explode. So, the fix was crude, but it worked. They put ram-air ducts on the sides of the fuselage to blow the fuel out."

"Well, maybe the fix for the one-eleven will be that simple."

"Maybe. But the Air Force'll spend whatever it takes. Right now, the Navy's got a lot better capability than we do for night, all-weather attack, and the one-eleven's the only thing we've got going to close the gap."

"Yes, sir."

"In a way, though, the one-eleven fiasco is this whole war in a nutshell."

"How do you mean, sir?"

"Well, we thought we could deliver a lot more than we did. When you cut through all the excuses and the bullshit, we didn't hack it. We thought we were going to win this thing with heavy-duty bombing of family-jewels targets in North Vietnam. What we found out is that our shit-hot jets dropping iron bombs weren't good enough. I'm not bad-mouthing the guys who flew downtown. They did everything they could do, and they had mucho balls. But they had to fly a lot of sorties and drop a lot of iron to take out each target, and the bad guys shot the shit out of us with old-fashioned triple-A," Burke said, meaning anti-aircraft artillery, the military-dictionary term for anti-aircraft guns. "Our losses got too high, and we had to stop going to Route Pack Six. Now we're reduced to trying to take out trucks hidden in the jungle one at a time."

"Well, sir, we didn't exactly fight this war the way we should have. Not with a build-up that took forever and all those stupid-shit bombing halts and political restrictions."

"Kevin, that's what we tell civilians who don't know any better. Even if we'd done this thing without all the interference from Washington, it still would've taken too many sorties, and our losses would still have been unacceptable. Sure, we would've lost fewer guys and been more effective with a quicker build-up and no bombing halts, but not effective enough to make the North Vietnamese quit. The truth is that the generals were making up Rolling Thunder as they went along, trying to find something to make Uncle Ho crack. But he turned out to be a tough little bastard. Our technology just wasn't good enough. Iron bombs aren't going to cut it the next time we go to war. We'll have to do a lot better. So, after I'm retired, and you and Charlie get to be generals someday, make sure we've got the stuff to take out targets the first time we hit them, without having to launch a hundred sorties a day for a week to do the job. And don't promise the folks back home more than you can really deliver."

"Yes, sir."

"Before all that happens, though, we need to finish out the war we're in right now the best way we can. So, as part of all that, we're going to upgrade you and a couple of the other new guys to element lead in a few weeks, and if everything goes okay, to flight lead in three or four months after that."

"That's good news, sir."

"And, since some of the old heads in the squadron'll be rotating home soon, we'll be upgrading a few others to flight lead. Maybe Sam Prentiss."

"Sam's a natural, sir."

"He seems to beam off in strange directions from time to time."

Don't sandbag a classmate. You owe him one from McConnell. "Well, sir, I think he'd be a good flight lead."

"Okay then," Burke said, looking at his watch. "It's about that time."

They walked inside to the auditorium to get the mass briefing with the other pilots flying late-afternoon missions.

* * *

With England still out of commission, and Rob on a five-day leave to Bangkok, they had drawn a two-ship flight. Thirty minutes after takeoff, Burke and his wingman closed on a tanker for refueling on their way to southern Laos, to hit a suspected staging area for trucks on the Ho Chi Minh trail.

"Firebird flight's cleared in. Check noses cold," the tanker's boom operator transmitted, reminding the pilots to make sure that their radars were off and that their guns were safe.

"Roger, Firebirds have cold noses." Burke moved to the refueling position under the boom as Kevin separated from his flight leader and eased to a formation position on the tanker's right wing.

"Firebird lead's full," the boom operator reported a few minutes later as excess jet fuel began venting out of Burke's fuel tanks, forming three spray trails in the air behind him.

"Roger, lead's disconnect," Burke replied as he released the boom from his Thud. He eased his jet up to the tanker's left wing and advised, "Firebird lead'll be off frequency for a couple of minutes to talk to Hillsboro."

"Roger."

Kevin slipped his jet into refueling position, moving directly to the boom from the right wing, skipping the steps of falling behind the tanker and then moving forward that he had used as a rookie. When he got his full load of fuel, he disconnected and went back to the right wing, waiting for his leader to return to the refueling frequency.

"Firebird lead's back. We've been diverted to Barrel Roll. It's ninety-five miles on the zero-five-zero radial, off channel seventy-nine," Burke said, giving the TACAN channel for a clandestine transmitter operating in northern Laos. In earlier days, flights headed to Route Package 6 had used channel 79 and other Barrel Roll TACANs to find targets in and around Hanoi. "There's a SAR in progress, and we're going to lend a hand."

"Roger, two" Kevin acknowledged.

"Thanks for the fill-up, guys. Firebirds will be separating down and left."

"Have a good one, Firebirds," the tanker's pilot responded. "Good luck in getting the guy out who's down."

"Roger. Thanks. Firebirds, go SAR primary."

"Two." Kevin looked at the mission card strapped to his right leg to find the new frequency.

"Firebirds check."

"Two."

As they headed north, they listened to a FAC, Raven 24, trying to orchestrate a rescue. It sounded like an athletic team, well behind, late in the final period of play, whose players were turning on one another in frustration.

Raven 24 called the pilot of a rescue helicopter with a Jolly Green call sign. "Jolly Green, can you make another pickup try now?"

"Negative! Negative! You've got to take out some of the shooters first. We took multiple hits on the last attempt. If you can't suppress some of the ground fire with the jets, we'll have to wait until the Sandys get here," the helicopter pilot transmitted, referring to the call sign of the slow-moving, propeller-driven attack planes that escorted the Jolly Greens. Called A-1 Skyraiders, they first saw action off Navy carriers during the Korean War. With their even slower speed, the rescue helicopters were staged forward on a short airstrip in Barrel Roll to cut down the time it took to fly to a downed pilot. The heavily armed Sandys, though, had to launch from a base with a longer runway in eastern Thailand, and it took precious time for them to fly north and rendezvous with a helicopter to form a rescue force.

"Okay, Mantis four, hang tight," Raven 24 advised the downed pilot. "I'm going to put in another strike with some F-4s I've got overhead. We'll take out more of the bad guys before we make another run with the Jolly Green. Keep your head down."

Firebird flight was too far south to hear the reply transmitted from the low-power, hand-held survival radio being used by the man on the ground. *Shit! He's one of ours,* Kevin thought, recognizing the Mantis call sign from Takhli.

"Okay, Joker flight, I'm going to put in a smoke rocket. I want you to put your nape," Raven 24 directed, using the slang for napalm, "right through my smoke on a line parallel to the road, one hundred meters east of the parachute in the trees. Acknowledge."

"Roger, Joker lead. Jokers acknowledge."

"Two."

"Three."

"Four."

F-4s and nape. That won't cut it, Kevin said to himself. He knew that the FAC wouldn't risk putting napalm in close to Mantis four. The fiery jellied gasoline could spill unpredictably anywhere. *And no guns for strafe either,* he thought.

Guns, the most-accurate ground-attack weapons, had been left out of early-model F-4s. The first F-4s were designed to be air-to-air fighters, and dogfights with guns were thought to be passe in the missile age. Their designers had apparently forgotten that, as far back as World War I, in one way or another, most dogfighters ended up coming down from their lofty perches to attack targets on the ground. *Those F-4s aren't going to take out many of the bad guys.*

Burke came to the same conclusion. He looked back at Kevin and made a visual signal for afterburner, moving his clenched fist from side to side. After getting his wingman's answering head nod, the flight leader snapped his head forward. The burners on both jets lit, and the bomb-laden Thuds accelerated as their engines began gulping fuel at nearly 50,000 pounds an hour. Time was getting short. It was late in the day, and the Jolly Green couldn't attempt a rescue pick-up after dark.

They sped northward as Joker flight completed its napalm attack. "Raven two four, Joker fight's winchester," the F-4 flight leader called, telling the FAC that his flight was out of ammunition. "Joker's exiting west."

"Roger," Raven 24 replied.

Burke called quickly. "Raven two four, this is Firebird flight."

"Go ahead, Firebird."

"Firebird's a flight of two Thuds with eight, seven-fifties and a thousand rounds of twenty millimeter each. We're coming north in afterburner. Give me your location and target elevation."

"We're twenty miles southeast of Sam Neua near a road," the FAC said, naming the town in northeast Laos that the Pathet Lao used as their headquarters, in the heart of darkness, twenty miles west of the border with North Vietnam. "The target's at three thousand feet elevation."

"Roger, we'll be there in about ten minutes. Give me the situation."

"Mantis four is down, west of the road. You can see his chute in the trees."

"Roger, tell me where you want the bombs. I want to get rid of them fast, so we can strafe in close."

"Roger, when you get here, you'll see smoke from napalm fires west of the road. I'll put in a smoke rocket at the north end of the fires, about a hundred meters north of the chute. Lead, put your bombs through the smoke on a line from east to west. Two, put yours east to west, halfway between my smoke and the chute. Acknowledge."

"Roger, Firebird lead."

"Roger, two."

"Firebirds, green 'em up. We'll bomb with fifteen-degree dive angles, at two thousand feet above the target and five hundred knots. Set one twenty-eight in your sight," Burke directed, telling his wingman that they were going to bomb with a seldom-used, minimum-range tactic to minimize errors in bombing close to the man on the ground.

"Roger, two."

After racing northward toward the TACAN fix, they picked up the smoke from the napalm fires, and Burke brought the flight out of afterburner. "Firebirds, fuel check."

"Two has five thousand." *Damn, we used up a lot of gas getting here.*

"Lead has five thousand. Call bingo at twenty-five hundred."

"Roger, two."

As the road came into view, Burke called, "Raven two four, we have the target area in sight. Put your smoke in now. We don't have any gas left to screw around."

"Roger. Raven two four's in."

Kevin caught sight of the FAC when the spotter plane's wings rolled to enter a dive. The Raven's small, slow, propeller-driven airplane, called the O-1 Bird Dog, looked like a castoff from a civilian flying school that had no business being in the middle of a war. The O-1 made a shallow dive, fired a smoke rocket from under its high wing quickly and pulled up, turning steeply to avoid ground fire. In a few seconds, dense white-phosphorous smoke floated up through the trees west of the road.

"Firebird lead has the smoke," Burke called as he headed toward the road, descending to attack altitude. "Raven two four, where do you want us to strafe on the next pass?"

"Strafe east of the chute, with south-to-north run-ins. Keep your strafe pattern to the west of the chute to avoid ground fire. The bad guys are coming toward Mantis four from the road. Work your hits progressively east from the chute to cover as much of the area as you can between the chute and the nape fires."

"Firebirds, roger."

Kevin moved his jet to the rear and right of Burke's Thud, taking spacing on his leader.

"Lead's in."

Firebird two pulled his airplane up to get more spacing by climbing until he could look through the lead jet to the smoke to match Burke's dive angle. "Two's in." He rolled nearly inverted and pulled the Thud's nose through the horizon quickly. He began rolling out for his bomb release as the lead Thud pulled up from its attack. As he rolled rapidly to wings level, to his right, Burke's bombs enveloped the white cloud on the ground with a line of soundless orange fireballs and black smoke. His own bomb release came quickly. His altimeter showed him hitting his release altitude as soon as he leveled his wings in his shallow dive.

After releasing his bombs, Kevin pulled up, jinking, following his leader toward the sun to set up for strafing passes from the south. Below him as he turned, he saw the Jolly Green in a tight orbit at low altitude, west of the chute, out of sight from the Pathet Lao gunners between Mantis four and the road, waiting to try another rescue run.

"Mantis four, stay down," the Raven called. "The Thuds are coming around to strafe,"

"Roger. I'm hunkered down."

Kevin began to see what the FAC was doing to set up the next rescue attempt. The Raven had put in strikes close to the road, to the north and east of Mantis four, to try to seal off the pick-up zone, and the Thuds' guns would take out the shooters between the downed airman and the napalm strike.

"Lead's in for strafe. Keep the pattern in tight." Burke fired a long walking burst, a strip of deadly flashes in the near-twilight from high-explosive ammunition igniting as it tore into wood and earth, a swath of fire that swept over twinkling points of flame coming from the muzzles of enemy gunners on the ground.

Kevin followed, his Thud's gun blasting a second trail of sparkling fire to the right of his leader's. He pulled off hard, turning left to follow Burke into another pass.

On their third strafing pass, their guns stopped firing when their ammunition gave out. "Firebirds are winchester," Burke called as he turned tightly through the sun for the last time, picking up a southerly heading toward Thailand, starting a rapid climb to altitude.

"Firebird two's bingo," Kevin called, climbing after his leader.

"Roger, Firebirds," Raven 24 replied. "Nice work, guys. How're you doing Mantis four?"

"I'm okay. You can send in the chopper any time."

"Okay. Jolly Green, let's try another pick-up."

"Negative," a new voice called. "This is Sandy two one. We're thirty miles out. Let's hold off until we can join up and escort the Jolly in."

"Roger, Jolly Green," the helicopter pilot called.

Sounding exasperated, the FAC replied, "This is Raven two four. Look, we've just hosed down the bad guys and the sun's getting low in the west. We need to make our move now."

"Negative," the Sandy responded. "I'm taking command of the rescue force. Let's use all the firepower we've got when we go in."

"Okay, Sandy," the Raven called, reluctantly passing control, "it's your show now, but you'd better hustle."

"Firebirds go squadron common," Burke called.

"Two."

"Firebirds, check."

"Two."

"How's your gas, Kevin?"

"Two's got a little over two thousand," Kevin said as he closed to spread formation on his leader.

"Okay, we don't have enough left to screw around trying to find a tanker. We're going to head straight for Udorn. We'll climb to twenty thousand, and then do a minimum-fuel let-down. Get wider, Kevin. We're going to clean everything off underneath to get rid of the drag. Hit the jettison-all button on my command. Ready?"

"Two's ready."

"Jettison."

Explosive charges in the Thuds' attachment pylons blew, and their wing tanks and centerline bomb racks flew away behind them. Burke climbed the flight to 20,000 feet. Thirty miles from Udorn, the two Firebirds entered a long, power-back glide as the first hour of night crept up on them.

"Brigham, this is Firebird flight of two," Burke called, using the call sign of the radar controller at Udorn who would clear their way to landing.

"Go ahead, Firebird. This is Brigham."

"Roger, Firebirds are thirty miles northeast, leaving twenty thousand. We're declaring an emergency for low fuel."

"Roger. Understand. Squawk emergency," the controller said, telling Burke to set his transponder to make a large, unmistakable symbol for an aircraft in trouble appear on the controller's radar screen. "Brigham has radar contact. I show Firebird flight twenty-nine miles northeast of the airfield. Udorn is landing runway three zero. Say your intentions."

"Roger, we're requesting single-ship, straight-in approaches. Firebird lead will drop behind Firebird two. Firebird two, say your fuel."

"Firebird two has eight hundred pounds," Kevin answered, calling out a fuel state below the Thud's emergency-fuel level of a thousand pounds.

"Roger, Firebirds. Say current speed."

"Firebirds are descending, holding best glide speed at three hundred knots."

"Roger. Firebird two, increase speed to three-ten. Firebird lead, hold current speed."

"Roger, Firebird two.

"Roger, lead."

Kevin lowered his Thud's nose slightly to increase speed ten knots and began pulling away from his flight leader, heading for the lights of Udorn in the distance, watching his fuel level drop slowly toward zero. Reaching down with his left hand, he found the ejection handle and gripped it, ready to pull it upward at the first sign of flameout. One of the warning lights in the stack under the master-caution light glowed FUEL LOW. He waited until he was two miles from the end of the runway to slow down, and he lowered his gear and flaps a mile later. The fuel gauge read 300 pounds remaining when final-approach speed showed on his airspeed indicator, and taking in a deep breath, he advanced the throttle to hold speed over the last half mile, hoping he had enough fuel left to make it to touchdown.

He flared the big jet as it approached the runway. With its light weight and clean wings and belly, the airplane sailed just above the pavement, not wanting to touch down. Kevin let it drop into a hot landing and yanked the drag-chute handle. He let his breath out as he felt the chute bite into the air behind him.

At the end of the runway, Kevin turned onto a taxiway and saw Firebird lead's bright landing lights just beyond white runway lights in the distance. Relaxing, he jettisoned his drag chute and began taxiing. After a long taxi in idle power on a taxiway leading to the transient ramp, as he started to turn toward a man with lighted wands in upraised hands, the Thud's engine began to unwind. "Udorn ground, this is Firebird two. You'll need to send out a tug to bring me the rest of the way in. My engine's just quit." While he waited for the tug, Burke taxied around him, parked his jet and got out quickly, hurriedly making his way to the base-ops building.

Ten minutes later, a tug arrived and pulled Firebird two across the last quarter mile of ramp to a parking space next to the lead Thud. Kevin got out to find Burke, walking around a yellow fuel truck that had arrived to fill their tanks. As he walked up a dimly lit sidewalk to the entrance to base ops, someone in the shadows said, "You're a little out of your regular neighborhood, Kev." A man with long brown hair and a mustache, both well beyond regulation length, stepped into the light. He was wearing a non-issue, dark-green jump suit with short sleeves and a holstered pistol on a wide cartridge belt around his waist.

It took a long second for the features of his senior-year roommate to register through the extra hair. "Josh?"

"Ayuh, it's me," Josh Pemberton said as he extended his hand.

"Well, I'll be damned," Kevin said, shaking hands. "This's a real surprise. The last I heard, you were in South Vietnam as a FAC with some Army outfit."

"Yeah, but that got to be a little boring. So, I volunteered for something a little more interesting. I'm operating up around channel seventy-nine these days with General Vang Pao," Josh said, naming the man who had rallied the Hmong tribesmen in the mountains of Laos to fight the Pathet Lao and their North Vietnamese allies.

"What're you doing there? You look like a real soldier of fortune in that get-up."

"I'm a Raven FAC."

"No kidding. We just finished working with one of your guys. Raven two four."

"Judging by the way you just ended your flight, it looks like you stayed with him a little past bingo fuel."

"Yeah. We were supporting a SAR."

"Did they get the guy out?"

"I don't know. We had to leave before the Jolly Green moved in. I guess that's what my flight lead's trying to find out now. Why don't you come inside and meet him?"

"Some other time, maybe. My lift's just arrived," Josh said, motioning toward the ramp.

Kevin turned to see a C-47, the military version of the DC-3 transport that dated back to before Word War II, swinging into a parking space on the transient ramp. It was painted gray with no markings. "Looks pretty spooky."

"Well, we GIs aren't supposed to be in Laos, you know. If we weren't, though, the bad guys would've overrun the whole place by now. The Pathet Lao and Uncle Ho kind of forget that it's supposed to be a neutral country. Anyway, I'll probably see you in the air one of these days, now that you guys are coming to Barrel Roll more often, now that you're not going to Route Pack One anymore."

"Probably so."

"Be on the lookout for Raven two nine."

"Okay. Got it. Raven two nine."

Kevin extended his hand. "It's great to see you again, Josh."

After their parting handshake, Josh trotted out to the waiting C-47, its engines running. As soon as its passenger was inside, the veteran transport's propellers gave out a short blast of power, and it began to taxi back into the darkness, out to the runway.

Kevin walked inside and saw Burke coming out of a door next to the operations counter. He was angry.

"Did they get Mantis four out, sir?"

"No. It apparently turned into a fucking goat rope. The guy at the command post at Takhli I just talked to said it took too long for the A-1s and the Jolly Green to get joined up, and it got dark before they could get to him. The Jolly should have made his move right after we finished strafing. He said that they'll try again tomorrow at first light."

"Who's Mantis four, sir?"

"It's that new kid, Jensen. He was in Sears' flight. If I find out that Sears was shooting up trees again when Jensen got knocked down, I am really going to get pissed. Well, let's not worry about that just now. Let's go get something to eat while they refuel our birds. There's supposed to be a flight-line snack bar out behind this building somewhere."

"Yes, sir."

Chapter 21

Friday, 27 December 1968

Kevin and Charlie were finishing breakfast at the officers' club. A Thai waitress poured each of them a second cup of coffee before taking away the cash covering their check. "Thanks, Somjit," Kevin said.

"Welcome, sir."

"So, Charlie, how did you meet up with Josh?"

"It was at the Chao Praya," Charlie said, naming the hotel in Bangkok where American military officers on leave and TDY were billeted. "I walked into the bar, and there he was, the Yankee wise-ass himself, off in a corner drinking alone. I might not've recognized him, though, if you hadn't told me about the long hair and the 'stache. Anyway, we had a drink together, and then he took me to this out-of-the-way restaurant so we could talk without everybody else listening in. He said that flying in South Vietnam as a FAC got to be too dull."

"Yeah, he told me the same thing. Josh didn't volunteer for a combat assignment out of Laughlin, so he had to take whatever came along. They gave him a FAC assignment, ran him through a quickie checkout course on how to fire a smoke rocket and then sent him off to South Vietnam. I'm not surprised that he finagled another assignment. What did he tell you about being a Raven?"

"They apparently live a pretty wild life at Long Tieng," Charlie said, naming the airstrip headquarters of Vang Pao's Hmong soldiers in the mountains of northern Laos, more commonly known among pilots as channel 79. "From the way Josh talked about the flying and the nights at the bar between missions, it sounds like something out of the foreign legion, except for the uniforms. He said that they wear civilian clothes everywhere, even when they fly, but he told me that the Raven guys are all active-duty Air Force. They have to have six months' experience as a FAC somewhere else before they can volunteer for the program."

"Like Josh said when I saw him at Udorn, GIs aren't supposed to be in Laos."

"He said that he works sometimes with guys who really are civilians, guys who fly for Air America and some others. They fly short-field airplanes and helicopters all over Laos. Reading between the lines, I'd have to guess that they're CIA. To top it all off, he said that the Laotian Air Force operates out of there too, on combat missions against the Pathet Lao. I guess you'd have to call channel seventy-nine the combat version of Shangri-La."

"Well, it sounds like the place suits Josh. He always had a wild hair up his ass."

"Like someone else we know locally."

"Yeah. For a while there, I thought Sam might mellow out some, after he and Nancy nurse started sleeping together. But he just seems to get wilder and wilder as time goes on."

"I think Sam's going to miss Hank Wise. I don't think he and your new squadron commander are going to get along all that well."

"Yeah. Sam really dug Wise's act, and Wise returned the favor. He moved Sam up to flight lead in minimum time."

"Well, Wise wasn't exactly what you'd call discreet. The man was a drunk, and everybody knew he was screwing that enlisted woman. When you guys started taking losses, it got pretty easy for the wing commander to make his move."

"It's unbelievable. It's been, what, five weeks since Roy Jensen disappeared after his SAR got screwed up? When Sears got shipped off to a desk job at Saigon, the other flight leads should've gotten the message. But they kept right on strafing dip-shit targets, and we lost two more guys. The one on Christmas eve was really bad."

"They might've gotten the message if Wise had tightened up, but I guess they don't teach that course in the all-balls, no-forehead school of leadership. I guess he thought everything would be just dandy if he let fighter pilots be fighter pilots."

"So, tell me about Fletcher," Kevin said, asking about the former operations officer in Charlie's squadron who had been moved quickly to fill the squadron-command void in the 357th after Wise had been unexpectedly reassigned, or as those who knew better said, fired.

"He comes from the tough-but-fair, tight-ship school. He's class of fifty-five from Annapolis. More important, he's part of the mafia from Kadena," Charlie said, naming the air base on the island of Okinawa where a wing of F-105s was stationed and sat alert with nuclear weapons. "I'm pretty sure he's one of the wing commander's inner circle, along with Rod Burke and some of the other guys who were stationed there together."

"I'll have to admit that I thought you were really reaching with your Kadena-mafia theory, Charlie, but you might be right. Burke got really pissed at Sears after Jensen was declared MIA. And then, bang, out of nowhere, Sears gets reassigned to Saigon."

"That doesn't surprise me. The story in the tight-knit fighter world seems to be that guys form pretty strong connections with other guys they trust as they go from one assignment to the next, and when they get to be senior commanders, they rely on the guys in their network for back-channel information and advice. No one admits it, but I think there's too much going on for anything else to explain it. I'd bet some serious money that the wing commander personally gave Sears the axe after talking to Burke."

"Well, Charlie, I'll have to take your word for it, since you're our resident expert on all matters political, big and small." Kevin looked at his watch. "I've got to go. Ten minutes until officers' call at the squadron."

"That's the first signal on Fletcher, by the way. If I remember correctly, Wise used to have all his officers' calls with you guys at night in the stag bar. With the new regime, I predict that you guys are going to be doing a lot less partying."

"Maybe so. See you later, Charlie."

"Right. Later, Kev."

Kevin walked outside and got on one of the Moped motor bikes parked near the club's entrance. After arrival at Takhli, most of the officers bought one to get around the base from someone completing a tour and going home. He made the short trip on his to the 357th's building and went inside to the day room where the rest of the pilots were gathering.

The largest room in the building, it easily accommodated all thirty of the 357th's aircrews, most of whom were already seated in naugahyde-and-chrome chairs that lined four masculine walls decorated with brass plaques, pictures of airplanes in combat and one war trophy. In a place of prominence, on the wall opposite the room's entrance, a Soviet-made AK-47 assault rifle rested in a presentation frame made of dark wood and silk. It had been given to the squadron by a grateful Vang Pao, after a hard-hitting air strike in northern Laos flown by the 357th earlier in the year.

Kevin found an empty chair next to Rob Johnson. "Hey, Rob."

"Hey," Rob replied in the short, hushed mode of conversation that the pilots had adopted for the morning's gathering, in the wake of the popular Wise's hasty departure the previous evening for a desk at Seventh Air Force.

The squadron's operations officer came through the door, and moving to one side, stood at attention. "Gentlemen, the squadron commander," he announced. The pilots got to their feet quickly and came to attention in front of their chairs.

"Be seated, gentlemen," Lieutenant Colonel Fletcher said as he strode through the room, moving to the far wall, under the AK-47. He turned and faced his new command.

Waiting until the room was completely quiet after the pilots sat down again, the new commander looked around, sweeping the pilots through the eyes. "This change of command probably seems somewhat abrupt to most of you. It's no more abrupt, though, than having your brother officers shot down and suddenly lost in the stinking jungles of Laos. There has been too much of that going on lately. Pilots in this squadron have been lost strafing things that only remotely resemble targets and that are not worth the loss of any one of us."

Fletcher paused for his words to sink in. "For those of you who haven't figured it out yet, let me be completely clear about what's happening. First, there are peace talks starting up in Paris to end this war. We are here to support our negotiators, in case the North Vietnamese need to be reminded that we can make things painful for them in downtown Hanoi again if we want to. Now that a new administration has been elected, after the inauguration, we may have to go back to Route Pack Six if the peace talks don't progress quickly enough. So, we have to keep our edge to be ready to do that. That's the main reason why you are flying combat missions in Laos. We are not here to hang our asses out strafing trees. If we do go back to Route

Pack Six, I can assure you that we won't be doing any strafing there. Is anyone confused about that?"

The room was completely silent. "Second, we are here to prevent supplies and ammunition from reaching the bastards in South Vietnam who are killing Americans there. I have seen very few, if any, targets along the Ho Chi Minh trail worth strafing. Where Barrel Roll is concerned, we are not here to fight to the death against the Pathet Lao and the second-string North Vietnamese helping them. Vang Pao's fight was going on long before we got here, and it'll be going on long after we leave. If he gets some help from our staying ready to go back to Hanoi, fine. The bottom line here is that I want you to concentrate on making your bombs count, not on getting your rocks off by getting down in the weeds to strafe. Is anyone not clear about that?"

Fletcher looked around the room again. No one spoke. "Good. Effective immediately, there will be no strafing by any pilot in this squadron unless there is an identifiable, tangible, militarily significant target worth attacking. We are not going to shoot up suspected truck parks or suspected anything else. I will be holding flight leads personally responsible for adhering to this policy. I will also be doing random checks of gun-camera film to make sure that it is being strictly observed. If I find any flight lead violating this policy, he will not be leading any more flights in this squadron. In fact, he will not be doing any more flying in this squadron. Are there any questions about that?"

The new commander surveyed the silent room once more. "Very well. I will be flying with every flight lead in the squadron over the next several weeks to evaluate the soundness of your procedures and tactics. I have a closing note for those of you who think that the loss of three good men from this squadron over the last five weeks was simply bad luck. I want you to know that I don't believe in luck, good or bad. That's all, gentlemen."

The pilots scrambled to their feet again as Fletcher started to walk out. They remained at attention until he said, "Carry on," as he left the room.

Kevin looked across the room at Sam Prentiss. Angry disgust showed on his face. Talking to no one, Prentiss walked quickly out of the room and left the building.

As the other pilots broke into small groups, talking in low voices, Rod Burke walked over from across the room to where Kevin and Rob were standing. "Kevin, could you round up the rest of the guys in the flight for a meeting in here in, say, half an hour? All the flight commanders are going to meet with Colonel Fletcher now, and I'll have some stuff to pass on afterwards."

"Yes, sir."

"I've already got one thing. Ask everybody to think about moving up their R and R dates. The training pipeline at Nellis and McConnell hasn't adjusted to the tour over here being extended to a year yet. They're still cranking out replacements based on a hundred missions over the North. So, we need to do some things to make room on the flying schedule for the new guys coming in. Maybe some of you can take your R and R a little early. Anyway, think about it."

"Yes, sir," they both replied.

As Burke made his way to the door, Rob said, "This's got to be fate. Sandra's just gotten a new assignment to Clark, and she's going to get there next month. She wants to meet me when she gets there, but I'd told her that I wanted to wait until my tour was half over before I took my R and R. The way things are going, I'd grab any reasonable excuse to change my mind. So, it looks like I'll be headed to the Philippines a little early."

"To do that one-knee thing?"

"Yeah. It's about that time, and besides, the woman's got a great collection of Motown LPs. How about you? When're you going?"

"I've already made reservations in Hawaii for March. The place was pretty well booked up, and I don't think I can change plans now. Well, I've got to round up the other guys for the meeting before they split. Wait here a minute, and I'll be back to hear more about your vanishing bachelorhood."

Chapter 22

Sunday, 16 March 1969

As the bus from Hickam Air Force Base turned into the driveway of the R and R center in downtown Honolulu, an Army enlisted man rose from the front seat and turned to face the other passengers. Speaking into a microphone, he said, "We're now approaching the starting point for five fabulous days and nights of R and R here in paradise. So, when you love-starved maniacs get off the bus, grab the best-looking woman you see and give her the kiss of a lifetime. You other guys, go ahead and kiss your wives."

The seated men in uniform responded with appreciative laughter and then crowded to one side of the bus to peer through its windows as it came to a stop. Wives and sweethearts waiting at the center's entrance smiled and began waving excitedly, one by one, as each caught sight of her man's face through the glass.

Kevin saw Teresa near the bus's entry door in front, and he moved forward quickly as it opened, joining a rush of eager males too long separated from their mates. Out the door, he ran to her and embraced her, drawing her tightly against him. She felt too good to let go, but the sensation of her body dimmed in the flooding softness of her lips that gently eased his mouth open. He moved his tongue lightly over hers.

She pressed against him as she ended the kiss and whispered, "Let's go to our hotel now."

"I'm your slave, ma'am."

Releasing her, he trotted to a row of luggage the bus driver was stacking by the curb and grabbed his bag. He held it in front of him as he walked back to hide the bulge visible through the tailored fit of his uniform trousers.

Holding hands, they walked to one of the cabs queued up on the street. "I can put your bag in the trunk, sir," the driver said as he opened the cab's rear door for them.

"That's okay. There's plenty of room for it on the seat. Royal Hawaiian Hotel, please."

"Yes, sir. Whatever you say," the man said as they slid into the back seat. He closed the door after them and quickly got into the driver's seat. Wheeling the cab expertly into traffic, he accelerated, passing other cars as he wove easily from one lane to another. Glancing into his mirror, he decided not to try to make conversation when he saw his passengers in the middle of a long kiss, closed off from everything else around them.

"Here we are, folks. The Royal Hawaiian," the cabbie said when he pulled to a stop in the hotel's driveway. "That'll be seven dollars, sir."

Kevin took a ten from his wallet and handed it to the driver. "Keep the change. Thanks for the quick trip."

"Thank you, sir. I remember how it was when I came back home to my girl here in Honolulu in fifty-three, after Korea," the man said. "I hope you and your wife have a great time here."

"I'm sure we will. Thanks again."

The hotel's doorman, wearing a bright Polynesian shirt and white slacks, opened Teresa's door as Kevin got out from the other side and came around the rear of the cab. "I can get a porter for your bag, sir."

"Thanks, but I need to hang onto it for a while."

"I understand, sir," the man said with a wide smile as he opened the hotel's entrance door.

Holding his hand, Teresa led him through a crowded, plant-filled lobby to an elevator being emptied by guests wearing shirts and muumuus with vivid floral patterns. As the last one stepped out, she pulled him inside, pressed a floor button and put her arms around him as the door closed. "I've missed you so much."

Kevin dropped his bag to one side on the floor. "You feel so good." He embraced her and kissed her again as their upward ride began.

Reaching down with her hand, Teresa brushed the front of his trousers lightly. "And I've missed Irish Rogue too."

Kevin smiled. "Rosa Linda's all he ever thinks about."

"She's going to be a very naughty girl this week."

They released one another at the top of the ride when the elevator door opened, and picking up his bag, he followed her as she walked quickly to a nearby door, searching for a room key in her purse. Inside, he dropped his bag and surprised her by picking her up and carrying her to the bed.

She laughed as he moved over her on hands and knees after putting her down. "Before you start tearing my clothes off, could you let me surprise you? I've been imagining right now for months. You'll like it, I promise."

"Is it very, very, very sexy?"

"Uh huh," she replied, drawing out her answer

"Okay."

"But you have to undress in the bathroom and wait 'til I call you."

"You're driving poor Rogue crazy, but I'll try to make him understand. He's such a simple fellow," he said as he got to his feet.

"Rosa Linda's impatient too. So, it won't be long."

"All right," he said as he went into the bathroom and closed the door.

He came out again when she called to him, a towel wrapped around his waist. He stopped when he saw her in the glow of candles she had lit and placed on a table in a corner of the room after she had drawn the drapes. She was lying on the bed with the quilt of their first lovemaking doubled over her. There was a slight scent of pine in the room from something smoldering among the candles.

"Do you have any idea how many times I've daydreamed about you waiting for me in that quilt, the day we made love for the first time?"

"I hope as many times as I've thought about you when I see aspen or ride alone or smell the pines in the mountains or see your face in Mary Clare's. Come here and be close to me."

He walked to the bed, slipped off his towel and got under the quilt with her. He rolled toward her to hold her, but she stopped him by getting to her knees and putting her hands on his shoulders. She eased her weight on top of him, straddling him, and smiled. "I'm not going to let you rest until I'm pregnant. You're going to have to work very hard this week."

"Right now, there's nothing I wouldn't agree to," he said as he cupped his hands lightly over her aroused breasts.

Her smile became wistful. "I want to memorize the way your face looks now," she said as she pressed on his shoulders, moving more of her weight to her hands. She closed her eyes dreamily as her lips parted and began moving her hips slowly in a gentle rhythm.

* * *

The next morning, they were silent for a moment as they sipped their coffee on the hotel's nearly empty terrace. The blue Pacific spread to the horizon in front of them, and a soft breeze moved the fronds of potted palms placed among tables covered with fresh linen.

"Breakfast at eleven may be a little decadent, but I like it anyway," Kevin said.

"It's on my long list of fantasies for this week."

"You have more surprises?"

"Of course. And they're all thoroughly researched. I talked to Clare, and she sent me all the trashy novels she read before she met Ed for R and R here last year."

"How's Ed liking grad school?"

"Clare said that he struggled a little at first getting back into the books, but he's doing fine now."

"How would you like to be stationed with them at the Academy?"

"Have you heard something?"

"It's my turn for surprises. Just before I left Takhli, my contact in the history department called and said that I've been accepted. They're sending me to Duke in North Carolina in September, and then I'll be teaching for three years, maybe four, after I get my master's. You're looking at Captain O'Dea, future history prof."

"That's good news, love."

It seemed to him that she said the right words, but something was missing. "You don't seem to be as excited as I thought you'd be."

"Of course I'm excited," she said, taking his hand after she put down her coffee cup. "It's just that being here with you now makes other things seem less important somehow. Now is more than enough for me. I want it to last until you're home."

"I'm glad that it's less than six months away."

"Mary Clare and I are counting in weeks. She keeps the tapes you've sent each week all numbered and stored in a little box in her bedroom. I've numbered the weeks on a calendar she has on the wall, and she crosses off a new number every time we get a tape in the mail. I've told her that you'll be home when we get number fifty-two. She's very organized."

"I really miss her."

"She misses you too. Everyone's being very attentive to her. Papa Miguel reads to her every night, and Karin and Jakob treat her like she's their own granddaughter. Juan's been wonderful too. When he comes home to the ranch from Denver, he spends hour after hour playing with her."

"Juan's right up there on my list of great guys of all time."

"Did I tell you that he's going back east to study?"

"I don't think so."

"It's a real plum. It's the divinity school at Harvard."

"Well, he's on his way to becoming one of those ferociously educated Jebbies."

"He was there last month, on his way to a conference in Toronto."

"Oh?" he said, starting to feel uneasy.

She held both his hands and said, "He saw Sean while he was there."

"How is he?"

"Juan said that it's good and bad. He's working as a teacher, and he's met a girl he likes a lot, but he really feels cut off."

"That's the choice he made."

"I know, love, but he made it when he felt cornered, when he felt everything was closing in on him."

"This's very tough for me, Teresa. The last thing I want to see is Sean hurting, but he hurt a lot of other people by running away."

"Couldn't you write to him?"

And who's writing to Roy Jensen, Kevin thought. "I don't know."

"Juan gave me his address."

"Love, let's not talk about this right now. It's just too hard."

"Okay."

"What should we do for the rest of the day?"

"I need to bring something back for Mary Clare for her birthday. Would you mind doing a little shopping? She'd love it if you picked something out especially for her. And I need to get something for Karin and Jakob, as well as Father and Juan."

"Well, shopping's usually torture, but okay."

"After that we could go to the beach for a few hours. I have a new swim suit I want to show you."

"I think that's a great idea. Rogue does too."

Chapter 23

Saturday, 22 March 1969

Charlie Rasmussen and Rob Johnson were sitting at the officers' club bar wearing khaki slacks and polo shirts when Kevin saw them and walked over from the club's entrance.

"Hey, guys, what's going on?" Kevin asked, walking up behind them.

Charlie and Rob turned around on their bar stools. "Hey, Kev!" Charlie replied. "How was Hawaii? Never mind. Judging by that grin, I'd say that you've definitely been laid within the last forty-eight hours."

"All the world loves a wise-ass," Kevin said, widening his grin.

One of the Thai bartenders came over. "Drink, sir?" he asked Kevin.

"Sure. Heineken, please."

"Fifty cents, sir," the bartender said as he got a bottle out of a large cooler and opened it.

Kevin exchanged two quarters for the bottle. "Thanks," he said, and took a long swallow.

As he put the bottle on the bar, he added, "Man, that tastes good after the flight back here from Bangkok on the Klong."

"How're Teresa and Mary Clare doing?" Rob asked.

"They're both good. Teresa said to say hi to both you guys. So, Rob, what's been happening while I've been gone?"

"Not much. Major Burke's on leave in Bangkok until Monday, and the weather's been dog shit in Laos. We haven't flown much all week. The mission I was on this afternoon got scrubbed after we briefed and stood by for three hours."

"I guess I haven't missed a lot then. Has the schedule for tomorrow been posted yet?"

"I looked for it about half an hour ago when I came in, but it wasn't there."

"Well, why don't I go take another look."

Charlie said, "I'll go with you."

"Okay."

Rob said, "That'll give me a chance to take a head break."

Kevin and Charlie left the main bar and walked to the deserted stag bar behind it. Inside, they went to a small bulletin board on the wall opposite the bar.

"It looks like it's just been posted," Charlie said. He looked at the morning missions assigned to his squadron. "Here I am. It looks like I've got the first launch tomorrow."

Kevin turned to the last set of flights on the last page of the schedule, those to be flown by pilots in the 357th. He found his name at the bottom of the page. "And here I am. I've got the last go tomorrow. It'll probably be a road-seed mission."

The last flights of the day often carried five-hundred-pound bombs with time-delayed fuses called road seeds. They were set to go off randomly during the darkness, when the North Vietnamese and the Pathet Lao put their trucks back on the road after hiding them under thick stands of trees during daylight. The last flights of Thuds hit choke points on a road and dropped road-seed bombs to bury beneath them, to catch trucks later when they were moving in the dark. At their most effective, road seeds cratered a road and stacked up the enemy's trucks, out in the open, for night flyers to attack. Road seeding also made being a member of the enemy's road-repair crews a hazardous occupation.

"It looks like your flight lead's Sam Prentiss," Charlie said, looking at the four names listed under the call sign, Dallas.

"Yeah, and Rob's flying number four, on my wing."

"Sam told me that he's going to put his papers in," Charlie said, meaning a resignation of an officer's commission.

"Well, Charlie, we've all threatened to put in our papers at one time or another."

"I think he really means it. He got really pissed one day last week while you were gone and showed me his resignation letter. He said he was tired of flying in a chicken-shit war with a chicken-shit squadron commander, who's afraid to fight, breathing down his neck. And he had a fight with Nancy nurse and broke up with her. Something's happened that fun-loving guy we all remember."

"Yeah, things don't sound so good. Well, let's get back to the bar."

"Okay."

Rob was waiting for them when they returned. "Was it posted?"

"Yeah, and we're in the same flight. We've got the last launch tomorrow."

"I guess I've got time for another beer then."

Kevin looked at his watch. "Why don't we all take in the eight-thirty flick instead? There's a good one tonight. *In the Heat of the Night.*"

"Seen it already," Charlie said.

"Me too," Rob added.

"Well, I've seen it too, but it's a great movie. Best picture and best actor for Rod Steiger. And what the hell, it's two more hours off the tour."

Rob said, "Okay, I'm easy. Count me in."

"I'm going to pass, Kev," Charlie said. "I really need to finish a tape I've started for Kelley, and I've got the dawn patrol tomorrow."

"Be sure to say hi from the O'Deas."

"Sure will."

"See you tomorrow, Charlie. Ready to roll, Rob?"

"Yeah. Let's go."

As the two of them walked from the club to the nearby theater, Rob said, "Sandra's coming to Takhli on leave in a couple of days. She's looking forward to meeting you."

"I'll enjoy seeing her too. Have you two set a date yet?"

"Yeah. October eleventh, a month after we get home. She's put her papers in, and we're going to go home together."

"That's great news, Rob. I'm really happy for you."

"There's one other thing."

"What's that?"

"I'd like you to be my best man."

Kevin stopped walking and turned to face Rob, extending his hand. "Absolutely. In a heartbeat." They shook hands and then continued walking.

Inside the theater, they got to their seats as the lights went down and the Stars and Stripes began waving on the screen. They and the others in the audience stood quietly at attention as the "Star Spangled Banner" played on the sound track. The anthem over, they took their seats and settled in as the movie's opening credits rolled and Ray Charles sang the title song.

Fifteen minutes into the film, Kevin became absorbed in the first, emotionally escalating confrontation between an elegantly cool Sidney Poitier as Virgil Tibbs and Chief of Police Gillespie, of mythical Sparta, Mississippi, played to redneck perfection by a gum-chewing Rod Steiger:

Gillespie, accusing out-of-town-stranger Tibbs of murder, said, "Yeah. And meanwhile, you just killed yourself a white man. Just about the most important white man we got around here. And you picked yourself up a couple o' hundred dollars."

Restrained, in a measured voice, Tibbs replied, "I earned that money. Ten hours a day; seven days a week."

"Colored can't earn that kind of money, boy. Hell, that's more than I make in a month. Now where'd you earn it?"

"Philadelphia."

"Mississippi?"

"Pennsylvania."

"Now just what you do up there in little ol' Pennsylvania to earn that kind of money?"

"I'm a police officer," Tibbs responded, staring Gillespie down.

Two rows ahead, three black enlisted men caught up in the drama jumped to their feet. "Yeah!" two of them shouted. A third shook his fist at the screen and yelled, "You tell him, Sidney! You tell him!" Then, realizing where they were, they sheepishly took their seats again.

Startled by the outburst, seeing the molten emotion lying just below the surface through the fissure the film opened, Kevin said to himself, *As far as we've come, we've still got a long way to go. I wonder if we'll ever get there.*

Chapter 24

Sunday, 23 March 1969

The pilots scheduled for late-afternoon missions listened as the wing intelligence officer continued his portion of the mass briefing, using slides and an overhead projector that illuminated a screen at the front of the darkened briefing room. He removed a slide showing the tally of the previous day's truck kills in southern Laos, as reported by Seventh Air Force in Saigon, and he replaced it with another showing a map of Barrel Roll. "In northern Laos, the enemy continues to press his offensive on the PDJ," he said, meaning the *Plain des Jarres*, or the Plain of Jars in English. Named for the huge stone jars that some forgotten culture had mysteriously left there before vanishing, the PDJ was a large plateau, northeast of Long Tieng, that was the natural invasion route into western Laos from North Vietnam. "Reduced air support to friendly forces, because of continued poor weather, has allowed the enemy to secure positions to threaten Long Tieng and the approaches to the Laotian capital at Vientiane," the briefer reported, pointing to locations highlighted on the slide.

"Finally, in another development, a usually reliable source has reported seeing occidentals living in caves around Sam Neua," he said, pointing to a red circle at the top right of the map. "This source reports that they appear to be closely guarded, suggesting that they may be Americans, rather than Soviet or East European advisors to the Pathet Lao and North Vietnamese. This report, however, remains unconfirmed."

I wonder if Roy Jensen's one of them, Kevin thought, as the briefer collected his slides before leaving.

"Any questions? None? Okay, I'll turn things over to the weatherman."

Another officer stepped to the projector on the briefing room's stage. His first slide showed a map of Laos marked with meteorological symbols. "Weather in target areas in both southern and northern Laos continues to be largely overcast, with low ceilings and poor visibility. Over the next twenty-four hours," he continued, pointing to a scalloped line he had drawn on the chart in grease pencil, "this front should continue moving south and provide significant clearing. There is thunderstorm activity along the front."

The briefer replaced his first slide with another marked with symbols and numbers next to a list of air bases in Thailand. "The weather south of the front is also affecting recovery bases. Ceilings are overcast with visibilities generally a mile or more. However, reduced visibility from intermittent rain can be expected throughout the region. Cloud tops are twelve to thirteen thousand." He turned off the projector and asked, "Any questions on the weather?"

"Yeah," one of the pilots called out. "Will we get better weather when we get a new weatherman?"

The briefer bantered back, "When I'm on that freedom bird back to the States at the end of the week, and the new guy starts briefing, you guys'll see how good you've had it. Okay, those of you who do launch this afternoon, have good flights."

The pilots got out of their chairs as the room lights came on and filed through the door to the briefing cubicles. The rest of Dallas flight followed Sam Prentiss to an empty cubicle, sat down and took mission folders from him as he handed them out. "If we git off the ground, we'll be doin' a road seed here in the Fish's Mouth," he began, pointing to a section of the border between North Vietnam and northern Laos, shaped on the maps inside the folders like the open mouth of a bass going for a minnow.

Companion photos in the folders showed a segment of dirt road west of the border, weaving among numerous bomb craters, that all of them had seen through their bomb sights before. "I don't think I have to go into a lot o' detail about what we're gonna do. We've all done this before. If we git released from the weather hold we're on now, we'll start engines at sixteen thirty, take off with thirty-second spacin', and join up on top o' the weather. Then we'll hit the tanker, fly to the target, puke off the road seeds and come home. We'll do individual approaches when we git back. Everythin' else's on the mission card. Any questions? Okay, let's go back to the squadron and wait to git canceled."

Prentiss left the cubicle first, followed by Dallas two, a junior lieutenant in the squadron named Bill Vincent. After the first two left, Rob stuffed his folder into his flight bag and said, "That's got to be the shortest briefing on record."

"Yeah, it was." *This is not good. I've got to try to talk to Sam tonight.*

Outside, the four of them sprinted through the rain to their truck. Prentiss took the wheel. After a silent drive to the squadron building, they went inside, and the three wingmen went to the day room to kill time playing darts while Dallas lead went to the ops counter. A few minutes later, Prentiss appeared at the day-room door and said, "I'm goin' to take the truck and go back to my room. Call me there when we get the word." He put his bush hat back on and went outside again.

An hour later, the squadron commander came into the room. "Panda, Bear and Cookie flights are weather canceled," he announced to the other pilots who had returned to the squadron after Dallas flight to wait with them. Fletcher walked over to Kevin. "We've just gotten the word for Dallas and Mantis to launch for road seeding, Kevin. Where's Prentiss?"

"He had to go back to his room for a while, sir. I'll call him there."

"Tell him to hustle. A recky bird," Fletcher said, meaning a reconnaissance aircraft, "just made a sweep and reported that your target's clearing. The A, B, triple C says to launch. Let's get a move on."

"Yes, sir." He walked to the ops counter and dialed the number he got from the squadron roster under the phone.

"Prentiss."

"Sam, we're on. The weather's clearing, and we're supposed to get to our target as soon as we can."

"Okay," Prentiss said and hung up.

Forty minutes later, the mission's rain-soaked preliminaries on the ground over, four pilots in wet flight suits moved their jets' throttles forward after lining up on the runway. Dallas lead roared into a takeoff roll, the orange glow of his Thud's afterburner bright in the gray light of an overcast sky. Water sprayed upward from its landing gear as the jet gathered speed on a wet runway. The Thud lifted off, and with afterburner still lit, the lead airplane disappeared into low, leaden clouds.

"Dallas lead's airborne, in a left turn to zero five five," Prentiss called to departure control, out of the other pilots' sight, three miles south of the airfield.

"Roger, Dallas lead. This is Takhli departure. Radar contact."

Vincent rolled thirty seconds after the leader, taking the prescribed interval for safe separation between aircraft in formation taking off in weather. Kevin started his cockpit clock to time his brake release as Dallas two accelerated to takeoff speed. Halfway down the runway, the afterburner glow in the tail of the second jet vanished, and its drag chute snapped open behind it.

"Two's aborting with a fire light," Vincent transmitted after he had slowed to taxi speed near the departure end of the runway, after braking his heavy, bomb-laden Thud through a tricky high-speed deceleration on wet pavement.

"Roger," Kevin answered. "Shut it down in the de-arming area after you turn off."

"Roger, two."

When Vincent cleared the runway, Kevin dropped his feet from the tops of his rudder pedals, releasing brakes, and moved the jet's throttle into afterburner. Feeling the familiar muffled bang of the hard-lighting burner, he concentrated on his Thud's engine instruments and warning lights, taking an extra few seconds to check them carefully before rising into the gloomy weather that waited above him. *Everything looks good.*

The airplane accelerated smoothly in the cool air and felt eager to fly. Airborne, Kevin entered the clouds soon after he raised the gear and flap handles, depending completely on the instruments in front of him as gray engulfed him and motion appeared to cease. They showed him in a climb, and he disengaged the burner, waiting for three miles to show on the DME before turning northeast. "Dallas three's airborne, in a left turn to zero five five."

"Roger, Dallas three," the ground controller replied. "Radar contact. Your leader's ten miles ahead, same heading."

"Dallas three, roger." He turned on the Thud's radar and selected its air-search mode. As his jet's nose came around to the climb heading,

Dallas lead registered as a bright return on the radar scope between Kevin's legs under the instrument panel.

"Dallas four's airborne, turning to zero five five."

"Roger, Dallas four. Dallas three's five miles ahead and lead's at fifteen. Call on top."

"Dallas four."

"Dallas lead's on top at thirteen thousand," Prentiss called a few minutes later.

"Roger, Dallas lead, departure control copies. I'll pass that to the weatherman."

"Dallas lead's level at fifteen thousand," Prentiss advised a short time later.

At twelve thousand feet, Kevin sensed the tops of the clouds approaching as light from the sun penetrated downward, brightening the last of the vapor that held him. At thirteen thousand, he shot out of a white, gently rolling layer of clouds that covered everything as far as he could see, into bright light from the sun behind him. He lowered the sun visor on his flight helmet and scanned the sky ahead and above him, trying to spot his flight leader. Glancing at his radar, he saw that Dallas lead had moved to within five miles. Looking ahead again, he saw a lone Thud off to his left, skimming the highest of the swells of the cloud layer beneath them. "Dallas three has a tally on Dallas lead."

"Dallas four's on top," Rob called a few minutes later.

"Roger," Takhli departure acknowledged. "Radar service terminated. Dallas flight is cleared en route. Cleared to refueling frequency at your discretion."

"Roger. Dallas, go two, sixty-three, point seven,"

"Three."

"Four."

After they had checked in on the new frequency, they closed on one another to spread formation and flew on in silence, their airplanes looking like dark migratory birds patiently traversing a strange, swelling sea of white. As they approached the border with Laos, Dallas lead contacted a radar controller at Udorn, and following the headings the controller gave him, Prentiss led his flight through a textbook intercept of their tanker.

"Nice to see you guys," the boom operator said as Prentiss moved in to take his fuel first. "We haven't had very many customers today."

"Yeah. Bad weather for bombin'," Prentiss replied in a flat voice that didn't encourage further conversation.

The veteran pilots of Dallas flight cycled easily through their refueling and soon dropped away from the tanker, heading north, taking up a course for the border with North Vietnam, using channel 79 to guide them. Ahead, placid stratus clouds gave way to a line of thunderstorms that towered above them in the distance.

Prentiss altered course slightly as he approached the buildups, using his jet's radar to find a path through the storm cells, a trail hidden to the eye by vaporous cloud layers that shrouded and connected the treacherous shafts of violent air. "Dallas four, take the left wing," Dallas lead ordered, as they closed on the wall of clouds.

"Four," Rob acknowledged as he moved from Kevin's right wing to the leader's left, forming a tight wedge of three Thuds in close formation, giving Dallas flight maximum maneuverability.

Kevin raised his sun visor and glanced at his radar scope before they entered the weather. The thunderstorm cells glowed up at him as a line of bright returns across his scope, and he saw that Prentiss had them aimed at the widest gap in the line to punch through. The air around Dallas flight went white as they flew into the front's misty outer veil, and his senses heightening, Kevin held on tightly to Dallas lead, feeling with his hands on the controls the smooth, gradual changes in course Prentiss was making to take them through. Spasms of light turbulence shook the Thuds when unseen storm columns seemed to grab out at the transgressors, not wanting them to escape, as they skirted by.

They burst into clear air. Ahead of them, remnants of the front hung as scattered clouds that offered faint cover for the enemy below. Looking past Prentiss, Kevin recognized the northern half of the Plain of Jars, and glancing at the TACAN display in his cockpit, he saw that their route through the thunderstorms had placed them about thirty miles west of their target.

"Dallas, green 'em up," Prentiss ordered as he dipped his right wing toward Dallas thee, signaling Rob to move back to his element leader's right wing As Rob slid right, Dallas lead rolled into a shallow right turn.

Kevin moved out from his leader as he armed his bomb circuits and set up his sight for the attack, searching ahead and to his right through the clouds for the target. He found it easily. The heavily bombed section of road just inside the Laotian border stood out as a light-brown sore on the surrounding jungle green. It moved through his windscreen and off to his left as Prentiss continued his right turn. Dallas lead rolled out heading east into the Fish's Mouth, paralleling the road that led to the target, setting the flight up for left turns into steep bomb runs to the west along the road, away from North Vietnam and into the low sun behind them.

As the target slid backward outside their canopies, Prentiss called, "Dallas'll do road recky when we pull off," meaning road reconnaissance, low-level flight along a road, crisscrossing it, to look for targets of opportunity.

Shit, Sam. It would've been nice to talk about this in the briefing, Kevin thought.

"Lead's in," Prentiss called as he rolled toward the road, diving his Thud as he turned westward.

Kevin followed, taking minimum spacing on the lead jet in case enemy gunners started shooting. "Three's in."

Prentiss was halfway through his dive when a string of five bursts of white smoke appeared well behind him, a tentative first volley from the gunners protecting the road.

"They're shooting, lead. Thirty-sevens," Kevin called over the radio, warning Prentiss that they were taking fire from Soviet-made, medium-range weapons, 37 millimeters in caliber, that dated back to World War II. "Keep it moving." He glanced at his airspeed indicator as his Thud plunged earthward. *Almost 500 knots.* He brought the throttle to idle to hold airspeed as he eased the pipper onto the road. *Dive angle's good. Three thousand feet to release.*

"Lead's off left."

"Four's in. They're tracking you, three! Move it!" Rob warned a few seconds later.

Kevin shoved his throttle fully forward and watched his airspeed jump past 550. Compensating for the extra speed, he dropped his bombs a thousand feet high, then rolled right and pulled back hard on the stick to defeat the gunners' aim, still diving steeply. "Three's off right," he grunted through the g's. Releasing the backward pressure in his hand, he snapped the jet to wings level, then pulled hard again to get the Thud's nose up. Continuing to jink, he ended his rapid, diving descent, then lost altitude gradually to begin road reconnaissance. He looking rearward, straining to find Rob.

Dallas four pulled out of his bomb run with a string of white bursts close behind. Rob banked to the left and pulled up, forming vortex streamers from his wingtips in the moist air from heavy g loading. Another string of flak blossomed in the sky to his right as he turned away.

"Keep it moving, four! They're on you!" Kevin called.

Rob reversed his turn, rolling right, keeping the streamers on, as another volley of five went wide to his left. "Four has three in sight," Rob called as he flew out of the gunners' range, continuing to jink.

Kevin looked ahead to find Dallas lead. A rolling motion caught his eye as Prentiss turned to cross the road from left to right. "Dallas three has lead in sight," he transmitted. As Prentiss flew across the road a half mile ahead in a shallow dive, Dallas three moved to the opposite side, easing his Thud down to a few hundred feet above the ground. Diving as they crossed the road, climbing as they turned back and then diving again, lead and three traded sides of the road in a butterfly pattern, flying westward at low altitude. Dallas four flew loose formation on Dallas three.

They flew past clusters of bomb craters that appeared around the road when it went through natural obstacles. What seemed impassable from high altitude looked different down low. Truck tracks stood out clearly, snaking around the huge holes, partially filled with water, in clear testimony to the determined skill of the enemy's combat engineers in keeping truck traffic moving toward western Laos.

Prentiss swung northward to follow the road when it changed direction for four miles before turning briefly east around high ground, then switching back to the west toward the PDJ, forming a beak-like section of road that pilots called the Bird's Head.

"Lead has a truck stalled on the road at the Bird's Head," Prentiss called as he flew along the left side of the road. "We're gonna extend to the east and set up for strafe," he transmitted as he started a climbing right turn to circle back to attack the target.

Kevin flew on to look at the truck, going by it on the right side. "Lead," he called, "it's already been hit. The right side of the truck's caved in."

"It looks like a tangible, militarily significant target to me," Prentiss replied with heavy sarcasm. "We're attackin'."

Kevin rolled right to follow Dallas lead. *Something's wrong here.* "This doesn't look right, Sam."

"Three, quit whinin', and just fuckin' fly wing!" Prentiss shot back angrily. "Lead's in for strafe."

Stung by the rebuke, Kevin watched Prentiss begin a tight descending turn to the west to strafe the truck broadside. Dallas lead rolled out, hurtling toward the truck, getting ready to open fire. Instantly, heavy tracer fire bracketed the lead jet. The Thud hemorrhaged flame as it broke off its attack. Its nose came up, trying to climb, but it slowed and began rolling to the right, mortally wounded. The jet's canopy came off, and its ejection seat followed, rocketing upward in the last frame of a quick-sequence nightmare. A few seconds later, a parachute opened to a shrill, pulsating sound over the radio on Guard channel as its emergency beacon, its beeper, began broadcasting a chilling, insistent distress call.

Oh, No! Oh, Jesus! It's a trap. Kevin reversed his descending right turn into the truck and pulled up hard to the east, gaining altitude to separate from the guns. "Rob! Break left! Now!"

Out of gun range, Kevin rolled right again to circle the crash site as the surviving Thuds continued to climb. Black smoke rose from the lead Thud's funeral pyre a mile west of the truck, and Prentiss's chute landed a half mile north. His thoughts raced. *Got to get the rescue force started. Oh, god, why didn't he listen? Can't think about that now. Got to focus. Got to save gas. Got 11,000 pounds. Not much daylight left.* "Dallas, go three, forty-three, point five," he ordered as the beeper continued to scream on Guard channel.

"Four."

"Dallas, check."

"Four."

He turned off his Guard receiver and called the C-130 transport that served as the ABCCC for northern Laos. "Cricket, Cricket, this is Dallas three."

"Go ahead, Dallas three. This is Cricket control."

"Dallas lead's been shot down at the Bird's Head."

"Authenticate, Dallas three."

Kevin looked at the code on his mission card that changed daily. "Bravo xray."

"Okay, give me coordinates, Dallas three."

Kevin looked to the console on the right side of his cockpit and read numbers from the readout on his doppler navigation system. "Nineteen degrees, thirty-six minutes north, and one-zero-three degrees, forty-nine minutes east." Glancing at his TACAN display, he added, "It's on the zero-six-one radial at fifty-eight miles off channel seventy-nine."

"Roger. Copy nineteen, thirty-six and one oh three, forty-nine. Stand by."

"Dallas three, standing by." *What more can I do? Got to save all the gas I can.* "Dallas four, jettison your centerline bomb rack on my command. I say again, centerline only. We'll keep our tanks in case we have to refuel. Acknowledge."

"Roger, four."

"Jettison," he called, cleaning off his Thud's belly.

As they orbited, the wait for help seemed interminable as the sun continued to lower toward the horizon. Cricket called back. "Dallas, are you in contact with the man who's down?"

"Negative."

"All right. Try contacting him on SAR primary. We'll monitor. We're not going to be able to get the Jolly Green through the weather, and it's too late for the Sandys to get that far north before dark. We're working something else. We'll be back in contact on SAR primary."

"Dallas three, roger. Dallas, go SAR primary."

"Four."

"Dallas, check."

"Four."

"Dallas lead, Dallas lead, this is Dallas three. Check in."

There was no response. Kevin turned his Guard receiver back on. It was silent. *Someone's turned off the beeper. Come on, Sam. Talk to me.*

They orbited for another half hour as the remains of Dallas lead's Thud continued to burn below them.

"Dallas three, this is Cricket. Do you have contact with the man on the ground yet?"

"Dallas three. Negative."

"Okay. We have someone coming your way. He'll contact you soon."

"Dallas three, roger. Dallas four, say your fuel."

"Four has eight thousand."

"Roger, call bingo at five thousand."

A weak voice transmission came next. The speaker sounded out-of-breath, talking through pain. "Dallas flight, Dallas flight. This's Dallas lead."

"Roger, Dallas lead. This is Dallas three. Say your condition."

"I'm bleedin' a little bit, and I'm a little winded from crawlin' away from my chute. I've found a hidin' place near a karst," Prentiss said, meaning a jagged limestone outcropping, one of the peculiar rock formations that jutted up randomly out of the trees in the Laotian high country.

"Okay, lead. Hang tight. Help is on the way."

"Thanks, Kev. I'm a real dumbass."

"Don't go soft on me now, Sam," he said, trying to hide his desperation. "Just hang in there until we get you out."

"Dallas three, Dallas three. This is Raven two nine."

Josh! "Raven two nine, go ahead. This is Dallas three."

"Raven two nine's been monitoring your last transmissions. Do you recognize my call sign?"

"Affirmative."

"Okay. I'm coming to you up the road that travels north to the Bird's Head. I'm staying low so that the gunners don't see me. What's the situation?"

"When you get here, you'll see a truck on the road. Dallas lead got knocked down on a low-angle strafe pass, attacking the truck from the east. It looks like a gun trap. The tracer looked like twenty-three millimeter," Kevin said, referring to a short-range anti-aircraft gun with a high rate of fire that made it deadly. "I can't see the gun sites. There's more than one. The guy on the ground is north of the road near a karst. You can see his chute."

"Okay. When I tell you, I want you and your wingman to make high-angle strafe passes to get the triple-A to start shooting. Just hose off a short burst, somewhere around the truck. Don't worry about hitting anything. Blow through fast and pull off high."

"Roger. Dallas four, make your run-in wide of mine, so that they can't track us both at the same time."

"Roger, four."

"Raven two nine has the truck in sight. Start your roll-ins."

"Roger, three's in." Kevin rolled his Thud inverted and pulled the pipper down to an area east of the truck. He rolled upright and began firing immediately. Answering fire came up at him in streams of tracer rounds, and he pulled hard to avoid them, jinking left and then right. As his jet bottomed out in its dive, he heard two sharp sounds. *I'm hit!* His eyes seized on his engine instruments and warning lights as the Thud's nose shot up above the horizon. *No indications. I'm okay.*

He rolled left and looked down, searching for Rob. The gunners had shifted their fire, but Dallas four pulled up from his pass before the tracer fire closed in on him.

Josh transmitted, "Dallas three, they got pretty close to you."

"Yeah, they nicked me, but I'm still flying. Did you see the guns?"

"I saw two sites, one west of the truck and one east. Stand by. I've got a call on another radio." After a long delay, while the Thuds orbited high and the Raven circled at low altitude, out of sight of the gunners, Josh came back on the air. "Okay, Dallas. I've been talking to the guys who're going to do the pickup. Dallas lead, can you hear me?"

"This's Dallas lead. Affirmative."

"I want you to pop your smoke flare now, so that some guys in a chopper can see where you are."

"Are they close? I'm hearin' voices, and I don't want to show my smoke if they can get to me before the chopper. I don't think I can move again."

"Sam," Josh answered, "the sun's setting now, and we've only got time for one pickup try. It's the best we can do."

"Okay." A hundred yards north of the chute, on the western edge of the karst, orange smoke drifted up, revealing Dallas lead's hiding place.

Josh came back on the air after a delay. "Dallas three, the guys in the chopper say that they can mask themselves from the eastern gun by coming in behind the karst, but you'll have to take out the western gun so that they can hover."

"I can't see the gun site."

"Okay. I want you and your wingman to come through again on another high-angle pass. When the guns open up on you, I'll pop up and mark the western gun site. As soon as you see my smoke, I want you guys to take out the gun."

"All right. Dallas four, after the high-angle pass, we'll have to get in close to make sure we get the shooter."

"Roger, four."

"Three's in." He pulled the Thud's nose down and lit its afterburner to increase speed as he dove at the truck from the east. He aimed west of it, and pulled the trigger for a long burst, hoping for a lucky hit on the gun site. Pulling off to the west, he adjusted his gun sight for close-in strafing while he turned hard and descended, back toward the truck, waiting for Josh's smoke rocket. It began billowing as Josh turned and dove away from the gun site, after popping up and firing while the gunners were diverted and shot at Rob.

Kevin pulled the pipper around to the target quickly, closing on it with the setting sun behind him to blind the gunners, rolling out for a long burst. Just outside the Thud's gun range, the gunners shifted their fire to him. He raised the pipper to the top of the white smoke and pulled the trigger. Easing the orange aiming dot slowly downward, he fired the rest of his ammunition in a long roar from the Thud's gun. The tracer fire got closer. As he yanked back on the stick to pull off at minimum range, the airplane shuddered as something boulder-like slammed into it. Searing pain exploded in his right leg.

Blindly, out of raging instinct, he put both hands on the stick and pulled. The nose flew up and the altimeter showed he was climbing steeply. He looked down, not believing what he saw. *Oh, god! No! It can't be!* Bright-red blood spurted out of a shattered leg and splattered his instruments. Wildly, he pulled the jet's nose around to the south and kept climbing.

"Shit hot, Dallas!" he heard Josh say. "You got a secondary out of the gun site. It's dead!"

He felt paralyzed as he looked down at the wound. Bone was sticking out through his g suit, and blood kept pulsing out, spraying more of the cockpit. *Oh, God, help me. Please help me.*

"Dallas three, this is four," Rob called. "Say your position. I've lost you."

Panic gripped him. *Got to climb. Got to get to Udorn.*

"Dallas three, this is four!" Rob called again, urgency rising in his voice. "Acknowledge!"

Fumbling, he thumbed the mike button, "This is three. I'm climbing. Heading south. I'm hit. Hit bad."

"Dallas four's turning south after you. Say altitude."

"Passing nine thousand."

"Hold down for a bearing," Rob called, telling him to depress his mike button long enough for the direction-finding equipment in the wingman's Thud to lock on and point in the direction of the leader's radio transmitter.

"Three's holding down."

"Four's got a good bearing. Say airspeed."

"Four hundred."

"Keep climbing and level at twenty thousand. Four's coming after you."

The radio calls pulled him far enough out of his shock for survival instincts to begin to take hold. *Got to stop the bleeding or I'll never make it.* He put the Thud into autopilot to hold his climb and took out a Bowie knife from a leather sheath sewn to the left leg of his g suit. Working quickly, he cut away layers of blood-soaked flight clothing from around the wound at the top of his shin. He took a strap tourniquet from a small pouch at the top of his survival vest and wrapped it around his leg above the shattered bone protruding through the skin. Increasing tension on the strap by pulling as hard as he could against its buckle, he managed to lessen the bleeding from a strong, rhythmic spurting to a gradual ooze.

"Dallas three, this is Raven two nine. We're moving in for the pickup. We'll need you to clear this frequency now. Hang in there, man. Kev, you did one hell of a job."

"Okay, Josh. Get him out."

"We will, Kev. See you."

"Dallas, go squadron common."

"Four."

"Dallas check."

"Four. Kev, stroke your burner to help me find you."

Kevin moved his throttle outboard and felt the soft jolt of the afterburner lighting. Its orange flame shone brightly in the twilight. After a few seconds, he moved the throttle inboard again.

"Four's got a visual on you, three," Rob called. Dallas four rejoined to close formation on his leader. "You've got a lot of battle damage on right side of your nose, Kev. Part of the radome's gone."

Kevin looked down at his radar display. *Dead.* "Yeah, my scope's blank."

"Let me look you over on the other side," Rob called as he slid his Thud back to cross under. As he pulled forward, he radioed, "You've got hits on the vertical stabilizer too. Are you okay?"

"Not so good. I've been hit in the right leg, and I don't have any feeling below the knee."

"You're going to make it, man. Udorn's only half an hour away."

"Yeah. Okay."

"Is anything else wrong with your airplane?"

"I don't see anything. No warning lights."

"How much gas do you have left?"

He wiped off the blood obscuring the fuel gauge. "A little under four thousand."

"Good. That's plenty of gas. Okay. We've got to get back through the thunderstorms. They're only ten miles away, Kev. My radar's working. Let me take the lead to get us through."

"Okay, Rob. You've got the lead."

Dallas three slid back to fly close formation on his wingman as Rob turned on his Thud's exterior lights. Catching the last of the light from the sun as it slipped below the horizon, the tops of towering thunderstorms ahead of them glowed white atop their gray base clouds.

They plunged into menacing, hazy ramparts hiding storm cells. Kevin's eyes locked onto the lights on Rob's jet that seemed to become disconnected from everything else. He hung on to them with all the strength he could find, calling on his last reserves of skill. He fought vertigo that took hold of him, that sharpened pain with fear, as the two jets remained suspended in a dark place that swallowed the camouflage paint on the lead Thud between flashes of lightning. Struggling against nausea from disorientation as turbulence began to buffet his airplane, he pulled his oxygen mask off to vomit, keeping his eyes fixed on the lead jet.

Rob looked back at him anxiously between glances at his radar scope, reporting their progress, giving encouragement. "We're almost through, Kev. We'll be out soon. Just hang on, man. You're doing great."

After what seemed liked hours, as Rob ended a radio call, they flew into clear air. The first stars shone above the rolling sea of solid stratus beneath them. Relieved, Kevin took his jet out wide to gather himself for his final battle with the weather, the descent to landing at Udorn. He cleaned his mouth with the back of his flight glove and put his mask back on.

Rob called him again. "Kev, I think you should let me lead you into Udorn. If something goes wrong with your airplane during the approach, it'll be a lot better if you're on the wing."

Pride reared up, then retreated. "You're right, Rob. You keep the lead." *The student becomes the instructor.*

"Okay, Kev. Let's get on Brigham's frequency and get you down. If anything happens, just flip to Guard channel and call. Ready to go?"

"Ready."

"Okay, Dallas, let's go two, thirty-four, point six."

"Three."

"Dallas, check."

"Three."

"Brigham, Brigham, this is Dallas flight."

"Roger, Dallas, this is Brigham. Go ahead."

"Dallas is a flight of two Thuds, forty miles northeast of Udorn at twenty thousand. We're requesting emergency descent and landing. My wingman has heavy battle damage and is wounded. I say again, wounded. Dallas is squawking emergency."

"Roger, Dallas. Copy all. Brigham has radar contact, forty miles northeast of the airfield."

"Say weather."

"Roger. Udorn is landing runway three zero. Ceiling is eight hundred overcast. Visibility is one mile in light rain. Winds are light and variable. Altimeter two niner point eight zero. Say type of approach."

"Roger, two nine, eight zero. Dallas requests radar vectors to an ILS final."

"Roger. Continue present heading. Descend at pilot's discretion. Call leaving present altitude."

"Dallas, roger. Break, break. Dallas three, I'm slowing us down to put the gear and flaps down. Let's see how your jet handles at approach speed before we get into the weather."

"Roger, three."

"After we break out, I'll go around and land after you."

"Okay."

"Dallas three, can you work your rudder pedals and your brakes?"

"Not on the right side."

"Okay. Then after you pop your drag chute, you'll have to get your tail hook down and take the barrier," Rob called, meaning a heavy cable stretched across the far end of a runway as a last-ditch measure to stop a runaway jet.

"Right."

"But remember, Udorn's an F-4 base, and they've got another barrier at mid-field. If you get your hook down too early and engage that one, it'll rip the hook right out of your airplane."

"Right. I remember."

"I think you should touch down a little right of the centerline. If the runway's crowned, and if you drift on the rollout, it'll probably be to the right. You can correct back left."

"Yeah. Okay."

"One last thing. If it looks like you're going to run off the runway, you can raise your gear and let the airplane drop on the wing tanks. Is your shoulder harness locked?"

He moved the locking lever. "It's locked."

"Okay, we're below gear-lowering speed. Let's see how your airplane handles." Rob led him through the lowering of the gear and flaps. "How does it feel?"

"Solid."

"Good. Okay, we're slowing to final-approach speed. How does it feel now?"

"It's good. Let's get on the ground."

"Dallas flight, this is Brigham. Turn right now, to a heading of two four zero. Cleared ILS approach, runway three zero. Report the outer marker."

"Roger, Dallas is cleared for the approach. We're descending out of twenty thousand."

Rob began a slow, turning descent into the ILS cone, and Kevin moved back in to close formation. *I can do it. Only a few more minutes. Got to hang on.* The cloud deck moved slowly upward, a low moon beginning to brighten one side of its hillocks and casting shadows behind. They eased into night clouds in a straight-ahead descent after Rob turned to the final-approach heading. Outside Kevin's cockpit, the green light on Rob's right wingtip glowed in a misty halo over the center of the white star on the lead Thud's fuselage.

Light on the star, he said to himself over and over, willing himself through weather and pain, as vertigo took hold of him again, as he fought off exhaustion by clinging to survival.

When they broke out, Rob had them lined up perfectly. "I'm on the go," he called to his wingman as he turned away. "Fly it all the way to the barrier, Kev."

White runway lights rushed up at him, and he flared the big jet to landing. *Touchdown.* He lowered the nosewheel quickly to the pavement then pulled the drag-chute handle. *Good chute.* The Thud tracked straight between white lights on either side of him. Passing a runway marker showing 5,000 feet of pavement left, he felt his landing gear thump over the mid-field barrier. *Hook down now.* Moving his left hand from the hook switch to cradle the gear handle in case he had to raise it, he tensed as the big jet rumbled on toward green lights 4,000 feet ahead at the end of the runway.

Slowly, the Thud's nose started to veer to the right. With his good leg, he eased it back with a thousand feet of runway left, and the big fighter tore past green threshold lights into the overrun. He pitched forward into his shoulder harness as the gallant, battered Thunderchief caught the barrier cable and lurched to a stop.

He sat still for a moment with the engine running and then shut it down. Raising his canopy, he leaned his head back against the head rest and felt cool, cleansing rain on his face as he took off his oxygen mask. *Thank you,* he prayed silently as he closed his eyes.

He felt completely drained when flashing-light bedlam surrounded his cockpit. A ladder slapped against the fuselage. "Sir, we'll have you out of there in a jiffy," someone climbing the ladder yelled up. A flashlight blinded him and then swept around the cockpit. "Jesus! Oh, Jesus! There's blood everywhere. Get that hoist over here! Now! Get the doc! Hang on, sir. Hang on."

Everything around him blurred as he was jostled, and surrendering, he let himself be swept away by a peaceful current he felt pulling on him.

He awoke on his back with a man in white kneeling next to him, stabbing something into his arm. He wanted to sit up, to resist, but straps across his chest and thighs kept him immobile. Metal doors at his feet banged opened, and he was sliding through them. More men in white appeared. "Surgery! Right now!" someone yelled as he was being rolled down a long, strange corridor.

He felt a strong hand squeezing his arm. He looked over. *Rob!*

"You're going to be okay, Kev. You're a warrior, man."

He put his hand on Rob's and looked him in the eyes. "I owe you more than I can tell you, Rob. See you in a little while, after I'm finished with the docs."

"Yeah. Later, Kev," Rob replied. He stopped walking, letting the gurney and its white-garbed attendants turn into another corridor through double doors where others in surgical greens waited to join the hurried procession.

Another orderly came over to him and asked, "Are you going to wait here until the surgery's over, Lieutenant?"

"No. I've got to go to base ops and report in to my home base. I'll come back after that."

"I can give you a lift to the flight line, sir."

"Thanks, but I'd rather walk."

"In the rain, sir?"

"Yeah."

Rob left the hospital and made his way toward hazy ramp lights glowing weakly in the distance. After he had walked a few hundred yards to a dark, deserted place between two dim street lamps, he stopped and looked up, letting soft rain wash moist places under his eyes. "I hate this fucking war!" he yelled at a sodden, indifferent night sky.

Chapter 25

Wednesday, 21 September 1983

The kitchen was chilly. Bending down, Kevin pulled two pieces of firewood from a wood box, put them into a large stove and latched it shut. After straightening up, he paused for a moment and shifted his weight from side to side to test his new prosthesis again. *This one fits a lot better with boots,* he decided as he walked to a cupboard to get the morning's coffee started.

"Hey, cowboy," Clare Walker said as she walked through the kitchen door wearing a sweater and jeans. "You're up awfully early this morning."

"Mornin', ma'am," he answered, affecting a western accent. "Well, I guess our guest room's goin' to lose its three-star ratin'. Important company's supposed to rack out 'til at least nine."

"What I like about your guest room is that it's centrally located, and I can keep track of everybody's comings and goings. I heard you in the hallway, so I thought I'd get up and get some of that strong Durango coffee you're so famous for."

"We aim to please. It's on its way," he said as he turned on a switch on the brewer.

"So, tomorrow it's back to where it all began for us," she said, taking a chair at a heavy wooden table. "I can't believe it's been twenty years."

"Yeah, a lot's happened since then. It should be quite a reunion."

"Who're you looking forward to seeing most?"

"Well, Charlie Rasmussen's coming. He's just gotten a new book published. It's a major tome. Compares the peace talks that ended the

Korean War with the ones that went on in Paris. He sent me a copy. Pretty massive. Lots of footnotes. He'll make a fortune, making all his students buy it."

"He's the one with the red hair. The professor at Auburn. Right?"

"Right."

"Ed thinks the end in Vietnam was pretty simple. He says that the North Vietnamese got serious after we sent B-52s to Hanoi."

"Well, as you might expect, Charlie thinks it's a little more complicated than that," he said, putting two mugs and spoons on the table. "According to Charlie, when we agreed in Paris to let the North Vietnamese keep their troops in South Vietnam after the cease fire, they got just about everything they really wanted to sign a peace agreement. That happened before the B-52s went north. He says that they really didn't give up all that much to get us to stop the bombing at the end. Anyway, if Ed and Charlie get into it with each other, you and I can just sit back and watch."

"I guess the arguments will just go on and on. I sometimes wonder, if John Kennedy had lived, if we would have escaped Vietnam."

"That's what the keepers of the Camelot flame have been claiming lately."

"It doesn't sound like they've convinced you."

"I guess not. A few nights ago, I read the speech Kennedy gave at graduation again. The most interesting part is at the end—where he said that America was going to be a force for freedom in the world, and that we were assuming this burden willingly, because if we didn't assume it, no other nation would."

"That's more than a little haunting."

"Yeah. Even though he never said the word Vietnam once in his speech, what took us to war in Asia is all there. There's a lot of New Frontierism in what he said, but I think he captured the mood of the times too. When Johnson sent us to fight, the country supported him. If Kennedy had lived, he would've had the same advisers Johnson did, and the same hawks in Congress breathing down his neck, all of them banging on him to keep Communists from getting another square inch of ground anywhere else in the world. I think what got us into Vietnam was much bigger than one man."

"God, those were terrible years, especially at the end. Ed and I just about divorced when he volunteered for a second combat tour. After he got shot down, I was a wreck. I think that the week I stayed here with you and Teresa kept me from cracking up completely."

"Naah. You're much too tough for that. And you're also looking pretty terrific, by the way."

"Why, thank you, sir. It's all part of my new colonel's-wife look, don't you know."

"I like it. Very assured, but subtle."

She laughed. "I remember when you and Ed were lieutenants at Williams. I thought colonels' wives were these mystical creatures who lived out in the ether somewhere. Now I am one. Pretty scary, huh?"

"A role you were born to play, my dear," he said as he brought the coffee pot to the table and began pouring. "Cream and pink stuff. Right?"

"Exactly."

"Pink stuff's in the blue bowl in front of you. I'll get you some cream from the fridge."

He came back, handed her a cream pitcher and sat down. "Let's see. Josh Pemberton's coming too. He's at Laughlin now. He's got one of the training squadrons there. I talked to him a few days ago. Like most of the guys in the class, he's sweating out the promotion list to colonel. They're all going to be jealous of your fast-burner husband at the reunion."

Teresa came into the kitchen in her bathrobe and slippers. "Hello, early birds. I thought I heard voices," she said as she sat down to join them.

"Let me get you a cup," Kevin said, getting up.

"Thank you, love. So, tell me again, what time does Ed's plane get in? I'll try to finish early at Karin's with the bookkeeper so I'm here when you get back."

"Around ten thirty," Clare answered. "Unless another crisis telephone call comes from SAC headquarters just as he's walking out the door to go to the airport, like it did yesterday."

"Well, I'm glad you came on ahead," Teresa said. "I enjoyed catching up last night. Do you want to come with me to Karin's this morning? I'm afraid that it might be boring for you, though, just watching us go over business things, billings and all that."

"I've got an idea," Kevin said as he sat down and poured a third cup. "Why don't I take Clare flying with me. That's why I got up early.

Since I've got to go to the airport anyway, I thought I'd get a hop in before Ed lands. With the fall colors out, it'll be gorgeous today. How about it, adventure girl?"

"Well."

"We were up together on Sunday, Clare, and it really is spectacular. You should go."

"Are you sure I can't help you with anything?"

"Positive. The kids practically get themselves off to school, and Father doesn't eat much for breakfast these days."

"Okay then. But let me whip up something to eat for the three of us while you dress, T."

After breakfast, Kevin and Clare walked outside as a bright sun climbed in a brilliantly blue sky above a ridge line to the east. It had started to melt a light frost on gray-wood fence rails that led to a weathered shed where he kept his pickup truck. They walked to it and got in.

"You've come a long way from sports cars," she said as he turned the ignition key.

The engine caught, and he eased the truck out of the shed. "Yeah. One of life's surprises. If I hadn't had to find a new line of work, I might not've found out how much I love ranching." He picked up speed when he reached the gravel road to the highway.

"I've never seen you so contented. You have a wonderful life here, Kevin."

"So, we're all in a Jimmy Stewart movie here?"

"Come on, Kevin, be serious."

"Well, I'd have to be an idiot not to be happy. I'm in love with a beautiful and talented woman, I've got four great kids and I'm living in the mountains in Colorado. Who wouldn't be satisfied with that?"

"There's something more. You had all that two years ago when Ed and I were here."

"Was I unhappy then?"

"No, but you seem to be happier now."

"Funny. I thought I was always this relaxed, easygoing kind of guy."

"Kevin, I promise. I'm not trying to play amateur shrink with you. It's just that I wish Ed were as far along as you seem to be in putting Vietnam behind you. He still has a lot of anger. It's well-hidden, but it's there. It worries me a lot."

"Clare, being a POW, even for just three months like Ed was at the end, was no walk in the park."

"But wasn't it worse for you? Being wounded and having your whole life turned upside down?"

"I don't know. It was different. Our experiences were completely different. Starting from the year before I went to Thailand."

"How do you mean?"

"I had this conversation with a guy who was working for the State Department when I was back in Washington on a cross-country. He laid the whole thing out for me, how we'd blundered into Vietnam without understanding the Vietnamese, North or South, and how we'd underestimated the people we were fighting. Did you know that they lost somewhere between half a million and a million troops, Viet Cong guerillas and North Vietnamese regulars, compared with the fifty-eight thousand we lost?"

"My god."

"That doesn't count the civilian deaths. They were a very tough and determined enemy. I guess you could even say fanatical. They've been that way for a long time in defeating invaders, like the Chinese, who expected to roll over them. We had no idea what we were getting into. He told me too that the air war over North Vietnam was going to come apart."

"He did?"

"Yeah. He believed that we couldn't force the North Vietnamese into a settlement with bombing unless we were willing to cause a lot of civilian casualties, like we did in Japan at the end of World War II. He was right, though, when he said that Americans wouldn't stand for that twenty years later. He was saying that even though we could have leveled Hanoi and every other city, town and village in North Vietnam if we'd tried to, the rules had changed. But I thought we could still hurt them enough by bombing their industry and military targets to make them want to quit."

"Well, don't you think we could have, if the politicians hadn't started running the war from Washington?"

"That's what I thought at the beginning. Yeah, Johnson's and McNamara's restrictions and bombing halts didn't help much. But that's only one part of the story. One day when I was in Thailand, my flight commander and I were talking, and he said something that really surprised me. When I said something about the politicians losing the war for us, he said, 'Kevin, that's what we tell civilians who don't know any better.' His bottom line was that we were having to fight a new kind of air war under the new rules, one that the generals were having to improvise, making it up as they went along, and fighting it with airplanes and weapons that couldn't hack it. As he put it, talking to me in fighter pilot, we thought we were going to win by bombing family-jewels targets in North Vietnam, but we found out that our shit-hot jets dropping iron bombs weren't good enough. That's tough to admit, I know, but now, I think he broke the code. So, any way you look at it, the guys in the fighter cockpits were caught in this no-win place, right in the middle of the crosshairs. And then there was Juan."

"Juan?"

"Yeah. I was here in Durango for Christmas, just before going to check out in the Thud. Juan and I had this after-midnight talk about the morality of what we were doing in Vietnam. It basically came down to whether or not keeping the North Vietnamese from taking over the South, and maybe other places too, was worth the human cost of the war. Not only our own casualties, but civilians in South Vietnam who got caught in the middle. Between our meat-grinder strategy of massive artillery fire, air strikes and search-and-destroy sweeps, and an enemy who didn't blink at using terror, who was willing to fight as long as it took to get us to leave. Juan didn't take a position one way or the other that night. But after I came home wounded, it pushed him over the edge. He went over to the anti-war side in a big way. He was at Harvard then, and he found plenty of places to apply his considerable talents. The Jebbies finally had to ship him off to Rome for five years to keep Nixon's radical hunters from throwing him in jail."

"I didn't know that."

"Juan's at the top of my list of great guys of all time. I can never repay him for what he's done for Teresa and me. When he went where he went out of conscience, I couldn't ignore it. In fact, I had to respect his integrity, the moral courage of what took him there. Gradually, it brought me back to what he said to me at Christmas."

"Where does all this leave you with Sean?"

He sighed deeply. "I don't know."

"Teresa told me that you saw him in March."

"Yeah."

"You don't have to talk about it if you don't want to."

"I can talk about it with you, Clare. It just takes a minute for the emotional surge inside to die down. Of course, the day I saw him just had to be the same date as the day I was hit over Laos. That morning, I'd been to the Vietnam Memorial for the first time with a classmate of mine, a guy named Paul Fortuna who's a major-league Washington lawyer now. He's one of the people who helped get the memorial built, and his law partner's the guy who was at the State Department, the one I just told you about. Anyway, I was pretty keyed up after seeing all the names I knew on those black walls." He stopped talking and took a deep breath.

Clare put her hand on his arm.

"I'm okay. After that, I was in the hospital with my mother and Juan, visiting my dad after his stroke, and, out of nowhere, in walks Sean. No one knew he was coming. I thought I'd worked through all the bitterness I'd felt when I was in the hospital recovering, after I got shipped back home and had to learn how to walk all over again. But it just jumped up inside. It just paralyzed me. Mom got up and hugged him, and Juan shook hands with him, but I couldn't move. I just sat there and stared. He looked at me, then he looked at my dad who couldn't talk, and then he just broke down and left the room. Juan went out after him, and my mom started crying." He eased the truck to the side of the gravel road, just before the intersection with the highway to Durango, and braked to a stop. "I've got to stop for a minute." He looked at Clare as she nodded, tears running down her face. He took another deep breath as she took his hand. "I went over to my mom and held her. And she said to me, 'Can't you see it, Kevin? You can't punish him any more than he's punishing himself.'" He turned off the truck's ignition and looked out silently through the windshield.

A car turned off the highway and accelerated past them, raising dust as it went by. "She was right, of course. He's my brother for Christ's sake, and there I was, tearing my mother's heart out, trying to sift meaning out of the rubble, out of this tragedy that overwhelmed everybody in it. Everybody lost. Men in Washington who should have been wise were blind first and deceitful later, trying to cover up their mistakes—and just about ripped this country apart. And men in Hanoi sent something like two million Vietnamese to their deaths—all for an illusion, this illusion of some new Vietnam that's become a bad dream for them now, now that they're actually having to live it. For me, though, the saddest loss was Sam Prentiss bleeding to death on the floor of a helicopter in the middle of nowhere for nothing. Finally, I had to ask myself: Was it worth it to lose my brother too?"

He started the engine, stopped briefly at the intersection and pulled out onto the highway. "Well, I couldn't even ask myself that question until I got back home, after a long talk with Juan in Washington just before I left, after Sean flew back to Canada without my talking to him. Finding an answer took another couple of months. Now, it's enough for me to believe that I did everything I could do by keeping the promises I made on graduation day. That's the only thing that really matters to me now. I don't need to bring Sean into it. I don't have to add to his demons. He's got plenty to handle on his own."

"Where do you go from here?"

"Well, I'll have to wait to see if I get an answer to a long letter I wrote to Sean about all this. It took me too long to get started writing it. And I've got to keep reminding myself that I've got some extraordinary people in my life. Teresa especially. After I wrote to Sean, she told me about the premonition she had while we were in Hawaii on R and R, about something going to happen to me. She said it was the hardest thing she's ever had to do, feeling the way she was feeling and not being able to tell me. By the way, I count you as one of those people I'm lucky to be close to. That's why I took a little break there from being relaxed and easygoing."

"You are a very good man, Kevin O'Dea."

"I'm glad you think so. With everything you've been through, I think you're pretty impressive yourself."

They said nothing more until they reached the airport located on a high mesa south of town. He took a back road to the area reserved for private aircraft and parked at the end of a row of metal hangars. A yellow biplane was parked in front of one that was open.

"That's still the most amazing story," Clare said after getting out of the truck.

"What is?"

"About how Sam Prentiss's dad just showed up in Durango one day and gave you this airplane."

"Yeah. He said that he couldn't sell something his son loved so much, and that I should be the one to have it," Kevin said, starting to walk around the Stearman, giving it a pre-flight inspection as Clare followed him.

"Maybe it was his way of letting his son go and making amends to you."

"Maybe. After he left, I found the maps he used for the trip here. He left them in the cockpit. He flew from Mississippi to Arizona, along the same route that he and Sam flew to get to Williams twenty years ago, then he flew north to Colorado. Well, Sam and I had some great times together flying the Stearman. I wish all our times had been that good."

"Maybe it's best now just to remember the good times."

"Yeah, probably so. And there've been more. Rob Johnson and I had a terrific time last month flying together when he came through with his family on the way to his new assignment. I'm really pleased that he's doing so well. He was one of the first in his class to make lieutenant colonel."

"I enjoyed meeting him and his wife—what was it?—five years ago?"

"Five years? Has it really been that long? I guess it has," he said, stepping up onto the airplane's lower wing, reaching into the front cockpit. "Here's your gear, Amelia Earhart," he said, handing her a flight jacket with a leather helmet and goggles folded inside. He retrieved his own jacket from the rear cockpit, the yellow in its dragon's-head and arrowhead patches dulled from many wearings. He put it on. "I had a wonderful trip three weeks ago. I flew Mary Clare off to Colorado College," he said as he put on his helmet and goggles next. "She's really looking forward to seeing you in Colorado Springs this weekend."

"You know, she's the closest I'll ever get to having a daughter of my own, after ending up with three boys."

"Well, godmother, I'd say your letters and presents over the years really meant a lot to her. So, are you ready to go?"

"Ready to fly, sir pilot, sir."

He helped her into the front cockpit, and she fastened her lap belt. "Okay, you're all set. You know the tradition, but after that, we'll just look at the scenery."

"Okay. It's a fine tradition."

A short time later, the engine propelling wings of memories having come to life, he took the runway and advanced the throttle without stopping to line up, remembering dirt-strip takeoffs from a place near Williams twenty years earlier. After lifting off, flying northward toward mountain peaks in the far distance, after climbing between two ridges of mountains bordering the river valley where Durango lay, he dove the Stearman slightly to accelerate, then pulled its nose up gently and rolled lazily once. *That's for you, Sam. I hope you're in a good place now. Sam, we did all we could do. We kept our promises.*

He flew on and climbed again, turning toward the sun over the mountain ridge to the east. Below him, groves of aspen announced themselves boldly in yellow, golden against the green of pines in morning sunlight. Seeing them from an open cockpit made him thankful for the years he had been granted since his wounding, and he drew strength from the timeless rhythm of their changing colors.

BVG